Larryn had to be dreaming.

But she continued to watch as the apparition of the duke paced before the carved desk that had probably once been his. Seldrake wasn't dressed in the picture's black velvet coat, but instead wore a gleaming white shirt with sleeves that billowed as he moved. His trousers stopped below his knees, and muscular calves filled out filmy stockings. His shoes had a gleaming buckle.

His hair appeared even longer than in the picture. It was parted in the center and curved down his shoulders in a mass of masculine waves that rippled as he walked.

Suddenly the pacing stopped. The duke's mouth opened. "I can heed her no longer," he said.

Seldrake headed toward the door. So did his dog.

So did Larryn . . .

Praise for the romances of Linda O. Johnston

Stranger on the Mountain

"Invigorating . . . inspiring. The pacing is fast, character development is excellent, and the setting abounds in natural beauty." —*Rendezvous*

"A warm and loving drama." —*Romantic Times*

Point in Time

"Readers will be entertained." —*Romantic Times*

The Glass Slipper

"A thoroughly charming update of *Cinderella,* complete with an endearing and wacky fairy godmother." —*Romantic Times*

A Glimpse of Forever

"The awakening of the young heroine to modern technology is priceless . . . An impressive, steamy, romantic adventure." —*Rendezvous*

ONCE a CAVALIER

Linda O. Johnston

JOVE BOOKS, NEW YORK

TIME PASSAGES is a registered trademark of Penguin Putnam Inc.

ONCE A CAVALIER

A Jove Book / published by arrangement with
the author

PRINTING HISTORY
Jove edition / June 2000

All rights reserved.
Copyright © 2000 by Linda O. Johnston.
Cover illustration by Franco Accornero.
This book may not be reproduced in whole or in part,
by mimeograph or any other means, without permission.
For information address: The Berkley Publishing Group,
a division of Penguin Putnam Inc.,
375 Hudson Street, New York, New York 10014.

The Penguin Putnam Inc. World Wide Web site address is
http://www.penguinputnam.com

ISBN: 0-515-12847-3

A JOVE BOOK®
Jove Books are published by The Berkley Publishing Group,
a division of Penguin Putnam Inc.,
375 Hudson Street, New York, New York 10014.
JOVE and the "J" design
are trademarks belonging to Penguin Putnam Inc.

PRINTED IN THE UNITED STATES OF AMERICA

10 9 8 7 6 5 4 3 2 1

In loving memory to:
Azorese Pandaemonium,
Italia's Lucia, and
Ubiquity's Micquey; and

With affection to my current lap-loving buddies:
Stapleton Sparquling Emily and
Ubiquity Sparques 'N Spice

Also:
To my brother Rob Osgood,
because he asked so nicely;
To Cavalier King Charles Spaniel owners and
breeders all over the world;
And, as always, to Fred, my own cavalier.

Chapter 1

"WHO IS HE?" Larryn Maeller had attempted to ask the question nonchalantly, but her tone was hushed, even awed.

She tried to tear her attention from the portrait on the far wall and look at her hostess, Chloe Seldrake, but all she could do was stare.

"That's my ancestor Thomas Northby, the first—and last—duke of Seldrake." Chloe stepped briskly up to the picture and wiped an imaginary speck of dust off the ornate gilded frame. She was a small septuagenarian who had surprised Larryn with her youthfulness when they had finally met in person half an hour earlier. "Isn't he wonderful?"

The portrait was larger than life and looked quite old. In it, a man stood beside the desk in that very room, the study in the suite Chloe had designated as Larryn's for her visit. The large desk was made of dark, burnished wood. Its sides and legs were carved with intricate geometric designs.

But the desk was not the picture's focal point. Oh, no.

The man was.

The colors in the antique oil painting had faded, but the man it depicted was still utterly impressive. Handsome, yet far from perfect. Cordial, yet arrogant.

His hair looked the cool shade of damp sand at the ocean's edge. It was wavy and even longer than Larryn's, when not pinned up in her usual professional chignon. He wore a flowing black velvet jacket adorned at the edges by a row of gilt buttons, and lace showed at his neck and cuffs.

Most imposing were his eyes. Emphasized by shaggy, ironic brows, they were as blue as the sapphire in the ring on his index finger. As sad as if he had experienced the greatest of human suffering. As penetrating as if he had asked Larryn a personal question. She even felt herself turn red as she stared.

How silly. Imaginative.

And Larryn was not an imaginative person.

Chloe tilted her head back to look up at the duke's portrait, and the ends of her perfect pageboy skimmed her shoulders. Her sable brown hair was given character by a stark white streak on the side.

"Handsome, isn't he?" Chloe continued. "And quite a nice man, from everything we know about him. He was a doctor, like you. He lived during the Restoration, at the time of the Great Plague. He risked everything to help people, and yet he got into some kind of trouble with his friend the king, poor dear."

She spoke as though she had met and liked the man. How wonderful, Larryn thought, to be so proud of one's family.

Then, many people were proud of their families. Maybe most people. She would be, too, if only her sister had—

Not a good time to think about that. "What kind of trouble did he get into?"

"I'm not sure," Chloe replied, "although I believe it has to do with his heroism. You see, during the plague, the law required that family members who were uninfected be shut up with those who were infected to stop the spread. That doomed the healthy ones to catch the disease, too, and die. The duke apparently saved dozens of uninfected children by spiriting them away from their quarantine early—though that was a crime."

"I see," Larryn said contemplatively. She recognized the

risk to the duke as well, in those days before the most rudimentary sanitation and other methods to stop contagion were known. He could have caught the plague himself.

"Isn't his dog wonderful?" Chloe asked.

In the portrait, the duke's hand rested on the head of a small red and white spaniel with a gold collar so jewel-encrusted that it nearly sparkled. The dog resembled the three live ones who scrabbled playfully around Larryn's feet.

"The Cavalier King Charles Spaniels of those days don't look quite the same as now," Larryn said. "Their muzzles were a lot more pointed."

"Yes, there are differences. For one thing, they didn't have such a complicated breed name; they were just known as the little spaniels King Charles II loved. The only cav-aliers were the king's champions, like Thomas. But I'll bet the dogs had the same sweet temperaments." Chloe looked down at her diamond-circled wristwatch. "Enough of that. It's late. You'll want to unpack and get ready for bed."

Actually, Larryn didn't. She had arrived in England that morning for the medical conference that had brought her to this glorious country for the first time. Though jet lag had nearly dropped her in her seat at the first interminable lec-ture, somewhere between the meeting, her taxi ride, and now, she'd gotten her second wind.

Still, she dutifully followed as Chloe finished showing her around her quarters, skirting the current Cavaliers, who frolicked and panted about Larryn's feet. Now and then she stooped to pat the sweet long-haired spaniels. She loved Cavaliers.

She had lost her own, Kit, only a few months earlier.

The study was part of a huge, antique-crammed suite, including an enormous bedroom and a spacious bathroom with an old porcelain sink trimmed with gold fixtures. The place could easily have been the mansion's master suite.

A horrible thought struck Larryn. "This is wonderful, but you haven't moved out of your own rooms for me, have you?"

"Of course not, Larryn. I've always reserved this suite for you."

That seemed an odd thing to say, but kind. "Thanks," she replied, putting down her overnight bag. Her luggage, woefully shabby for such luxurious surroundings, had been deposited beside a tapestry-lined wall in the bedroom. She had noticed a couple of maids when she'd arrived—efficient and unobtrusive, judging by how quickly and quietly they had gotten her things here.

Chloe led her back to the suite's study. "Now I'll leave you." She held out her perfectly manicured hand. When Larryn took it, the older lady unexpectedly pulled her forward until she was enfolded in a surprisingly hearty hug. She wasn't used to such close contact with anyone. It made her uncomfortable, especially when it stretched on for several long seconds.

Chloe's head barely reached Larryn's chin, and she felt fragile in Larryn's arms. "You can't know how long I've waited for your visit." Chloe's voice was vehement with an emotion Larryn couldn't interpret.

"I've looked forward to it, too." But Chloe's comment seemed strange to Larryn. She *had* looked forward to her visit, for longer than she had needed to. She had been scheduled to arrive around the same time the previous year, but when she'd had to postpone at the last minute due to a work emergency, Chloe, to Larryn's great disappointment, had put her off about rescheduling, until now. Coincidentally, it was just a year later than originally planned. The timing turned out perfect, right at the same time as a London medical conference Larryn had wanted to attend.

"Good night, Larryn." Chloe paused at the door. She was a pretty lady, with high cheekbones and a dainty little chin—very youthful. But Larryn noted wrinkles at the corners of her hazel eyes, and a network of small veins crisscrossed her cheeks. Now her sweet, sly smile held a message that Larryn couldn't understand. "Sleep . . . well." She looked over Larryn's shoulder, then hurried from the suite, followed by her dogs.

Larryn turned to see what she had been looking at. It could only have been one thing. Behind her was the bigger-than-life portrait of Thomas Northby, duke of Seldrake.

Larryn stared again for a long moment. The guy certainly had been imposing. Noble. Handsome.

And had lived a long, long time ago.

Why was it she felt so drawn to him? As though his long, aristocratic fingers had lifted from the back of his dog and beckoned to her.

As though those arresting blue eyes saw into her soul.

Larryn sighed. She was being ridiculous. A psychiatrist would have a field day with her. She had no interest in a relationship with a real man, so it was safe for her to fall for the one in the portrait. There was no possibility that the attraction could be returned.

Besides, she knew deep inside, that the duke, when he walked these halls, would have been as big a turn off as any man she had ever met. He was from the Restoration era. She knew a little about that age because of her interest in King Charles's small spaniels. It was a time of revelry after the ousting of the Puritans. A time of excess, when men changed mistresses more often than they bathed.

She gave a glance of scorn to the gorgeous man peering from the portrait. His brilliant blue eyes beneath those ironic brows seemed much too amused.

Shaking her head at her own overactive imagination, she went into the bedroom and began to unpack.

A yap woke Larryn.

She had not realized she'd been asleep. She had only lain down in the huge, hard-mattressed bed at eleven be-cause it was her usual bedtime at home, and she wanted to get used to English time. But she hadn't closed her eyes— or so she had thought.

She did not at first raise her head from the comfortable down pillow. It was still night, wasn't it? The room was dark.

Almost.

Part of the room was lit by a soft glow. Funny. When she had arrived by cab, she hadn't noticed street lamps near enough to wash light into the house, although there were several other houses along this country lane. The only illumination to welcome her had been from a dim gas lamp flickering from a pole at the arc of the circular drive and the vibrant light that streamed out through the mansion's many windows.

This late, the house lights would be doused. The gaslight outside might still be lit, but this glow didn't flicker. And didn't her room face the back?

A movement caught her attention, and she gasped. Then smiled. It was a dog. The one whose noise had awakened her, of course. One of the dogs she had met earlier.

Except . . .

The pup was different from Chloe's three Cavaliers. It looked more like the one in the portrait: lankier and with shorter legs, a pointed muzzle, and ears set higher on the head. It was the same coloration—the white with red markings that was known as Blenheim. Its hair was fluffy and long.

The jewels on its collar glinted in the strange glow that had somehow moved to encompass the dog. An optical illusion, Larryn believed. The light had to be coming from outside the window.

But before she had lain down, she had loosened the thick cords and dropped the heavy velvet curtains over the mullioned windows.

Obviously the door to the suite had gotten open. Yet she had checked to ensure it was shut; in case she failed to sleep, she didn't want the dogs to hear her restlessness and disturb anyone.

Besides, she had wanted a final look that night at the marvelous portrait of the duke.

But if the door had been shut, how had this dog managed to get in?

Now the small creature sat on the floor, regarding her with head cocked and tail wagging. Where had Chloe found a jeweled collar so like the one in the portrait? Had she had it made—or could the real thing have been passed down through the centuries?

"Hi, pup." Larryn's voice sounded groggy, even to her. The tail wagged faster, and the big brown eyes brightened. "What are you doing here?"

The dog stood, crouched, and yapped again, then ran off.

Strange. There was no carpeting on the beautifully polished tongue-and-groove hardwood floor where the animal had been; the Turkish carpet beneath the bed didn't extend quite that far. But Larryn heard no skittering of doggy nails.

She sat up, stretching. Her long brown hair, unbound for sleeping, tickled her bare shoulders, and she used the back of her hand to brush it from her face. She decided to shoo the pup away so it wouldn't be left behind when the other dogs were let out for their constitutionals when morning arrived.

"Where did you go, fellow?" she asked, then looked in the direction of the glow. Unsurprisingly, it came from the door to the study. She must have left a light on.

There was no need for her pulse to begin racing as though something really odd were going on. But it did anyway.

She swung her legs slowly over the bed, trying to convince herself her sudden nervousness was for nothing. The glow had a perfectly logical explanation. So did the presence of the light-footed, unusual-looking dog. She was simply in an unfamiliar place. No need to feel uneasy.

It was a long way to the floor, but she eased her way down, her feet searching the rug for her terry-cloth mules. Her sleeveless white cotton nightgown reached to just below her knees. Though she wasn't likely to run into anyone rambling around the house at this hour, she grabbed her blue satin robe from where she'd draped it over the top of a bedpost before lying down. She threw it around her and tied the belt.

As she reached the door, she gasped in shock, and her hand flew to her throat.

The dog was no longer alone. And now he looked translucent. That odd glow no longer followed him; it emanated from him.

Just like it emanated from the man he was with.

The man who also stared down from the portrait on the wall.

Standing in the study was the life-size, transparent figure of Thomas Northby, duke of Seldrake.

Chapter 2

IMPOSSIBLE! Larryn grabbed the sturdy door frame for support as her legs nearly failed her. Her heart thumped crazily inside her chest, and her teeth chattered.

Bad enough that she was imagining the specter of the man in the imposing portrait, but the dog, too? Who ever heard of a ghost dog? She had to be dreaming.

But she continued to watch as the apparition of the duke paced before the carved desk that had probably once been his, his strides long and decisive. His pet kept up, loping at his heels. The glow followed them up the room and back.

Larryn's breathing grew audible as she watched. Tiny moaning sounds of fright issued from her throat.

Seldrake wasn't dressed in the picture's black velvet coat but wore a gleaming white shirt with sleeves that billowed as he moved. His trousers stopped below his knees, and muscular calves filled out filmy stockings. Buckles gleamed on his shoes.

His hair appeared even longer than in the picture. It was parted in the center and curved down his shoulders in a mass of masculine waves that rippled as he walked.

His eyes no longer looked merely piercing and sardonic,

but angry. Those light, shaggy brows she had seen in the portrait were drawn together in an irate frown.

The detail in this dream was incredible.

Larryn shook her head, feeling her hair twist about her. She blinked, she wiped her moist eyes, and still the specters remained.

"Okay," she rasped aloud in a tremulous voice. "What's going on here?"

Neither man nor dog reacted as if they had heard her. Of course not. No one had ever said ghosts could hear.

But what rational person ever said ghosts existed?

Suddenly, the pacing stopped. The duke's mouth opened. "I can heed her no longer," he said. His resonant baritone reverberated hollowly through the room in an accent that sounded nearly Shakespearean. No, that was wrong. Shakespeare had been Elizabethan, more than fifty years earlier than the Restoration.

Seldrake seemed to put something on his desk. Then he headed toward the door. So did his dog. So did Larryn.

She had actually heard the ghost speak.

Who was the "her" he'd said he couldn't heed?

"I thought ghosts had no substance," she whispered. But this one, though transparent, twisted the doorknob, flung open the heavy wooden door, and hurried on.

Larryn's suite was on the second floor of Seldrake House. At the arched doorway to the hall, she grabbed on to a column. She had an urge to run back to bed and hunker down under the covers. Maybe she *was* still in bed beneath the blankets. If so, why was she shaking so hard?

She heard no footsteps as man and dog continued down the corridor. She didn't even hear Chloe's Cavaliers; what kind of watchdogs were they?

But they wouldn't bark at what happened in her dream.

The two ghosts had reached the end of the hall. Urged by an impetus she didn't stop to analyze, Larryn ran after them.

She felt the hallway below her slippers, heard her own scuffling steps on the long, red runner as she chased the glow and its spectral contents. Why was she following? As frightened as she felt, she had to be nuts!

She passed a procession of closed doors of decorative carved wood. The antique tables and bric-a-brac that had looked so grandly ornate under the lights when she had arrived now cast eerie shadows in the faint, fading glow.

Fading? Where had they gone, the unreal man and his spectral dog?

At the end of the hall, Larryn saw an open door. The glow shone from somewhere beyond. She glanced inside. It contained a narrow stairway, with steps leading both up and down. The pale light gleamed from the upper end. Larryn hesitated. She didn't really want to follow. She should go back to bed.

What if this wasn't a dream?

Somehow, she no longer thought it was. She must be awake. Bodies didn't quake so fearfully in dreams, did they?

Taking a deep breath, she grabbed the handrail and began to ascend. No! she told herself. But a sense she couldn't explain compelled her upward.

Judging by the steepness and narrowness, she assumed it had once been a servants' stairway. She passed a door on the first landing, probably leading to maids' quarters in the attic. A blast of cool air bombarded her as she continued upward, and her satin robe billowed about her. In a minute, she was at an open door. She walked outside into darkness lit only by the glow.

She was on the roof. It was flat there. She hadn't noticed its pitch when she had arrived at the mansion the night before. All she had seen was the size of the house, its geometric detail, its many mullioned windows from which light had poured.

The man and dog were some distance ahead. Though terrified, she took tentative steps in their direction. The dog darted about. Its excited yaps sounded as though they came from deep inside a tunnel.

What was the man doing? He stood nearly at the edge

of the roof, beside a white wrought-iron rail that reached only to his shins. In the glow that emanated from him, his chin looked raised. His hair blew in the breeze. So did his white shirtsleeves. His hands were outstretched, as though beseeching someone Larryn couldn't see.

She heard his voice, like the dog's, as though it were distant. She couldn't make out what it said, but the tone sounded cajoling. At first. As she slowly walked toward him, the volume grew louder. His stance tensed. "You cannot!" he shouted. "I shall not let you hurt that—"

Larryn could make out no more, for ghostly man and dog were suddenly sheathed in something gray, thick, and swirling, like liquid smoke. She smelled something humid, yet burning. She ran toward where she had last seen the specters despite the fear the smoky substance—the whole scene—instilled in her. "Wait!" she cried. "What's happening?"

The roof went black. Larryn gasped. For a moment, she could see nothing, hear nothing except the pounding of her own frantic heart. She was afraid to move, unsure how close she was to the edge.

As her eyes adjusted to the darkness, the moon emerged from behind a bank of clouds. In its light, she saw she was still a few feet from the rail around the roof.

She edged closer. The spirits, if that was what they had been, had disappeared. She had no reason to think they'd fallen over the roof. And yet, she had an urge to look down.

There were no lights on in the house below, and she felt as though she were looking into the blackness of a bottomless well.

She swallowed hard. Not that ghosts could be hurt, but if they, or anyone else, fell from here, they'd be—what? Killed? Who could kill something that didn't exist?

And then she heard a rustling behind her.

Barely breathing, tears moistening her eyes, she turned.

Man and dog stood a short distance away. They were still translucent. Glowing.

The man held out his hands toward her. She could see

him in even more detail now, for she was closer. His great, shaggy brows were knit in a frown above those piercing blue eyes. His nose was long and aristocratic. The wide mouth, so expressive in his portrait, was twisted in a grimace that shouted of anguish, of horror.

"Help me," he said.

Thomas Northby, duke of Seldrake, seldom asked anyone for anything. He knew not why he pleaded with this woman. Except that . . . something was terribly wrong.

He had failed. A failure so dreadful . . .

But he could not remember.

He heard August whine. He looked down to see the little dog. Did he like dogs? He did not know. But this one, he felt certain, had belonged to someone dear to him, which made the animal dear to him. But why could he not recall?

His mind. He had long prided himself on its keenness. But now . . . now, its sharpness had softened into utter confusion.

Who was this woman? How did he believe she could help him?

In the dim light of the moon, he stared at her. She reminded him of . . . who? She was lovely, with her long hair—brown, burnished silk—blowing in the wind, though he had a recollection of it swept up severely, free of the wigs, frills, and curls favored by other ladies of his acquaintance. Ah, but she was different in so many other ways as well.

Though he recalled little else, he was certain of this.

There was a near feline quality to her face, with her large, dark eyes tilted up at the corners, her full lips so demure in repose, rarely curving up into a smile, but when they did, their taste gave more delight than the sweetest of the fruit from his orchard. Her jaw was just a touch too strong, underscoring the determination within her that drove him to distraction.

Now, she stared at him with an expression darkening her

delightful face that he could interpret only as . . . horror. And pity. For him?

For Thomas Northby, the first duke of Seldrake? How utterly ridiculous!

"How?" whispered a melodious, quavering voice. The woman spoke to him.

"How what?" he asked. His voice sounded hollow, even to him. And as rusty as a bell in an abandoned churchyard.

"You asked me to help you." She sounded a trifle impatient. "What would you like me to do?"

Ah, her spunk was showing. No longer was she so afraid. But . . . "Do?" He did not know. Something was appallingly wrong, yet he did not understand what it was. "There is nothing you can do for me, Larryn."

Her beautiful dark eyes widened, then she blinked. "How do you know my name?" Her sweet voice shook with fright.

He had no answer. He had simply . . . known. He had not meant to frighten her. He held out his arms in supplication.

Only then did he notice he could see right through them. He could not feel them. He glanced about himself. There was no substance to him at all! And as he watched, his arms began to disappear. In alarm, he roared, "No!"

What was happening to him?

"Larryn," he whispered, his voice sounding so terribly far away. "I will come back."

Somehow, despite the darkness of the stairwell without the ghosts to light her way, despite the trembling in her legs, Larryn made it back to her room.

She had seen a ghost. *Two* ghosts.

The specter of the man had known her name.

He had promised to come back.

She closed the door behind her and turned on the overhead light. The brightness hurt her eyes. She leaned against the wall while whatever starch had been left in her legs drained out. She sank to the floor, closed her stinging eyes, and shook her head. What was happening?

Something warm and furry leaped into Larryn's trembling lap, and she stifled a scream. As her eyelids popped open, a wet tongue slurped at them. It was a dog. A Cavalier puppy. A *real*, Blenheim Cavalier puppy, one of Chloe's dogs, that she could, and did, hug. It had a soft muzzle that showed its youth plus a coveted red lozenge spot between its matching red ears, at the top of its otherwise white crown. "What are you doing here?" Larryn asked.

The puppy whined in response.

"Did you see them? The ghosts, I mean." The pup replied only by licking at the air as though trying to taste her breath. Larryn laughed despite herself. "Well," she said, "I don't think I'd better take you back to your buddies at this hour or we'll disturb the whole household."

On the other hand, maybe she should wake Chloe. Tell her the whole horrible tale.

But what if Larryn really had been hallucinating?

The ghosts were gone. Telling Chloe could wait till morning—and by then Larryn might have thought of a rational explanation.

That was as likely as the pup on her lap reciting love sonnets. "How about spending the night here?" Larryn scratched behind the dog's ears. The idea of canine company, after all she had been through, sounded appealing.

The pup lay on the floor, its small head between its paws. It looked at her, enormous brown eyes peering soulfully from the red mask formed by the short fur of its face.

"Poor thing, you look tired." From the bathroom, Larryn got a towel that looked older than the rest. "Hope you're housebroken." She put the towel on the rug, then got into bed. "Good night," she said. "Keep that tail wagging." Now, if only she could settle her own pulse rate so it didn't keep time with that tail as the pup happily pawed at the towel to make a nest.

As hard as Larryn tried to settle into the comfortable bed, her mind turned cartwheels. Ghosts, indeed! Had she gone mad? She didn't think so. But the alternatives were that she had dreamed everything, which she no longer believed . . . or that she had really seen them.

How had the duke of Seldrake's ghost known her name?

He had said he was coming back. She should have been terrified. She *was* terrified.

Then why, Larryn wondered as her eyelids grew heavy, did the thought of his return make her smile?

A yap woke Larryn. Her eyes popped open. Not again!

But it was daylight. No ghost dog barked. The pup who had come to visit had somehow gotten onto the high bed and stood on the covers near Larryn, sounding off.

Someone knocked on the door. That explained the pup's behavior. It had heard the person first.

"Just a minute," Larryn called groggily, then grumped to the barking pup, "Keep your watchdogging to yourself." She glanced around. The room was filled with the warm light of day. No glare from a frightening, though gorgeous, hallucination, thank heavens.

"Doctor Maeller?" called a high, female voice. "Miss Chloe asked if you was awake, for she wants to come see if you'll breakfast with 'er before your meeting."

"I'll be dressed soon," Larryn called to the maid. "And Miss Chloe can come in whenever she wants." She hopped onto the floor and lifted her robe from the post.

"Thanks." The voice was Chloe's. The door opened, and Larryn's hostess walked in. She was dressed in a short-sleeved hunter green sweater over a brown tweed skirt. Her streaked pageboy was neatly combed, and her hazel eyes, in their nest of fine wrinkles, appeared well rested.

Unlike, Larryn was sure, her own. She began to tie her robe and found its sash was wet and full of tiny teeth marks.

"Oh, dear." Chloe picked up the puppy. "We'll get you a new dressing gown."

Larryn shook her head. "It's nothing."

"That's very sweet, Larryn. I hope this little imp didn't disturb you. She always strays from the others."

"No, she didn't bother me." She helped me, in fact, Lar-

ryn thought. She was still considering whether to tell her
hostess her house was haunted.

"Your friend, here, is looking for some special attention."
Chloe sat on the edge of the bed, petting the pup.

"She's adorable," Larryn remarked. She cast aside her
memories of the night to organize her clothes for the day:
a tailored gray suit, a white blouse.

"I'm glad you think so. She's the only one left of my
last litter, and I wish to give her to you."

"Oh, Chloe, you don't—"

"It will be good for her. And for you. You can easily
take her home. The only horrible quarantine is when you
come here."

Larryn would never subject a dog to six months in quarantine. But the United States didn't impose the same re-
strictions as England. Chloe had even sent Kit to her a few
years back.

Even though they had only just met face-to-face the day
before. Until then, they had simply been Internet friends.
They had corresponded by bulletin boards and E-mail for
years, since Larryn was an undergraduate student, when
Chloe had turned into Larryn's angel. She had already
given Larryn so much. And was it fair to the pup? "A dog's
a lot of responsibility, Chloe. With my work, I'm gone a
lot."

"Only during the day. It isn't as though you have a medical practice."

Larryn felt her back stiffen defensively. "Research has
its own demands," she said.

Chloe placed the puppy on the floor and took a step
toward Larryn, her slender hands outstretched. "I didn't
mean what you do isn't important. It is vital that someone
discovers what to do about all those horrible viruses. But
you tend to work regular hours. You hadn't any trouble
keeping Kit, did you?"

"No." Larryn had bought a townhouse with a doggy door
into a locked garden so the dog could take a constitutional
when he wanted. She still lived there now. Alone.

Lonely.

The imposing figure of the duke of Seldrake—confusion in his eyes—zipped into her head, and she zipped it right back out. She didn't need a phantom to keep her company. She was content. She had her work, and her coworkers, and her friends.

But no family, a small voice taunted inside. Not anymore.

Not after what had happened to her sister.

She said to Chloe a bit too brightly, "Thanks, I'll think about it. What's her name?" Why should she care? She wasn't going to take on another pet—was she?

And have the heartache when she lost this one, too? Kit had contracted a doggy disease that not even she, a human infectious disease specialist, had been able to conquer.

Not that she had been successful with her sister, either.

"Poor nameless thing," Chloe said. "After I sold her brothers and sisters, I couldn't decide what to do with her, so I just kept her around. I've called her 'pup' or 'baby.' She's nearly six months old. Even if you don't take her, why don't you name her?"

Larryn knew that if she named the pup, she would feel even more attached to her. "I'll think about that, too," she said.

"Good." Chloe smiled, staring at Larryn with her head cocked, as though she expected something.

Larryn hesitated, not wanting to sound rude. "I'd better excuse myself to get dressed for my meeting."

"Of course." Looking disappointed, Chloe headed for the bedroom door. "Breakfast is in the morning room. After, I'll have you driven to the nearest train station."

"Thanks," Larryn said, "for everything."

"You're quite welcome." Chloe paused at the door to pick up the pup. "I'll put her out with the rest. Now, hurry so you've time to breakfast with me." Her mouth turned up into a smile that looked . . . well, crafty. Even more so than the sly smile Larryn had thought she'd seen last night. "I was hoping you'd bring it up yourself," she said, "but since you didn't . . . well, I'm dying to hear how you spent your night." She left, closing the door behind her.

Chapter 3

SHE KNEW! LARRYN could think of little else while she showered and put on makeup.

Larryn had wondered why Chloe had rushed her upstairs the night before. She had assumed her elderly hostess was tired. But Larryn now suspected that Chloe had intended that she be there waiting when the specter appeared. Specters. She couldn't forget about the dog.

Nor could she forget the man. His look of anguish as he disappeared into the fog. His plea for help. The fact that he knew her name.

He had said he was returning. The idea made her quiver—not entirely from fear, but from anticipation as well. How bizarre!

All this was too incredible. Maybe Chloe was playing a trick on her. But why?

She threw on her clothes and pinned up her long hair into its professional chignon. Then she picked up purse and briefcase and hurried down the grand staircase.

The entry hall was more magnificent in daylight than it had been the night before. The whiteness of the marble floor gleamed in the sunlight streaming through windows around the front door. The gold trim on the lowboy tables along the walls sparkled, setting off the figurines on their tops. Even the oil portraits and country scenes along the painted walls seemed brighter.

Larryn stopped at the base of the steps and looked around. She heard a thundering of tiny pawbeats, and suddenly she was leapt upon by the three dogs, including the puppy. She laughed.

"Dr. Maeller." A thin maid in a pink uniform stepped out of a doorway. "Miss Chloe says you're to meet 'er in the breakfast room, mum. It's this way, if you please."

Accompanied by the rowdy dogs, Larryn followed the maid, who opened a door and led Larryn into a long room with glass walls. It was warm inside. Sunlight streaked through the windows. Outside, down a gentle slope, was a vast, gorgeous garden, with trimmed trees, squared hedges, and beds of flowers—obviously well planned, and beautifully symmetrical. "Oh," she murmured.

"Do you like it?" Chloe asked in her cultivated English accent. She had been at a table at the end of the room reading a book. A pair of half-glasses perched near the end of her nose. She pulled them off and reached down to pet the dogs.

"It's lovely." Larryn took the seat that Chloe indicated. "Your home is wonderful. It's got such magnificent atmosphere. I'd imagine it's quite old, and that—"

"Did you see him?"

Larryn blinked at the older woman, momentarily speechless. "See whom?" Her voice caught, and she cleared her throat.

"The duke, of course. The man in the portrait."

Larryn said cautiously, "I noticed the portrait again this morning."

"But did you see *him?* His ghost. And the dog's."

Larryn stood, disturbing the dogs. "They scared me half to death, then led me to the roof in the dark. I don't know why I followed, but—"

"You had to." Chloe's voice was gentle.

Larryn closed her eyes in amazement. Chloe was acting as though they were having an ordinary conversation, but what they were saying was incredible. "Is this a joke?"

"Not at all."

"If it's real, and you knew about this . . . this haunting, why didn't you warn me?"

Chloe lifted the edges of her mouth in a patronizing smile. "Would you have believed me?"

"Of course—" she began indignantly, then hesitated and finished more weakly, "—not." She gave an answering grin. "Americans are brought up to believe in the possibility of a flying saucer cover-up, but not, necessarily, in ghosts."

"Well, then . . ." Chloe waved her small hand, with its red polished nails, in the air. "Now, tell me about it."

"First, explain, please: Why did you set me up?"

"All in good time, Larryn. I need to know what happened."

The maid brought Larryn's breakfast. Larryn took a bite, considering how to begin. "I heard a dog," she said, then told the whole tale.

Chloe's hazel eyes barely blinked as she stared at Larryn, obviously enthralled.

Larryn tried to explain what she had seen on the roof. "The . . . duke was upset, arguing with someone I couldn't see. Then he disappeared into a bank of . . . well, fog." She paused to take a bite of toast.

"Was that all? I mean, wasn't he . . . didn't he . . . ?"

"He returned," Larryn said.

"Wonderful! Did he speak to you?"

Larryn shuddered as she nodded slowly. "He asked me to help him. He . . . he knew my name." She drew in her breath. "And he said he'd be back."

"Splendid!" crowed Chloe, clapping her hands. That brought the dogs to attention. "This is even better than I'd hoped."

"You hoped?" Larryn cried. "Chloe, I deserve an explanation."

"Yes," the older woman said, "you do. Have you finished

breakfast?" Larryn nodded. "Good. Come and walk with me."

Larryn looked at her watch. "I haven't much time."

"Let's hurry." Chloe led Larryn through a glass door and down stone steps into the garden. The dogs barked and ran ahead.

The path was strewn with wood chips, and the fragrance of pungent hedges mixed with aromatic fall flowers filled Larryn's senses. A dilapidated stone outbuilding sat off to one side.

"Chloe . . ." Larryn prompted, treading carefully in her high-heeled pumps.

"I knew about your visitor last night, Larryn," her hostess said, "because I've seen him every September fifteenth since I was a child."

Larryn stopped as though suddenly tethered. "Do you mean you—?"

"I suspect the duke of Seldrake comes here on the anniversary of some major event, maybe even the night he died." Chloe stooped to pick a dead flower off a rosebush beside the path. "But though this house has been in my family for generations, I only heard whispers. Some English families take pride in family ghosts, but mine apparently did not." She began walking again.

"Chloe, tell me, please. Why did you set me up?"

"I'll get there, but you need the background. Like you, I saw the duke's ghost; heard him, too. He acted the same as you saw. The first times I saw him, he disappeared in the fog, but after several years, he began to come back and beg me for help."

Larryn wasn't sure why she felt so deflated. Surely she hadn't hoped that she shared something special with the ghost. "Then he called your name and said he would return," she prompted, trying to sound cheerful.

"No. He never knew me. And he certainly never said he would return."

Larryn felt guilty at the pleasure that washed through her. "But he did come back?"

"Not till the next year."

The next year? Something inside Larryn seemed to plum-met to the ground. The last thing she wanted was to have to worry about a ghostly visitation for a whole year. No, the last thing was to have to *wait* for a year. Would Chloe even invite her back?

Chloe hadn't stopped speaking. "Things went differently for you, Larryn. I knew they would. Maybe this time I'll get an answer. If he said he'd be back, perhaps it means right away."

A ray of hope lit inside Larryn. "Why does he return?"

"I wish I knew." Chloe sighed. "I've consulted experts. It could be as simple as that something highly emotional to him happened on this date years ago, perhaps his death. That's a common reason persons do not find rest. Their emotional energy becomes imprinted in time at that very moment. But because he asks for help . . . well, I've con-cluded he left unfinished business."

"What kind of unfinished business?"

Chloe sighed. "It's not for lack of trying that I've failed to learn."

"You said the duke is your ancestor. Is there a clue in your family history?"

"Actually, we're not direct descendants. There is confu-sion as to whether he even had children. No sons, or there would have been subsequent dukes. Daughters, perhaps. We think he was married. We know his sister was."

Married? Larryn's knees suddenly wobbled. Of course he would have been married. Nobles always married to continue their lines. But why did the ghost's marital status make her feel so miserable?

Chloe glanced at her watch. "You had better hurry to your meeting."

"Of course." Larryn started back up the path, then stopped. "But Chloe, you haven't explained why you brought me into this."

The older woman smiled. "We'll talk later."

•   •   •

At the conference, Larryn forced her mind to concentrate on lectures on infectious diseases, her specialty. At least she tried.

When the day's talks were done, as she'd previously planned, she took a combined walking and bus tour around London. Many buildings seemed quite old. Had they been there during the days the duke of Seldrake had lived? He might have seen some of the same structures. Walked on the same ground.

For someone with limited imagination, she was certainly being fanciful.

Finally, exhausted, she returned to Seldrake House. She stood outside, grinning at the sound of the excited dogs from inside. There were smaller homes down the road from the three-story stately house. It was deep gray and geometric, with as many windows on one side as the other. All were mullioned, and light gleamed on the front lawn from most of them. Steps at the house's center swept up to the covered entry.

Larryn's gaze rose to the roof. The center was flat, though the front was sloped and contained a row of small and skinny chimneys.

Before Larryn knocked, a maid opened the door. "The dogs thought they heard something," she said. "Welcome back, Dr. Maeller. Miss Chloe is waiting in the front parlor." The dogs leapt at her legs and licked her hands.

Her hostess was in a caftan of flowing blue satin. She hurried toward Larryn, hands extended. "How was your meeting?"

"Great." Larryn permitted Chloe's brief hug, then followed her to a beautiful Queen Anne beechwood settee, with carved scrolling arms and acanthus leaves at the back. They sat, and Chloe told the maid to bring tea.

A furry weight leapt onto Larryn's lap, and she looked down. It was the pup Chloe had offered to her. Larryn laughed.

"You don't have a choice about accepting her," Chloe said. "She's adopted you."

"We'll see." But Larryn couldn't help thinking Chloe was right as she stroked the warm pup's silky red and white fur.

"Tell me about the conference," Chloe said.

Larryn obeyed, keeping her comments brief.

"All right, then." Chloe's small features beamed. "You've been patient, my dear. You wanted to know why I asked you here in time to see the duke's ghost."

It was what Larryn had dwelled on all day. That and her impossibly enticing mental image of the handsome, tortured ghost.

"Wait here a minute." Chloe rose and left the room.

While she was gone, one dog climbed onto the antique settee, and Larryn shooed him down, unsure of the house rules. Perhaps she'd broken them by allowing the pup on her lap.

If she kept her, what would she name her? She glanced down, seeing the ID tag on her briefcase on the floor. It was adorned by . . . a caduceus. Of course! She would name the pup Caduceus. Caddie, for short. "Hi, Caddie," she whispered. The dog stretched up and licked her nose.

The decision had been made for her. Caddie was hers.

Chloe returned, carrying a small box. She sat beside Larryn, who nearly trembled with curiosity.

"The tale is long and involved," Chloe said.

Larryn's heart sank. Wasn't she going to get immediate answers?

"It began when I was a child, the first time I saw the duke's ghost," continued Chloe. "I was fascinated. Later, I realized I'd become obsessed with him. But even knowing that, I didn't want to stop. I wanted to know all I could, to help him."

Larryn identified with that.

Chloe's fine skin seemed ageless in the parlor's dim light. "This house dates from before his time. I knew there were relics from then. I began, at age twelve, to comb the place: the bedrooms and studies, attics, servants' quarters—everywhere."

"Did you find anything?" Larryn leaned eagerly toward her. Had the contents of the box on Chloe's lap been the duke's?

"Eventually. Interestingly, it was in an outbuilding called a banquet house that had once, I believe, been used as a kennel. For Cavaliers, for Seldrakes have kept the small spaniels since then."

"I can understand that," Larryn said, giving Caddie a little squeeze. The pup looked up from her lap, her panting resembling a silent laugh.

Chloe smiled. "Among some fascinating but moldering medical journals from the sixteen hundreds, I found other items that were clearly the duke's. There was the sapphire ring he wore in his portrait. Plus, there was the jeweled dog collar." She opened the box. The familiar-looking jewels sparkled inside.

"There's a special compartment in the collar," Chloe continued. She ran her fingers along the heavy gold, and Larryn noted a thicker area. Chloe popped it open with her thumb.

"This was particularly fascinating to me," Chloe said. "In fact, it triggered my life's quest."

She pulled out a small locket. Inside was a miniature painting.

Larryn stared at it. The woman portrayed was a dead ringer for her!

She wore her hair in the same severe chignon Larryn favored. Her eyes, the same shade of dark brown, tipped up at the corners in the way Larryn found so annoying.

"Who . . . who is she?" Larryn couldn't stop the shaking in her voice.

Silently, Chloe popped the portrait out of the locket.

Written in tiny letters on the back was: *Dr. Larryn Maeller.*

Chapter 4

"I . . . I DON'T understand." Larryn could hardly speak. She reached for the tiny portrait, studied it for a moment, then dropped it onto the table as though it had caught fire. The face seemed to stare back at her. *Her* face.

"I'll make a story that spanned many years very short," Chloe said. The smile on her aging face was sympathetic. "When I found the locket, I began trying to find a historical reference to a Dr. Larryn Maeller. If she lived in the duke's time, she would have been an anomaly. And brave. Women acted as healers and midwives then, but any who styled themselves doctors were either deemed mad or persecuted. But for the longest time, despite becoming quite obsessed with my quest, I found no mention at all, not in reference volumes, diaries, family histories, church records . . . until several years ago, when I saw the name 'Larryn Maeller' on the Internet, of all places. But—"

"But that was me," Larryn whispered. "I was just a college student who wanted to become a doctor."

Chloe nodded. "Yes. I was certain after you sent me a picture of yourself. And although I did not understand, I knew what I had to do."

"You helped me." Larryn's breathing was shallow, and she wondered if she was going to hyperventilate. "You found me the money to get through medical school. And you encouraged me."

She had adored this faraway woman who had taken such an interest in her. She still did. But now she knew that there had been an ulterior motive. A very bizarre, impossible motive: to create the "Dr." Larryn Maeller of that portrait.

"That's right, Larryn, my dear. And now . . ."

"And now what?" Larryn forced her voice to become stronger. "Are you trying to tell me that somehow I am this same Dr. Larryn Maeller depicted in a locket that's nearly three hundred fifty years old?" She laughed. "Chloe, I appreciate everything you've done for me, but I really can't believe—"

"And did you believe in ghosts before last night?"

That stopped Larryn. She bit her lower lip. "What is it that I'm supposed to do?" she asked quietly, convinced that she did not want to hear Chloe's response.

Chloe shrugged so her narrow shoulders brushed the bottom of her pageboy. "I don't know what you will do, my dear. But I am quite certain that you will do something."

Larryn did not expect to sleep at all that night. Even so, she was awakened by a yip.

Caddie had been sleeping on the bed with her. It was the puppy who had roused her. Larryn did not want to know why. She kept her eyes closed . . . at first. But Caddie wriggled about on the bed, as though greeting someone.

With a deep and nervous sigh, Larryn gave in. She forced her eyes open.

The phantom dog was on the floor beside the bed, a light around it. A matching glow appeared in the adjoining room.

Hadn't Chloe told her that the ghost only appeared once a year? But more had happened to Larryn than Chloe had seen before. And Larryn had known something would occur. What else but the return of the duke of Seldrake?

She lay there shaking. Why did the woman in the locket look like her? have her name?

Did she really want to find out?

Did she have a choice?

Of course. She could stay where she was, allow the phenomena to disappear without getting near them again. Without getting involved.

Without helping, as the ghost of the duke had begged. . . .

With a deep sigh, she realized she had to face what awaited her. She couldn't go home now, knowing of this mystery, without understanding what it was about. She doubted she could help, but she was a doctor. She had given an oath that she took seriously. She had to help people in distress.

Even if they were already dead . . . ?

Caddie whined beside her. "All right," she whispered to the puppy. "You win." She turned on a lamp, comforted a little by the light. She threw the covers off, blanketing the puppy till Caddie wiggled out from beneath the sheets and leapt to the floor. The phantom dog and the pup seemed to sniff each other, the way any ordinary dogs did when they met. Larryn shook her head in amazement.

Now what? If she went into the other room, the specter of the duke might be there. Would he stalk back up to the roof? If so, she would follow. This time, she was not about to go up the cold stone stairs and onto the wind-tossed roof in her nightclothes. She put on underwear and grabbed the first thing she could find: the long-sleeved blouse and tailored skirt she had worn that day to the conference. She skipped the suit jacket.

Taking a deep breath, she ventured into the next room.

The duke of Seldrake was there. Rather, his specter was—as imposing as the night before. He was dressed again in the antique shirt and short trousers that looked so good on him.

He followed the same scenario as he had the previous

night: pacing in anger, grumbling, "I can heed her no longer."

In moments, he stalked from the room. Larryn could still change her mind and go back to bed. She did not have to—

She continued to argue with herself as she followed him. His phantom dog was by his side, and Caddie trotted happily beside Larryn.

As before, no one in the rest of the house stirred. Larryn again trembled in trepidation as she followed the ghost and his dog up the stairs, but this time she was filled with anticipation, too. Was she about to learn why she was the subject of that antique locket?

Would the ghost again ask her for help? Would she somehow figure out what to do?

At least this time she was prepared to come back downstairs. She had stuck a mini flashlight into her skirt pocket.

On the roof, the wind blew even more fiercely than it had the previous night. Seldrake appeared oblivious to it, instead enacting his one-sided scene once more. "You cannot!" he shouted. "I shall not let you hurt that—"

The gray and swirling miasma returned, its hot, burning smell hurting Larryn's nostrils. Caddie whined.

For a moment, Larryn saw the ghost dog's form partially surrounded by the fog. It peered out, its nose seeming to touch Caddie's. The puppy stepped forward—and was immediately immersed in the smokiness. "No!" Larryn cried and took a step toward her pup.

In moments, she, too, was engulfed by the vapor. It was freezing. It burned her. It slithered up her body, from her legs to her chest until it seemed to crush her. It whirled about her face until she was paralyzed by its odor of brimstone and ice. She was choking. She couldn't breathe. She felt herself falling . . . falling . . . and then she felt no more.

The early August eventide was unseasonably cold. So thought Thomas Northby, duke of Seldrake, as he stood upon the parapet of his rooftop, surveying the nighttime sky. A myriad of stars illuminated the darkness, overshadowed to the east by the brilliance of the near-full moon.

There was much to occupy Seldrake's thoughts. He had word of a new child in distress, one whose circumstances were such that he might be able to help. But as always, such assistance required a plan that would involve stealth, trickery, perhaps bribery or treachery.

And the utmost caution.

First, he would need to consult with his sister, Adele. It was because of her that he—

A loud thud interrupted his thoughts. It was followed by a shrill bark from August, who had, as usual, accompanied him to the roof.

As Seldrake turned, he heard an answering bark from a second dog. How odd! He had but one pet, and that due only to the loving memory of his dear Charmian. How could another animal be in his home, let alone atop the roof?

He espied the dog beside his Augie. The two examined one another, as such animals did. The strange dog resembled his pet: the same height, the same red and white coloration. But its muzzle was more round, its head more flat.

Its presence was not the oddest matter that demanded his attention, however. Lying near the pole that supported his family's banner was a woman, unconscious.

How came she to his home? To his roof? And in such a state of undress! Her attire was scandalously brief; it appeared that someone had ripped the skirts from her body, leaving her with only the shortest, plainest of her petticoats. It had hiked up, to be sure, as she lay on the ground, but even stretched to its fullest he did not believe it would reach longer than to just below her knees.

Had someone attacked this stranger here, breached the sanctity of his home? But who? And was it somehow a warning to him related to his own illicit activities?

"Madam?" he called, hurrying to her side. Seldrake knelt and reached out for the wrist of the arm that rested upon her bosom. He noted that her breast rose and fell; she was alive. He had not studied under the noted royal physician William Harvey, who had died nine years earlier, but he subscribed to Harvey's theories on the circulation of the blood. He lifted the woman's wrist to check the pulse within her. Her arms, at least, were covered by her shirt, and yet the style was like nothing he had ever seen: plain, with buttons of an unaccustomed substance. Even the shirt's material was not familiar. Mayhap she was a foreigner.

The question remained: How had she come here?

Her pulse seemed quick, yet not overly so. She moaned, and he placed her arm back as it had lain. He stared at her. She was a most comely woman, with a strikingly lovely face that stirred him even in her unconscious state. Her long hair appeared a soft brown in the light of the candle he had brought with him to the roof, a straight and silken pillow beneath her head. Perhaps she was a bit underfed, for she was more slight than the women of his acquaintance. He could not help a glimpse at her bared legs . . . slender but well shaped.

"Fool!" he growled at himself. He had no business noting the appearance of this woman. He had to awaken her, learn why she had invaded his home, and send her on her way . . . if he dared. "Madam!" he said urgently. He lifted her head.

Her eyes opened. They were an unusual hue, deepest brown, as the mahogany imported from the wilds of Africa that was used for his favorite furnishings. They seemed at first not to focus, and they closed once more.

"Madam, you must awaken." He attempted not to sound as angry as he felt; affrighting her would not assist him in obtaining the answers he needed.

Her eyes opened again. "Where am I?" Confusion showed on that most attractive face, which reminded him ever so slightly of a cat: wide mouth, large eyes tipped slightly up at the corners.

"You are at my home, madam. I am Thomas Northby, duke of Seldrake, and this is Seldrake House. And now that you have your answer, I demand mine: How came you here?"

She blinked, sat up slowly, and reached toward him. She fingered the sleeve of his shirt, then grasped his arm. She gasped, then allowed her palm to caress the side of his cheek. It was his turn to gasp at her wantonness, but the feel of her hand—slightly callused as though used to toil, yet without the harshness of a servant's—sent a thrill through his body.

"Who sent you?" he demanded harshly. Perhaps she was to seduce him so that he would tell her his many secrets. A woman as lovely as this must have wiles aplenty. But he was no fool. "Tell me," he demanded again at her silence.

"You're real." She seemed to breathe the words, as though she did not herself believe them. "I must be dreaming."

" 'Tis no dream!" he roared. "You are in my home, and I insist that you tell me who you are and why you are here."

She closed her eyes anew, and when she opened them again she shook her head as though to clear a haze from her brain. Her silken, straight hair billowed about her shoulders. "My name is Larryn Maeller." Her voice was most pleasingly pitched, but Thomas had never heard her name before. Nor did he know of her family. "I suppose you could say that Chloe Seldrake sent me," she continued, "though that's not entirely true. In a way, *you* sent for me, though I doubt that you know it." She stopped for a moment. Tears filled her lovely eyes.

He would not allow her artifice to sway him. "I most certainly did not send for you, Mrs. Maeller," he said coldly. "And I know of no 'Chloe' in my family."

"I figured you'd say that." A look most rueful washed over her face. "I'm not married, so you don't need to refer to me as 'Mrs.' "

The woman was quite old enough to have married, yet she was a spinster. Why did he feel pleased to hear that? Still, he said coolly, "I refer to all women of my acquaintance who are of good character as 'Mrs.' I might call you

'Miss,' however, should your character be less than spotless."

"I don't suppose you'd call me 'Doctor' Maeller, would you?"

Seldrake felt shocked. This woman called herself a doctor? "Unlikely, madam. Have you a barber-surgeon license? Have you been examined by the bishop of London?" He laughed aloud.

"I don't suppose you'd recognize a medical degree from UCLA and a license from the State of California, would you?"

"What nonsense is this? I know of no institution styled 'UCLA.' And 'California'—is that not the whimsical name the Spanish have given to some remote area they discovered beyond England's New World colonies?"

"Er . . . right." She appeared to hesitate for a moment, and then she said, "Could you possibly tell me right now what kind of help you need? Maybe it's some kind of business you have to finish. I'd like to get this over with so you can go to . . . wherever it is you are supposed to go."

"Help? You are here to give me help?" Thomas threw back his head and roared with laughter. But he sobered in moments. "I would believe that as much as I would believe that I sent for you, *Mrs*. Maeller. I am not going anywhere, of that you may be certain, for this is my home. And I will not toss you out on your ear until such time as I do understand your purpose for being here and your method for getting into my residence. Is that understood?"

"Sure," she said. Her words were decidedly English, yet their use, and her accent, were most foreign. He could not determine from them from whence she had come.

This woman must have quite a tale to tell, Thomas was certain. If only he could extract it from her.

"Since you are to be my . . . guest for the present," he said, "I cannot allow you to remain in such an unclothed state." He allowed his eyes to range suggestively over her body. She, after all, was the one to invade his home in such a condition. She must wish his lustful intent . . . not that he would succumb to it.

But confusion wound through him as the woman turned a becoming and embarrassed shade of pink, as though he had mortified her.

Who was she? And why did he feel so discomfited by her uninvited and unwelcome presence in his own home?

He would have his answers from her. By God, he would!

Oh, lord, Larryn thought, rubbing her eyes. This could not be happening.

She watched as the duke—the real, corporeal duke, with substance she had felt—stood beside her. "Come." He reached a hand down for her.

"Please, give me a minute." Her attempt at a pleasant smile failed miserably. She trembled all over. She was certain she would not be able to stand—not now.

"Of course, madam, but I can assure you it is warmer inside than it is here."

But the cold was not why Larryn was shivering.

She felt dwarfed as she remained seated on the roof. Vulnerable, too. She hadn't been able to tell from his picture or from his specter, but the duke was a large man.

And now, he was an angry man. He thought she had broken into his house and he wanted to know why.

She couldn't blame him. She would have the same irate reaction if someone unexpectedly appeared in her townhouse.

This couldn't be real. Ghosts did not suddenly become corporeal. But she had thought ghosts did not exist . . . and apparently they did.

"Caddie," she called. Her puppy was sitting a few feet away, beside the dog Larryn had last seen as a ghost. It, too, now appeared to have substance. It wore a beautifully jeweled collar—like the one in the portrait of the duke. The one that had hidden away the locket with Larryn's likeness. . . .

Caddie wagged her tail and lumbered in her cute, eager

puppy gait to where Larryn sat. Larryn pulled the pup to her and hugged it—her sole connection to reality.

Unless, of course, she was dreaming this, too. Or hallucinating. That was what she had thought before. It might still be true. But if so, how could she wake up or make the delusion go away?

She tucked her quivering legs under her on the hard surface of the rooftop. The duke kept staring at them, as though he had never seen a woman's legs before.

An unlikely scenario. A man as handsome as he would have had many women fawning after him, particularly in a time known to be licentious. Chloe had said that the duke of Seldrake lived during the time of the Great Plague. That was during England's Restoration period, the days of King Charles II, known for the bawdy excesses of king and courtiers.

No, Thomas Northby was probably no different from other men of his time. He'd likely had his share of women and then some.

The thought of his probably dissolute ways irritated her enough to stop her shaking. She stood, ignoring the hand he proffered again.

"Would you care to go inside?" the duke asked.

Good idea, Larryn thought. She wouldn't worry now about interrupting her hostess's sleep. This time, she would scream until Chloe came. Chloe could decide what to do now that the duke was real.

Would he explain to her how he needed her help, so she could do whatever it was and he could dematerialize again?

In the meantime, he was bigger than Larryn. She did not want to argue with him.

She wanted Chloe.

"Sure," she said. "Let's go in."

Chapter 5

LARRYN TRIED TO remain calm as she followed the duke, Caddie at her heels. The flickering candle he held in one hand made his sapphire ring sparkle. Where had the candle come from? She supposed it made as much sense that he would have materialized with his own light as that he would have materialized at all.

The illumination, while not much, was certainly better than the last time she had groped her way downstairs in the dark. She would have reached for her flashlight, but Seldrake had insisted on taking her hand. She presumed that, in his time, it was courteous to illuminate a woman's way down a stairway, to steady her by holding her hand. But his touch bothered her. He gripped her firmly. His hand was much larger than hers. It was warm, confining, terrifying . . . for it was real. *He* was real. Ghosts did not come to life.

What was nearly as strange was that his grasp also felt comforting, as though she found it less unnerving for him to be real than a specter.

There was something more, too. Something she despised herself for: This unreal being's clasp sent waves of sensual awareness pulsing through her.

Well, why not? She had allowed no real man to arouse her for ages. As she had found the duke's picture to be seductive because it was safe, why not find his presence enticing, too?

Only it wasn't safe. Not now. Not when he appeared actually to exist.

They reached the second floor. The dogs circled them, then Caddie yipped and chased the other dog down the hall.

Larryn gasped. The hallway was completely different! It was illuminated by rows of wall sconces, each holding lit candles. The odor was warm and somewhat rancid, with a slight overlay of spices. It reminded her of a demonstration she had seen once of candlemaking in a reconstructed European village, where old homemaking skills were demonstrated for tourists. Tallow—that was the smell.

But where were the electric lights? She glanced at the walls. They had been painted before, but now they were paneled in a rich, burnished wood. Chloe's paintings were gone, replaced by a gallery of oil portraits of people dressed in clothing from Thomas Northby's era or earlier. Along the hall's perimeter was an occasional table, carved as beautifully as Chloe's antiques but holding silver candelabra instead of precious knickknacks.

"I . . . what . . . ?" Larryn could not put into words all the questions that tumbled through her mind. She had assumed, on the roof, that the ghost of the duke had somehow materialized. As unthinkable as that was, she was afraid now—terrified that something equally bizarre, yet with more dire repercussions for her, had occurred.

Could she have wound up in the time when Thomas Northby, the duke of Seldrake, had lived?

"Oh, no," she finally managed. That couldn't be. "Excuse me." She pulled her hand from the duke's and hurried down the hall. The wooden floor was uncarpeted except for a runner of woven wool. She pulled open the massive wooden door to the suite that Chloe had given her . . . and stopped.

The outer room was similar, yet different. The large, ornate desk was there, but it was in use, strewn with papers. On it was a large plume stuck into a bottle that obviously contained ink. There were more candelabra on the desk. A silver seal was tipped onto its side, and beside it were used blocks of sealing wax. The wall behind the desk was bare; it did not contain the portrait of the duke.

"What do you wish in my chamber, madam?" roared the man behind her.

She cringed. "I . . . I thought it was my room." Her voice was small and despairing, and she immediately realized what she had said. "I mean," she said more strongly, "you said you would lend me some clothing, and I thought I would find it here."

"In *my* chamber?" he repeated in an outraged and incredulous tone.

She turned to face him. His shoulders were stiff beneath his loose-sleeved white shirt, his chin was raised, and he glared down at her imperiously with flashing blue eyes.

"Obviously I don't know this house," she said, attempting a nonchalant shrug. "I thought this was a guest suite."

"Indeed?" Seldrake snorted. "And how would you—"

Larryn did not wait to hear what he had to say. She thrust open the door to the bedroom. It, too, was different—more opulent than in Chloe's time. The canopy and curtains around the elegantly carved bed were deep brown and russet, definitely masculine.

Larryn still did not want to believe it, but she knew what was likely to convince her. She hurried to the bathroom door.

"Madam!" came the indignant shout behind her.

It was not the bathroom she had left only a short while ago. The room was illuminated by the candlelight behind her; she saw no electrical fixtures. There were a basin and a tub, but what had been a toilet was now a wooden platform. There was no plumbing to the toilet, no plumbing anywhere. Servants must haul water in and wastes out. . . .

"Oh, lord," she said in despair, leaning against the paneled bathroom wall. "It must be true." She shook all over, and her heart felt as though it was contracting into nothingness. Why had this happened to her?

"Thomas!" An excited feminine voice resounded from the other room. "It's been confirmed. There are two young children in a terrible situation."

"Hush!" hissed the duke.

The voice lowered, but Larryn could still hear her words. "You do not understand. Both their mother and father were just stricken—no symptoms until today, but already the guard is there, their house is nailed shut, and—"

"Adele!" Seldrake interrupted, then whispered, "There is a stranger here."

Larryn heard the woman called Adele gasp. "Oh, my heavens. I didn't . . . I— Oh, Thomas, have I condemned us?"

"Not if I can prevent it." The duke's voice was grim and determined, and it made Larryn shudder.

From the little Chloe had told her, Larryn realized the problem. Taking a deep breath, she strode out of the bathroom. "Don't worry," she said. "I'm all for saving children before they can become infected. Bubonic plague is a terrible thing. Maybe I can help. I am a doctor, whether or not you believe it."

She glared defiantly at Thomas Northby, whose shaggy brows were raised in an incredulous expression. "Are you mad, madam?"

"Stop calling me 'madam.' And 'Mrs.' If you won't believe 'doctor,' then just call me Larryn." Larryn stepped toward the woman who stood near the doorway to the suite. She was a pretty young lady of maybe nineteen or twenty. Her hair, as light as the duke's, was curled in tight sausages that hung from her temples to her shoulders, and she wore a long burgundy dress cut low in the front and off the shoulders. "Hi," Larryn said. "You're Adele?"

"Yes," said the soft voice. Adele glanced in obvious confusion at the duke. Her eyes were blue, though not as brilliant as Seldrake's. Still, there was a resemblance between them. "Who is she, Thomas?" Adele asked.

"It's a long story," Larryn broke in before Seldrake could reply. "Are you a relative of the duke's?"

"She is my sister." Seldrake's voice was icy. "But that is not your concern, madam."

"Larryn," she corrected immediately.

"Of course. Larryn." Adele swept forward in her wide, rich skirt and stopped before Larryn. "I am most pleased to meet you." She glanced down at Larryn's clothes, then hurriedly back at her face, as though she were embarrassed at seeing a woman in such abbreviated attire.

On the other hand, Larryn thought, she tended to dress relatively modestly for her own time. Her skirt reached to her calf, and her shirt skimmed her throat. Though she'd had a revealing evening gown or two in her time, she wouldn't be caught dead during daylight hours in something as skimpy at the neckline as Adele's dress.

"I'm glad to meet you, too," she said to Adele. This was not the time to criticize the customs of this era. But her mind whirled. These people were going to want an explanation of why she was here. She could try the truth, but weren't women hanged in this era if suspected of being witches? The alternative might be incarceration at Bedlam— or its equivalent—for madness.

This era. Oh, heavens, she believed it! She somehow was in the past.

"Enough of this charade," Thomas Northby said. "This woman is not a guest, Adele. She has invaded our home for some reason of her own." He stood beside his sister, drawn up to his full imposing height, and looked down his imperious nose toward Larryn. "If you are not here to spy on us, then perhaps, madam—I mean, *Larryn*"—he made her name sound like an epithet, and Larryn cringed—"then perhaps you would be so kind as to grace us with an explanation of your presence."

She needed time to come up with something credible. For now, she groped with a response they might buy. Putting on a haughtiness of her own, she said, "I have attempted to tell you." How should she address a duke? She guessed. "Your lordship." His scowl grew only slightly more ominous, but as he said nothing she supposed it was okay. "I am a . . . healer." Maybe that was more acceptable than a woman's being a doctor. "I have heard of your work, and I am here to help you."

"I do not know what you believe you have heard," the duke said through gritted teeth, "but I wish for you to tell me the source of these vicious rumors."

So that was how he wanted to play it? Well, Chloe had said that spiriting kids away from houses quarantined for plague had been illegal. He was probably just protecting his own behind. Adele's, too.

"Your cousin Chloe told me," Larryn said. It probably made sense to tell the truth when possible, even if they might neither understand nor believe it.

Adele looked at her brother with her brow folded into wrinkles of confusion. "I do not believe I know our cousin Chloe, Thomas."

"That," he said, "is because she does not exist." He took one long stride that planted him right in front of Larryn. "And I am determined to learn the truth from you, ma— er, Larryn. So, for now, you shall be our honored guest." The irony he inserted into his last words made Larryn flinch.

At least he wasn't throwing her out. And, best of all, he wasn't turning her over to either the witchhunters or this time's equivalent of the men in white coats. Or the police.

"Thank you, kind sir," Larryn replied, knowing her tone reflected her sincerity.

"And," Thomas Northby said, "for our safety, and, perhaps, for yours, you shall remain our guest until you have given us the truth."

A scratching sound, followed by a whine, woke Larryn.

Woke her? That meant she had actually fallen asleep. How had she relaxed enough?

Disoriented, she blinked, surveying her surroundings.

The bed she lay on was soft and lumpy. Its frame,

though, was opulent, with posts carved with cherub faces and flowers leading up to a canopy hung with yards of red satin.

Was it true, then? Or had she just dreamed that she had gone into the past, to the time of Thomas Northby, duke of Seldrake?

Of course she had dreamt it. It couldn't possibly be real.

But why, then, was she in a different room? And she still wore the nightgown she remembered putting on last night, after borrowing it from Adele. It was long-sleeved, of a wrinkled muslin, and it reached the floor. Her own lingerie was usually short, of comfortable cotton or shimmery nylon.

No. This was impossible. Shivering, she glanced around. Although the draperies were drawn shut, she could tell that dawn was breaking outside the windows on two sides of the chamber; she was in a corner room. She sat up, slid from the high mattress, and drew the curtains open. The glass in the windows, though clear, was gray and irregular—not at all the normal, clear glass she'd looked through in Chloe's home.

From below, in a walled courtyard, came the sound of horses' hoofs and coach wheels on cobblestones. A large carriage careened into the courtyard as Larryn watched. No cars were visible, and a retinue of servants swarmed from the house to meet the coach.

If this were a hoax Chloe had dreamed up, it certainly was elaborate.

Or had Larryn gone insane? Died and become a ghost, like Seldrake's? What had happened to her?

She couldn't find out by staying here. She looked around for her clothes. They were tucked into the corner of a cabinet, but inside a huge and ornate marquetry armoire were the two outfits Adele had brought in last night. One was peach-colored, the other blue. Both appeared similar to what Adele had been wearing, and they consisted of many pieces: full skirts and underskirts, bodices trimmed in lace . . . and with incredibly revealing necklines.

Until she figured out what was going on, she had better pretend she belonged here. With a sigh, she pulled out the pieces of the peach ensemble. She changed into it as best she could without help lacing up the bodice's back. It was too snug and left her more bare on top than was comfortable. Her own underwear certainly wouldn't work with this. What did women in this time do? She would have to ask Adele.

The whining and scratching that had awakened her sounded once more. Caddie! Larryn hurried to the bedroom's door and turned the knob.

The door wouldn't open.

Damn! The duke had made good on his threat. She was a captive. Not that she had anything better to do, if she truly were in the past, than to hide out while she thought of a story to explain her presence. And at this moment, she was inclined to believe that she was, somehow, incredibly, in another time.

But if she was in the past, was she here for a reason? The duke's ghost had asked for help once. The second time she had seen him, she had wound up here. Was there a connection?

She hoped so. Maybe then, if she learned and did what was needed, she would go home. She couldn't, after all, stay here . . . could she?

The duke, though, would die. That angry, vibrant, altogether too imperious . . . too handsome . . . man was going to die, probably soon. In any event, he would cease to exist long before Larryn came into the world.

The thought made her sigh aloud.

A responsive yip sounded from the other side of the door. "Oh, Caddie," Larryn said. "I'd love to let you in. Better yet, I'd love for you to find a way to let me out."

More yips turned into a series of barks. Then there was a steady scratching sound, as though the puppy were attempting to dig her way through the door. Larryn felt like laughing and crying at the same time. Her one and only friend in this era was her puppy, and the two of them had been cruelly separated.

" 'ey now, what's this? Ye must be a new companion to Augie." The high masculine voice was muffled. "Y'er goin' to scratch that door to pieces, and 'is Grace is not goin' to be pleased. Nay, 'e is not."

Larryn heard Caddie scratch some more, accompanied by further barks.

"Are ye trying to get at something inside?" the voice asked. And then, blessedly, Larryn heard a key turning in the lock.

She pulled the door open slowly but forcefully, not allowing her rescuer to change his mind. She was immediately assailed by an energetic ball of fur. She laughed, kneeling to hug the puppy. "Hi, Caddie. Thanks!" She was thrilled to see at least one small tie to her life before coming here—or insanity, if that were the answer.

As she rose, she looked at the man who had opened the door. He was small and wore a shapeless hat, leather vest, and coarse shirt over baggy britches.

She couldn't be insane. Her mind would not have invented such an odd character as a servant—would it?

He stared at her with wide eyes and a mouth that made an O of surprise. He was grizzled, and his mouth was sunken as though he had a scarcity of teeth. "Madam, I did not mean to disturb ye. 'is Grace did not tell me of 'is guest, and—"

"That's perfectly all right," Larryn said and swept past.

"But—"

Larryn hurried down the main stairway. She could guess what the duke was doing with that closed carriage arriving at dawn. If she was right, she had to help.

But she did not know the house well. The servant had followed. "Can I help yer ladyship?" he asked when she reached the bottom of the steps and stopped, looking around in confusion.

"Yes," she said. "What's your name?"

"Ned," he replied.

"Ned, I need to get to the courtyard at the back of the house. I overslept, and the duke will be angry if I do not get there to help him."

"Oh, but—"

"Take me to him!" she demanded. She took a guess. "I'm supposed to help the duke with the children." Ned's eyes widened. She hated to sound as tyrannical as the duke. On the other hand, Ned and other servants around here must be used to obeying shouted orders.

"Yes'm. Please come with me."

He led her through a labyrinth of hallways on the house's first floor. Caddie stayed close on her heels. They passed other servants, who nodded courteously at Larryn with heads lowered, but their looks were curious. If she'd been in her own time, she'd have smiled and said hello, but she wasn't sure of the protocol here.

Finally, they reached the huge, stone-walled room that had to be the kitchen. If Larryn had continued to harbor doubts that she was in the past, they vanished. This couldn't exist in the present, except, perhaps, in some reenactors' display of how people used to live. Biting her lower lip in anxiety, she knelt again to pat Caddie for reassurance. The puppy's gaily wagging tail lifted Larryn's spirits, if only a little.

A contingent of servants was busy preparing what was probably enough breakfast for a small army. Most looked up and stared at her, then looked quickly away, talking quietly among themselves. Larryn supposed that guests of the duke didn't often appear in the kitchen.

There were huge, blackened pots hanging over fires in two enormous fireplaces. Below them were spits where what appeared to be entire cows were being roasted. The smell of burning wood and cooking food was delicious and made Larryn recall that she hadn't eaten since dinner last night—or three hundred fifty years from now, whichever the case might be.

But she didn't have time now. She hurried through the kitchen and out the door at the far end, Caddie close behind.

Except for the coach, and a stable hand taking charge of the horses, the courtyard was empty.

"Damn!" she muttered under her breath, then looked around to make sure no one had heard. She doubted it was acceptable for genteel women to swear in this age.

On the other hand, if the Restoration era's reputation was correct, it was acceptable for them to bed nearly every man in sight.

She sighed and looked around the courtyard. There were several large outbuildings. One of them appeared to be a stable. And the others . . . ?

Holding up her skirts so she could hurry over the cobblestones, she approached the closest building, which resembled a large cottage. She thought she heard the muffled sound of a child crying. This had to be it!

The duke's dog, whom she had learned was named Augie, appeared from around the building. With a bark of pleasure, Caddie took off after him.

Larryn pushed open the heavy wooden door and stopped. Inside was a large room, empty except for several wooden chairs and a huge stone fireplace. Tapestries covered the walls.

This could not be the place she sought. But then she heard the crying once more. It was muffled, as though it came from behind the walls. Behind the tapestries . . . of course!

She pulled up the hanging on the nearest wall. Behind it was a door. She opened it.

"Leave!" boomed a familiar, commanding voice.

Larryn pursed her lips in annoyance at the duke's continued rudeness. At least she had guessed right. She stepped inside, shutting the door behind her.

"Do you not understand, madam?" The duke stood near the door. In his arms was a toddler, whom he rocked gently. Beside him was another child, a young boy who held on to Seldrake's full sleeve and regarded Larryn with fright. "This is a dangerous place," Seldrake continued, his angry blue eyes holding Larryn's. "Whether you are here as a spy or not, you must be warned: These children have been exposed to the plague."

"I figured as much," Larryn said. That meant that Seldrake had been as well, not to mention everyone else in the room, which included Adele, in a plain brown gown with a neckline higher than on the dress she had worn the night before, plus a man and a woman Larryn did not recognize.

The duke stood tall, sheltering and protecting the children about him despite the danger they posed to him. Notwithstanding the man's vile temper, she had to admire his guts.

She looked around. The room was small, filled with cots in rows, one on each side of the room. Two other children sat up in their beds—one girl about six and the other a little older. They were in small muslin gowns similar to the one Larryn had worn to bed, and they watched the exchange between Larryn and the duke warily.

"Adele, did you not tell the servants that Mrs. Maeller was to be left alone while she rested?" Seldrake's words were clipped and obviously angry. Damn! Larryn hadn't intended to get Adele in trouble; the younger woman had seemed pleasant, a possible ally, and Larryn did not want to alienate her. She was clearly deferential to her brother and might not want to do anything to rile him.

"I am sorry, Thomas, but in all the excitement, I forgot that we intended to keep Larryn locked in." Her words were correct, her eyes downcast as though she were contrite, but she shot a small glance at Larryn that told her that Seldrake's sister was not, after all, intimidated by her brother. Larryn restrained herself from cheering.

Instead, she turned back to the duke. "Tell me how these children have been exposed to the plague," she said in a cool, businesslike tone. She needed Seldrake's cooperation, but she would do what she needed to in any case.

He stared at her. "It is best that you do not know, madam."

"For whom? Not for the little ones; I can help them if I know their story."

The duke raised one eyebrow incredulously. When he spoke, his tone sounded as though he issued a dare. "You can help? Well, then, I shall tell you—and I shall also keep close watch to ensure you do not betray us. Matters shall go ill with you if you do." His glare was menacing.

Larryn waved her hand in the air to hurry him. "Yes, yes. I figured that. Now, please, go on."

He spoke through gritted teeth. "Know, then, that these two are our latest arrivals. Their parents took ill just today. The others came two days back. This is the place where we bring the children at first, to isolate them from the rest."

"The rest?"

"There is another cottage. Those who have been at Seldrake House longest, after we believe danger to them is past, remain there. Mistress Clydia, there, has survived the plague and wished to help others." He nodded toward the thin woman in servants' dress near the other man in the room. "She tends to our newcomers."

Did he realize that Clydia had acquired immunity by her survival? This was long before vaccines would be invented, after all. Larryn did not want to start another controversy by mentioning a concept that might not yet be known here. Instead, she walked to the boy at Seldrake's side and knelt. "Hi," she said softly. "My name is Doc—er, Larryn. What's yours?"

"John," came the tiny, frightened voice.

"How do you feel, John?"

"Fine. But me mummy and papa are sick."

"I see." Larryn stood and hurried to a small washbasin on a table in the corner. She scrubbed her hands, though there was no soap. Then she returned and pulled up the boy's shirt. She felt his small body for fever and swollen glands and examined him for the ugly plague sores known as buboes.

It had been a long time since her residency, which had been the last time she had examined patients. She was certain, of course, that she remembered how. She only wished she'd brought at least her medical bag—but she had hardly known she would wind up centuries in the past. She would make do as best she could.

After a minute, she stood and rinsed her hands once more. Then she held out her arms for the baby. Despite his scowl, Seldrake handed her the child, and Larryn examined her, too. She felt even more comfortable this time with the process.

"Nothing obvious," she said, pleased with her sense of accomplishment—and relieved she had found no symptoms. "Now, let's set some ground rules. The plague is spread by bacteria carried by the fleas from rats—*Yersinia pestis*, I believe. I don't think you know about bacteria yet, but they're tiny living organisms of sorts. The disease is highly contagious, as you know. Unfortunately, I don't have antibiotics with me. So, we'll start with these kids, since they're the most at risk. I noticed you're not lacking for servants, which is good. Go to your kitchen and order them to boil a lot of water. We're going to need soap, too. Let's see—what is soap made of these days?"

Seldrake stared as though she had gone completely insane. She whirled and looked at Adele. "I don't think your brother wants to listen to me. He can believe me mad; that's fine, as long as he pays attention. The best thing you can do right now to protect these kids and yourselves is to make certain everything is clean. I want this place scrubbed, and everyone and everything in it. Please, Adele. You haven't any reason to trust me, but I can assure you that I know what I'm talking about. Sanitation is important."

"What she says makes sense," said the strange man. He approached Larryn. He was dressed in a long, woven jacket of black that flared at his hips enough to resemble a skirt. His curly hair was nearly as long as the duke's, though it was darker and coarser, and Larryn realized it was probably a wig. His pale brown eyes were somewhat prominent, though he was pleasant-looking. "I am Henry, Lord Wyford, a physician. In such desperate times, any suggestion that might limit the contagion is most welcome, madam."

He smiled, then bent with a sweeping gesture to kiss Larryn's hand.

"Glad to meet you," Larryn said, trying not to blush at the chivalrous gesture. Mostly, she was grateful that she might have another ally here.

"We have heard that cleanliness is helpful," Adele agreed with an apologetic look toward her brother. Then she moved to Wyford's side and glanced up at him.

Ah! Larryn thought. There was a hint of adoration in Adele's eyes. She obviously had a thing for the young doctor.

"There are those," Adele continued, "who say that where the London ditches are the foulest is where the greatest concentration of plague victims have dwelled."

"See?" Larryn turned toward Seldrake. "What I'm suggesting won't hurt, certainly, and I can assure you it will help."

For a long moment, the duke simply stared at Larryn, the sapphire blue of his eyes glinting in obvious anger and mistrust. And then he said, "So be it. Adele, you must tell the servants to boil water and gather soap. We have work to do."

Chapter 6

SELDRAKE STILL FELT exhausted when he strode down the grand stairway early the next day, in his usual state of morning undress: shirt, britches, and stockings, but without coat and stock.

Not only had his entire family remained hard at work long into the night, but when he had finally attained his chamber and bed in the wee hours, he had been unable to sleep.

Who was this strange woman who had insinuated herself into Seldrake House? Were they all in danger of being found out, thanks to her presence? For himself he did not care, but he would not abide any danger to Adele or to the rest of his family, as he and others of his acquaintance styled their households, including servants. They each were at risk, including his friend Wyford—both of catching the plague and of incurring the wrath of the king for failing to obey the laws. They needed nothing, and no one, to make the latter peril more imminent.

This day, he would have his answers from Mrs. Maeller. No . . . Larryn. *Doctor* Maeller? Ludicrous . . . was it not?

As was his wont, he went into the dining room to break

his fast. He lifted the bell from the table beside his favorite chair and rang it to summon Ned.

Instead of his chief manservant, however, Augie hurried into the room, accompanied by the strange but similar dog who had come here with Larryn. The spaniels leapt on him in greeting, and he absently stroked their furry heads and long ears and beneath Augie's jeweled collar. Where was Ned?

The dogs soon frolicked about the room, ignoring him, like everyone else in the family this day. Seldrake's stomach growled. He wished his morning meal. But again when he rang the bell, nothing happened.

With a snarl, he strode from the room. No serving folks were about the hallways, so he sped toward the kitchen.

And stopped at the door. The place looked much as it had last night before everyone had retired. It was filled with servants moist with sweat as fires blazed in the several hearths beneath kettles of boiling water.

Ned turned at Seldrake's appearance. He had been hastening out the door, using rags in his hands to prevent himself from being burned by the steaming buckets he held. "My lord." He inclined his head and placed the buckets on the floor.

"What is happening?" Seldrake demanded. "I thought we completed this . . . this whim of our guest last night." He realized he was being unfair. What Larryn had said about cleanliness helping to stop the relentless spread of contagion held logic. The worst concentrations of plague seemed to occur in areas where houses were closest together and streets were filthiest. But that the suffusion of the disease had to do with rats bearing fleas that themselves carried living creatures so tiny that they could not be seen . . . that stretched possibilities.

"It is Larryn, Y'r Grace—your guest."

Seldrake noted Ned's use of the lady's first name. Apparently she had no qualms about familiarity with persons of all stations. Seldrake was unsurprised . . . and found this idiosyncrasy, unlike many of her others, appealing.

Ned continued, "She said we must scrub the second cottage, where the rest of the children are housed. Lady Adele agreed."

"Adele?" Not hungry any longer, Seldrake skirted the buckets on the floor and stalked out the door. He paid no heed to the dampness on the cobblestones. Before he reached the small house once used for banqueting, he heard voices.

He froze, then turned to look around the courtyard to ensure that they were in no peril from visitors or tradesmen, then he threw open the door. The outer room was meant to be empty, a precaution against prying eyes spying the children he spirited away. Not so today. It was a jumble of children and servants, babbling at once as they scrubbed walls and floors. Merry laughter assailed his ears—until the room grew progressively silent as first one person, then another, noticed him.

"Good morning." Seldrake would have recognized that mellifluous voice anywhere.

"Good morning, Larryn," he said.

She stood by a window, a sopping rag in her hand. She wore an old gray shift that he recognized as Adele's, and at its bosom she had tucked a concealing scarf. Why did he wish to whisk it away? Her modesty was no concern of his.

Her hair was pulled into a neat configuration at the base of her neck, from which a few strands had escaped to dangle moistly beside her flushed and lovely face.

How could a woman in such dishabille cause him to ache so to drag her off to his chamber?

Angry with himself, he continued, "So you have not yet completed your disruption of my household?"

"No, I guess I haven't." She sounded not in the least contrite. Did she not have a father or brother who had taught her to respect a man and his fury? "Thank heavens these youngsters haven't caught the plague, but I decided it would be best to scrub things down here, too. I did, after all, find quite a collection of fleas and mice and other ver-

min, especially in the bedroom . . . ugh!" She shuddered.
"Anyway, just because you've been lucky and haven't gotten the disease here yet doesn't mean you or anyone else
is actually immune, you know. Except perhaps Clydia,
since she had the plague and recovered." She glanced toward Clydia. The servant smiled up at her as she knelt on
the floor, rags in her hands as she scrubbed.

Seldrake said nothing as Larryn's gaze returned to him.
There was nothing subtle about the defiance in her look.
Bold and aggravating woman! She brazenly dared him to
berate her for taking over his household.

He opened his mouth to do just that, but was stopped by
a soft touch to his shoulder. "Thomas, you're awake!" His
sister stared anxiously up at him, as though at least *she*
feared his chastisement.

He growled, "I understand, Adele, that you sanctioned
this labor."

"Yes." Her tone was as unrepentant as Larryn's. Was
their confounded, brash guest fomenting a revolution from
his sister as well? "I spoke with Henry—er, Lord Wyford—
before he departed this morning about the measures Larryn
suggested. He said cleanliness would do no harm and
might, in fact, be beneficial. I assumed you would agree,
so—"

"So why did you not ask me?" Seldrake knew he
sounded petulant. He did not like that. He *was* not like that.
He strode into the inner room, stopping where two children,
girls with their hair bound up in kerchiefs, sat on the floor
scrubbing at wood-and-rope bedframes from which the
wool-stuffed mattresses had been stripped. He saw them
leaning against a wall, drying. They, too, had been sub-
jected to this cleaning frenzy.

"Is it not more likely that these little ones will take ill
now from the dampness?" he demanded of Larryn.

"We'll make sure they're all dried off, but for now it
gives them something to do. It's like a game to them and
keeps their minds off the fact that"—she lowered her
voice—"they're here without their families, poor things."

Seldrake felt his heart, which had grown as hard as rock at this subversion within his home, begin to melt. He glanced down at the children at his feet, then looked about the room at the other young ones, who swiped at walls and windows. "Mayhap you are right," he allowed. "Now, has anyone a spare rag to lend?"

Larryn doubted it was customary for the duke of Seldrake to perform manual labor alongside his servants. Why, then, did he work beside her as she scrubbed the cottage's windows and walls?

She asked. "For speed," he replied. "We must hurry to put things aright quickly, in case we have unexpected visitors; it would not do for these children to be found here." He paused. "Besides, you have indicated that this is a way to halt the plague. I wish to learn your secret. Is it a magical spell?"

Amazingly, there was a teasing tone in his deep voice. His bushy brows were raised over his twinkling blue eyes as he waited for her answer. He had pushed up his sleeves, revealing strong and sinewy forearms, and water had dripped onto his loose, silky shirt so that it clung to him—revealing a well-honed, muscular body beneath his clothing. She felt certain the duke did not lift weights or have a gym in which he worked out. Therefore, his muscles must be genuine, developed by work. Maybe, despite his illustrious title, he didn't shirk from manual labor after all. He certainly hadn't hesitated about digging in and scrubbing.

Now, though, he had paused as though her answer mattered. It *did,* to her. She didn't want to admit to anything that arguably smacked of witchcraft. Though she couldn't recall when people were no longer hanged in England for such things, she didn't want to find out the hard way.

"Magic?" She forced a laugh. "Not me. I'm the most down-to-earth, realistic person you could ever hope to meet."

She swallowed hard when she realized that she had told a whopper. It might have been true a week ago, before she had ventured to England, seen the ghosts of this man and his dog, traveled back to his time. . . . She nearly tripped as she bent down to soak her rags in the bucket of water beside her.

He caught her arm. His grip was strong, and it sent a thrill of awareness through her that this man, no matter how he had appeared before, was real. He had a body. And if the physique hinted at by the dampness of his shirt was any indication, it was *quite* a body. She usually shunned contact, but to her own surprise she waited for a few moments before gently pulling away.

"Do be cautious, Larryn." Her name now tripped off his tongue as though he said it naturally, with no sarcasm. "You do not wish to drown in the very bucket you have commissioned for your cleaning purposes, do you?"

"No," she agreed. "I wouldn't want to drown in *anything*—bucket, basin, or bathtub."

He smiled at her! She couldn't help returning his with one of her own. His eyes, even more brilliant a blue in person than in his portrait, continued to regard her, and she felt lost in them, as though she were falling upward, into the eternity of the sky. . . . But their expression segued from flippancy to puzzlement. "I would like to know," he said, "where you got such notions: tiny beings on fleas that cause the plague, which can be scared away by scrubbing. And why you first professed to be a doctor."

Oh, lord. If she didn't want to be prosecuted as a witch she couldn't even hint at the truth. But she doubted he'd leave her alone if she refused to answer.

Behind her, she heard the eager chatter of Adele and the servants as they continued their ministrations, the sloshing of water, the excited shouts of the children as they attempted to help. The earlier fetid odor of the place had been replaced by the pungency of strong lye soap, though there was a faintly olive smell where the servants had attempted to soften the harshness by using castile soap as well. Her hands felt wet and raw from the soap's alkali, but she ignored the sting.

"Well . . . have you ever been to northern Scotland?" she finally blurted, her mind racing.

"No," he replied, "I have not."

"Oh, well, that's where I'm from." She prayed he hadn't any friends or relations to whom he'd turn for verification, but at least she could make up something that might satisfy him . . . for now. "Things are different there. Women can call themselves doctors if they have knowledge of healing and midwifery. And though some of our practice comes from . . . from old legends passed down through generations, we've found a lot of things that work. Like cleanliness. It helps to keep wounds from getting infected, diseases from spreading, that kind of thing."

"I see. I am surprised, for I do not hear the Scottish tones in your voice—although your words are sometimes strangely foreign to me. What part of northern Scotland are you from?"

"Er . . . it's a really small town. If you haven't been up there, you wouldn't have heard of it."

"And how," he said, "came you to be unconscious on the roof of my house?"

He wasn't making things easier. "I wish I knew," she said with a shrug. She picked at a stubborn spot on the window with her fingernail, which was difficult since her nail was soft from being wet. "I don't even know how I got to . . . to this part of England. Maybe I was abducted, or—"

"Ought we to summon the authorities?" His tone was clipped once more. She didn't look, but she was sure he was scowling.

And they had been getting along so well . . . for all of a minute.

"I wouldn't want to do that," she said. "It might get you into trouble."

"Do not threaten me, madam." The volume of his voice did not change. Neither did his friendly tone. But Larryn recognized the threat.

She turned toward him once more. She leaned against

the windowsill and felt her fists clench about the wet rags she still held. He watched her, his face a hard mask, and she had a momentary pang of regret that their former truce had disappeared so quickly and completely.

"I'm sorry if it sounded like a threat to you. I was quite serious. Although most of my memories are intact, I'm uncertain about how I got here." That was true; how could she explain time travel? "I just sort of . . . well, appeared. And until I have something more concrete to tell the authorities, it's hardly worth jeopardizing your situation by contacting them." She paused for a moment. "No matter what you may think, I'm on your side. I find what you're doing for these children wonderful, and I'm glad to help. Please believe that."

His expression remained stony as he continued to stare into her eyes. And then he said, "If your strange methods help to save lives, Larryn, then no matter your real purpose, I am glad you are here, too."

Larryn was amazed at how quickly the day passed. She was used to the complex but nonstrenuous work of observing specimens under microscopes, not scrubbing dirt and killing fleas. But the more she did, the more she felt energized and alive.

Maybe it was because the duke worked at her side.

It wasn't that she was attracted to him. Far from it. Despite how good-looking he was, he was a male chauvinist to the utmost degree. She supposed she couldn't blame him. Assuming women to be soft, brainless, and obedient had been bred into him, probably taught by seventeenth-century society from the moment he was born.

Never mind the reality of women's intelligence and pluck here. From the little she knew of Adele, she could see the duke's sister had a mind of her own. And enough sense to get her way by maneuvering around Seldrake's masculine ego.

But Larryn doubted her own ability to manipulate the duke. In fact, she tiptoed about as though the cobblestones were eggshells to avoid getting kicked out into the inhospitable world of Restoration England . . . or worse.

To deal well with Seldrake, she pretended that her ideas had come to her from men in her family or from legends.

What rot!

Still, he was a charming man when she got him talking.

That afternoon, to keep him from asking more questions, she inquired about Seldrake House and his family.

"This has been ancestral land for many generations," he told her while wringing a rag into a wooden pail filled with water. "The house was built but twenty-five years ago, though. I was born in the prior, smaller house that once stood here, as were my father and grandfather."

Larryn searched her mind for what little she knew of this time in English history. "What was life like under Oliver Cromwell?" she asked.

Bad topic. The scowl he turned on her was glacial. "I would not know, madam. My family were devoted Royalists. We accompanied His Majesty to France. In fact, that was why I was given the hand—" He stopped abruptly and turned his back on her. He scrubbed the wall with such vigor that he appeared intent on sanding it away.

Given the hand . . . ? Chloe had said he was married. Larryn remembered that only too well—and her own absurd dismay. But since she had been here, she had not seen any indication that Seldrake had a wife.

She could not ask him. But maybe Adele would explain.

Larryn groped for a less upsetting subject. "What you're doing for these kids is wonderful. Have you been a doctor long?"

That caused him to turn back toward her, suspicion narrowing his eyes.

"I'm asking because I'm interested," she said, "not because I'm trying to get you to betray yourself."

He relaxed a little and moved his head so that the deep sand-colored waves that fell below his shoulders flowed back. His hair looked natural, though Larryn had been able to tell that Wyford's longer hair had been a dark wig.

Didn't most aristocratic men wear wigs in this era?

"I have been a doctor for quite a few years," he responded to her question. "And I have known about healing for more years than that. My father was also a physician. In fact, he was physician for a while to His Royal Majesty, our first Charles."

"Really? What does it take to be a king's physician?"

"Learning, and an ability to heal. Plus, my father had journals of remedies that had come from his father and his father's father. Each generation of Seldrake physicians has annotated and added to them."

"Have you, too?"

Seldrake nodded. "They are perhaps my most prized possessions."

"And I thought Augie was," Larryn teased. But once again she realized she had unwittingly said something wrong.

"Not mine," the duke said in a muffled voice; "but my wife's." This time, he did not merely turn his back on her; he stalked toward the opposite wall of the cottage, took a rag from an obviously tiring child, and began to scrub even more vigorously than before.

They were finished. Larryn helped a couple of friendly servants bring the midday meal of bread and cheese out to the children in the house they had cleaned that morning. The kids squealed in delight; obviously, the exercise had made them hungry.

As for the children still in quarantine, Larryn knocked on the door of the other cottage. Clydia answered. Before Larryn handed over the filled dishes, she asked Clydia if everyone seemed all right.

"Oh, yes'm," the older woman said, bobbing her head as she gave a grin that revealed gaps where two of her teeth should be. Her snug white cap hid all but a shock of her gray hair. "My young charges are doin' nicely." She leaned conspiratorially toward Larryn. "Not a hint of the plague in here, there ain't."

"I'm glad," Larryn said, then told Clydia to send for her if there was a sign of any illness, no matter how minor.

Tired from her earlier exertions, she dragged herself back into the withdrawing room in the main house and sat in a chair with carved arms and legs that appeared to be polished mahogany. The dogs followed and sat at her feet.

In a moment, Ned followed. "We'll serve your meal in the dining room, if you please, m'lady," he said.

"Is anyone else eating there?" Larryn hadn't seen Adele or Wyford for a while, and Seldrake had left on horseback earlier, saying he would return by supper.

She wondered if he was attempting to escape the memories she had stirred up . . . of his wife. She didn't live here. Had she left him? Larryn doubted that was done much in these times.

Perhaps she was dead.

In any event, the duke was obviously distressed by thoughts of her. And despite how absurd her feelings were, that bothered Larryn. A lot.

"No, m'lady," Ned replied to her, "no one else is eating in the dining room, but—"

"I don't want anyone to go to any bother serving me," Larryn said firmly. "I'll eat where everyone else does."

"It's no bother, m'lady."

Larryn sighed. Apparently, despite their earlier camaraderie, the servants had decided she was not one of them. She wasn't part of the duke's echelon, either.

She simply didn't belong here.

Well, no use feeling sorry for herself. She had a mission, after all. Didn't she?

"What do you think, Caddie?" she asked after Ned had left the room, Augie at his heels. Larryn's little spaniel wriggled at the attention, and she lifted the puppy into her lap.

Why *had* she come here? It could have been some kind of cosmic fluke, but she didn't think so. After all, she'd seen Seldrake's ghost, it had asked her for help, and soon after, here she was.

So, it was logical that she had come to help him. But how? According to Chloe, ghosts returned because of deep emotions, even death, occurring at the site where they appear. Larryn had seen Seldrake's side of some scene on the roof that had apparently affected him greatly. Had he died there? Possibly.

The thought made her shudder.

Well, then, she simply had to keep him away from the roof.

On the other hand, the duke might have turned into a restless spirit because he had left some unfinished business. That, too, could have occurred on the roof. And to finish it, he might need to go back up there to work it out. In that case, making him stay away from the roof would not solve anything.

Larryn sighed. "I don't know how to figure this out, Caddie," she whispered sorrowfully.

Caddie laid her head down on Larryn's chest and seemed to listen sympathetically.

"I have to do something," Larryn continued, "if I want to get back home. Right?"

Caddie's long, pink tongue appeared and she licked Larryn's chin in commiseration.

"Of course, maybe we'll never get back home." Larryn wasn't sure how she felt about that. Oh, she knew she didn't belong here. But now that she had met Seldrake, the duke whose portrait had so enthralled her—well, she supposed there were worse things than living in the seventeenth century.

Like not seeing him again.

A thought filled her with further misery. "Do you think, Caddie, that the duke's unfinished business has something to do with his wife?" The idea constricted Larryn's heart. Dummy, she told herself. She had no business caring one way or the other about Seldrake's significant other. More than likely, in this time, Seldrake had plenty of significant others besides his wife. Restoration-era men had a reputation of faithlessness to uphold.

She clenched her fists. That, if nothing else, made her hope she was here just long enough to fulfill a purpose, then go far away from Seldrake—*very* far away . . . as in centuries.

If he did have unfinished business that involved his wife, how could Larryn help?

Maybe it instead involved the children he was saving. Now Larryn was saving them, too.

Yes, that had to be why she was here.

"Come on, Caddie." Larryn was still in the dirty shift she had worn for scrubbing. If she was to eat in the dining room, even alone, she wanted to change clothes. She went up to her bedroom, poured water into the porcelain basin to wash up, and put on a dressier outfit, with the help of Adele's maid, Marie-Louise.

She soon sat alone at one side of a vast wooden table on which rested several huge, unlit candelabra; plenty of light streamed in from the mullioned windows. The walls were of dark wood, and at one end of the room was a huge stone fireplace that had been swept clean. The room smelled of smoke and burned candles.

But she wasn't completely alone. Both dogs sat on the floor beside her, their large brown eyes regarding her every move, their fluffy tails wagging, sometimes in unison and sometimes in opposition. "Beggars!" she said affectionately.

Her meal consisted of a slab of mutton, coarse bread that she felt certain contained plenty of healthy fiber, and yellow cheese that was strong yet tasty. Then there was the red wine, served in an ornate metal goblet that looked like pewter; she hoped it didn't contain much lead.

Knowing she shouldn't, now and then she dropped small pieces of mutton and bread to Caddie and Augie, who wriggled appreciatively . . . then begged for more.

Larryn wondered where Adele and Wyford had gone. Maybe they were with Seldrake. But as she finished eating, she was glad none of them was around. She knew what she wanted to do that afternoon. She was curious about the journals Seldrake had mentioned, wondered if she could find them and learn more about the state of medicine at this time. Were they the same journals Chloe had mentioned finding? On the chance Larryn was here to help the children, she ought to know what she was up against.

Where might Seldrake keep them? Logically, it had to be someplace where he spent a lot of time. His bedroom? Maybe he kept them in that lovely carved desk that had somehow survived the centuries.

Followed by the dogs, she started there, armed with a story that the duke had asked her to clean his quarters. But no one questioned her being there. Neither, though, did she find the journals.

Where else? She had passed a couple of rooms with open doors on the way to the dining room. One appeared to be a study. Maybe Seldrake kept the journals there.

The mansion's first floor was busier than the upstairs. Servants bustled everywhere, carrying wood for the many fireplaces as well as cleaning materials. She passed a couple of the maids who'd boiled the water they'd needed for the cottage cleaning. They paused to smile and wish her a good day, then resumed sweeping the marble floor of the huge entry hall with brooms made of some kind of coarse bristles tied together around the end of a stick.

When she reached the door to the study, she looked around. Seeing no one, she ducked inside, the dogs close behind.

She kept her ears open as she went through the drawers of the large, ornate cupboards that lined the room. Fortunately, none of the servants seemed interested in coming in. She could tell why; the room was already immaculate. Its wooden floor gleamed with whatever they used for polish, as did the massive mahogany tables with thick, carved legs. The room smelled of burned logs, but all the ashes had been removed from the huge fireplace. Its mantel was trimmed with a small gilt rail, and the brocaded chairs and settees were plumped up and inviting—apparently ready for guests.

The first of the large wooden cabinets contained silver-ware and ornate plates, trimmed in gold. No books there, though Larryn was surprised it hadn't been locked.

In the second cupboard, the first drawer Larryn looked at contained papers—apparently records of medical treatments. This looked promising. When she pulled open a stiff door inlaid with decorative wooden trim, she found several thick books bound in black leather. She opened one carefully.

The front page read: *Seldrake: Medicus*. Success! Larryn carried the volume to a settee, curled her legs under her, and began to read.

It was primarily an herbal, describing hundreds of natural remedies, from something called "adder's tongue" to yarrow. It was handwritten, annotated in several different cramped scripts—and it was fascinating!

Many of the plants and herbs Larryn had never heard of. Others she was surprised were even known at this time: lettuce, for example. She visualized great, sumptuous feasts here of roast beef or venison, with courses of soups and potatoes and fish. Did they eat salads, too?

Sometimes the plants were to be ingested alone or mixed with other herbs she felt to be of dubious efficacy. If some of these concoctions didn't cure the patient, they might well kill him—or at least get him to purge himself of anything harmful inside.

Sometimes the plants were just to be formed into plasters and placed on the body; others were to be hung around the neck, their odors supposedly having some medicinal effect.

Larryn smiled but caught herself. Physicians of her time had learned that not all old wives' tales were false. She would ask Seldrake if she could study his journals, even inquire which of the so-called cures he had used and how well they had worked.

Seldrake. Her smile widened at the thought of him. Sure, he was an arrogant son of his time. But he was undoubtedly as skilled as any other physician here. He hadn't known that sanitation helped defeat the spread of plague—but he was bold enough, brave enough to defy all edicts to try to save children.

He had thrown himself into her cleaning project right alongside the servants and her. He had seemed interested in her theories of halting contagion, even if he did not believe in them.

He was intelligent, he was brave, he was admirable. . . .

And he was unattainable, even if she had any interest in attracting him. Which she didn't.

Her smile turned into a moue of grim determination. She had a journal to read. She turned the page of the book in her lap and began studying the difficult script.

The room was warm. She had learned from one of the servants that it was the second week in August. She had left her time in mid-September. Apparently, someone who traveled in time from one year to another didn't necessarily arrive on the same date. Curious, she thought idly—but no more curious than the whole idea of time travel.

She returned to her reading. A while later, she glimpsed the dogs sneaking out of the room, even as she felt herself nod in her exhaustion. . . .

A noise startled her awake. It wasn't loud—a whisper. A giggle.

She was slumped on the settee, the journal still in her lap. Heavens! Was Seldrake back? She should have asked permission to look in his family's treasured volume. What if he considered it secret? Could she put it back without his realizing she had seen it?

Cautiously, she raised her head—and found herself staring.

Near the closed door, Adele was held tightly in Wyford's arms . . . and the kiss they shared could have ignited a fire in every hearth in the house.

Chapter 7

LARRYN MUST HAVE made a noise, for Adele
pulled away from Wyford with a gasp. She looked around,
her blue eyes widening as they lit on Larryn. "Oh," she
said. Redness crept up her pale cheeks, clashing with the
rose shade of her gown.

"Sorry." Larryn felt embarrassed herself. She slid the
book onto the seat, hoping they could not see it over the
back of the settee. "I . . . I must have fallen asleep. I'll leave
you two alone."

"Oh, no, that is all right," Adele murmured. "We were . . .
discussing a new idea for keeping the children safe, and—"

She broke off as Wyford planted himself protectively in
front of her, straightening his long coat. The waves of his
dark wig spilled over shoulders much more narrow than
Seldrake's. "Mrs. Maeller knows what we were doing, and
we were not *speaking* of anything."

Larryn smiled at his bluntness. "It's none of my business."

"No," Wyford said, "it is not." Larryn had thought the
man amiable before, but there was nothing friendly now in

his cold gaze. His prominent, light-colored eyes had slitted, and he regarded her as though he were determining whether to murder her.

Larryn made herself shrug nonchalantly. "If you'll excuse me . . ." She glanced down. She couldn't leave the journal there, but how could she return it to the cabinet?

Adele rushed over and sat beside her. Her eyes widened further when she noticed the book. "Did my brother tell you about this?"

Larryn nodded. "He said the journals are his most prized possessions."

Adele managed a wan smile. "He obviously did mention them, then, for that is how he always speaks of them. Did he give you permission to look at them?"

Sheepishly, Larryn shook her head.

"Then," Adele said, "we each know something about the other that must be kept from my brother." Her smile was friendly but held a touch of triumph, sadness—and relief. She glanced at Wyford, who still did not relax. "It will be all right," she told him. "Larryn will not tell Thomas what she saw, will you?" She turned back to Larryn.

"I take it," Larryn said dryly, "that your brother doesn't approve of your kissing Lord Wyford."

"That is a mild way of describing a powerful truth." Wyford's voice was tinged with irony.

"But why?" Larryn stood and faced Wyford. "You are obviously well trusted, or he wouldn't let you know what goes on here."

"Henry is a second son. He is from a good family but has neither title nor fortune." Adele's tone dripped bitterness. "That makes him worthy enough to be a friend, but not worthy enough to marry into the family."

"I see." Anger rose inside Larryn. Who was the duke, to dictate whom his sister could or couldn't marry? He was a creature of his time, sure, but he'd seemed somewhat enlightened.

Somewhat.

Could this new bit of insight relate to some unfinished

business of Seldrake's? Could he have died without providing for his sister, without allowing her to marry the man she loved? But how might the scene Larryn witnessed on the roof fit in?

If this was it, though, Larryn would take pleasure in making certain that the duke regretted his absurd despotism.

Wyford had left. Larryn had returned the journal to its place in the cupboard with the others.

Now, Adele and she sat in the withdrawing room next to the study. Caddie and Augie slept at their feet. Coffee had been brought by one of the servants.

"Thomas is not a bad man," Adele said to Larryn. She had tucked her skirts beneath her. Larryn kept her eyes on her hostess's face, not really wanting to look at where her breasts plumped out from the low bodice.

She glanced at her own borrowed outfit, chosen by Marie-Louise. It was too large. If not for the kerchief she had tucked inside the neckline, she would have been even more exposed than Adele. That was the fashion, she reminded herself. Bosoms here were in; legs were out.

"I understand my brother," Adele continued, her small lips curling into a tolerant smile, "although Henry does not. He cares for Thomas. They have been close friends for a long time. Yet Thomas fails to open his eyes to possibilities around him."

"Possibilities like his sister caring for a very nice man who happens to be beneath her station?" Larryn tried without a lot of success to keep her tone light.

"He wants the best for our family and for me," Adele said simply. "And he believes he knows what that is. You see, his title did not come easily to him. It was not handed to him by our father; Thomas earned it, and now he wishes to ensure that its benefits are made available to our entire family."

"Really? He earned it?" That captured Larryn's interest, though she tried to pretend otherwise. She took a sip of the coffee. It was bitter and rather disgusting, and grounds floated at the bottom of her cup. She put it down.

"Yes. You see, our family was against the Roundheads—the Puritans, who were eventually led by that hateful Oliver Cromwell. My father, who was physician to King Charles I, went into exile with the younger Charles before our sovereign was executed." Adele gave a small shudder.

"Thomas—the duke went with them?"

Adele nodded. "As did I. Our mother was already dead, and I was quite young. The French were kind, but our people wanted to return home, Thomas particularly. When he was old enough, he acted, with our father, as physician to the court in exile. I remained in France with our father, who died there. Thomas went with Charles as he attempted to gain the throne: to Holland, Scotland, Spain. And then, when the Lord Protector Cromwell died and there were no strong successors, Thomas assisted Charles in his negotiations to return to the throne. He preceded Charles to England's shores at great peril to himself and assured the English people he met that their true sovereign stood ready to return to lead them. That was why, once Charles returned to London six years ago, he made Thomas the duke of Seldrake."

"I see," Larryn said. And now the duke acted against the very king he had supported by breaking laws designed to try to keep the plague from spreading.

If Larryn recalled her history lessons, despite the gaudy clothes and blatant excesses of the Restoration era, there was nothing wishy-washy about the power of King Charles II. Seldrake could be in big trouble for defying him.

"Thomas's bravery on behalf of the king is also why he married Charmian DuPrix." Adele must have known she was dropping a bombshell, for she looked at Larryn with her arched brows raised over blue eyes so like her brother's.

"Oh?" Larryn again tried to insert indifference into her tone.

Adele laughed and touched her arm. "You need not pretend, Larryn. I know you are attracted to my brother." She sobered. "I do not know where you came from, or whether you are good for him. I am aware, however, that he is also fascinated by you, although neither of you wishes the other to know."

Larryn stared at Adele, then shrugged. "Your brother's a good-looking man, even if he's a bit stuffy sometimes. And domineering. Any woman would find him appealing, in a chauvinistic kind of way."

But Larryn knew she found him more than appealing. She had traveled a long way to get here—much longer than she could ever tell this pleasant young woman.

"Chauvinistic?" Adele sounded puzzled.

"Egotistical. In my ti—I mean, where I come from, the term is usually used to refer to the way men mistakenly think they're better than women."

Adele laughed. "Chauvinistic. Yes, that fits my brother and many other men I know. Not Henry, though." She pondered for a moment, then amended, "At least not as much as some."

It was Larryn's turn to laugh, but only briefly. "I am curious about the duke's wife." She hoped Adele would take the cue.

She did. "Charmian was the daughter of a Frenchman who supported our king, and the man's English wife. Her family was wealthy and powerful, and everyone knew whoever married Charmian would make a fine match. When Thomas returned to France for me after the king was restored, Charles interceded with Charmian's family. The contract was made; Charmian married Thomas. She was a very amiable woman, though when we came here she missed her home." A look of sadness washed over Adele's face.

"What happened to her?"

"Thomas had promised her a trip home, but he became so busy as court physician here. . . . He brought her to Whitehall one day to meet with Charles, and our king gave her August."

"August?"

Seldrake's spaniel at her feet suddenly sat up at attention, followed by an interested Caddie.

"Oh, Augie," Larryn said.

"Yes, Augie. Augie and Charmian were inseparable. She loved that little dog. And then . . ." Her voice trailed off.

"And then?" prompted Larryn.

"Then Charmian began to spend more time in London, riding her carriage in the parks, showing off her little dog. She came home with . . . with the plague. Last year. Thomas tried so hard to save her. He would have given his own life, but she died."

"He must have loved her very much." Larryn felt tears choke her for the man Seldrake must have been: warm, caring, loving. So different from the cool side he had mostly shown to her.

But, then, he did not love her. He barely tolerated her—unsurprising, since he believed her a spy.

"He felt so guilty that he, a doctor, could not save her."

Larryn drew in her breath. Her cheeks were suddenly wet. "I know how that can be."

"You do?" Adele sounded surprised.

Though Larryn didn't want to talk about it, she felt she had to. "As I told you, I'm considered a . . . healer where I am from. My sister contracted a horrible disease that also had no cure." Not the plague, she thought, but in some ways as bad in her time. Her sister, her sweet, defiant, reckless sister, rebelling against the responsibility pressed on her so early as guardian to her little sister, Larryn, had contracted AIDS.

And Larryn, who by then had been through medical school, had been forced to watch her waste away and die.

Larryn heard a sob, and realized it was hers. "I—I'm sorry," she managed. Feeling a furry body pressed against her leg, she reached down and lifted Caddie onto her lap. She hugged the puppy tightly.

"Your sister died?" Adele asked.

Larryn nodded against the warm dog fur, and Caddie

squirmed around to lick her tears with her long, rough tongue.

"And you could not save her? Yes, I believe you understand how Thomas felt. He is a good man. When he cares about someone, he cares deeply. He wishes the best for them. He wishes the best for me." Adele's voice broke, and Larryn looked through her tears to see that Adele, too, was crying.

Larryn cleared her throat, willing herself to calm. "And the best is Henry Wyford?"

"Yes," Adele said. "Henry is definitely the best."

"Henry is the best at what?" questioned a sardonic male voice.

Larryn startled, nearly knocking over her coffee cup. Caddie leapt down and ran with Augie toward the door. Seldrake had entered the room. He leaned against the wall near the door, looking rakish in his flowing shirt and britches and very, very handsome. He bent to pat the dogs.

Larryn felt embarrassed. She could only hold her own with this arrogant man if she remained strong in his presence, yet he had caught her crying. She dashed away her tears and stood, regarding him calmly. "We were discussing physicians and surgeons," she told Seldrake. "Your sister described your skills in healing people. She also told me that, except for you, Henry Wyford is the best physician she has ever met."

One of Seldrake's bushy eyebrows raised in obvious skepticism. "Yes, Henry is quite skilled. He also has no hesitation at attempting new approaches to healing." He threw a hard look at his sister. "However, I have a feeling that you were discussing other charms of my friend Wyford, were you not?"

Adele paled. Larryn wanted to holler at Seldrake to stop him from intimidating his poor sister. Instead she said smoothly, "He's a charming man. Adele tells me he isn't married. She said she hopes I have an opportunity to get to know him better." There. Maybe some pressure would be off Adele if Seldrake thought she was matchmaking between Wyford and Larryn.

Seldrake's expression appeared startled. When he turned toward Larryn, Adele threw her a grateful look. "Yes," Adele said. "Larryn, as a healer herself, might be a wonderful helpmeet to a doctor. And Henry has mentioned that he has need of a wife."

"And you believe that he should take on this woman Larryn, who suddenly appeared on our roof with no explanation?" Seldrake's unexpected roar made Larryn jump. "We do not know her business here except to disrupt our lives, to take over the servants' time with excessive cleaning, to—"

"Don't talk about me as though I weren't in the room," Larryn interrupted, angry herself. She wondered what had gotten him so upset; she'd thought he would be pleased at the suggestion that Wyford was interested in someone other than Adele. "I'm trying to help you, even if you're too stubborn to acknowledge that. If I choose to go after Wyford or anyone else, it's not your concern."

"Oh, but you are wrong," he said softly, moving to stand directly in front of her chair. She rose to face him.

Seldrake's sand-colored waves cascaded down his shoulders, and he was close enough that she could smell his pleasant aroma of horse and leather.

The dogs stood at his feet. Their long, feathered tails, which usually wagged, were still, their large eyes anxious, as though they reflected the tension in the room.

Seldrake's blue eyes flashed. "The seduction of my acquaintances concerns me, madam. I will warn Wyford, you can be certain of that. I will not allow him to do anything so foolish as to marry a woman whose background is highly suspect."

"Don't you think he should be the judge of that?" Larryn asked defiantly. "When two people get together, it's their concern, no one else's." She glanced briefly at Adele, who nodded her gratitude ever so slightly.

"It is the concern of everyone involved with them," Seldrake contradicted. "It is certainly *my* concern. Wyford is my friend."

"And mine," Adele said softly.

Seldrake glared at her. "Enough of this discussion for now. We will continue it at an appropriate time, preferably when Wyford is present, since we are deciding his fate, are we not?"

Larryn laughed and shot another look at Adele. Adele would warn Wyford to be prepared for an offtarget command from Seldrake not to blindly marry a mysterious stranger like Larryn.

Seldrake had lost his wife. He had loved Charmian. Why wouldn't he want his sister to marry the man she loved?

His reason to stop Larryn from marrying Wyford was to protect Wyford. He didn't care what Larryn felt. Well, that was fine with her.

But why did a little worm of misery begin to crawl inside her?

"We're discussing my fate, too," Larryn reminded him testily.

"And your fate is in my hands, Larryn." An emotion she didn't understand radiated from his eyes, wrapping around her and stealing her breath.

She managed to contradict him anyway. "Don't count on it." She stooped to pick up her puppy, who had been by her feet beside Augie. She stroked Caddie's soft head, hugging her tightly.

For a moment, Seldrake said nothing, but she felt his fury rise. He didn't vent it. Instead, he said through gritted teeth, "I sought the two of you out just now to convey some news. I have been summoned to the king's presence at court tomorrow." He glanced at Adele. "I will take you with me."

"That will be most pleasant, Thomas," Adele said. "Thank you."

He turned back toward Larryn. "I will take you as well."

She stared. "Me? To court?"

His laugh was harsh. "Did you not expect to see again so soon whoever it was who sent you here? Or will someone recognize who you really are and disclose it?"

"I don't know anyone at court," she replied stiffly. "I'm sorry you don't trust me. But I would think that, with the work you're doing here, court would be the last place you would want to go."

"When one is summoned," Seldrake said, "one complies. And I have already informed you that you shall be my 'guest' until I have determined your reason for being here. I am certainly not about to leave you here unsupervised. Therefore, you shall come along. I intend to keep close watch over you."

Close watch over her. The thought infuriated Thomas, who had better things to do than to supervise a woman whose intentions were quite unknown and wholly incomprehensible.

The same thought intrigued him, much more than he wished to admit. For, as maddening as Larryn was, she was also like a mysterious flower whose secrets he wished to unveil, petal by petal.

"You don't need to watch me." She sounded both defiant and petulant. "And you don't need to drag me off to court. I'll stay here."

"No, you will not," he said lightly, though he was certain she could not fail to comprehend the look he shot at her; she was not to argue with him.

And yet, this woman always argued with him.

He despised idle arguments. With Larryn, however, he found himself enjoying each new challenge. And with Larryn, challenges appeared to be endless.

A match between Larryn and Wyford, indeed! He suspected that was a new stratagem by Adele to make him accept that his close friend paid court to her. As much as he liked Wyford, he required better for Adele. An arranged match with someone with a title would suit; her children, too, would be titled.

Mayhap Seldrake himself would wed again for the good of his lineage, but for now and for the foreseeable future such was unthinkable. Should he never bring himself to remarry, the brief dukedom of Seldrake would, sadly, die out upon his own childless demise.

Yet hadn't his own arranged match with Charmian, before there was love between them, worked out well? Adele would come around. She would do her duty for the family they both loved.

And the idea of Larryn wed to Wyford—never!

It wasn't solely the thought of his friend being caught by this woman's wiles that made Seldrake rage. The very idea that someone other than he would bed this contrary and difficult woman . . . he did not wish to consider it. He refused even to ponder why it bothered him.

"You *will* come along, madam," he repeated more sternly.

"All right, if it's that important to you. But you'll be embarrassed by me."

"You will do nothing to shame me, Larryn, or you will be sorry." Standing directly in front of her, he glared down with menace in his eyes in an attempt to intimidate her.

She did not back up even one step. He found himself gazing down at the deep brown eyes of the pup she held, and the similarly dark eyes belonging to Larryn—eyes that were as defiant as ever he had seen them.

"I won't do anything intentionally to shame any of us," she said. "But I have nothing appropriate to wear to court."

"Ah." Thomas nearly smiled. Mayhap Larryn was not, in some respects, so different from other women. "Adele has lent you some of her clothing. Perhaps she would see what else in her wardrobe might be altered to render you suitable for presentation to the king."

His sister's grin was wide. "I would be most happy to help. Come, Larryn. We shall see what we can find."

As they left the room, Larryn looked back at him. She had picked up the red and white spaniel pup, and Augie, the traitorous canine, trailed along. "You really don't have to drag me with you," she said sadly. "You can trust me enough to leave me here. I won't go anywhere, not until I know that I've helped you."

He believed, right then, that he could trust her to remain at his home without causing mischief. But he intended for her to go along for other reasons as well. "I wish to introduce you to His Majesty, Larryn," he told her, although he could not have explained to her just why. "And there is more. The summons came because there is someone dear to the king who is ill. His Majesty wishes for me to attempt a cure. He is, for now, at Hampton Court Palace, since this summer the plague is again besetting London, though less than last year. Mayhap you can assist me by demanding that the entirety of Hampton Court be scrubbed clean, as you did here." He smiled at her.

She smiled back. "Sure," she said. "Maybe that's where I can be of help."

Chapter 8

"THIS STUFF IS so darned uncomfortable," Larryn grumbled to Adele early the next morning. "How do you wear it all the time?"

She regretted her words immediately, for Adele's blue eyes widened as though she were scandalized. "What do you wear in your home in Scotland?" she asked. "Do you never dress for parties?"

They were in Larryn's bedroom, with clothing draped all over the tester bed. Adele had been kind enough to assign Marie-Louise to alter a perfectly stunning outfit for Larryn to wear, in a gorgeous shade of azure silk. Adele herself was in a low-cut cream-colored gown that Larryn now recognized as consisting of many pieces: stays and stomacher, sleeves, underskirt, skirt . . . all decorated with lace and ruffles. On her, it looked wonderful.

The clothing Larryn had borrowed before had also been Adele's, but it had not been altered to fit Larryn, and her hostess was rounder than she. It had fit loosely, which had made Larryn even more uneasy with the deep décolletage, but otherwise it had been comfortable.

But now . . .

She had to answer Adele. "I don't follow fashions very well at home," she admitted. "I believe in comfort as well as style."

"But those items you wore when Thomas found you—do you consider them comfortable?"

Her blouse and skirt had fit just fine. They suited her lifestyle, particularly when she wore them with a tailored jacket. "Yes," she said. But she knew that Seldrake hadn't thought them at all becoming. He had rushed her inside from the roof to ensure that her legs got covered quickly. She shouldn't care what that autocratic, opinionated man thought of her clothes or her appearance . . . but she did.

"But the . . . the thing you wore to restrict your bosom," Adele persisted. She flushed. "I hope you do not mind, but I saw it in the drawer where your other things are kept."

Her drawer? Did Adele see her flashlight, too, hidden in her skirt pocket at the bottom of her meager pile? How would she explain it?

But Adele finished, "I did not quite understand how it would fit, but I am very certain I would not like to wear one."

Her bra? "You get used to it," Larryn said. "Probably more easily than this bodice." She had put on a dressing gown for modesty until the maid returned with the rest of her outfit. She pulled the top back. She wore a sheer, low-cut shift. On top of it, a ferociously stiff garment hugged her from her chest to below her waist. Covered in front with an attractive piece called a "stomacher," the bodice was laced down the back and stiffened everywhere with stays. Its snugness squeezed her bust upward—the better, she was certain, to be all but revealed by the depth of the neckline of the outfit she had tried on before. Marie-Louise had removed the skirts to take the waist in to fit her better.

"Larryn, I did not think to ask before, since I judged you from your bearing, but . . . are you perhaps of the serving class rather than from a station similar to ours? I do not mean to embarrass you, for I will not regard you ill even so, but . . ."

How could she answer that? "Where I'm from, we try not to judge people by what they do but more on who they are. I recognize that's not the case here. I suppose that, because of my profession as a . . . healer, and because my family was also held in high esteem"—her late father had been a doctor, too—"I would be considered among the elite by most people."

Here, it would be important for her to be thought part of the aristocracy. Otherwise, Seldrake would deem her beneath his notice. And then she would never be able to help him, if that was why she was here.

She abhorred the idea that he was such a snob.

But she abhorred even more the thought that he might wind up ignoring her.

"In any event," Adele continued, "you shall be treated with the utmost respect at court when you come with Thomas. His Majesty esteems my brother, considers him an excellent physician. That is why Thomas has been summoned, although I wonder who is ill, and with what. I pray it is not the plague."

"Me, too." Larryn doubted she'd be of much help if the entire court had already been exposed to the horribly contagious disease. At least she didn't recall such a disaster from history books. "We should hurry, don't you think?" She had suggested this before but the process had, if anything, slowed down. "If someone is sick, it's better to get there quickly than to worry about how we look."

"If we dwelled farther south," Adele said, "we could make the journey to Hampton Court more swiftly by barge along the Thames. But from here, we must use the roads. In any event, at court appearance is important." She spoke firmly. "We must finish your ensemble. Let me see again what you have chosen."

With a sigh, Larryn pulled back the robe.

"Good." Adele examined the stomacher, which covered the front of the bodice. It actually was quite pretty, with rows of pink ribbons that Adele had called "echelles." "I have a muff and cloak that go well with these. Oh, and also a fan. I will get them for you while you wait for Marie-Louise. She will also dress your hair." She examined Larryn critically. "Is it the fashion where you come from to pull your hair back so severely, with no curls at all?"

"Not really," Larryn said truthfully. But she had always considered her tight chignon professional-looking, and she had no time to waste on playing with new hairstyles.

"Well, Marie-Louise is an artist. She will make your beautiful hair even more lovely."

"But—" Larryn's protest was lost as Adele swept from the room.

This was Larryn's opportunity. She slipped behind the embroidered screen Marie-Louise had brought to protect the scant modesty Larryn had left; she had needed help with almost every aspect of dressing.

She dropped the dressing gown to the floor and reached behind herself to untie the bow at the bottom of the lacing up her back. She worked her fingers upward to loosen the ties so she could breathe once more. When she was done, with the bodice so loose it nearly fell off, she inhaled deeply, gratefully, and smiled.

She had seen few people, but guessed she was more slender than most women of this age. How did those with greater curves learn to breathe with this stiff contraption holding them in?

Her smile froze as she heard a rap on the door. "Come in," she called, expecting Adele. How was she going to explain what she had done? Did fashionable women ever loosen their stays? "I had to sneeze," she began without peeking from behind the screen. She heard panting and scrabbling at her feet. It was Caddie and Augie. "Hi, pups," she said with a laugh, glad she could bend down to pet them.

But then Augie barked and ran away. Caddie yipped and followed. In moments, the two dogs were chasing one another madly around the room. "Hey, calm down!" Larryn called, but it was too late. One of them careened into the screen, knocking it to the floor with a crash. The noise sent the dogs fleeing from the room.

Only then did Larryn realize that her visitor wasn't Adele. It wasn't even Marie-Louise, returning with her altered clothing.

It was Seldrake. He was staring at her.

She drew in her breath.

She had thought the most dressy men's attire of this time to be nearly effeminate, with its skirtlike coats and snug stockings. But on Seldrake, even with his long, wavy hair, it appeared the most masculine clothing ever created. He wore a large, loose coat of black over a long waistcoat of a blue as deep a color as the sapphire in his ring. His britches, also of blue, were tucked into stockings fastened at his knees. A touch of lace appeared at his wrists and throat—and he looked totally, awesomely gorgeous.

Larryn, on the other hand, realized she was clad only in her loosened bodice over a very sheer and gauzy shift. Fortunately, the front of the bodice was long and came to a strategic point. But still, she felt certain that he didn't have to use his imagination to see her breasts and her legs. If the duke had been scandalized by seeing her in her calf-length skirt, right now he must consider her the most disgraceful creature he'd ever had the misfortune to meet.

But he did not seem angry. He did not seem shocked. His brilliant blue eyes were wide, and he looked her slowly up and down as though he could not help himself.

"I apologize for this intrusion, Larryn." His voice was hoarse. And when his gaze met hers, she felt as though the nuclear age must have arrived centuries early, for she felt immediately consumed in raging fire.

"That's all right," she managed, though she could not move, could not force herself even to stoop to retrieve her dressing gown. Instead, she stood immobile, as though she had been immediately turned to stone by his stare. Or to ashes, for she could have sworn her bones no longer existed. She simply waited for . . . whatever was, inevitably, to occur.

• • •

This woman. This stranger. This interloper to his home.

This gorgeous, seductive creature turned Seldrake into a stammering subaltern with no will of his own.

Her shift was so sheer as to be near nonexistent. Light from candles along the wall behind her danced through the fragile garment, revealing all her charms beneath.

He stared at her as though to look away would cause his death. Perhaps it would—for want of her.

She was slender, much more slight than his beloved Charmian. But despite his suspicions of why she stood before him flaunting her state of undress, there was an embarrassed sweetness about Larryn as well.

And beauty. Definitely beauty in her long, shapely legs, her slender arms held rigidly at her sides . . . everywhere.

Flaunting her state of undress? She had not demanded that he come to her room with those playful spaniels. She had not knocked over the screen behind which she could have maintained her modesty.

He took an involuntary step toward her. And then another.

She did not shrink from him, although her soft brown eyes widened as though she were a doe engirded by a ring of hunters. But there was not truly fear in them. No. A wariness, perhaps . . . and a wanting?

Or did he simply wish to see a need in her as intense as the one that caused his body to tighten near painfully?

"Why are you—I mean, is there something you wanted?" She stopped speaking at once, as though she had realized that her words might be taken as invitation. Her breathing, quick and irregular, caused her lovely bosom to rise and fall in such a manner as to incite his imaginings all the more.

Imaginings? Why but imagine? This woman was a seductress, was she not? Had she not come here to entice him to lower his guard, to betray him to those who would give much to know of his treasonous actions in saving those unable to save themselves?

She had offered him no other explanation of her sudden
appearance in his home, her knowledge of his affairs, so
what else was he to think?

His discreet inquiries at court and of his trusted friends
had yielded no knowledge. He failed to place her strange
accent.

Yet she, too, had attempted to save the children. She
might be in as much difficulty as he, if found out.

"I came to learn how soon you might be ready to depart,"
he finally said, attempting to sound as though unperturbed
by the vision before him.

"I—I'm not sure. Marie-Louise hasn't returned with the
things she was altering to fit me, and Adele went to find
some accessories. . . ."

"Your Grace, mademoiselle, may I enter?" came a timid
French-accented female voice from the doorway. It was
Marie-Louise.

"Yes. Please." Larryn's voice sounded as relieved as it
ought, Seldrake thought. He but imagined a touch of regret
in it.

"How long will it take to complete Larryn's dressing?"
he demanded of the plump, auburn-haired maid who had
once been Charmian's servant brought with her from
France. She had wanted to return there until Adele had
convinced her to stay.

"We must put on her skirts, arrange her hair. . . ."

"Do it quickly," Seldrake demanded, hoping that his own
regret at having the moment end was not evident. Imperiously, he turned on his heel and left Larryn's chamber.

Larryn lost track of time.

Marie-Louise, at Larryn's okay, immediately finished
dressing her, tightening the bodice once more and adding
to it and her stomacher full, detachable sleeves, a petticoat,
the azure overskirt and pale blue underskirt that she had
fitted to Larryn, knit stockings of a deep blue as well, and
silk shoes with an embroidered front but no heel, so they
fit Larryn despite her feet being larger than Adele's.

Adele returned with a satin cloak and matching muff in sable brown that went well with the outfit. Larryn sat still while Marie-Louise dressed her hair in a style that seemed strange to her: nearly flat on top, with ringlets dangling from her temples.

But Larryn did not complain. She hardly said a word.

Her mind remained at the moment that Seldrake had come into the room and the screen had fallen. It was as though the voracious look in his eyes had driven her libido mad. She almost felt those strong hands on her arms, her legs . . . and the rest of her might as well have been bare, for all the cover the shift had provided. She had certainly felt his gaze on every revealed part of her, and the recollection still sent continuous surges of desire to the most sensitive areas of her now-clothed body.

How ridiculous, she kept telling herself. Even if Seldrake was real here, she wasn't. She wouldn't stay. Couldn't stay, if she had anything to say about it.

Which she doubted, for she had certainly had no say in getting here.

Her mind was playing games. He could not be as handsome as she thought. His stare could not possibly have been as lustful, and it could not portend a passion as wonderful as she imagined.

Damn it all! So what if he was the incredible lover that his gaze had suggested? She, of all people, was not the kind to just sample passion, then leave—even though that was the fashion in this time.

Hadn't she learned how superficial, how dangerous that attitude was from her sister, Cathy? Cathy, who had died for her reckless, fruitless quest for love.

Larryn shuddered.

"Are you cold?" Adele asked, shattering the spell Larryn had woven around herself.

"Yes," she said. She was definitely chilled to her bones. How had she allowed a hungry look to affect her that way? "But I'll be fine."

She permitted herself to be led to the ornate mirror in

Adele's room. Was that her? The eyes of the woman in the glass were soft yet glowing, as though she hid a secret. She looked as if she had emerged from a painting from the past.

No, this present.

Larryn knew she was ordinary-looking. Yet the woman who stared back was—she had to admit it to herself—quite striking. More . . . pretty.

She smiled ruefully at the reflection, even as Adele echoed her thoughts. "You are lovely, Larryn! Just wait until Thomas sees you."

Larryn snorted silently inside while thanking Adele for the compliment. As if the way she looked now, fully clothed, would matter to Seldrake. The man was a product of his time, undoubtedly flitting from one gorgeous, well-bred paramour to the next. That was the only reason he had stared at her before, when she had been practically bare. She probably reminded him of his latest dalliance. Or two. Or three.

She heard the dogs bark in the distance. "We'd better get going," she told Adele. "Your brother will wonder what kept us; he tried to hurry me along before Marie-Louise was finished, while you were looking for things."

"Oh, dear," Adele said. "We must join him immediately."

Larryn squared her shoulders as she walked down the grand stairway beside Adele—carefully, so as not to expose any more of her bust than already showed.

As she had told herself before, she did not care whether Thomas Northby, duke of Seldrake, noticed her as a woman, as long as he somehow gave her the deference due to her as a doctor—even if he didn't believe her.

As she glided to the base of the steps, Seldrake, who had been engaged in conversation with someone just inside the withdrawing room, turned to look at her.

His eyes widened—with what appeared to be appreciation this time, not lust. "Larryn, you are most beautiful," he said softly, taking a step toward her. He appeared to stop himself as he noticed Adele by her side. "As are you, my dear sister."

Adele was, of course, lovely in her court finery. Still, Seldrake's telling her so in the same breath as his compliment to Larryn took away some of the thrill.

But any possibility of pleasure for Larryn was totally eradicated the moment that the person he had been speaking with stepped into the house's marbled entryway.

The woman swept to Seldrake's side and put her dainty gloved hand possessively on his arm. Her coppery gown, trimmed in jewels and lace, had a deeper neckline than any Larryn had yet seen, revealing a full, curvaceous bustline. Her waist was slim, her hips large. Pearls adorned her neck and her black, curling hair. And her face . . .

"Please be so kind as to introduce me to your little friend, dearest Thomas," said the most beautiful woman Larryn had ever seen.

Chapter 9

LARRYN WAS SURE that the coach they rode in was the epitome of modern transportation in this time. It appeared incredibly luxurious: a broad, flat top decorated at the edges with the most ornate of scrollwork, tapering gracefully to fit neatly between large iron wheels. It was made of gleaming, polished wood with an intricate inlay pattern, and was drawn by a team of six matched gray horses. Their trappings were of red leather, and the coachman, too, was dressed in red.

It was even sumptuous inside, with seats and sides richly upholstered in padded brocade.

But it was the worst ride Larryn had ever taken.

First, there was the utter discomfort. The thing not only swung from side to side; it jounced tortuously up and down on potholed roads that could only have been designed to keep riders from obesity thanks to constant nausea. The odors of sewage and horse emanating from outside the carriage did not help.

Even worse was the miserable atmosphere inside.

"You must not spend every moment with that ill child, Thomas," said the woman who had come to sweep them away to Hampton Court. Her name was Bess, Lady Main-waring, and she had clung to Seldrake's arm as long as Larryn had been in their presence. Now she looked up into his face earnestly from beneath lowered lashes. "From the message that came to me, I fear there is little that can be done for him. You shall examine him, of course. And then you must sup with His Majesty. I, of course, shall be at his table as well."

She would be flirting with the king, too. Of that Larryn had little doubt. Unless . . . unless Seldrake was the object of all of her flirtatious intention.

That made Larryn's stomach lurch as much as the hor-rible ride. She wondered if a trip on the river, as Adele had described, would have been as bad. At least it would have been faster.

Larryn sat beside Adele and directly across from Lady Mainwaring. She had little option but to study the beautiful woman. Seldrake obviously studied her, too. Closely. And that gave Larryn the urge to kick him, no matter how awk-ward that would have been with her full skirts in the cramped coach.

Okay, idiot, she told herself. She had stepped into the middle of a play that had begun, and would end, without her. She was just an insignificant extra thrust into its mid-dle, and she would not, could not, influence its outcome.

But surely Seldrake, an intelligent man, could see through Lady Mainwaring. She was hardly subtle in using her feminine wiles on him. And she certainly seemed to have a lot of wiles. Femininity, too, darn her.

Bess's face was a perfect oval, framed by a curled mass of raven-black hair pulled back into a single coil that draped over her shoulder. Her full lips, never still, pouted prettily as she reacted to everything Seldrake said. If her eyes were somewhat shallow, she nevertheless used them expres-sively. With Seldrake, they were all innocent fascination, all pleasure.

With Larryn, they had been scornful. Suspicious. Surely

the woman didn't consider her a rival for Seldrake's attention.

Because Lady Mainwaring's cheeks were so pink, Larryn assumed that at least some women in this time used cosmetics. Bess needed no mascara, though, for her eyelashes were as full and prominent as her arched brows.

And her body—well, if Larryn had been concerned that her own bust was in danger of spilling out, her peril was nothing to Lady Mainwaring's. The woman's décolletage would surely be the first to burst.

"I shall sup with His Majesty if he wishes it," Seldrake responded to Bess's comments. "But the boy's health is of greater concern."

"Of course." But Lady Mainwaring did not sound pleased.

"And how is my lord Purvis this day?" Adele asked.

The look Bess shot at Seldrake's sister was surprised at first, as though one of the leather straps along the top of the vehicle, which they all grasped to brace themselves, had suddenly spoken. She smiled sweetly. "My husband is not well these days, poor man. His gout, you know. It is painful. That is why he did not join me."

Larryn had a feeling that the woman would have squeezed her husband's painful feet into too-tight boots if it would have given her this opportunity to spend time with Seldrake.

How ungenerous, Larryn chastised herself. Maybe Bess really did care for her poor, suffering husband.

To atone for her ugly speculation, Larryn blurted without thinking, "Maybe I could take a look at him. There may be something that could make him more comfortable."

This time Larryn was the recipient of Bess's stare. It was disgusted, as though a mouse had reared up to squeak at her. "I am most certain you cannot," she said crisply. "The duke, here, a most excellent physician, has already examined my husband and determined that little can be done."

That could be true, Larryn thought sadly. The drugs of her day that helped to deal with the high levels of uric acid in people with gout would hardly be available now. "You're probably right," she told Lady Mainwaring, who quickly turned away from her as though she had disappeared.

Larryn no longer wanted to kick Seldrake; Lady Mainwaring's oh so snobby knees would do instead.

"And Lord Terence?" Adele asked. "How is your son?"

The atmosphere in the coach, uncomfortable before, suddenly crackled with some emotion Larryn didn't understand. Seldrake lifted one shaggy eyebrow in apparent amusement at his sister. Bess drew in her breath as though about to deliver a speech, but she obviously reined it in.

Her voice, when she spoke, was light. "My son grows bigger and healthier each day. He is at court, of course. You will see for yourself. He will be pleased to meet with you."

"Of course." Adele's eyes never left her brother's.

Larryn wondered what the subtext of that little exchange had been, but she could not ask. When it ended, the only conversation inside the coach, for the longest time, was a friendly exchange of gossip between Bess and Seldrake about rumored liaisons at the court of King Charles II. If their discussion had even an ounce of truth to it, all Larryn had ever heard about the licentiousness of the Restoration era was true.

And it was hours before they reached their destination.

Larryn drew in her breath at her first sight of Hampton Court. It was huge! Even the gatehouse appeared to stretch forever. It was at least five stories high. The red-colored edifice was the epitome of an opulent castle, with domes and peaks, a multilevel, crenellated rooftop, and mullioned windows. They passed a similarly structured clock tower inside an inner courtyard.

Servants greeted them and hustled the duke inside. Larryn followed with Adele. They were shown first to a lavish parlor, but Seldrake was immediately summoned away.

That left Larryn with Adele and Lady Mainwaring. The

atmosphere grew more tense than in the coach, even after a crisp team of liveried servants provided them with wine and some hors d'oeuvres that Larryn did not even attempt to identify.

Instead, she walked around the stone-floored room, studying the walls. Of carved wood panels below, they were adorned with opulent tapestries of battles and pastoral and religious scenes around the upper perimeter.

"Lovely, are they not?" asked a voice beside her. Adele strolled alongside as she completed her circuit of the room. In a moment, she whispered so that only Larryn could hear, "I do not care for Lady Mainwaring, but there are reasons I must—"

She was interrupted by the appearance of a male servant even more elegantly dressed than the others. He stopped in the open doorway, and Lady Mainwaring started to rise. "Has the duke sent for me?" she asked with a catty glance toward Larryn.

"No, m'lady," the servant replied. "The duke of Seldrake requests that Lady Larryn Maeller join him."

Lady Larryn Maeller? It wasn't as good as "doctor," but at least Seldrake had provided her with a title that might lend her status at court. And she was fast becoming convinced that having no status in this time amounted to having virtually no identity.

Adele grinned at her. Larryn smiled back, then lifted her chin and said in her haughtiest manner to the granite-faced servant, "Please take me to the duke."

Larryn glanced toward Lady Mainwaring as she left the room. The seated woman glared as though ready to spear Larryn with one of the lances held in the gauntlets of the barren suits of armor standing guard around the hallways. Obviously Lady Mainwaring had expected a summons from Seldrake. Hers had not come.

Larryn's insides danced with glee.

But she had no time for smugness. Seldrake was waiting in a small but well-appointed bedroom that had royal blue satin decorating the bedposts and tester. Several women in elegant gowns stood at the fringe of the chamber, speaking quietly among themselves. They glanced frequently toward the bed. On it lay a young boy, whose face was flushed. He was coughing harshly.

Larryn rushed toward him. "What's wrong?" she asked Seldrake, whose strong brow was creased with worry.

He had removed his coat and stood beside the bed with his loose white shirt tucked into his britches at the waist. His hands were on his hips, his loose sleeves furling about his arms.

"I do not believe it is the plague," he said. "In fact, I do not believe he is seriously ill. Yet I wish another opinion, if you will be so kind as to examine him." He looked at her with an intense expression she could not interpret. Was he challenging her—or did he actually believe in her?

It didn't matter. "I'll need soap and water to wash my hands," she said crisply. "And a clean towel."

Seldrake nodded at the servant who had brought her to the room. The man returned a minute later with all she had demanded.

After washing and drying her hands, Larryn sat on the side of the bed. She hesitated. It had been a long time—by choice—since she had examined someone she knew was ill. Since she had treated any patients.

After the death of her sister, she had purposely distanced herself, whenever possible, from the hands-on practice of medicine. It was one thing to espouse sanitation, to examine children with no symptoms. But this boy was obviously ill.

And with her knowledge so much greater than anyone else's here, at this time, she could not turn her back on him, no matter how uneasy she was.

The boy glanced up at her listlessly. He was dark-haired, with a long nose and big brown eyes rimmed in red. He wheezed with each labored breath.

"Hello," she said cheerfully. "My name is Larryn. What's yours?"

"Apsley," he replied feebly. "I do not feel well."

"I can see that. Let me take a look at you so we can

figure out what will make you better. Is that all right?"

He gave one small nod that sent him into a new parox-ysm of coughing. Larryn drew in her breath as she fingered the child's neck. "His lymph glands don't feel swollen," she told Seldrake. "That's a good sign." She looked at where her hands had been. "No obvious buboes, either." She put her forehead down on the child's. "If he's got a fever, it isn't very high. Have you examined anything he's spit up?"

Seldrake nodded. "There was no blood."

"Good." Larryn did not believe that stethoscopes had been invented yet. "Have you listened to his lungs?" With-out waiting for an answer, she laid her ear on the child's chest. She couldn't tell much that way. She looked up at Seldrake. "I need something to enhance the sound." What about the horns that were sometimes used by the hard of hearing before hearing aids? Weren't they called "ear trum-pets"? She described one to him.

"I know of no such thing, but it sounds a marvelous invention." The duke appeared pensive, and Larryn won-dered if ear trumpets would soon make their debut before their time.

"Okay, then," she said. "How about some stiff paper?"

Seldrake went again to the group of women. One in a pale green dress slipped out the door. He returned to Lar-ryn's side. "His mother expressed concern that young Ap-sley may be afflicted with consumption," he said. "I do not believe so, however."

Tuberculosis. Like the plague, it was highly contagious, and in these days there would be nothing to prevent—or stop—it.

"I don't think so either," she said. "We might be able to tell better when—"

The woman in the green dress returned carrying several stiff sheets of parchment. She handed them to Seldrake, though she stared curiously at Larryn.

Before Larryn could take the papers, another woman swept through the door. She was short and pretty, with dark, sloe eyes, and she appeared to have been crying. "How is my Apsley?" she demanded hoarsely of Seldrake. "Will he be all right?"

"We are still diagnosing his malady, Lady Anne," Seldrake told her. "Please remain with the others until we have something to tell you."

"But the king. He has already laid his hands upon Apsley to cure him, but thus far it has been to no avail. His Majesty will want to know my son's progress, and I must—"

"Please," Seldrake urged.

Larryn wondered who Lady Anne was, and why the king was apparently interested in her son's welfare. It didn't matter, of course. She had a patient to deal with. She untied the top of the child's nightshirt and pulled it down in front. Then she rolled the paper into a cone and placed the narrow end to her ear and the wider end upon the child's chest. She listened as he breathed.

His breathing was uneven and labored, but his heartbeat was regular. Though his lungs sounded congested, they did not seem dangerously so—if Larryn could rely on her makeshift stethoscope. Which she did not.

She looked up at Seldrake. "If I were to hazard a guess right now, I'd say this young man just has a nasty cold."

"My thoughts as well." Seldrake's glance at her was surprised. This *had* been a test, then, and he'd expected she would fail. "The boy's signs may also bespeak of mere rheum or catarrh."

"Right." If Larryn recalled correctly from medical school, those were obsolete names for the same thing. She chose to keep her irritation with Seldrake inside—for now. "But in case it's something more serious, we'll need to keep a close eye on him."

"Fine," Seldrake said. "I shall prepare my equipment so we can bleed him as soon as possible."

"Over my dead body!" This time, Larryn blazed without thinking. And then she wondered if she had given him ideas; the way he looked at her was murderous. "I mean," she said placatingly, "he'll need all the energy he can mus-

ter to fight off whatever he's got, cold or not. Drawing out
blood saps energy. Now, what I would suggest is that buckets of water be brought in and that a fire be lit over there."
She pointed to the idle fireplace. "The heated water evap-
orating into the air will make it easier for him to breathe."
She thought a moment. "I don't know if you have anything
like camphor, but a little of that tossed into the water might
help, too. If you don't have camphor, maybe mint."

He had the gall to argue with her. Well, why not? Bleeding had been thought to help people way into the nineteenth
century, if Larryn recalled correctly. But how could she
help the ailing boy if she remained embroiled in an argument with Seldrake?

"Look," she said. "Maybe Apsley's phlegm is out of balance, not his blood." Wasn't that one of the "humours" they
tried to deal with in these days? Also, black bile and yellow
bile, if she remembered correctly. "If my method doesn't
help," she continued, "you can always bleed him later."

"Should he survive until later," Seldrake grumbled.
"Still, we can add catmint, or mayhap onion and mustard,
to the decoction which the child may breathe." He spoke
to Lady Anne. She hurried from the room to return with a
team of servants. In a while, the fire was blazing and water
boiled over it. A pungent odor, from all the cooking herbs
and other remedies, filled the room.

"Now," Seldrake told the others, "leave us. Lady Larryn
and I will watch over the boy this night."

"But—" Lady Anne began, looking frenzied as she
stared from the boy to Larryn and back.

Larryn rose from the bed and took a step toward her.
"You're Apsley's mother, aren't you?"

Lady Anne nodded.

"The duke and I will do everything we can to heal him.
Please believe that."

Lady Anne bit her bottom lip as she studied Larryn, her
dark curls askew as she tilted her head. Then she nodded
slowly. "Yes, I believe you will. Thank you."

She turned and herded the other women from the room.

Larryn was alone with Apsley and Seldrake.

"And so, Doctor Maeller . . ." There was a tinge of sarcasm in Seldrake's voice, but did she catch a hint of admiration, too? In any event, his ironic smile did not appear to make fun of her. "Do you truly believe this boy will heal without a bleeding?"

"Of course." Larryn glared at him. Her eyes ranged between the duke and the child, warning Seldrake that, though Apsley appeared to have fallen asleep, he could be listening. "He'll be a lot better by tomorrow morning. I'm sure of it."

Seldrake raised his thick eyebrows. "Yes, I believe you are quite certain of your healing power, are you not?"

No, she wasn't. Not when she was so rusty at it. But she couldn't let him know that. "I'd do better with . . . with all my equipment and medicines. But I'll do the best I can here."

She watched over the boy for a long time. He seemed to breathe a little more easily. She felt relieved that her first patient, after so long, appeared slightly improved.

She took one of the towels that had been brought in and soaked it in the water; after wringing it out, she placed it on the boy's head. "This will help cool him down if he does have a fever," she explained.

She watched as Seldrake drew two ornately carved chairs beside the bed. "We have a long vigil this night," he said. "We might as well rest as we can."

"Thanks." Larryn leaned her head back and closed her eyes. When she opened them again, Seldrake was staring at her.

She was reminded of the way he had looked at her that morning, when he had caught her with only a sheer shift and loose bodice on. Desire seemed to spark from the depths of his blue eyes, igniting her as well.

Her breathing suddenly seemed as erratic as the child's. She must be dreaming, she told herself. There was nothing sexy about this situation. Nothing sexy about her.

She rose to hover over the boy, making sure that the

towel stayed on his forehead and the covers were pulled up to his chin.

"Why did you send for me?" she asked as she sat again, wondering if he would acknowledge he had been testing her. She ventured a look at Seldrake. The passion she'd thought she had seen was no longer there; he regarded her with amusement.

"You have made it clear you believe you can heal," he said softly. "Your ideas of cleanliness may be overzealous, yet I do see your sincerity. Your knowledge appears greater than I anticipated." He'd admitted he had been trying to catch her in a lie! But that wasn't all, she realized as he continued. "And I did not wish to leave any possible diagnosis of young Apsley untried. He is too important."

"Who is he?"

"Lady Anne, his mother, whom you met, is . . . someone of whom His Majesty is very fond."

She was the king's mistress, Larryn realized. One of them, at least. That meant . . . "Apsley is his son?"

Seldrake lowered his voice. "Indeed, yes. The king cannot fully acknowledge him, of course, for he is not a legitimate heir. But His Majesty cares deeply for the boy."

His Majesty would not be pleased if his illegitimate son were to die. If she had failed his test—or even if she hadn't—had Seldrake called for her to be a scapegoat in the event he couldn't save poor Apsley?

She studied him. He was a sensual man. He had a temper, and he was judgmental. But he was not a coward. He would do what he could for the child, listen to her if it suited him. But if something happened to Apsley, he would not blame her.

"I know you'd try to save him even if the little guy had only peasant blood." His eyes flared in warning, but she was only teasing. She was certain there were no bugs planted in this bedroom in these days, but she could not be sure whether there were alcoves or holes in which eavesdroppers might hang out. She was not about to betray Seldrake. "But particularly since he's the king's child, we'll do all we can. He'll be a lot better by morning." She hoped. "You'll see."

Seldrake smiled at her so warmly that she felt enveloped in it. "And why, Lady Larryn"—he drew out the syllables caressingly, as though they were an endearment rather than a title he had made up—"do I believe you?"

Was this his unfinished business that she might need to fix? Was she here to make sure little Apsley got well? This certainly had nothing to do with the roof at Seldrake House, and yet . . .

Somehow, suddenly, she could not work up the same enthusiasm she'd arrived with for figuring out if she were here for a reason, handling it, and leaving Seldrake behind. She tried to put smugness into her own uneven smile. "Because, Duke, you know that I haven't lied to you yet."

"And you are a doctor?" One eyebrow quirked mockingly.

"Yes," she said with enough conviction to convince them both. "I am a doctor."

Late into the night, Seldrake sat in one of the two chairs he had drawn up such that Larryn and he could remain at the child's bedside. Larryn sat in hers as well, as they kept vigil.

Although the sweet and bitter smells of their jointly prescribed decoction filled the chamber's air, he was well aware of the scent of the woman who sat near him: sweet, near floral, all womanly.

She had pulled her hair, so nicely arranged before they had left Seldrake House, off her face such that it appeared nearly as severe as when she had worked about the children secreted in the banquet cottages. This must be the way she wished it when she had work to accomplish. It called attention to her face—her near-feline wide eyes, her smooth skin—unadorned by any decoration such as a stylish coiffure or a fashionable patch.

And it was quite, quite lovely.

Now, in the wee hours of a new day, she nodded at his

side, nearing sleep. Her pert, small chin fell to the expanse
of her part-exposed, most attractive bosom.

Her own movement startled her awake, for she caught
herself and drew herself up stiffly. She hazarded a look
toward him.

He permitted himself to grin. She scowled in discomfi-
ture at his having noticed her being less than fully alert.
But then she relaxed. Her return smile lightened the room
more than did the merrily blazing fire at the hearth along
the outer wall. "You caught me," she said.

Would that he *had* caught her. Caught her in a lie—and
yet she did appear to have a physician's knowledge, a physician's skills.

Mayhap, then, he might have caught her not only in his
gaze, but in his arms and—

Nonsense. That untoward musing was one which he
would not allow, not now and not ever. He wished no
closeness with any woman, not after his loss of sweet Charmian.

"You may sleep if you wish, Larryn. I will keep watch."
He did not attempt to withhold the chill from his voice.

Her pretty, arched eyebrows rose, then fell. Her mouth
drew into a line that appeared pained.

Brigand! he chastised himself. He need not be so unkind
as a result of his own untoward thoughts.

"It is late," he said softly. "You are tired, as well you
might be. This day has been long. Sleep, Larryn."

"Only if you wake me in an hour. That way, I can check
on little Apsley, and then it'll be your turn to nap. Deal?"

He was silent as he endeavored to interpret the latest of
her odd phrases. Did she ask if they had pledged a bargain?
It would seem so.

"Deal," he replied with a smile.

But a short while later, he regretted that he had been so
accommodating. Larryn had, as promised, gone to sleep in
her chair beside him. But instead of her head falling forward as before, she had slumped sideways. Toward him.

Her head rested on his shoulder. He could smell even

stronger her womanly fragrance. Feel the gentle burden of her head upon him. Look down the front of her where her small breasts peeked from her bodice, rising and falling gently as she breathed.

It was not the weight of her that made him uncomfortable. Oh, no, for his discomfort was not in his shoulder but in his britches.

He wanted this woman.

But such desire was folly. He did not know her, not truly. He did not know whence she came, what she wanted from him.

What she might do to him.

Besides, was not Adele attempting to matchmake between Larryn and Wyford? Not that Seldrake believed in such a farce. He knew how Adele felt toward Henry—no matter how inappropriate.

And he would not tolerate a match between Henry and Larryn any more than with Adele. It would be most unsuitable because . . . because he forbade it!

He lay awake long into the night, aware of his own unslaked stiffness below . . . but unwilling to move Larryn's sweet head from his shoulder.

Chapter 10

WHEN THE MORROW arrived and sunlight streamed through the chamber window, Seldrake was even more disposed to believe that the Lady Larryn had a physician's skills, even if somewhat unconventional.

With his deep cough, his listlessness, little Apsley had appeared last eventide to Seldrake to be ill, yet not mortally. Seldrake had nevertheless intended to bleed the boy, to ensure that all his humours returned to proper balance.

But Larryn had been correct; bleeding had been unnecessary after all. Although young Apsley sniffed and coughed upon rising, the child appeared much improved.

"I wish my mama to come," he demanded, sitting up in his sickbed. "And I want to break the fast with a quince tart. Mama always lets me eat quince tarts when I have been ill."

"Well," Larryn said, "I guess we'll have to have someone check the king's kitchen to see if quince tarts are available." She examined the child anew, checking his pulse, holding her forehead to his, again looking for buboes and swelling at his throat. She returned her gaze to Seldrake, her eyes glowing with such pleasure that they ignited a similar delight within him. "He's much better today," she told him. There was relief in her voice. Mayhap, despite her brashness, she had the same uncertainties that he, as a physician, sometimes had about his diagnoses, his treatments.

Not that he would ever admit that to a patient, for fear of removing hope. And not that he would ever admit any uncertainty to Larryn. He, after all, was the physician. *She* was . . .

She was an enigma he had yet to solve.

A knock resounded on the door. "Enter," Seldrake called, at the same time as Larryn said, "Come in." She obviously was of the opinion that she had charge of this sick chamber. Mayhap he would disabuse her of the idea . . . later.

Lady Anne Farswell hurried in, her morning gown swaying. Her pretty face was a grimace of concern. "How is he?"

Seldrake glanced at Larryn. She appeared a trifle put out, as though the child's mother should have come first to her. Seldrake did not wish her to feel badly. She had, after all, been of great help.

And those hours sitting with her pressed against him . . . He had not wanted to move. And now parts of him ached from the strain of such stillness. But he did not rue it. He had, for reasons he did not wish to examine, cherished her closeness.

"Your son is fine, Lady Anne," Seldrake said. "For that you may thank Lady Larryn, a skilled healer in her home. She suggested the treatment, and I found it worthy of essaying. And it worked."

Lady Anne moved immediately to the bed, where she hugged her son—who demanded his quince tart. "Of course, my sweet." Lady Anne's smile was wide. She rose and took Larryn's hands in hers. "I cannot express the depth of my gratitude to you, Lady Larryn."

"No need. Besides, I can't take the credit. The duke is a wise man and knew just what to do."

Seldrake laughed aloud. Her words had been precise, although she doubtless believed she had taken full charge of the treatment. In her estimation, his knowledge of what to do consisted of obeying her. What a brazen woman!

What a fine, wise—desirable—woman.

Her brown eyes had turned to him, and she smiled. That self-satisfied smile was not, however, chiding. It seemed full of pleasure, as though she embraced the gladness of the child's recovery. As though she embraced his efforts at heeding her advice and not taking the credit with Lady Anne.

As though she embraced . . . him.

It reminded him of his futile attempts not to stare down her bodice the night before. Again his body recalled that he was a man. He wished, suddenly, that this chamber was his own, that Lady Anne and young Apsley were somewhere far removed.

But such thoughts were foolish. He did not doubt any longer that Larryn was a lady. He had no reason to believe any lascivious advances on his part would be favored.

Nor should they be. Larryn did not appear a woman to be trifled with. And although he might be required to marry again, he would choose a woman appropriate to his station—certainly not one who kept her antecedents a mystery. He would assuredly harbor no deep feelings for a woman again, not after his loss of Charmain. Thus, there could be naught between Lady Larryn and him.

Why did such knowledge pique his temper?

"So," he said crisply to Lady Anne, "I believe that Apsley has reminded me of the time. I am hungry, are you not, Lady Larryn?" He glanced at her sternly, insisting by his glare that she not reply. "Let us all go break our fast."

Following Lady Anne and the duke as they walked the opulent halls of Hampton Court, Larryn wished she understood why Seldrake had turned so testy. His masculine ego should have been well massaged by her extolling his prowess as a physician—even if the most skillful thing he had done last night was to listen to her.

To a man of his time, and as arrogant as the duke was,

that actually was an accomplishment. She was grateful. He could have ignored her, bled the poor little boy so he'd have had little stamina to fight off what ailed him. Her prescribed treatment was common sense for her time but would be considered risky now.

And it had worked, thank heavens.

Not only had Seldrake listened to her; for a while this morning, he had seemed complimentary. Even amused. Charming.

Well, she wasn't here to learn his many moods. She just wished she knew why she *was* here.

Behind Lady Anne and the duke, Larryn was able to take in her sumptuous surroundings: gilding and tapestries and molded ceilings. Guards in red uniforms stood at attention in rows along the corridors. Men wearing ballooning britches and huge, feathered hats strolled beside women in dresses even lower in front and frothier than the one Larryn had borrowed from Adele. Most ladies flirted from behind frilly fans. Many wore fake dark patches on their skin that resembled moles in geometric shapes—the height of fashion here, Larryn believed.

She was actually at King Charles's court in the extravagant Restoration era!

Lady Anne turned back toward Larryn. "We dine in the Great Hall this morning." She gestured toward a massive door.

The duke had not forgotten his manners. He bowed his head and swept his arm forward to usher Larryn into the room.

She stopped inside, amazed at the opulence of the Great Hall. Its name was appropriate; "great" described not only its size but its decor, particularly its magnificent, multi-arched ceiling decorated by carvings and gilt and painted pendants. Huge, detailed tapestries hung on the lower section of the walls. Above were stained glass windows.

Then there was the noisy crush of people seated at tables. Dogs were present, too—a whole host of Cavalier King Charles Spaniels! Snuffling around the floor and begging for food, they looked like Augie, thinner and with more pointed muzzles than the Cavaliers of her day. Some were tricolor: black and white, with just a touch of red at their eyebrows and legs. The rest were Blenheim, like Caddie.

She suddenly missed both dogs. Was Caddie being well cared for in her absence? Surely so; Seldrake's servants wouldn't dare mistreat Augie, and they would take care of Caddie, too.

On a dais above the rest sat the man she recognized from portraits as His Majesty, King Charles II. He was certainly imposing. The long, wavy hair of his dark wig contrasted with the gleaming silver fabric of his coat. He spoke animatedly with the man at his right. At his left sat a small, shy-looking woman who concentrated on her food. Of all the women present, only she wore a black dress—though richly trimmed—and one that covered her front to her throat. Could that be the queen? Larryn thought she recalled reading that the pious Catherine of Braganza did not dress as sumptuously as other women at court.

Seldrake took Larryn's arm and whisked her to one of the long tables. She was pleased to find herself seated beside Adele. She was less pleased to see that, as soon as Seldrake sat down, Lady Mainwaring planted herself beside him.

"I have heard of your miracle of last eventide," Adele said, her blue eyes shining as she squeezed Larryn's hand. "So has the entire court, I feel certain."

"Fortunately, little Apsley wasn't very sick, despite everyone's fears," Larryn said. "I'd imagine that all the cases of plague have people spooked, ready to believe the worst."

"You are too modest," Adele replied. "You saved the child; I am convinced of it."

"She doubtless did a fair job of heeding the instructions of your brother." Lady Mainwaring smiled sweetly at the duke as she fed his already robust ego.

But to Larryn's surprise—and pleasure—he didn't just accept the praise. "It is I who heeded Lady Larryn's behest," he allowed. He did not return Bess's smile but grinned at Larryn as though sharing a secret with her. "Her methods were not unsimilar to mine, although we chose not to bleed the boy until we saw his progress. Now, cutting him will be unnecessary."

Larryn met his gaze and grinned her thanks.

"But Thomas!" Lady Mainwaring sounded shocked. "What if your listening to that . . . to Lady Larryn had caused the bleeding to come too late to save young Apsley?"

"It did not." His scowl stopped Bess from saying more.

Bess mirrored it, though, when she glared at Larryn. "One must be cautious when treating a person beloved of His Majesty," she said slowly, as though instructing someone backward.

"I agree," Larryn said sweetly. "That was why bleeding him would have been the worst thing possible."

"But—"

A servant brought a platter, and Larryn made a big point of thanking the man, effectively cutting off Lady Mainwaring. Larryn started a conversation with Adele as she ate but kept one eye on the duke. Bess returned to flirting with him. He seemed to enjoy it, darn him! Well, it wasn't Larryn's business.

She concentrated on the food. Breakfast was not like anything Larryn was used to—no coffee or orange juice. Instead, wine, served in silver goblets, was the drink of the hour.

She dined mostly on bread and butter, served on plates trimmed in gold, though she sampled oysters, anchovies, and carp. She even forced herself to taste a little of the pie Adele told her was made of swan.

Seldrake clearly had an appetite after their sickbed vigil last night. If he had any compunction about eating swan, she didn't see it in the large portion of pie he ate. Even something as petty as her misgivings about this era's food underscored the differences between them. All the more reason for her to find a way to return home.

Noting movement at the king's table from the corner of her eye, Larryn looked up. The king had risen. He went to the table where Lady Anne sat eating, surrounded by others whom Larryn did not recognize. King Charles conversed exuberantly with them all, appearing not to single out Anne. But when he spoke with her, she nodded toward Larryn's table.

The king gazed toward Larryn, though he might just as well have been seeking out the duke. Or even Lady Mainwaring. Larryn had no idea of the protocol when looked at by the king, so she bobbed her head uneasily and concentrated on her food.

Before she had eaten much more, someone cleared his throat behind her. She turned to see a man with a small, dark mustache like the king's but a much weaker chin. "Lady Larryn," he said, "His Majesty has requested that you meet with him."

Larryn realized that a request by the king was a command performance. "Certainly." She glanced at Seldrake to find him regarding her with a dark expression. Surely he couldn't be angry with her because the king had summoned her.

Maybe he *was* worried. She knew enough to inform against him, have him punished for breaking the law. As his "guest" so he could keep an eye on her, she had seen a lot of what was going on. But if her knowledge concerned him . . . Larryn felt incredibly hurt. He didn't know her well, but she had told him she wouldn't betray him. She might even be considered a conspirator with him.

But he didn't trust her.

"I am Lord Hubert Browne, m'lady," the courtier told Larryn as he escorted her back through the hallways of the palace. "I am the king's lord-in-waiting." His pace was brisk; obviously, he wanted no delay in reaching the king.

Larryn managed to stay at his side. "My name is Larryn Maeller," she said. She didn't even attempt to give herself the title of "Lady" as Seldrake had, for she didn't want to attempt a false explanation of where it had come from. And she had learned her lesson about using her true title of "Doctor."

"I know, m'lady." Browne nodded his acknowledgment. His long, black hair, obviously a wig, rippled as he moved his head. His coat was a brilliant scarlet, and he wore a white lace jabot beneath his chin. His clothing was as rich-looking as that worn by most of the male guests. Larryn wished she understood the protocol here; the lord-in-waiting, though a messenger of the king, must be more than a servant.

She supposed, then, that although in this time one did not make conversation with someone considered a social inferior, it was probably not incorrect to speak with Browne. She asked, "Do you know why His Majesty wanted to see me?"

Did she imagine the snide sideways glance? It was gone in an instant. "No, m'lady. However, I believe he wishes to meet the woman whose name is become celebrated at the palace, thanks to the praises of Lady Anne Farswell. She has said that you, and not Seldrake, saved the life of her son."

"Not at all," Larryn said quickly. "He's the doctor. I just made suggestions." Was her treatment of the barely ill child going to get both of them in trouble? She hadn't done much. But maybe, instead of helping Seldrake, she had hurt him. Nervously, she nibbled her bottom lip.

"The duke of Seldrake, although an esteemed lord and reputedly able physician, is not always successful at saving lives, m'lady," Browne said. There was a testiness to his voice.

Did he dislike Seldrake for some reason?

Larryn sighed. She didn't belong here. She didn't even understand the politics of her time, let alone here, in a foreign court so distant in time and customs.

"He's a skilled and caring physician," she defended firmly. She couldn't say much more; she didn't dare allude to the young lives he had preserved from the plague.

"Mayhap," Browne said with a shrug. "Please follow me." He gestured to a narrow stairway. The ceiling displayed elaborate frescoes. As Browne climbed, his lace-trimmed britches and thin, stocking-clad legs emerged from the front of his long, red coat.

Larryn held up the sides of her dress so as not to trip. Browne got ahead of her on the stairs. "Where are we meeting the king?" she asked.

He glanced down at her. "In the Haunted Gallery."

Larryn started but still managed a small laugh. She knew now that ghosts existed but wasn't about to say so to this courtier with a bad attitude. "And who haunts this gallery?" she asked lightly.

"They say many have heard the screams of Queen Catherine Howard begging her husband, King Henry the Eighth, to keep her from the scaffold." There was a ghoulish relish in Browne's voice that made Larryn shudder.

She didn't say anything. Expressing her horror on behalf of the poor woman might be considered an insult to the monarchy, and therefore to Charles as well as his predecessor.

She wished Seldrake were with her. She could have followed his lead. Despite his arrogance, he had protected her. But she supposed that one didn't invite oneself along to an audience commanded by the king.

They passed through an area Browne identified as the Horn Room, beyond the Watching Chamber, and into the long, Haunted Gallery. Tapestries lined the walls. At one end stood Charles II, engrossed in conversation with several men in dark coats.

At Larryn's approach with Browne, the king waved the men away. With amazement, Larryn thought she recognized one, a young man with a large nose and full lips, from a famous portrait: Samuel Pepys, a civil servant whose diaries had survived the centuries, giving detail and color to the Restoration era.

"Ah," King Charles said, "Lady Larryn." He dismissed

Browne with a glance, and the lord-in-waiting quickly moved away.

The king's sparkling eyes looked down at Larryn.

"Your Majesty," she replied, unsure what to do or say next.

"Our very good friend Lady Anne Farswell has been telling us about you. She says you saved little Lord Apsley last even."

The king's son, Seldrake had told her. "I worked with the duke of Seldrake to help the boy," she said carefully. "I was delighted that he was much better this morning."

"As were we all. Come." He motioned her to a matched pair of carved chairs at one side of gallery. She sat in one, and he took the other. "Now," he said, "tell me what you think of the duke."

She clasped her hands together in her lap. What was he looking for? "He is a very compassionate man, Your Majesty, and an excellent doctor." She weighed the words, making sure nothing sounded as though there were a hidden meaning.

"His father was a fine physician, too," King Charles said. "The family accompanied me into exile, you know." A sadness washed over his prominent features. "Those were trying times."

"So I understand," Larryn said.

"Did you not find them so?" the king shot back. "How did you pass the cursed time of the Protectorate of Cromwell?"

Oh, lord. Had she inadvertently offended him? "I'm afraid I'm not well versed in politics, Your Majesty. I tried not to pay attention to what went on."

"Where were you? Did you and your family not take sides?"

She didn't know how to reply. "We . . . we passed some of the time in Scotland. No matter how we felt, Your Majesty, we did what was expedient."

"Scotland, eh? Well, then you must have had an opinion about our dear friend George Monck. He marched from the north to confront Parliament, to permit our return."

Larryn groped for something appropriate to reply. "I certainly am glad he was successful."

The king's laugh was long and merry. "As are we, Lady Larryn." When he stopped laughing, he looked at her. His glance at her bared neckline was not in the least subtle. "And now you are the houseguest of the duke of Seldrake, are you not?"

"Yes, I am." Larryn tried not to let her discomfort show. The king's reputation with the ladies was legendary. She certainly didn't want to be one of his conquests—nor did she dare to brush off the all-powerful king of England.

"And is he treating you well?"

Oh. The king must think that she was Seldrake's mistress. Maybe if he thought that, he wouldn't hit on her.

Or maybe he would, if he thought she was that kind of woman.

She took a deep breath before saying, "The duke has been very kind." There. Let him read into that whatever he wanted.

She met the king's eye briefly. His look was speculative, but he said offhandedly, "Has the duke told you much of our adventures together?"

Larryn shook her head.

"You must tell him to do so. He and his father were most helpful to us. We remain grateful . . . and would not wish for the duke to find himself in trouble." This time, his gaze deep into her eyes was obviously intended to impart a message. Before she could fathom what it was, he rose. "A pleasure to have met you, Lady Larryn," he said. And then he strode down the gallery.

Browne was inquisitive as he led Larryn from the Haunted Gallery and back downstairs. "May I ask what His Majesty wanted of you, m'lady?"

No, she wanted to retort, *you may not.* But she was concerned about the repercussions of antagonizing anyone here—particularly someone who might have the king's ear.

And the king had clearly issued a warning to Seldrake. . . .

She just said softly, "He most certainly is charming." Browne could make his own interpretation; she hoped he would consider it a flirtation by a man known to be over-sexed.

The problem was that, if the king asked him, Browne would undoubtedly say that His Majesty could make another easy conquest if he wanted.

Larryn sighed, then asked, as they passed the door she recognized to the Great Hall, "Where are we going?"

"Outside, m'lady. All are gone to the park, at the head of the Long Water, I do believe."

The Long Water was an extended canal, lined on both sides with a garden area replete with lime trees. The entire breakfast crowd appeared to have come out here. Larryn noticed that Anne Farswell sat with a group of other women at one end of the park, watching some young children play. Apsley was not among them but it was, of course, too soon, even if he felt better.

Lady Anne rose as she spotted Larryn. "Oh, Lady Larryn, please join us."

"Thank you for guiding me," Larryn said to Browne, glad for an excuse to leave his presence. The man bothered her.

"You are welcome, m'lady," he said. He glanced around. "Ah, I see your . . . patron, the duke. You might wish to tell him how much you appreciated my company."

Larryn blinked as she regarded Browne. What on earth had he meant by that? Was there some message she didn't understand that he wanted her to impart to Seldrake? Well, she wouldn't. She hadn't really appreciated Browne's company, after all.

She turned and saw the duke, too, standing near the edge of the canal. He seemed engrossed in conversation with Lady Mainwaring, who smiled hungrily up at him as though they were alone in a bedroom. . . .

He could have a dozen desirable women here at court at his beck and call. He probably did. Larryn didn't care.

But the problem was that she did. He obviously hadn't noticed her return. Or if he had, it hadn't mattered to him enough even to glance away from the woman who so obviously wanted to get him off by himself.

Anger welled within Larryn. She wanted to leave this place. Now. Go back to her own time. The duke obviously did not want, or need, her help.

Then there was Browne, who remained beside her. "The man is a thief, m'lady," he whispered harshly in her ear. "He steals hearts and souls." With that further cryptic remark, Browne turned and strolled toward a group of men clustered on the path.

Her shock at Browne's barely suppressed fury made Larryn forget her own ire for a moment. What was that all about?

She turned to Lady Anne, hoping to get a clue from her. But Anne didn't seem to have heard Browne's odd remark. "I understand that His Majesty desired to thank you in person," she said to Larryn with a large smile.

"Thanks to you," Larryn said. "I really didn't do much but work with the duke." For both their sakes, she had to tone down this woman's praise. A misstep could cost Seldrake dearly. Her, too. She appreciated Lady Anne's notice, though, here where she was a stranger who didn't dare admit to what she did best.

"Even Thomas allows that you did more," Anne said. She nodded toward the Long Water.

Seldrake, his head bent toward Lady Mainwaring, was still engrossed in conversation with her.

"I appreciate the duke's kindness." Larryn had to work to keep the chilliness from her voice. She turned from the rankling scene, only to find Lady Anne regarding her speculatively. Larryn made herself smile. "Since the duke appears to be occupied, I'd like to check on Apsley."

"I will accompany you, but let us take the long way around. I visited my son but a short while ago, and although he was progressing splendidly, he had laid his head down for a nap."

They strolled past the area where the other children played, some splashing in the water of the canal. Larryn wanted to ask if they were all the king's offspring but didn't dare. She wasn't even sure that Lady Anne admitted to everyone about Apsley. Instead, she said, "I had no idea there would be so many children at court."

"Usually there are not," Anne said. "But since last year, when the plague was so rampant, courtiers who join the king in this pleasant but necessary exile also bring their families."

That didn't make the infamous Restoration dalliances as easy to carry out, Larryn surmised. "I see."

"You might be interested to learn that the boy in the corner with both hands in the water is Lady Mainwaring's son, Lord Terence," Anne said, stopping at the edge of the water. Her voice sounded grim.

Why would I be interested in that? Larryn thought with a glance, despite herself, toward Seldrake. He was shaking his head as though disagreeing with the woman before him. Finally!

Or was it just a lover's spat?

Larryn quickly turned back to the boy. He had light, wavy hair and was dressed, as were the other youngsters, as a miniature courtier, in britches, jacket, and feathered hat. He was a good-looking boy of about seven, though he didn't seem to resemble his mother much.

"Is Lord Mainwaring at the palace with his wife?" Larryn asked, wondering if she had his title correct. She would have to ask Adele, discreetly, for a lesson in aristocratic terminology.

Anne's eyes widened. "Oh, no. Lady Mainwaring's husband suffers much from gout and seldom leaves his home in Sussex."

"That's a shame," Larryn said involuntarily. She felt sorry for Lord Mainwaring, with a wife like Bess. She couldn't help feeling a little sorry for Bess, too, if her husband was an invalid. She imagined here, with men so domineering, that a woman raising a child virtually alone would have a difficult time. Of course, if she were of Bess's class, she would have the help of servants.

"Oh, Lady Mainwaring does quite well at court," Lady Anne said in a disparaging tone.

Larryn wondered at Lady Anne's obvious dislike of the woman. Lady Mainwaring apparently thought no better of her, judging by her attitude when she had come to fetch Seldrake to help little Apsley. Were they rivals in some manner?

And then it came to Larryn. They both had sons. Lady Anne's had been sired by the king. And Lady Mainwaring's son Terence? Maybe Larryn was jumping to conclusions, but Bess apparently did not stay home with her invalid husband. . . .

"Larryn, there you are." Adele joined the two women by the fountain. "How was your audience with His Majesty?" Though her tone was light, there was a touch of concern in her eyes.

"Delightful," Larryn said with a touch of prevarication. It had certainly been interesting, but "delight" was too strong. She would tell both Adele and the duke that she believed the king had issued a warning, but not here, and certainly not now, with so many people able to eavesdrop. She looked toward Anne. "I was so pleased to meet the king. He was really effusive in his praise. But what was most important was that Apsley was better."

"Of course," Anne said with a smile.

"We were just going to check on him," Larryn told Adele.

"Then I shall come along," she said. But before they had gotten more than a few steps closer to the palace, Browne broke away from a group of men and approached them.

"Ah, Lady Adele," he said. "I trust you have been staying well ahead of the plague."

His snide look suggested to Larryn that he knew what Adele and Seldrake had been up to, and she narrowly avoided shuddering.

"As well as anyone can in these days, Mr. Browne," Adele replied lightly.

"Your brother, now—he is a physician. Should he stay away from houses of plague, one might brand him a coward. And yet the duke has the reputation of being a brave man."

Larryn blinked. How could Adele respond to this? She was hardly likely to claim her brother was a coward, yet she couldn't admit to his attempts to save children from death.

Adele obviously sensed the trap. She regarded Browne with haughty blue eyes. When she opened her mouth to reply, Browne laughed. "No matter, Lady Adele. Whether your brother is a fool or a coward has little to do with you. I will call on you someday soon, if I may, Lady Larryn. Perhaps you will go riding with me." He doffed his hat and bowed low, then walked away, leaving Larryn feeling as though someone had just dumped a cockroach down her dress.

Chapter 11

As Larryn walked with Lady Anne and Adele back into the palace, she caught Adele's disapproving frown. *I didn't encourage the creep,* she wanted to tell the young woman who had been so kind to her.

She had no idea why Browne wanted to call on her. And she was certainly not about to go riding, or anything else, with him.

Unless, of course, it had something to do with why she was here—if there even was a reason. She hoped she'd figure it out soon. She didn't understand this time or its intrigues. She didn't belong here.

And she certainly didn't enjoy standing by watching Seldrake, whom she believed she was supposed to be helping, ignore her and hit on the lovely Lady Mainwaring.

Larryn had become a bit familiar with the look of the palace's vast and winding hallways. She still couldn't help staring, though, at the detail of the painted ceilings and portraits on the walls.

Little Apsley was sound asleep when they reached his room. Larryn checked his pulse and temperature nevertheless. While she was bent over him with her forehead on his, she listened to his breathing. Though he snored slightly, as if his nose was still stuffy, he seemed much better.

"I will sit with my son for a while," Lady Anne said.

That left Larryn alone with Adele. They headed back toward the park. Larryn was not surprised when her companion broached the subject of Browne. "I will not presume to tell you from whom you should receive attention," Adele said, staring straight ahead with her chin high. "But I believed, from your words and actions, that you wished to assist my brother and me and Henry—I mean, Lord Wyford—in our . . . activities. That you did not wish to harm us."

"That's true," Larryn agreed.

"Lord Browne . . . is no friend of my family's. Not now. In fact, had he any proof of Thomas's deeds, he would immediately betray him to the king."

They had reached the door back out to the garden. Larryn paused. "That was one thing I wanted to be sure to tell the duke and you."

"What is that?" Adele's tone was puzzled.

"The king hinted he might be aware of your . . . activities."

Adele's blue eyes widened in shock. "What said he? Are we to be accused?"

Larryn shook her head. "I don't think so. He made a comment like he was grateful for the help the duke and his father had given before, and that he would not like to see Seldrake in trouble. I took that as a warning."

"Then he does know." Adele's voice was small and frightened.

Larryn touched her shoulder. "If so, he didn't sound as though he's going to act on it—though maybe if your work continues he could change his mind."

"I must warn Thomas." Adele's gaze swept the large garden.

"He was near the canal with Lady Mainwaring last time I saw him." Larryn's tone must have been dry, for Adele's pale brows shot up.

"Mayhap we shall still find him there."

Mayhap you *will,* Larryn thought. She didn't have anything to say to the duke while he flirted with Bess. But she didn't have much choice, as Adele begged, "Please, come with me."

"All right."

Adele paused on the path for just a moment, letting a richly dressed couple gazing into one another's eyes pass by. "You must understand," she said when they were gone, "why Lord Browne is my brother's enemy."

That took Larryn aback. "Enemy?"

"Yes. You see, Browne and his family went into exile with the king, too. Browne's father was quite close to Charmian's—a distant cousin, I believe. Browne had understood that someday the king would bless his union with Charmian. But our Charles had little enough to award those who had done him special service. When our father suggested that Charmian and my brother wed, and neither objected, he granted it. Browne has not forgiven him—most especially since Thomas, though a physician, was unable to save Charmian's life."

"I see," Larryn said slowly. And Browne, as lord-in-waiting, whatever that entailed, was around court a lot. He had the ear of the king. He could spread rumors—viciously untrue or not. Those who knew the source and the reason might understand. But there would always be others. . . . "We'd better watch out for this Browne character and keep out of his way."

"Yes," Adele agreed. "We should all keep far out of his way."

The group of children was no longer playing at the edge of the canal. Maybe Bess had gone wherever her son was.

No such luck. Bess was beside the duke, hanging onto his arm. Seldrake did not look overly pleased at how their conversation was going, though. That almost made Larryn smile. She wished she knew what they were talking about.

Seldrake looked up as Adele said, "Thomas, do you not think it time that we started for home?"

"Yes," he agreed with no hesitation. "As soon as we take our leave from the king."

Beside him, Bess glowered. "But Thomas, about my sweet Terence. We have not settled—"

"We shall settle it another time, Bess." His firm tone did not invite an argument. "And now we shall find the king."

Seldrake was pleased to see His Majesty, accompanied by three attentive and beauteous ladies of the court, stroll from the palace door just as he approached. Seldrake, too, was accompanied by two most comely women: his sister, Adele, and his enigmatic . . . what should he call the exquisite, intelligent Larryn? His guest? His prisoner, perhaps, for he did not dare let her out of his presence for long; she could do him immeasurable harm.

He only prayed she had not said something untoward to the king or to Lady Anne, who had the king's ear.

And at the king's behest Larryn had spent much time in the company of that insidious and resentful wretch Browne. That might have been the most harmful contact of all.

He would find out all from her on the way home.

"Your Majesty," he called as he neared his king. "We must, unfortunately, take our leave. It grows late, and we do not wish to presume upon your hospitality for another night."

"You may partake of our hospitality at any time, Thomas," Charles II said. His eyes were not on Seldrake, however, but on Larryn. "So long," he continued, "as you bring along your most pleasing . . . friend, Lady Larryn. We wish to see much of her."

"You're very kind, Your Majesty," Larryn said. She blushed prettily as His Majesty bent to kiss her slender hand.

An ugly wisp of poisonous choler meandered its way through Seldrake's blood as the king regarded Larryn in the way that had grown familiar to Seldrake in the long months of exile spent in Charles's company. It was the lusting look his king used when he found a new woman most appealing.

When he wished to increase his acquaintance with her.

Seldom had a female refused, even before Charles's throne had been restored. Even more seldom was he refused now that he was monarch.

The king's interest mattered only because of the harm such familiarity with Larryn could do to his illicit enterprise, Seldrake insisted to himself. Women held little interest for him. They made demands, like Bess Mainwaring, who used her near-irresistible beauty like a lodestone.

Or they died, like his sweet Charmian. His Charmian, whom Browne still coveted.

His Charmian, whom Seldrake had failed to save.

"It may be some time before we return to court, Your Majesty," Seldrake said, endeavoring to keep himself from sounding churlish. "There are family obligations, you understand."

"That is most unfortunate, Thomas," said Lady Beatrice, one of the women who had accompanied the king from the palace. The wife of Lord Redding, she was known for her enthusiastic escapades in the beds of men other than her husband's. "I had hoped to ask you to see to my . . . medical needs." She smiled most engagingly at Seldrake.

He glanced at the king, who was known to partake of the lady's bed skills now and again. His Majesty seemed but amused.

When Seldrake met Larryn's gaze, however, it appeared quite a different matter. Amusement was not the word Seldrake would have used for the inquisitive glint in the lady's eye.

"If you must leave, Thomas," said the king, "then so be it—for the nonce. We are aware that you are a skilled physician. And Lady Larryn is a most able assistant, although she gives all credit to you. In any event, should we need medical attention for ourselves or for our favorites, must we hesitate to call on you for fear your family obligations hold you elsewhere?"

"Never, Your Majesty." Damnation! Seldrake felt as if he strode through a bog in which he was threatened, with

each step, to be sucked in deep over his head. He had no
wish to fall into the king's ill graces. "You need but call
on me. I find nothing more important than to please you."

"Remember that, Thomas." The king's brow knitted severely as he regarded an uneasy Seldrake. But Charles gave
a smile most charming as he bowed his head toward Larryn.
"And you, Lady Larryn. May we count on your return
should we need . . . attention?"

Larryn was no fool. Her lovely dark eyes widened at the
king's double entendre. "It looks as though you have a lot
of attention around you, Your Majesty," she said with a
smile toward the women attending him. "As for me, I think
I can do best at aiding the children at court. I'll be happy
to help them whenever I can."

Had the woman dared to rebuff the king? That made
Seldrake's heart soar, even as he allowed himself to cringe
internally as he awaited the king's response.

To his surprise, Charles laughed. And then he said, "Ah,
are not the oldest of men but children at heart, Lady Larryn?"

With that, the king walked away, leaving Seldrake uneasy.

They had been on the road for a couple of hours. Somehow,
despite the rough ride, Adele had managed to fall asleep.
Larryn had already told Seldrake about the warning from
the king. He had seemed concerned but not surprised.

Except for the creaking of the coach and the clopping of
the horses' hoofs, all was silent now.

Lost in thoughts about all she had seen and heard in the
last couple of days, Larryn was startled when Seldrake's
deep voice broke into the quiet. "What thought you of our
visit to court, Larryn? You seemed much at home."

She stared at him. At home? The court of King Charles
II was nothing like her home.

Her home was a condo, where she lived alone, and her
lab, where she did research. Both were a long, long way
from here.

"It was very . . . interesting," she managed. Her nostalgia inserted a catch into her voice that she hadn't anticipated.

"Then you had not been to court before?"

Despite her helping him with the children, despite her passing along the king's warning, Seldrake obviously still suspected that she was a spy. "No," she said calmly though hurt pulsed through her in near palpable waves. "I had never been to court, hadn't met anyone there before—except for Adele and you, of course. And Lady Mainwaring." She paused. "Is this coach yours? I thought it belonged to her."

"It is Bess's," Seldrake agreed. "She decided to tarry longer at the palace and allowed us its use to return home."

Was the loan of something as valuable as a coach and matched team done all the time, or had Lady Mainwaring lent it because she wanted something from Seldrake?

Or did she already have what she wanted from him?

Larryn looked at the duke. Despite the relentless jouncing of the carriage, he sat up straight, his posture impeccable. Adele only took up a small portion of the seat; Seldrake occupied the rest. He watched Larryn quietly, his blue eyes unfathomable, yet not unfriendly. In her time, few men, if any, wore their hair in such long waves. There, it would have been a feminine hairstyle. On Seldrake, it enhanced strong features that were definitely, fascinatingly masculine.

One corner of his mouth quirked upward as though he were amused at her scrutiny. Damn! She didn't want him to think she was admiring him—even if she was. The man was arrogant enough.

"Do you go to court often?" she asked to make conversation.

"I once did, when my wife was alive." His voice was curt, but Larryn could hear the pain behind his words.

"I'm sorry for your loss," she said softly.

His eyes had turned the blue of glacier ice. "It was more than a year ago. And many have suffered losses due to the plague."

"That doesn't make your hurt any less." Without thinking, she reached forward and touched his knee sympathetically.

His leg was warm and muscular beneath his britches. Amazed at her own impulsiveness, Larryn began to draw away, but her hand was captured in Seldrake's strong clasp, held tightly to his leg. A tremor rocked through her as she became more attuned to the duke's sensuality. Her breathing grew unsteady.

"No," he said. "It does not lessen the hurt. But that is why I must help the children. And why I shall allow nothing to interfere."

Again was the implied suspicion, the overt threat. Larryn tried to pull her hand away, but he did not let go. Instead, he turned it and began stroking her palm with his thumb.

The soft, erotic gesture filled Larryn with a rush of desire unlike anything she had ever felt before. She wanted to pull back. She hated to be touched, she reminded herself.

She swallowed, then made herself speak steadily. "You don't need to tell me that. I helped you before, and I'll help you again." *Until I determine what you really need,* she thought. *Until I can figure out why I'm here and learn how to get home.*

But the idea of leaving did not enthuse her a fraction as much as it had when she had first arrived here.

She chuckled ironically and audibly at herself.

"What amuses you, Larryn?" The duke's deep voice thrummed through her body.

"Me? Amused?" This time her laugh was shrill. "That's the last thing I am." She managed finally to draw back her hand. Despite herself, she practically cradled it in her lap as the echo of the duke's touch continued to reverberate through her.

Beside Seldrake, Adele stirred in her sleep, murmuring something unintelligible.

"We need to speak more softly," Seldrake said, "lest we wake my curious sister. Instead, I wish to satisfy my own curiosity."

The levels of their communication confused Larryn. Anyone eavesdropping on their words would hear nothing but a remote conversation between the merest of acquaintances.

But the undercurrent, caused by his look, his touch . . . it was electric. Or would have been, if electricity had yet been named in this age so distant from her own.

Seldrake's lustful, incisive gaze captured Larryn's, nearly hypnotizing her. If he asked her to tear off her clothes right here and now, she had a wayward fear that she'd obey him. "About what?" she whispered.

"Tell me about your family in Scotland." His tone was low and sensual.

But Larryn felt as though he had thrown her into the Long Water at Hampton Court. His sweet seduction had been an act to put her off guard. To get her to reveal something about herself that he hadn't been able to learn another way.

Well, it hadn't worked.

"My family?" She spoke through gritted teeth. "I haven't any."

"Everyone has a family," he insisted. "I wish to know about yours."

"Of course you do," she replied. "You want to know more than that, don't you? Well, I can't tell you everything about who I am and where I'm from, your lordship." She spat the last words at him ironically. "Just take it at my word that I came from northern Scotland. It's more believable than the truth."

She watched his eyes widen in surprise at her rash revelation. His full lips parted, but before he could ask the questions she saw written on his face, she interrupted.

"The one thing that is true, Duke, is that I am not here to harm you. I'm here to help you, though the only way I can convince you of that, I'm sure, is to show you. So far I have demonstrated it, haven't I?" She gave him no time to answer. "Okay," she continued. "You want to know about my family. I'll tell you about my family. I had one—

once. My parents died young. So did my sister. Like your wife, she died of a terrible illness."

Her sister, who had thrown herself despairingly into a life of looking for love . . . and it had killed her when she contracted AIDS.

Larryn remembered Seldrake's long, apparently emotional conversation with the gorgeous and tempting Lady Mainwaring. The way that Lady Beatrice, when Larryn had met her with the king, had made her interest in the duke oh so obvious.

Men like Seldrake, men who seduced women—they, too, had killed her sister.

That was why she had no interest in any man. Why she hated to be touched.

"I am sorry," Seldrake said, mirroring the sentiment she had shown when he had mentioned his wife's death.

"Thanks," Larryn said curtly.

"Thomas? Larryn? Is everything all right?" Adele had wakened, and she looked in alarm from one to the other.

"Everything's fine," Larryn said, her eyes locked on Seldrake's. "But I think it's my turn to take a nap." She deliberately lowered her eyelids.

Chapter 12

LARRYN HAD NEVER been much of a gardener. Though she had, now and then, managed to keep a few houseplants alive for more than a week, she'd had even less success growing things in the little space in the yard of her townhouse. The few times she had tried, her sweet and lively Cavalier, Kit, had dug everything up.

She sighed, thinking of Kit, whom she had lost months ago. But as she looked about, she smiled. "Here, Caddie," she called. "Augie, come!" Both dogs came running through the dirt, leaping on her where she knelt in the verdant Seldrake House herb garden and nearly knocking her over. She laughed and hugged them both. After Caddie leapt up to lick her chin, Larryn batted the pup playfully away. In moments, Caddie was back for more. Augie joined in the roughhousing, too.

Little August, though his nose was more pointed than Caddie's, had the same red-and-white coloration. He often, though not always, wore the jeweled collar that Chloe had found in the future. He didn't have it on now. Augie was as loving and playful as any Cavalier Larryn had met in her time.

And he had belonged to Charmian, the duke's wife, whom he had so painfully lost.

Larryn's pleasure with the dogs grew suddenly subdued. "What was she like?" she asked Augie softly. "Was your mistress beautiful?" What about her had the duke loved?

And what would it be like to have the duke's love, the way his wife had? He was such a demanding, arrogant man most of the time, yet he sometimes teased, too. When he spoke of losing Charmian his pain was nearly tangible.

He wouldn't have acted so suspicious of *her,* Larryn was certain. He wouldn't have tried to trick information from her. He probably had been kind and attentive. And in bed . . . ?

"Are you nuts?" she chastised herself. That wasn't something she should wonder about.

But she wondered just the same. And she knew why. Even though he'd had an ulterior motive the day before, just the feel of his leg, the clasp of his hand, had caused such fire to leap through her that she couldn't help it; her imagination ran wild.

Wild? That couldn't even begin to explain the way she had fantasized in bed last night about Seldrake, her fury with the man notwithstanding. How she had imagined how the duke, with his smoldering eyes and sensuous touches, would undoubtedly drive a woman out of her mind with his lovemaking. Her body grew molten once more at the very thought.

She closed her eyes and clenched her fists. "Cut it out," she told herself. She despised physical contact, after all. And the guy probably hadn't even been true to his beloved Charmian, not in this era.

That halted Larryn's lustful musings. The man was a product of his environment. She had seen how women fell all over him to get his attention—most especially Lady Bess Mainwaring.

But Larryn did not intend to be just another notch in his belt—or whatever held up those damned sexy britches. She snorted in ironic laughter.

The noise caused Augie to bark, bringing Larryn's attention back to the dogs. "I need to keep my mind on you, don't I?" She played with both dogs for a few more minutes, keeping her mind carefully blank.

It helped. A lot. She finally said, "Okay, you two. Thanks for keeping me company, but now you can get back to whatever mischief you were into."

She was ready to get back to gardening. She watched the pups cavort off together, skirting the inside of the high stone wall that surrounded Seldrake House. The wrought-iron front gate was closed securely; she had made certain of it when she had first come to the garden, since she did not want the dogs, who'd followed, to get outside. Seldrake House was at the junction of two wide dirt roads. She wasn't sure how busy they were, but it wasn't good for the dogs to be outside the grounds unsupervised.

There was another gate from the rear courtyard onto the road perpendicular to the one at the front of the house, but she was told it was always kept shut except for comings and goings of the household horses and coaches.

The house looked much as it did in Chloe's time, with its three-story oblong shape, mullioned windows, and roof sloping up to a flat center. It was a much lighter gray in color now when nearly new, attesting to how its surface had become dirtied over the years. The windows were of bubbled glass in a greenish gray.

The lovely gardens behind Chloe's house filled the area where the courtyard sat in this time. Only one of the cottages, where the duke secreted the children whom he so courageously saved, had survived the centuries—but not very well.

The gardens now were at the front, between the house and the wall that Larryn now knew provided privacy from the main carriage road outside. The road that eventually led to Hampton Court and the king.

The road on which they had ridden in Bess's carriage, in which Seldrake had taken her hand. . . . Damn!

Forcing her mind once again off that path, she smoothed

the skirt of the worn shift that Adele had given her—one
of heavy muslin, appropriate for gardening. She longed for
her ratty old T-shirt and denim shorts. How that would
shock Seldrake! But not even the knee-length men's
britches here would have felt any better than the loose dress
she wore, so she hadn't complained.

The britches certainly looked good on Seldrake, she
thought. His strong calf muscles were revealed by the knit
stockings he wore beneath them. And she had touched his
leg. . . .

Enough! she commanded herself. She was going to concentrate on gardening.

Adele had brought her out here earlier and explained the
contents of each small patch of herbs and other plants. The
physicality of kneeling on the earth weeding around medicinal herbs was exactly what she needed. Maybe she
would try some herbs herself. She needed some purging,
after all—to get the duke out of her mind.

She glanced toward the rear of the house, where a corner
of one cottage was visible. Seldrake and she had checked
on the kids first thing when they returned the previous
night. The little ones in quarantine seemed fine. They would
remain there a while longer just in case, but the likelihood
of their having contracted the plague grew slighter as each
day passed.

The others were well, too. And clean. With prodding
from Lord Wyford, who had looked after the children while
they were gone, Ned and the other servants had seen to it.

Wyford had been waiting upon their return. He had been
pleasant, businesslike, and quietly friendly with the duke.
But Larryn had seen the way his eyes surreptitiously met
Adele's. And how the duke's sister blushed in the young
doctor's presence.

And how the duke had scowled the one time he had
caught the illicit flirtation.

Keep out of it, she told herself. Unless making Seldrake
act sensibly with respect to his sister and the man she so
obviously loved was Larryn's reason for being here. . . . But

she would only learn that with vigilance and patience.

In the meantime, the children had all seemed restless. Cabin fever had set in.

That could be dangerous to the duke and his brave household. Restless children made more noise. Became more visible.

Brought more attention.

She knew what would keep them occupied: school. Could that be the duke's unfinished business? Was she supposed to help him teach the children in his charge?

She shook her head. "When hens make holy water!" she whispered aloud, then laughed. It was an expression she had heard Adele use when Seldrake had told her that it was too dangerous to help him any longer, that she must cease coming along to help rescue children. It meant "never." And since the duke turned the children over to surviving family as quickly as possible, Larryn figured her idea held no merit.

She turned back to the part of the garden she was weeding. Seldrake's journals would tell her the uses made of the plants she tended. She hoped to return to the study and read them more thoroughly—preferably with the duke's permission.

In the meantime, she pulled up a clump of weeds, inhaling the fresh fragrance of earth and pungent greenery. She wished she knew what everything was but she could not recall even half the herbs Adele had identified.

She recalled some, though—either because of their familiarity or because of their odd names. She whispered their names as she pointed at them, hoping that she knew her crowfoot from her clove. "Balsam herb," Larryn said, weeding around one group of plants. Adele had also called it costmary. "Dill, endive, fennel, and feverfew." She walked slowly to another area. "Lavender, marjoram, and mustard." She knelt again. When she'd gotten nearly every weed in sight, she strode to yet another area of the flat, vast garden. "Rosemary and thyme," she said, wondering if she'd missed the parsley and sage of the song "Scarborough

Fair." "And garden rue and garden tansy and jack-by-the-hedgeside."

There were dandelions, too, which Larryn would have pulled as weeds had Adele not extolled their medicinal qualities for internal cleansing and assisting in relaxation. Larryn had, of course, heard of dandelion wine.

The patch of pretty daisies also had healing qualities, Adele had said.

Fascinating, Larryn thought. She had learned over the years that many old herbal cures had genuine merit in application, though none replaced medical breakthroughs like antibiotics and vaccines.

She could learn a lot here, she was certain, if she remained long enough.

But did she want to stay? Her mind immediately focused—yet again—on the duke of Seldrake.

So what if she was turned on by the man? She wouldn't act on it. That, at least, she could prevent.

But she also didn't want to like him. Or care about him. Or admire his courage, or enjoy his sense of humor the few times he had let it show.

But despite herself, she realized that the man was infinitely more appealing than his portrait that had drawn her in the first place. Sure, she had to get her libido under control around him. Worse, her emotions had become even more entangled than they had been when the man's ghost had pleaded for help. . . .

His ghost. The thought brought her up abruptly. "He's going to die," she told herself softly, looking at her earth-covered hands. There was nothing she could do about that. Everyone died. But this brave, arrogant, appealing man, who had so captivated her imagination . . . and, she was beginning to fear, was starting to capture her heart—he was going to die centuries before she would ever be born.

"Oh, Seldrake," she whispered. "I can't care for you. I simply can't."

But seeing the logic did not make it so.

She heard an excited bark, followed by another. When

she looked up, she saw Caddie and Augie hurtling themselves through the open gate.

Open? But it had been closed. And Larryn heard the
rumble of a carriage, the clopping of a horse's hooves.

"Oh, no!" She ran toward where the dogs had disappeared, her long skirts in her way. "Augie! Caddie! Come
back!"

From the corner of her eye, she saw a movement at the
front of the house. She didn't stop to see who had come
out. She strained to hear the dogs. If they were barking,
they were still all right.

Was that just one bark? In her mind, she could see a
small red-and-white form crushed beneath a horse's hooves.
"No!" she screamed. She had reached the gate. She threw
it open farther and raced through.

Outside was the hard dirt road. Across from it were fields
of wheat tended by Seldrake's tenants. She saw no one
there.

"Caddie!" Larryn cried. She looked up the curving road,
then down. No dogs. At least neither had become roadkill.
But where were they?

She heard a voice she couldn't quite make out, the crack
of a whip, the creak of a carriage. A large brown horse
appeared from the side road. It plunged around the stone
wall. "Caddie! Augie!" she called, terrified. Were they
around the corner? Had she missed them because they were
already lost? She ran toward the carriage—and froze. The
horse galloped straight toward her.

She waved her hands. "Hey!" She tried to dive off the
road. The stone wall was in the way. She had nowhere to
go. The horse kept coming. . . .

Could she get to the far side of the road in time, fling
herself into its ditch?

The horse was nearly upon her.

And then . . . a bark sounded at her side, and then another. Two small red-and-white shapes hurled themselves
toward the horse, yapping and nipping at the hooves.

The horse reared. The small carriage it pulled nearly toppled. The dogs' diversion gave Larryn enough time to throw herself across the road and into the ditch.

The driver got the horse under control. Gathering speed, the carriage continued down the road. It wasn't large, but horse and vehicle could have done one unprotected person a lot of damage. Larryn hadn't made out anything of the driver, who was hidden beneath a cloak.

"Larryn!" A deep, masculine voice shouted from the gate. In moments, Seldrake knelt beside her. "Are you injured?" His hands ran down her arms, still sheathed in her borrowed shift. She knew he was examining her for broken bones, yet again his touch electrified her.

"I'm fine," she tried to say calmly, but her voice quivered. "The dogs—"

"I shall flog them for placing you in such danger." The anger in his voice made her shudder.

"No. No, they saved me. They scared the horse, and it hesitated enough for me to get out of the way."

"Who was the driver? Did he not stop to ensure your safety?"

Larryn shook her head. "No. In fact . . ." She hesitated.

"What?" he demanded.

"I'm probably wrong, but I had a feeling that . . . that the driver intended to run me down. There was no hesitation, and I heard a whip crack, and—"

"Describe the carriage." Seldrake spoke through gritted teeth. "I arrived too late to see, with that bend in the road."

"It was smaller than the one we rode in yesterday. It had only one horse."

"Was it a carrier's cart, a post coach, or a private coach?"

"I . . . I'm sorry. I don't know."

The duke's blue eyes blazed, as though his fury were turned on her. "Where in Hades are you from, Larryn Maeller, that you do not even recognize the type of coach that nearly killed you? Do not tell me Scotland. You have admitted that is a lie."

She laughed bitterly. "Maybe I really am from Hades." Tears filled her eyes, and she looked away.

She felt his hand beneath her chin. Firmly, her face was turned so that she faced him.

"You are truly unhurt?" This time, Seldrake's voice was quiet, yet there was a tremor in it as well.

"I'm all right." But she was crying nonetheless.

In moments, she was lifted to her feet and snugged close against Seldrake's hard chest, the top of her head resting beneath his chin. He held her tightly until her crying stopped.

"I'm sorry," she whispered.

"As am I, that you should be so endangered while in my charge." Her chest was still against his, and the vibration of his voice sang through her entire body.

"I'm not in your charge," she contradicted, pulling back. "I'm—"

But she did not finish, for her mouth was suddenly occupied as Seldrake kissed her.

Her fantasies of the night before still left her unprepared for the reality of this man's lips making their sensual demands of hers. His mouth commanded hers to open, to allow his tongue access. Despite how she argued with every order he had issued, in this she had no will of her own. She didn't want to fight. She wanted to yield to the demands of this man's heated, searching mouth, his ravaging tongue that mated with hers even as he pulled her tighter against him.

There was no mistaking how aroused he was, for his hardness pressed against her stomach. She pushed herself even closer, wanting pressure on her own needy, sensitive parts that yearned for solace.

He muttered something against her mouth, then drew his away. Her own small sound of protest turned into a gasp as he kissed her neck, then pulled open the top of her shift to press his burning lips there, below her neck but above her breasts. Why, now, wasn't she wearing one of those damned revealing dresses that would have afforded him better access? She rubbed her cheek against the softness of his masculine hair, planting mindless kisses among its

waves, trying not to sink to her knees right here, at the side
of the road, as his mouth continued its relentless, arousing
quest—

The road! Was she crazy! Here they were, in plain sight
of anyone who came along. Even someone on the highest
floors of Seldrake House.

"Wait," she said breathlessly. "We can't do this here."

He froze at her words. His mouth was just skimming the
top of her right breast, and she could feel her nipple straining as though waiting for his moist caress.

With a growl, he pulled away. Larryn immediately
reached to grab the flaps at the top of her shift, tying the
laces shut. When Seldrake looked down at her, his eyes
were hooded, his mouth a straight line of frustration.

"You are right, Larryn," he said, his breath rasping. "We
cannot do this. Please, come into the house. We shall as-
certain that you are unharmed, and then we shall determine
who attempted to injure you."

Seldrake sat alone in his study less than an hour later, mull-
ing over his indiscreet folly with Larryn Maeller, the mysterious woman in his charge.

Had his wits grown addled? His concern about the
woman's well-being had turned him into a rutting fool in
broad daylight at the side of a well-traveled road. Anyone
could have happened upon them: his tenants or neighbors,
the townsfolk from nearby Seldrake Forest . . . Adele.

Worse was that, had Larryn not spoken and brought him
to his senses, he would have torn off her garments there at
the roadside, taken her before his reason gained control of
his bollocks.

The woman had muddled his mind, turned him into a
mad creature that belonged in Bedlam.

But his derangement would have been boundless had she
been harmed.

She had said that the carriage—why could she not tell
him the kind?—had lain in wait at the side of the wall until
she had emerged through the gate in search of the dogs.

Had the driver been after Larryn, or simply anyone at Seldrake House who happened to come after the animals?

"No matter!" he raged aloud. Those within his walls were under his protection. Despite the lack of information, he would find the knave and deal with him soundly.

Thank the heavens that the dogs had come when they had and startled the steed that bore down on Larryn. He had told the head cook to reward them richly with tempting bones from his own supper.

But none had seen the carriage as it tarried at the side of the wall, any more than anyone had seen it careen nearly into Larryn.

Seldrake shuddered once more at the thought of what might have happened to that woman of infinite beauty. Of intelligence and knowledge like none other of his acquaintance.

Of boundless wit and endless lies and shrewish tongue that made him wish to shake her at the same time as he wanted, over and over, to finish what had been so precipitously started that day on the road. . . .

"Have you bewitched me, Larryn Maeller?" he asked aloud. Despite the ugly accusation in his strong words, he felt his lips curve in a fond grin. For if she had bewitched him, he had no wish for her to end the spell.

Only for her to complete it, so he could feel her slim body writhing beneath him in bed.

Mayhap then the spell might be lifted. Or mayhap that would but constitute the beginning . . . a most appealing thought.

"Y'r Grace?" Seldrake heard Ned's words before the rap at the study door.

"Yes, Ned. You may enter."

The shriveled and elderly manservant who had been with the Seldrake family for many years pushed open the door and shuffled into the room. "Sorry to disturb you, Y'r Grace, but there is a visitor at the gate who says he must speak to ye right away."

"Did he come in a carriage?" Mayhap it was the scoundrel who had attempted to injury Larryn. Had he returned to complete the job?

Yet why, if he had managed to get safely away, would he thus imperil himself?

No, it was unlikely.

Ned's words confirmed Seldrake's doubts. "Nay, sir. He came on horseback."

"Do you know the man?"

"Nay, but he says he knows you, sir."

"His name?"

"Warflem, sir. He says he has come about a child."

Seldrake felt himself straighten. A strange name, and not one he recognized. But what stranger would know of Seldrake's interest in children? Was his presence a threat?

"Show me to him," Seldrake said, then followed Ned from the chamber.

Chapter 13

WARFLEM AWAITED SELDRAKE in the kitchen, as was appropriate for a man of his obvious station. The man was unfamiliar to Seldrake, but he was clad as a common laborer, with leather britches and a coarse and soiled shirt. He had a curved back and did not meet Seldrake's eyes as he spoke, whether from nervousness or deference Seldrake could not tell.

"Y'r Grace," he said in a nasal voice, "I am sent to request y'r help, I am. It is about three children in a house about to be locked due to plague."

"And why would you come to me about this?" Seldrake purposely kept his tone cold and angry, although inside he allowed himself the merest quake. Should he make but a single misstep here, should he trust the man and be in error, his fate might be the gallows.

And not only his own life might be forfeit. Adele, Wyford, and others, too, would be imperiled. Mayhap even Larryn. The idea turned him as cold inside as the ice of the North Sea in winter. He dared not be less than prudent now.

But mayhap there *were* children in peril. He might be able to salvage another life or two. He, who had been unable to save the life dearest to him from the ravages of the most fiendish of diseases.

"It were Nessie Janes that sent me, sir."

"And who is that?" Seldrake knew well who she was. The old, impoverished woman made her living as a searcher of the dead. Searchers listened for the parish bells that tolled the latest to succumb. From home to imperiled home they ventured, obtaining the most vile of statistics to be recorded in the Bills of Mortality, by which authorities kept track of the numbers and causes of London's deaths.

Nessie was not above increasing her meager earnings by taking a few shillings from the duke. In return, she told him of children about to be locked away with their dying families. But Seldrake held the woman's fear as well as respect. If the wrong persons learned she took bribes, her life, too, would be forfeit. Thus, Seldrake and she participated in a most uneasy bargain. They had come to trust one another. She would not betray him.

Yet might she have told another of his activities, his payments? He had warned her never to do so. She had always come herself to tell of salvageable children. But how would this creature know of their bargain had Nessie not revealed it?

The man named Warflem appeared confused. "Nessie said you know her, Y'r Grace. She gave me this list of other children who might be in y'r charge." He held out a grimy piece of paper.

As he glanced at it, Seldrake assumed a look of the utmost disdain, despite his increased malaise. It contained names of some of the children hidden carefully within the cottages and others already returned to surviving families. "I do not know these persons," he snarled nevertheless. "Who are they?"

Warflem shrugged his narrow shoulders. "I would not know, Y'r Grace. I does not read. But Nessie do. She gave me this." He waved the list in the air. "I has not come for payment. I has received enough from those what wants these children saved."

"Thomas?" Adele had come into the kitchen. Seldrake felt his teeth clench. He turned slowly, intending to tell her with his eyes that she must go.

But she was not alone. Larryn accompanied her. Now she, too, would be endangered, as when the carriage had set after her.

He had put trusted subalterns to the task of finding who had nearly run her down. They had so far learned naught. If their efforts remained barren, he himself would take over. Soon.

But he bade his thoughts return to the most immediate concern. "I am discussing men's business," he stated coolly. He glared at his sister, who paled and glanced at Larryn. Was Adele now taking cues from this woman who never obeyed? This could not continue.

But now was not the time to chastise either woman. Larryn's gaze was as stubborn as he had yet seen it—and he had seen her appear as stubborn as the most recalcitrant of untrained horses.

"Maybe we can help with your men's business." Larryn's voice was as sweet as if she licked honey from an abandoned beehive—until her pronunciation of the last two words stung as though the swarm had returned.

"I think not," he told her pleasantly, though he hoped his scowl conveyed his rage.

If it did, it failed to deter her. She stood beside Adele, and both continued to regard both Warflem and him expectantly.

Furious that the woman did not heed him—even in front of this stranger, no matter how inconsequential—Seldrake forced himself to fake a yawn as he turned back to Warflem. "Leave your information if you wish. It is of no interest to me."

"What shall I tell Nessie, Y'r Grace?"

"You may tell this Nessie anything you wish." He spoke through tight-clenched teeth.

"And the children, sir? They are very young, the offspring of a public servant who begs your help, a public servant as has done no one no harm."

"Except perhaps to spread the plague? I think it time for you to leave."

With that, Seldrake nodded to Ned, who stood watchfully at one corner of the empty kitchen. He approached. " 'ere, I'll show you out now."

Warflem looked reproachfully at Seldrake. "They'll die, Y'r Grace, if ye don't save 'em."

Seldrake turned his back and stalked from the kitchen.

"This is foolishness." Larryn couldn't help criticizing even as she followed Seldrake into the coach. It was less opulent than Lady Mainwaring's. In fact, it appeared rather old and worn.

The better, she figured, not to be identified if anyone saw them.

"My prudence might well be lacking," Seldrake agreed, seating himself on the wooden bench at the coach's back. "Which is why you shall stay here. I will not give the order to leave until you have departed this carriage."

"You'll be sitting here a long time." Larryn sat down facing him. It was better than being beside him, where they would undoubtedly be jostled as the coach started, making them touch each other—whether they wanted to or not.

And she did not want to touch Seldrake. Never again. It engendered too many wayward emotions inside her.

"We shall come, too, as always." Adele got into the coach as well, followed by Wyford.

"There is no need for everyone to come," Seldrake snapped. "If there is danger, I must be the only one imperiled."

"Why should we miss all the fun?" Larryn asked with a grin she hoped was as sardonic as one of Seldrake's. "Besides, it's not exactly safe around here, either, with mad carriage drivers on the road."

A look she could not interpret flashed across Seldrake's face, but she knew she'd made her point.

"We shall say we were all out for a drive, should we get stopped," Adele added.

"And you may need assistance should these children already be ill," Wyford said. "If so, we cannot take them with us, of course, yet we will want to make them as comfortable as possible."

"There will be less room for children in the carriage if we all take a constitutional in the most stricken areas of London. And thus far we have all been most fortunate not to have contracted the disease. We know not enough about this situation to understand if peril is more imminent." Seldrake still wasn't giving in without a fight.

But Larryn suspected, without knowing why, that this trip had something to do with why she had come to this time. And if Adele and Wyford wanted to help—well, they might need all the help they could get. "I thought the plague was everywhere in London," she said.

"The worst of the plague in recent history was last year," Wyford explained. "Although the disease has not disappeared, there are fewer deaths in this year of Our Lord sixteen sixty-six, and therefore fewer areas currently affected. Yet the disease is no less agonizing."

"I see," Larryn said. She turned to Seldrake with a final argument. "By the way, since I'm your prisoner, if you leave me without guards aren't you afraid I'll escape?"

With a sharp shake of his head that sent the waves of his hair rippling, he bent toward her. She drew in her breath. Had she gone too far? He wouldn't strike her. Adele and Wyford would be watching.

But maybe men were permitted to hit women in this time, just as they were allowed to control them.

On the other hand, last time he had gotten so close, he had kissed her. . . .

She braced herself, but instead of hitting or kissing her he stood and rapped on the underside of the front of the coach. The signal to the coachman worked, for they started rolling.

Larryn would have laughed at her own imagination—if

she'd found it funny instead of pathetic. Her fantasies about this man simply wouldn't quit.

She sat beside Wyford. There had been no more said about Adele's alleged matchmaking between them. Just as well. Larryn doubted that Seldrake had bought into it for a moment, and reminding him might just stir his annoyance at Adele's interest in the supposedly unsuitable young lord.

"Why," she asked once they were under way, "are you listening to that guy—what was his name? Warflem? From what Lord Wyford and Adele have said, you have a system for hearing about kids who need your help, and that fellow wasn't part of it."

"He mentioned one of my most reliable sources," Seldrake replied. "And he said he was paid by a public servant who required assistance. There is no proof of validity, and yet I am curious. We will simply observe the situation at first. If it appears there are children who can be helped at no peril to us, we shall help them."

"Sounds simple," Larryn said.

"It is not simple in the least," Seldrake retorted as though he had not heard the irony in her voice. And he was right. If something was wrong, there might be no way to save themselves.

But Seldrake apparently was ready to put himself in jeopardy for the sake of some unknown, ragtag kids whose lives he might not even be able to save. She had a sudden urge to hug him for that.

No, she didn't. She shrank from hugs. But she admired the man for trying to save the world, a couple of kids at a time.

"I'm looking forward to seeing London." Larryn settled back onto the uncomfortably hard seat. "Don't turn the carriage around on my account."

"Nor on mine," Adele said forcefully, though she didn't meet her brother's eyes.

They did look like a jolly party of aristocrats out for a drive, Larryn had to admit. Wyford and Seldrake were dressed in brocaded coats over their britches, and both wore large plumed hats. Maybe she was getting used to the garb of this time, but both of them looked really good—Seldrake in particular. His coat was stretched tightly over his broad shoulders and tapered to his slender waist before billowing out over his britches. His knit stockings hugged his muscular calves. His large sapphire ring was on his index finger.

Larryn doubted she would ever get used to wearing women's clothing here. She was in yet another tightly laced bodice that squeezed her breasts up, though not quite out. She sported several layers of skirt, too. Her outfit was in shades of green; Adele's, similar to hers, was in yellow.

At least she had shied away from the spiral curls of this time. She had pulled her hair back in the severe bun she favored. It was professional-looking and she might well have to treat patients at the end of their journey.

The ride to London took over an hour. When they arrived, Larryn could hardly believe that this was the same town she had toured only a few days earlier.

London in her day wasn't like New York or any big United States metropolis. It wasn't crammed full of closely spaced skyscrapers. A lot of its buildings were charmingly antique. It had a lot of bridges. Its main streets tended to be wide thoroughfares, covered with cars and double-decker red buses and old black taxis that appeared to be of 1940s vintage.

Here, there were horses and carriages, but mostly tightly packed pedestrians, including noisy street vendors hawking their wares. Some roads were paved, some not. Though they passed a couple of huge, ornate buildings that may have been palaces or mansions, they also swung through crowded residential neighborhoods. The streets were narrow, made all the more claustrophobic because the houses' second stories were cantilevered out over the street on both sides so that they nearly formed a canopy that blocked sunlight.

Then there was the sanitation—or, rather, lack of it. The entire place stank. If there were any sewers, any means of disposing of rancid food or human waste other than by throwing it in the streets, these people were too lazy to use it.

No wonder plague had gotten a foothold. With conditions like this, it could decimate the entire population.

Eventually, they stopped before a house on a street that wasn't the worst they had traversed, but it wasn't the best, either. At least the houses here didn't all overhang the street, which kept it from being too dark. The coachman called down, "We has arrived, sir."

"You will all please wait here." Seldrake stared first at Adele, then at Wyford.

When his gaze met Larryn's, she raised her eyebrows. "I'll come with you," she said. "We'll check out this place together."

"You will wait here," he repeated, his voice a growl.

But Larryn had already opened the carriage door. "I don't suppose one of you gentlemen would be kind enough to help me down, would you? I wouldn't ask if it weren't for these dratted long skirts; they get in my way."

"I will assist you, Lady Larryn," Wyford said, but before he could help her Seldrake leapt from the carriage and offered her his hand.

She ignored his menacing scowl. "Thanks."

Seldrake gave the coachman orders to pull around the corner with Adele and Wyford still inside. Good idea, Larryn thought. If this were a trap, the others could still get away.

She looked around. The street seemed empty, and no wonder. Painted on several doors were red crosses and the words that struck utter terror into this era's hearts: LORD HAVE MERCY UPON US! The inhabitants had been infected by plague.

The house where they'd stopped had neither the cross nor the sign. If the inhabitants had the plague, they hadn't yet been locked in. That might indicate that Seldrake and she could save the children.

Or that this was a setup.

The duke went to the front door and knocked.

As it was pulled open just a little, three men exited the house next door. They were dressed in coats and britches in dark colors, and each one's frown seemed more officious than the next. They were government officials of some kind, Larryn was certain. "State your business," one called.

"We are just visiting some family," Seldrake said calmly. He didn't look at Larryn. He would want her to play along, whatever he said.

Her heart hammered viciously in her chest. She should never have let him come—as if she could have stopped him. That little weasel Warflem had undoubtedly betrayed the duke. But why?

And how was Larryn going to get him out of this predicament? If some unfinished business had brought her to this time, this might well be it. Though what this had to do with the scene on the roof . . . ?

"What family might that be, your lordship?" asked another of the men. He did not wear a wig, and his white hair, though shoulder-length, was wispy.

"My family," Larryn interrupted. "His lordship has brought me home."

"Home? And what might your name be?" The third man regarded Larryn disdainfully. Didn't her bust bulge enough? She swallowed the hysterical laugh that bubbled inside her. This wasn't funny. It could be life and death—hers and Seldrake's.

He would die one day soon. She knew it. But it wouldn't be at a time when she could save him—she wouldn't allow it.

It wouldn't be now.

A plan suddenly came to her. It was a risk, sure, but she had to try it. She began, "I'm Doctor Larryn Maeller. Some family of mine will live here in about three hundred fifty years. That's when I come from, you see. I've traveled in time to come back to help this gentleman." She pointed to the duke without naming him; with luck, they would never identify him.

"You claim you're a doctor, and you've traveled in time?" The closest man stared with bulging eyes and a slack jaw.

"Didn't you hear me?" She flew toward him with her hands raised as though she would claw him.

"Yes. Of course." He stepped back hastily.

"In my time, right here, beneath this street, there will be long vehicles that move in tunnels by their own power— subways, they call them in my country. The Tube, the Underground—that's how Londoners refer to them." The officials' apparent terror gave Larryn the impetus to continue. "There will be cars—horseless carriages—driving on the streets, and a sewage system, and neon lights at Piccadilly. I don't think we visited there yet, did we?" She glanced at the duke, who stared as though she had gone insane— which was, of course, the whole idea. She turned again toward the ill-at-ease men. "But I just can't wait to return so I can fly in an airplane—that's like a carriage that flies." She looked up at the sky, then hesitated. Had she gone too far? What if they thought she was a witch, ready to take to the air on her broomstick? She stared at the nearest official. "You," she barked. "Did you hear me?"

She glanced at Seldrake. This wouldn't work if he didn't play along. But surely he understood.

His eyes had narrowed, but now he opened them guilelessly and held out his hands. "Gentlemen," he said in a soft voice. "If you will be so kind as to allow us to look in this house, then I will take my charge back to where she belongs. She will be calmer then, you see, and easier to handle."

One man cleared his throat. "Er . . . Bedlam is it, sir?"

Seldrake frowned and put his index finger up to his mouth in a gesture obviously intended to silence the man. Larryn took her cue and hissed, rushing toward the speaker.

Seldrake deftly caught her around the waist. "Now, Doctor," he said. "Mayhap we will take a quick look at this house, then go on our way, shall we?"

Larryn glanced at the men. One nodded as though signaled over her head by the duke.

Once again the duke knocked on the door of the house. It was pulled open a crack once more. "No one can come in," grumbled a sour female voice. She was dressed in an apron. "This is a house of plague."

"There are no signs," Seldrake said.

"There will be." Larryn assumed the woman was one of the searchers of the dead; she did not appear to belong in this middle-class neighborhood.

"Who is inside?" asked one of the men.

"Alls who should be," the woman said. "A man and woman stricken down with plague, and their young."

"Show us the children," demanded one of the men.

They had been betrayed! How else would these fellows have known they were here for the children? Seldrake should never have trusted that weird Warflem.

Yet Larryn felt with certainty that Seldrake would not have turned his back on children who had not yet contracted the plague.

The door was pulled open wider. The woman tugged three children to the entrance, two boys and a girl. The girl was crying. The boys, older, stared out in sad-eyed resignation.

"Keep them inside," one official ordered. "And you, sir." He turned to Seldrake. "You and your . . . charge best be on your way."

Seldrake nodded. "We will." He grasped Larryn under her arm and half dragged her down the street.

She looked back at the house. "I can't leave here!" she cried, waving her hands. "I must go back to the future!" She allowed herself to cackle as though she had gone absolutely mad.

Seldrake passed the street where the carriage had turned, obviously concerned that the officials would follow and find Adele and Wyford. He pulled Larryn down several blocks, then turned the corner in the opposite direction.

"We will double back in a short while," he whispered to

her. As they continued on, he said in a low voice, "That was most resourceful on your part. And such a maniacal story—they will be talking of it at their supper tables for weeks."

"I'm sure," Larryn said dryly.

In a while, they turned back in the direction they had just left, but on a street several blocks away.

The carriage stood in a blacksmith's yard. The horses were happily being fed. At Seldrake's appearance, the coachman pulled them gently from the feeding troughs.

Seldrake helped Larryn into the carriage, then got in. Adele and Wyford were there. Adele hugged both Larryn and Seldrake. "How did you get away?" she demanded, tears streaming down her cheeks.

"We feared you were lost," Wyford agreed.

"Wait until I tell you the tale Larryn invented," Seldrake said in an admiring tone with a shake of his head. "Her imagination is more fertile than even I had believed."

Larryn heard a small sniffle and looked down. A trapdoor had been pulled up in the bench seat. She saw a pair of wide, frightened eyes staring at her.

The children? she mouthed to Adele, who nodded with a big smile. She pointed to the seat where Seldrake and she sat, indicating that the other children were there.

"I think we all have stories to tell," Larryn said, settling into her seat for the ride back to Seldrake House.

On the way, Wyford explained that Adele and he had surreptitiously peered around the side of the house to watch the confrontation with the officials. Although they could not hear what Larryn said, her performance had provided a prolonged diversion. Despite fearing for the safety of Seldrake and Larryn, Adele and he had gone to the back of the residence and gotten one of the adults to pass the children outside.

" 'Twas perfect," Seldrake said with a laugh. "I could not have planned it better if I had assisted Larryn in creating her absurd story."

Irrationally hurt by the way Seldrake continued to poke

fun of her story, Larryn felt an irritated retort spring to her lips.

But she swallowed her words. It *was* absurd . . .

. . . even though it was true.

Chapter 14

LARRYN STOOD ON the flat part of the roof of Seldrake House, where everything had begun. Or at least her sojourn in Restoration England had started here.

"Oh, Caddie," she sighed, staring into darkness illuminated only by the quarter moon, a myriad of stars in the skies and the dim reflection of candlelight shining from the windows of Seldrake House onto the courtyard and garden. She had blown out her own candle and placed its silver holder onto the rooftop beside her. A gentle breeze wafted her skirt about her legs. She might as well be looking over a dark ocean, for beyond the walls of the house she saw only blackness.

The pup rubbed against her ankle, obviously maneuvering for attention, and Larryn picked her up. Caddie's warm fur smelled vaguely sweet, as though she had been into something in the kitchen.

"What am I doing here?" Larryn whispered sadly as the pup licked her cheek.

"You are standing on the roof in the dark, madam," stated a gruff masculine voice, "holding a spaniel." Startled, Larryn turned to see Seldrake, his face illuminated by his own candle, standing at the doorway to the stairs. He was in his usual state of undress at home—flowing shirt and dark britches. He looked roguish. He looked handsome. And Larryn was immediately in a quandary. Should she insist that he leave the roof or stay? It might be dangerous for him here.

While she pondered, she forced a grin; the duke had attempted levity. "Am I really on the roof? As confused as I was earlier, I might have thought myself on a bridge over the Thames."

"At some time hundreds of years hence, was it not?" Seldrake's deep, pleasant laugh resounded into the silence.

He didn't know he was laughing at her, of course. He believed he was laughing with her.

Still, it hurt.

"Of course," Larryn managed lightly. "In the year two thousand." She was horrified at the catch at the end of her words. She was not going to cry.

But when was she ever going to learn why she was here?

And why was she beginning to feel as though she never wanted to leave?

"Does something trouble you, Larryn?" The duke had drawn closer, and concern radiated from his voice. His sudden kindness was almost more than Larryn could bear. She buried her face in Caddie's fur, but the little dog squirmed to get down.

Larryn knelt and deposited Caddie on the roof. With a yap, Caddie headed toward the stairwell. An answering bark indicated that Augie was waiting below.

Without even the puppy to hold, Larryn felt terribly needy. She made herself rise nonetheless and pretend that something in the inky distance had captured her attention. Her back was to Seldrake, so he couldn't possibly know about the tears that dampened her cheeks.

He hadn't begun to enact the scene on the roof she had viewed before—when he was a ghost. Tonight was probably not the night. . . .

"Larryn?" He touched her shoulder, bare, as usual, in one

of Adele's borrowed gowns. Warmth radiated from his callused flesh, and he squeezed gently. "Is something the matter?"

"Not a thing," she said lightly, though she knew the hoarseness of her voice belied her words. She wanted desperately to throw herself into his arms, seek the comfort of his closeness.

But that was ridiculous. She hated to be touched. Her sister Cathy had hugged her. Her sister Cathy had hugged many . . . and had died.

Larryn especially did not want Seldrake's nearness, his caring. She needed to keep her distance. She was only here to help him, and then, with luck—her wayward, absurd yearnings to remain in his presence notwithstanding—she would go home.

She missed the modern medicine of her own time, though she wondered if she ever would feel right slaving over a microscope again. She had an urge, for the first time since her residency in internal medicine, to work with real people, in a time where she might actually effect cures of dire diseases—some, at least. Her success with little Apsley, though a minimal challenge, had made her proud.

But her townhouse, where she lived alone . . . after Seldrake House, after the duke—would it feel like home?

"You may tell me what ails you. I shall not bite, I promise."

She almost preferred when Seldrake barked at her. His foul temper, his arrogance, kept her hackles raised, and that prevented her from feeling sorry for herself. But the gentleness in his voice now . . .

A sob escaped her. In moments, she was pressed tightly against Seldrake's solid masculine chest, and she cried despite her determination not to.

"I do not understand," he whispered against her hair. "The latest children to arrive are fine. Wyford and Adele saw to their scrubbing in the manner you demand. You do not weep because of them?"

Unable to speak, Larryn shook her head in the negative.

"Is this because those men affrighted you today? I could not help but admire your ingenuity in unnerving them right back. Machines that carry people through tubes beneath London streets. Other machines that carry people through the air. Such an imagination you have, my dear, when you need it."

Larryn's laugh through her tears was tremulous. "Yes, I suppose I do."

"Why, Larryn, do you weep?" His strong fingers stroked her cheeks, smoothing away the dampness. She turned toward them and allowed her lips to brush them.

Why had she done that? She couldn't explain it. But as the tips of his fingers traced the outline of her mouth she closed her eyes.

The tenderness of his gesture was her undoing. "I'm crying because there's so much I don't understand," she whispered.

"Mayhap I can explain," he said. "Simply tell me what you wish to know." In a moment, his mouth had replaced his fingers.

His kiss was gentle and soothing, as though he wanted to take away her hurt. His tongue prodded hers gently, teasingly, daring her to cheer up. The silkiness of his long hair furled about them in the breeze.

She threw her arms around his neck and deepened the kiss. She wanted contact. Oh, yes. But she didn't want softness; she wanted fire to burn away her sorrow.

With no hesitation, Seldrake obliged. His lips covered hers, even as he pulled the pins from her hair. As her loosened hair fell to her shoulders, he buried his hands in it and held her fast. She tried to pull back, to breathe, to regain control, but he didn't let her. Instead, he lowered his head and let his tongue range in the valley between her partially bared breasts.

She gasped and held him as his hands traced the path of his tongue and below. His fingers found one stiff nipple and teased it, pressing it and allowing it to spring back into his waiting touch. She moved slightly, allowing him access

to the other breast, the other nipple, irritated that the tightness of the bodice prevented him from baring her altogether.

One of his knees pressed against her skirt, parting her
legs. His leg insinuated itself between her thighs, high up,
and she rocked against him, damning the voluminous
clothes that acted as a barrier. His erection strained against
her abdomen. She needed more.

"We must go inside," he muttered against her mouth. "I
want you in my bed."

That stilled her. She wanted him, too—in bed, on the
roof, wherever they happened to be. But she had promised
herself long ago that she would never take lovemaking
lightly.

And there could be no relationship with the duke of Seldrake—short term or long term. They were, literally, worlds
apart . . . even though, for the moment, she lived within his.

She pushed gently away, trying to get her uneven
breathing under control. "I'm sorry," she said. "I can't."

"Why?" he demanded. He had placed his candlestick behind him, and in the flickering backlight his incredibly
handsome face was awash with angry shadows.

"Because there's no future with you." She laughed bitterly, realizing that she stated more truth than she could tell
him. She could hardly reveal that she knew he would die
one day soon—and become a ghost. And that in some un-
imaginable way she had been sent here, she believed, to
help him.

He stared at her. "No," he finally agreed, "there is no
future between us."

Why did his words, confirming her own, pierce her as
though he had stabbed her with a dagger?

"Yet we can still have a present," he continued, taking
her arm. "Or is your half-seduction a means of throwing
me off my guard for a reason of your own, Lady Larryn?"

She drew in her breath. "If nothing else, you surely know
by now that you can trust me," she said.

"I have learned that you think swiftly. And that you make

me wish to take you in the most inopportune places—a coach, a ditch, a rooftop. This might be part of your scheme, for you have yet to tempt me in a place where I can easily turn the seduction upon you such that you will not wish to stop me."

"You're rather full of yourself, Seldrake." His arrogance had returned. Larryn was glad. This, she could deal with.

Couldn't she?

"Ah, but I would much rather that *you* be filled with me, Larryn." His voice turned as smooth as newly churned butter, and Larryn felt her knees weaken.

If she took one small step forward, she could be in his arms once more. Feel his mouth, his touch . . .

"You wouldn't be so certain if you knew the truth," she blurted, needing something to turn off herself as much as him. "What if I told you that I wasn't totally acting crazy with those officious sons of guns this afternoon? That I'm actually from the future, and what I said was real."

He was silent for a long moment. And then he said, "Do you think I am smitten enough with your charms to believe such absurdity?" There was a chilliness in his voice.

Larryn stopped breathing. She hadn't meant to blurt that out. She'd gone too far.

Would he really drag her off to Bedlam now?

"I . . . I'm sorry. I couldn't think of any other way to make you realize there can be nothing between us. I'm not crazy; at least I don't think so. But the answers I need . . . you can't give them to me. No one can."

"Why do you not ask your questions, madam, and then we shall see." The coldness had not left his voice. He stooped to retrieve his candle and held it toward her face. She felt exposed as the candle's flickering light nearly blinded her.

"All right, then," she managed angrily. "I want to know why I'm here. Why it's now. Why I don't feel as though I belong here, but I'm not ready to go home. And most of all, I want to know why I . . . why I . . ."

"Yes?"

"Why I want to kiss you again. But I won't, believe me."

She stared at him defiantly for a moment before stooping to pick up her own candle. She had to face him just long enough to light the wick from the one that blazed before him.

There was a bemused expression on his face, but he did not come any closer.

Then, turning carefully so as not to blow out the flame, she hurried toward the stairwell. She stopped when she reached it. Did she dare leave him by himself on the roof?

By himself. That was the key. He could not repeat the scene she had witnessed if no one was with him.

Once she left him, he would be alone . . . and so would she.

Seldrake stood on the rooftop. He looked over the courtyard and the banquet houses that contained the rescued children.

The children who had all been scrubbed, along with the cottages, due to the intervention of Larryn Maeller.

Doctor Larryn Maeller, she called herself.

True, her skills at healing were partly untested. Young Apsley had not, after all, been as ill as had been feared. But Larryn had insisted on unconventional treatment methods—partially. The child had not been bled. Yet they had boiled water containing herbs for the boy to inhale, an ancient remedy. Apsley had recovered overnight. Might it have taken longer had Seldrake bled him? Might he have failed to recover at all due to lack of energy, as Larryn had suggested?

None of the children here, thank the Lord, had taken ill with plague. None had even before Larryn's arrival, so her demand for cleanliness proved nothing.

She had an explanation for the contagion that none of his acquaintance espoused: bites from fleas on infected rats. Rats bred in filth. Fleas bred on rats. Tinier creatures yet bred on fleas. Eliminate the filth, and the contagion would ease.

Mayhap it was true. But . . . Where was he going with

his musings? He knew, as much as he knew he was alive, that there was something different about Mrs.—no, Doctor—Larryn Maeller.

Was he commencing to give credence to her incredible tale of coming from a time in the future when men flew in machines?

"Hah!" He laughed aloud, but the noise sounded hollow.

She had, after all, appeared from nowhere upon this very roof. Her ideas were different from any he knew about. Her strange use of words, her unknown accent did not divulge her antecedents—Scottish or otherwise—nor even her social class.

She was certainly not similar to any woman of his acquaintance. There were those better endowed with curves, for she had a thinness about her. And yet she made him lust as though he were a mere boy wishing for his first woman. At the very thought, he felt his groin tighten.

He wanted her. And yet, she had been correct. Wherever she hailed from, his destiny did not involve hers. He wanted no woman permanently, particularly not one whose words spoke of madness—the future and flying machines, indeed! But she did not seem deranged, only confused. Sorrowful. In need of understanding.

"Damn!" Turning so abruptly that his hair blew about his face, he headed for the stairway.

In minutes, he was outside her room. He rapped soundly on the door. "Madam . . . Doctor Larryn, I wish to come in."

"Why?" Her voice was strong, and yet there was a hint in it that she had not yet recuperated from her inexplicable grief and confusion atop the roof.

"I wish to continue our conversation."

"I don't."

Confound the woman! Did she feel compelled to turn even a gesture of kindness on his part into a dispute?

And yet . . . was he there out of kindness to her, or because of a need in him?

"Larryn, please," he said. "I, too, have questions. Mayhap even if I cannot answer yours, you can respond to mine."

"Right!" She sounded irate, and yet the door opened. She turned her back as she walked away from him. "Come in, if you want. But I think we'd both better give up on getting answers." She whirled to face him. "I just don't believe any more that there are any."

Was she a witch? He did not believe in such crones or their supposed powers.

Yet if Larryn was not one, how did she hurl the despair in her dark brown eyes into him? She must have done so, for suddenly he, too, was filled with anguish—for her? for himself?

He stepped forward with no hesitation and gathered her into his arms once more. "Oh, Larryn," he whispered against the silken, fragrant hair that he himself had released from its confinement. "Doctor Larryn, if you wish. Pray tell me why it is that you stir such passions deep inside me, why I wish to argue with you as much as I lust after you . . . nearly."

He heard her draw in her breath. "I don't know, Seldrake. I only know that I feel the same way."

"Mayhap I should release you from the prison of my home." He wished immediately to retract the words. What if she agreed? What if she left and he never again saw her, never held her to him as he did now?

The question must have stirred her as well, for he felt her trembling. "Sure," she said after a moment. It was not relief he heard in her tone, nor delight, but resignation. And could it be . . . certainly it could not be fear. But she continued, "I've never liked having my freedom curtailed."

"Fine, then." He had begun this conversation. He would follow it until its conclusion. But not now.

Neither could he follow through on his earlier desire to bed this alluring woman. Was that not why he had come to her room? He was the duke of Seldrake. He had no wish for involvement with a woman after his loss of Charmian. He most certainly had not come here to comfort the pain he had seen in Larryn Maeller; that was not his wont.

But he would not bed her, not now and not ever. He knew that, once he had had her, he would want her again. And again.

Mayhap Doctor Larryn had indeed bewitched him, for even without bedding her he felt as though he wanted nothing more than to remain in her presence. And yet, he still knew nothing about her. She told absurd stories. He wished to trust her, yet he could not dispel the belief that someone who had appeared from nowhere as she had might betray him.

And if she was not a spy, if she were truly there to assist him, he was endangering her. Should something happen to her, something caused by him that he could not prevent . . . He had suffered agony over Charmian. He would not allow that again.

"Good night, madam." He abruptly released her. "I shall see you on the morrow. We shall discuss this situation further."

He did not seek her glance as he strode from the room—for he feared seeing the pain in her eyes once more.

Chapter 15

"IS SOMETHING AMISS with the oysters this morning?" Adele asked Larryn from across the dining table the next morning. "You have eaten not a bite."

"They're fine," Larryn said, even though the shellfish, despite being well cooked and seasoned, caught in her throat. She had surreptitiously fed a little to Caddie, who leaned against her leg under the table.

"Mayhap Larryn is pleased about a matter we commenced discussing last night," Seldrake said. He sounded irritable, but when Larryn glanced at him he appeared engrossed in tearing off a hunk of bread from the loaf. Nothing appeared wrong with *his* appetite this morning—and why should it? He probably felt righteous and proud of himself. He had suggested granting his prisoner her freedom.

Larryn sipped some wine. She usually didn't imbibe at breakfast, despite the custom of the time, but this morning she was happy for the drink. She vowed to take just a little; she didn't need her senses dulled by alcohol. She had nearly decided to skip breakfast where she would have to interact with other people. She had to think.

She had lain awake all night trying to figure out a so-
lution, but nothing had come to her. What was she going
to do if Seldrake did cut her loose? Where would she go
in this time? She hardly knew anyone. She had little means
of making a living—she wasn't about to style herself a
doctor here and possibly get herself institutionalized or condemned to death.

She could probably get a job as one of those poor
"searchers of the dead." Heaven knew whether she would
survive the plague, even knowing what she knew about
sanitation.

And if she left this house, how would she ever determine
the manner in which she was supposed to help Seldrake?

What would she do if she never saw him again? She
took another quick sip of wine.

Ned appeared at the dining room entry. "There is a messenger at the gate, Y'r Grace," he said. "He says he comes
from the king."

"By all means let him in," Seldrake commanded.

In moments, a man garbed in ballooning britches and an
overshirt of a style Larryn had heard called a "jerkin"
stepped into the dining room. Both Caddie and Augie
barked and leapt up on the stranger until Ned firmly led the
dogs from the room.

"Y'r Grace," he announced, "Me name is Trice. I've a
summons from court to deliver." He waved an envelope
sealed with red wax in the air.

Seldrake stepped forward to take it, but Trice held it
away. "Sorry, Y'r Grace, but this is for Lady Larryn
Maeller."

Larryn felt her jaw drop. She looked at the duke.

"You must read the king's missive, Lady Larryn." His
voice held no inflection.

She rose and took the envelope from Trice, whose stare
with pale gray eyes made her uneasy. She used her finger
to slit it open. The message inside read, "His Majesty
wishes the favour of the presence of Lady Larryn Maeller

at once." It was signed "Charles R." *R* for *rex*, Larryn knew—the Latin word for king.

"D-do you know why His Majesty has sent for me?" she asked the messenger.

Trice stared as though she had just spoken to him in gibberish. "I am just the messenger, m'lady," he said. "His Majesty is in residence at Hampton Court. I am to bring you back with me, if you please."

It didn't matter whether she pleased or not. It was a command performance from the king, and Larryn knew it.

She glanced at Adele, who appeared afraid. Then she looked at Seldrake. He had plastered one of his unreadable expressions upon his face, but she knew he wasn't happy. Not at all.

"I'll get ready," she said to Trice. "Did you bring a coach?" At his nod, she said, "I'll meet you there shortly."

When the man had left, she took a few steps toward Seldrake.

"It's a real summons, isn't it?" she asked. "I mean . . . well, I was almost run over by a carriage. No one is setting me up for a kidnapping—I mean, abduction—are they?"

"It appears a genuine invitation from the king." Seldrake's voice was quiet and chilly.

"I am not a spy." She enunciated each word. "In fact, you're welcome to come along and keep an eye on me."

"His Majesty would have included me in his invitation had he wished me to attend."

"But you brought Adele and me with you the last time," Larryn said.

"I was summoned for a purpose, and I brought you along to be of assistance. I doubt I can help with what the king has in mind." Seldrake's grin was jarring. It did not reach his wintry blue eyes. Larryn realized what he was thinking and felt a shudder pass through her. Well, even if it were true, she would find a way to gently dissuade the king. She would have to.

"Of course you are not a spy." Adele had joined them.

She placed her hand gently on Larryn's shoulder. "It is merely . . ."

"That I'll be in a perfect position to betray you, if I choose. Or even if I don't so choose, if I'm not careful." Larryn did not even try to keep the bitterness from her tone. "Well, this is an ideal opportunity, isn't it? You wanted me to leave anyway; you made that clear." She tried to make her expression as blank as Seldrake's as she turned back toward him. She didn't want to betray her hurt that he no longer wanted her around. "Maybe I can figure out a way to stay at court." *Short of encouraging the oversexed king,* Larryn thought. "In any event, you can be sure that I have no intention of telling anyone of the good work you do here. And I hope that I've enough intelligence, even though I'm a woman, not to allow it to slip out when I'm not paying attention."

With that, she lifted her skirt and pivoted, hurrying toward the door.

The king's coach was indeed elegant, trimmed in gilt and leather. His Majesty had not sent along his finest horses, however, Seldrake noted. He stood beside the coach as Larryn emerged from the house, the dogs August and Caddie at her heels. She was dressed in one of Adele's most fashionable ensembles, yet, as usual, she wore her brown tresses pulled starkly from her face—emphasizing, rather than detracting from, her beauty.

Seldrake wished to grab her by her bared shoulders and shake her. Did she not understand what appearing so lovely in response to the king's summons would mean?

While Larryn had prepared for her journey, Seldrake had attempted to engage the courier Trice in conversation in case the varlet knew more than he had revealed about the summons or the king's intentions, but Seldrake had learned naught. He continued to fear the worst—betrayal or bedding or both—for what other reasons might there be?

Larryn stooped to pet the dogs on their heads. "I'll miss you two," she said softly. The animals wriggled at her feet and pushed their noses into her palms as though begging for a morsel.

Would she miss him, as well? The unwelcome question penetrated Seldrake's thoughts, but he forced it away.

Then Larryn nodded to Seldrake in barest acknowledgment as she prepared to climb unaided into the carriage.

Stubborn woman! She attempted at first to ignore the hand he offered. But the step was high, and she finally had to resort to his assistance.

Did she feel the same bolt of awareness and desire that he did at this touch intended to be as innocuous as a newborn babe's? He could only believe so, for her lovely, dark eyes widened and her hand convulsed in his, even as she made no further move to climb into the coach.

She loosened her hand from his, however. She took her bottom lip in her teeth and looked down at the cobbled ground where the dogs still sat at her feet.

How could he allow her to go? If His Majesty had sent for her . . . Despite the political favor Seldrake knew he enjoyed, he did not always admire the king and his scruples. His Majesty was as much a man as he was a king, and he allowed himself to be governed much by his passions.

If he was sending for a woman as beautiful as Larryn, it may well be to appease his lust. The thought made Seldrake wish to shove his fist through the coach's thin and elegant wall.

He needed to forewarn Larryn. Mayhap, though, she needed no warning. Mayhap this was planned as a part of whatever purpose had brought her here.

Yet he realized that, deep within him, he did not think so any longer. She had told him such was not true. He believed her, because he wished to believe her. And if she had not planned this summons, if she wished not to accede to the king's rutting pleasure, he needed to alert her. For despite her brazen, outspoken ways, she appeared most naive about so many matters. It was almost as if her strange tale of the future could be true. . . .

Nonsense!

Still . . . Seldrake glanced about. Ned was speaking with the coachman and messenger. None would hear what he said to Larryn.

"Larryn, I wish you to know that His Majesty's summons of young women . . . they are sometimes due to his wishes to get to know one better."

"In other words, he wants to add me to his list of mistresses," Larryn said bluntly.

Seldrake smiled despite his concern. He ought to have known he did not need to spare this woman's sensibilities. She was direct, and she feigned no swoons at others' directness.

"Mayhap," he agreed. "If you wish not to accede, he will not insist; of that I am certain, although I would counsel you to make pretty apologies and not vent your anger on His Majesty the way you oft do with me."

It was Larryn's turn to smile. "Don't worry," she said. "I can be tactful when I need to be."

He had not finished his thought, although the remainder seemed to pierce his soul painfully. "Should you wish to consent to the king's wishes, I do not know if you have sufficient knowledge of the court and its ways to ensure your future. Should you wish my counsel on this as well, you need but ask."

Was that anguish that pinched her lovely features so direly? "Is that what you think?" she whispered. "That I'd go to bed with the king to take care of my future? Well, believe it or not, Duke, my future is just rosy, as long as I can figure out why I'm here and get home to it."

With that, she again said her good-byes to the dogs, then put her hand out again as though commanding Seldrake's assistance.

He took it in his, but he did not, at first, help to lever her into the coach. Instead, he bent his head and touched his lips to the smooth, warm flesh at the back of her hand. He lifted his eyes to meet hers.

"I meant no insult, Larryn." His voice held a huskiness, which he did not disguise. "And should you wish, after you learn what His Majesty wants of you, to return here as my guest—not as my prisoner—you are most welcome."

With that, he firmly assisted her into the coach. He did not intend to meet her gaze again.

Yet, as the coach pulled away, he walked alongside it in the courtyard, Caddie and Augie at his heels . . . and his eyes held Larryn's until the coach's turn at the gate.

Seldrake wasn't kicking her out! Larryn's heart sang practically the entire long and grueling ride to Hampton Court.

If she ever went there again, she might insist on taking the river. She had seen that Hampton Court sat right on the Thames, and even going the long way around to get to a boat had to be better than this miserable bouncing.

At least she was alone, for Trice rode on the outside seat beside the coachman. She had a lot to think about and didn't really want to make small talk with a stranger.

Whatever the king wanted, she would deal with it as tactfully as she could, then ask to be taken back to Seldrake House. She had a place to stay.

More than that, Thomas Northby hadn't attempted to dispose of her.

She only cared, she insisted to herself, because she had to learn if she was here for a reason, figure it out, and, if at all possible, get home. Plus, she knew Caddie, though well cared for, would be waiting for her to return.

She admitted to herself that it was more. The duke of Seldrake had gotten under her skin. She had begun to care for the arrogant, handsome duke and his imperious, yet endearing, ways. A lot.

She had to get home. She missed modern conveniences. Modern medicine. Her life.

But how would she ever leave when the time came?

The coach finally pulled through the large gates and into the main courtyard at Hampton Court. In moments, Trice stood at the coach's door. "I am to show you where to go, m'lady."

He helped her down; his bony fingers and weak grip

made Larryn yearn for the duke's strong and sure assistance.

He showed her into the palace. Like the last time, well-dressed courtiers milled around the vast, gilt-trimmed hallways. Uniformed guards with lances stood at attention, and servants with filled arms bustled by. No one paid much attention to her. No person, at least. She was greeted by a wave of the king's spaniels. She laughed and petted the few she could reach.

The messenger did not appear amused. "Okay, pups," Larryn finally said. "I'll see you later."

The long hallway where Trice led her, with its rows of tapestries and molded ceiling, appeared familiar. But instead of turning toward the Great Hall or where Larryn believed the king's audience chamber to be, he led her to the stairway she had seen before. At the top, they turned right and walked through the Horn Room, the Watching Chamber, and the Haunted Gallery. Larryn could not help peering around for the specter of the ill-fated Catherine Howard. They passed through several other rooms and into another hallway, and then Trice said, "I will leave you here, m'lady. You may rap on yon door."

He pointed to a closed wooden door, then turned and left.

Strange little man, Larryn thought. She steeled herself with a deep breath, then knocked.

The door was drawn open immediately. But it wasn't Charles II that stood there, but Lord Browne. "Ah, Lady Larryn. Please, enter." He gestured sweepingly into the room. As before, he was dressed in a richly red coat and billowing britches, and his black wig's waves cascaded over his shoulders.

Uneasily, Larryn remained in the hallway. "I believe the king sent for me," she said.

"Of course," Browne said smoothly. Had he trimmed his dark mustache to an even smaller size since she had seen him before? It only served to emphasize the weakness of his chin. "I am to entertain you until His Majesty is ready to see you."

"Oh. Well, if you don't mind, I'd rather go out to the park. If you would be so kind as to show me the way—"

"We must talk first, Lady Larryn." His small eyes had grown eager. "I have questions to ask you about . . . shall we say some of the duke of Seldrake's less public activities?"

"What activities?" It was time, Larryn thought, to take a lesson from Seldrake and act remote, condescending, and not just a little arrogant with this courtier who overstepped his bounds. But she felt as if her bones had frozen. Could she pull this off without betraying Seldrake's trust?

She had to. She had promised.

"You know, I am certain, of the activities to which I refer. Please, I must ask some questions."

Two men strolled by with an elegantly dressed woman between them. All three stared at Larryn, and she inhaled sharply. Maybe she should get out of the hallway, where curious eyes might wonder what was happening.

She swept past Browne into a small chamber that looked like a miniature study. It was dark, its only light trickling in from a long, thin window with a pane of wavy glass within it. She took a seat on the room's only chair, of rough leather.

"Now," she said, "why don't you check with His Majesty about how long it'll be before he's ready to see me."

"I cannot do that," Browne said. He closed the door behind him, which made Larryn uneasy. "His Majesty does not like to be hurried. He will send for you in his own good time."

Larryn rose again. "I'm not going to wait for him here, Lord Browne. Please show me to the park."

"First, I wish to hear about the duke's latest rescue of endangered children. I heard there were some . . . difficulties."

He knew. Or he suspected. But Larryn had no reason to trust the man.

"Tell me," he commanded. "I must know."

Larryn approached Browne, only because he stood in front of the door. "I do not know what you are talking about," she said frostily. "I insist on waiting for His Majesty in the park."

She skirted around him, careful to allow no part of her gown to touch him, which was not easy due to his proximity to the door.

"I know everything," Browne muttered behind her. "But I require further information. And I will obtain it, never fear."

Larryn *did* fear—for Seldrake, mostly. "I think, Lord Browne, that you are gravely mistaken. And I suggest that you do nothing to harm the duke of Seldrake or his reputation, or he will make you very sorry."

With that, she swept by him and out of the room.

Pretty good, she commended herself. She was even beginning to speak a little like an arrogant aristocrat from this time.

She wasn't sure how else to get to the park, but she retraced her way to the Haunted Gallery. There, she paused before a portrait of King Charles I—who had a spaniel at his feet. Like father, like son, Larryn thought.

She had intended to return to Seldrake House soon, of course. But now that she had probably antagonized Browne, who might know about Seldrake's saving children—should she insist on going back earlier, to warn him?

Of what? Others probably had their suspicions, too. And she still did not know what the king wanted from her.

She needed to find that out before returning to Seldrake. Maybe, if she had a reason to be here, if she was supposed to help him, this was somehow related.

The Haunted Gallery certainly wasn't haunted by a large number of courtiers that day. Larryn grew uneasy as she stood there alone. It was time for her to find the park.

She headed for the narrow stairway, but she couldn't help pausing for just a moment to stare at the fresco on the decorated ceiling above—which was a big mistake.

She barely heard the fast-approaching footsteps before a figure in a hooded cloak was upon her. In a moment, she was being wrestled toward the top of the stairway.

"Hey!" she cried. "Stop it!"

Whoever it was didn't respond but continued to manipulate her till the steep flight of stairs loomed below.

She grabbed at the wooden cap to the wrought-iron railing. Held tightly with both hands as her body pivoted sideways. Screamed louder. But the shoving at her back was relentless.

She couldn't let go. She didn't dare.

The person at her back shoved harder.

She felt her grip fail.

Chapter 16

A<small>S HER HANDS</small> flew free, Larryn reached out. One hand grabbed on to the wrought-iron rail. The sharp edges gouged her fingers. Damn, they hurt! But she held on.

Her feet were tangled in her long skirt so she couldn't run. Couldn't climb up the step she'd fallen down so she could ram her assailant. She tried to turn to see who it was, but the hood was huge and concealing. Larryn thought she saw a mask beneath it.

She held on, screaming, as the person kicked, through the cloak, at her hands. As a foot connected with her wrist, she nearly let go.

Where was everybody in this huge, busy palace?

Over her screams, Larryn heard barking. The pack of spaniels ran up the steps toward her. "Get out of the way," she called. If she fell, she didn't want to squash a Cavalier; they were too small to break her fall.

They plunged around her. Some growled and snarled. One bit her assailant, then another.

The person froze. Larryn heard a muttered imprecation, then the figure turned and ran down the hall, Cavaliers in pursuit.

Only then did several courtiers appear at the bottom of the steps. "What is the matter, madam?" yelled a man in a bright blue hat with white plumes. He began climbing toward her.

"Someone tried to throw me down the stairs."

"Who?"

"I don't know, but the dogs chased him that way."

Once he and his two companions reached her, they glanced into the Watching Chamber. Two of them ran in the direction she pointed. The other eased Larryn to a sitting position at the top of the steps. "Are you all right, madam?"

"I will be." But Larryn's voice was shaky. Someone had wanted to kill her. The person had been relentless in his attempt to shove her down the stairs.

Maybe it was the same person who had driven the coach at her two days earlier.

But why? She hadn't been in this time long enough to make enemies.

The two men returned. "We did not find anyone," said the shorter. He had a small mustache like the king's, and his dark wig sat slightly askew on his head. He looked at Larryn dubiously, as though she had wanted only to create a spectacle of herself.

"It doesn't matter," she managed. "I'll just finish my business here and go home."

"You are all right?" The man in the blue hat eyed her as though she would faint on the spot.

"Just dandy," she said. Lifting her skirts, she climbed the step she'd fallen and knelt shakily to pet the Cavaliers who'd come to her rescue—unlike the people at this palace.

The king had sent for her. She supposed she had to see him before she left. But what she really wanted was to go home to Seldrake House.

Home? To the duke's house? She shook her head. She must be more rattled than she'd thought. "Please point me toward His Majesty's chambers," she said haughtily. "He summoned me."

One of the men called over a servant who had stopped to gape. "Take this woman to His Majesty," he demanded.

The servant obeyed, showing Larryn through one connecting room after another. There appeared to be few halls in this part of the palace. " 'ere y'are, m'lady," the servant finally said, bowing slightly.

They were before a closed door. Two red-uniformed guards stood at attention before it. "Is His Majesty in there?" Larryn asked.

"He does not wish to be disturbed," said one of the men.

After all she had gone through, Larryn was not about to be put off by an officious guard. "He sent for me," she insisted. "I don't think he would be pleased if you didn't tell him I was here."

Giving her a skeptical glare, the man asked in a surprisingly respectful tone, "What is your name, m'lady?"

Larryn told him.

"I will see if His Majesty wishes to be disturbed." He opened the door and walked in. There must have been an inner door, for Larryn heard a knocking from inside.

With fingers still aching and trembling, she smoothed her skirt as she waited and ran her hand across her hair to attempt to push back the errant strands that had escaped from the bun at her nape in her struggle. Maybe she shouldn't have come now. Hadn't Browne said His Majesty would send for her when he was ready for her?

Well, he would simply have to understand, under these circumstances, why she couldn't wait for his command.

The guard returned. His eyes were chilly. "His Majesty is not pleased, but he will see you now."

Not pleased? Larryn considered fleeing, but she had already disturbed him. She went into the anteroom, then toward an inner door that was slightly ajar.

"May I come in, Your Majesty?" she called.

She heard something more but could not make it out. Had he told her to enter? She decided to wait.

In a moment the door was pulled farther open. His Majesty, King Charles II, was nearly undressed. And not nearly in the way the word "undressed" was used in that time, to mean wearing informal attire, but in a silk nightshirt. "We did not send for you, Lady Larryn." His tone was haughty. But then he looked at her. "What is wrong?"

"I had a little . . . mishap. I didn't mean to disturb you. I'm sorry."

"Come in and explain this 'mishap.' " He turned away, obviously expecting her to follow. She did so timidly.

Inside the room was a huge bed on a platform. And in the bed, beneath voluminous covers, was Lady Anne Farswell. "Lady Larryn, how pleasant to see you," she said, sitting up. She held a coverlet to the tops of her breasts, apparently bare beneath.

Embarrassed, Larryn said, "I apologize for bothering you. I'll go now."

But the king insisted on Larryn's telling what had happened. When she had finished, he said in an angry tone, "We will make inquiries, never fear. We will learn who used our name to summon you, and whether it was the same person who attempted to injure you. Now, have you a way back to Seldrake House?"

"No," she said. "The messenger brought one of your coaches, I believe, to pick me up."

"You shall stay at least for supper. And then we shall send you home in a more splendid coach. Is that satisfactory?"

"Oh, yes, Your Majesty," she said and made an attempt at a curtsy in the manner she had seen other women do it here.

"You should visit with Apsley, Larryn," said Lady Anne. "He is outside with the other children. He is well, thanks to you."

"And we are most appreciative, as you know," added the king.

"I'm just glad I could help," Larryn said. "And I will go check on him now." It was a good excuse to leave the couple to what she had so obviously interrupted.

Mortified, upset at everything that had happened, Larryn took several wrong turns before she found her way to the park. By the time she reached Long Water, she wanted to holler, to kick something. But that wasn't even appropriate in her own time, let alone suitable behavior for a supposed lady here.

The air was brisk and breezy, and the scent of fall flowers filled it. The garden plots in front of the lime trees were full of blooms in warm, golden colors. The area was less crowded than the last time Larryn had seen it, yet courtiers conversed in small assemblages throughout the well-maintained grounds. Larryn couldn't help it; she stared at one group, then another. No one wore a cloak and disguise, of course.

Anyone could have been her assailant on the stairway. If only she could go to each group and quiz people on when they'd come into the garden—and what they had been doing before.

That supposed a stranger had tried to hurt her.

Still, she had met so few people here: the king, of course, and Lady Anne and her son, but none of them could have been her cloaked attacker. It seemed as unlikely that her assailant would be the odd messenger who had come for her, Trice; if he had meant her harm, he could have done something on the way to the palace.

Her bet was on Browne. Why had the man been so insistent on accusing Seldrake of spiriting children to safety? Had Larryn's protective attitude toward Seldrake antagonized the lord-in-waiting? Had he thought he would exact revenge on Seldrake for Charmian's loss through Larryn? She wouldn't put it past Browne to have been the cloaked person who shoved her down the steps. He could have followed her.

"Lady Larryn!" A young voice interrupted her thoughts.

"Lord Apsley," Larryn said, looking down. "It's great to see you outside." The boy was grinning and rosy-cheeked, and he and the children with him were attired like their overdressed elders. The plumed and embroidered outfits made the kids appear like adorable dolls, and Larryn had an urge to hug each of them.

Strange, she thought. She wasn't the effusive type. And physical contact with other people used to make her cringe.

"I am pleased to be outside," piped the reedy, formal voice. "My mama is inside now doing important work for the king."

So that was how she described it to her son.

"But she told me," Apsley continued, "that if I saw you again to make sure you know I am grateful for your help."

"No need." Larryn felt herself redden at the child's earnest stare. In her own time, she could say helping people was her job. Here, she simply added, "My reward is in seeing you look so healthy. Are you playing with the other children?"

Apsley nodded. "We play tennis often in the king's tennis court, when we are permitted to do so."

Tennis? Larryn hadn't known it existed this early in history, let alone that the king had a tennis court.

"It is over there." Apsley pointed toward a path. As Larryn followed his gesture, her eyes met those of Bess, Lady Mainwaring, who stood near the other side of the canal speaking with a group of women. So Bess had returned? Or perhaps she had never left. Maybe she was a fixture at the court—not surprising, if her son had been fathered by the king.

With Bess, Larryn thought she recognized one or two of the women from Apsley's chamber the night of his illness. Bess's look was a cool, assessing greeting that made it clear she thought of Larryn as a gauche interloper. Larryn tried to insert self-assurance into the gaze she shot back—wondering how ill-kempt she must appear after her incident on the stairs.

Bess was another person here who knew her. But she could hardly be jealous of Larryn's nonrelationship with Seldrake. And what other motive would she have for harming Larryn?

The ladies from Apsley's sickroom knew of her, too. But what motive did *anyone* have to hurt her?

"Will you join us in a game?" Apsley's small voice was

so earnest that Larryn almost agreed out of impulse.

But she caught herself. "I'd love to, but I can't. It's time for me to leave now." Despite the king's invitation to supper, Larryn felt it was long past time to go. She hadn't really been summoned here. She had nearly been killed, she had interrupted the king, and now she appeared to be engaged in a contest of wills with Lady Mainwaring, without knowing the rules.

After a protracted good-bye to little Apsley, Larryn made her way back toward the palace. At the door, she stood aside while a group of men filed out.

Among them was Browne, the man she suspected of trying to kill her on the stairs. He might even have tried to run her down in the carriage near Seldrake House. He stared at her with a cold expression that would have done Bess Mainwaring proud.

Larryn smiled sweetly. She had won, after all, thanks to the king's Cavaliers. She had not been hurt. She wanted to ask to see Browne's shins to determine if the dogs had nipped him.

Boldly, she approached. "Lord Browne, His Majesty offered me a coach for a ride back to Seldrake House." Home. The place where the duke would be . . . as silly as it was, Larryn could not wait to get back to his irritatingly protective presence. "Would you see to it now, please?"

She saw a flash of annoyance in his small, cunning eyes but it disappeared. "Right away, Lady Larryn."

Larryn wondered if she should check the coach he chose for her to make sure that the wheels wouldn't fall off or that the driver was neither an outlaw nor a drunk.

As the coach pulled up to the wrought-iron gate at Seldrake House Larryn gave a big sigh of relief. She had made it safely!

She planned to find Seldrake immediately and alert him to all that had happened. He needed to be told, and she needed a friendly shoulder to lean on, if just for a moment.

The broad, masculine shoulders that Seldrake's loose shirts had hinted at would do just fine.

But except for the men who pulled open the gate, the only person who came out to the cobblestoned courtyard to greet her was Ned. The elderly servant was hardly able to assist her from the palace coach. The coachman had not been an outlaw or a drunk, but a subaltern full of himself for being the king's minion. He had acted disdainful of Larryn; she could only guess what Browne had told him. As soon as she alit, he drove the team of four horses back toward the road.

"Where is the duke?" Larryn asked Ned, stooping to pick up Caddie, who had come out to greet her. She smiled as the pup licked her nose, then she knelt to hug an excited Augie.

The old man tipped his graying head toward the main house. "Inside, Larryn. They's in an uproar, they is."

"Why?"

But Ned would say no more.

Larryn hustled inside through the kitchen door, the dogs in close pursuit. She heard raised voices as soon as she entered the far hall and followed them to Seldrake's study.

The door was closed. As Larryn raised her hand to knock, she heard the duke shout an angry oath, then say, "You will marry whomever I choose, Adele."

Adele's voice was softer, and she obviously was crying.

It was a family matter. Larryn shouldn't butt in. Nevertheless, she entered the room. Caddie and Augie followed.

Adele was on a tapestry chair, head bowed. Seldrake stood stiffly beside her.

"Hi," Larryn said. "Looks like I've missed a little excitement."

Seldrake turned on her. "This is between Lady Adele and myself, madam."

Adele threw herself across the room and into Larryn's arms. Larryn hugged the shorter young woman. "Oh, Larryn," Adele sobbed. "Thomas has demanded that Henry— Lord Wyford—leave and return only upon his invitation."

"Why?" Larryn met Seldrake's glare with a quizzical raise of her brows.

"I found them in here, in my study, in a . . . compromising position."

"Would it have made a difference if they had been in another room? No, I see from your glower that it wouldn't." She stepped back from Adele.

"Do not interfere, madam." Larryn had never heard Seldrake sound more menacing.

"Of course not." Larryn considered what to do next. She knew the man wasn't used to having his authority questioned, particularly by a mere woman. That hadn't stopped her from arguing with him before—but now, for Adele's sake, she would need to tread more lightly. "But this is your sister, Your Grace." She hoped she managed to sound meek. "I am very concerned about her well-being."

"As am I." His expression was glacial.

"I just have a couple of questions." Larryn aimed a placating smile at the duke but felt it falter as he continued his ominous frown. She took a deep breath and plunged ahead. "Adele, do you love Wyford?" She heard Seldrake's growl and hoped her cringe was only internal.

"Yes." Adele's voice was timid as she defied her brother.

"And does he love you?"

"Yes." Adele stopped, then blurted, "And he wishes to marry me. He told Thomas so."

"Well, then," Larryn said to Seldrake. "Don't you think—"

"What I think, madam"—Seldrake spoke through gritted teeth—"is that Lord Wyford's title is a minor one, as is his fortune. In any event, I am Adele's guardian, and she shall wed whomever I select for her."

Tommyrot! Larryn wanted to reply. Instead, she tried for her most conciliatory tone. "Wyford *is* titled, after all. A lord is better than a plain mister here, isn't it?" Adele nodded. The poor kid's eyes were red, her cheeks puffy. Larryn surmised that this discussion had been going on for some time.

She planted herself before Seldrake. His breathing was rapid, expanding his already expansive chest beneath his loose white shirt. As much as she hated confrontations with the man, they seemed to be the norm—and she had to admit that an aggravated Seldrake was a particularly sexy Seldrake.

"Wyford is also a doctor," she continued. "He's compassionate, and he has helped you to save children. I vote that you let him marry Adele."

"You have no vote in this matter, madam, any more than you would have a vote in whom I shall marry."

"That is part of the problem," Adele said softly. "Just after Charmian died, Thomas vowed he would not marry again, despite his need to pass along the title. It can only go to a male heir, and he believes he will have none. But Thomas is a good and dutiful man. Once he has done with mourning for poor Charmian, I believe he will wed again for the good of the family. His marrying me off now to someone whom he deems suitable for our posterity will become for naught." Her pleading gaze fell on her brother's still-unyielding scowl.

No matter what he ultimately intended, Seldrake would not marry again. Or at least he would not leave an heir or pass along the title, according to Chloe's information.

But she wasn't sure whether it hurt worse to realize that this strong, virile man would soon become a corpse—and a ghost—or to know that he'd loved Chairman enough not to want to marry again after losing her.

For Larryn was falling in love with Seldrake, as foolish as that was, and the feeling would never, could never be returned.

"My future plans are not under discussion," Seldrake said, his rage barely contained. "And if I deem it necessary to wed again one day for my family's sake, then so be it, but it is for neither of you to determine." He looked at Larryn. "I grow weary of this situation. You first appeared uninvited in my home, making extraordinary claims of traveling through time. Then you direct what I must do while heeding none of my behests. Did you reveal our transgressions to the king? Or did he invite you to Hampton Court so that he could bed you more easily without the interference of the man who somehow has become your host?"

Adele gasped. Exhausted from trying to be the voice of reason with this unreasonable man, Larryn finally erupted. "What are you accusing me of, Seldrake? Hopping into bed with every man who looks at me sideways? I wouldn't do that even with a king—let alone an earl or a duke or a lord. Or a plain old mister, for that matter. On the other hand, I wouldn't put it past a man like you to seduce every woman who gave you a second look. Bess Mainwaring, for example, obviously wants to get her hooks into you—if they're not there already."

"My relationship with Lady Mainwaring is not your concern any more than are my plans for my sister, madam." Seldrake's voice was icy—and it chilled Larryn deep inside. He had, in effect, admitted to a relationship with Bess. Jealousy leapt through Larryn but she immediately thrust it aside. How many times did she have to remind herself that Seldrake was right? His affairs—figuratively and literally—were not her business.

"In the meantime, Lady Larryn, while you were doing whatever the king bade you"—his words were clipped, and Larryn knew he still suspected her of betrayal or bedding the king—"we suffered a crisis with a child this day. One of those now in the quarantine cottage fell ill. I was preparing to dose him with medicines and to bleed him to balance his humours when he became hysterical, calling for the 'lady doctor.' Clydia had to rock him to sleep, and I never was able to treat him. And then came this . . . this incident with Wyford. Mayhap you will be so kind as to check on the child instead of throwing yourself into matters of no concern to you."

A lump grew in Larryn's throat. "An ill child. It couldn't be plague, could it?"

"The symptoms are different. But since you deem yourself the expert, madam, I will defer to you." He swept an imaginary hat off his head and bowed.

This first meeting with Seldrake since her harrowing day at Hampton Court had been nothing like she had imagined. A broad shoulder to lean on, even for an instant? She hadn't even gotten a hint of civility from the difficult man.

And the fact that she had begun, against her will, to care for him . . . Larryn felt tears well in her eyes. She hid them by stooping to pet the dogs, who had stayed by her feet.

"There are things that happened at the palace that you should know about," she said quietly without looking up. "I think everything's all right now, but I need to tell you. I'll check on the child first."

She lifted her skirts and, with her head bowed, hurried from the room.

Blast! Seldrake turned his back on Adele and followed Larryn from the study. He was a man, a duke, who had comported himself well in exile with the king. He comprehended the manners of court and of leadership.

Why could he not fathom the ways of women?

Most particularly of Larryn Maeller. For before Larryn's arrival, Adele had been most tractable. And now she had adopted the defiant attitude that so exemplified the character of the beautiful, blunt-spoken, perplexing Larryn.

Seldrake had been fearful when the king had summoned Larryn. Whoever she was, she was a novice at court. He fretted whether she would say or do something to garner the king's disfavor.

He fretted even more that she had garnered the king's lustful attentions. He did not wish this woman to bed anyone . . . but him.

Ah, yes. That was the crux of it, he mused as he followed her fast footsteps on the cobblestones of the courtyard, the dogs at her heels. He wished to bed her himself.

More, he wished to consult with her about how to care for this indisposed child. To learn from her how her day at the palace had transpired.

In short, he had come to wish to pass all concerns by Lady Larryn, for he cared much for her replies.

He cared much for *her*.

They had reached the cottage. Larryn instructed the dogs to remain outside. After she walked in, she called out such that those hidden behind the door beneath the tapestry would know that it was she.

Clydia emerged. "Oh, Larryn," the haggard woman said, wringing her hands. "It is one of the newest children. He had a fever, and now he has spots. What shall we do?"

Spots? Those with plague did not develop spots.

Seldrake pushed past Larryn, consumed with worry. Were they now beset by smallpox as well?

Chapter 17

THE SICK BOY was Bevin. He was one of the kids sneaked to safety after the ordeal in which Larryn had saved the day by pretending to be crazy—simply by telling the truth.

She had a particular soft spot in her heart for nine-year-old Bevin. All the kids had had a hard time of it, being wrested away from their ill families. But Bevin had actually seen his father die and had protected his younger sister by pretending their papa had merely gone to sleep.

Their mother had succumbed to ravages of the plague too rapidly to care for them. The third child with them had been a young cousin. The kids could all so easily have come down with the disease, too. . . .

But that wasn't Bevin's problem. Larryn could tell that right away from the small spots all over his body.

"So, Doctor Maeller." The duke's voice at her ear was filled with his usual irony, but when she turned to glare at him she could see the deep concern etched into his blue eyes. "Is the lad's problem smallpox?"

"Smallpox?" How should she know? The disease had been eradicated in her time, so she had never seen a case, had only seen descriptions of the viral disease and a history of its vaccinations in medical school texts. She knelt beside Bevin. "How are you, sweetheart?"

"I don't feel good, Doctor Larryn," he replied.

"Tell me just how you feel."

His itchiness about the rash, fever, and runny nose were definitely symptomatic of measles. Plus, the rash had only reached his face and neck. But Larryn did not know whether these were also symptoms of smallpox.

She checked him over thoroughly, then stood. "I think it's measles," she said, "but could you examine him for smallpox?"

"Ah . . . the infallible Doctor Maeller from the future is requesting the assistance of a mere physician from today?"

Larryn winced. His words and tone were no more sarcastic than usual, but she realized how superior and hurtful her own attitude must sometimes seem—especially to a man who still could not accept her fantastic story. "I don't know anything about smallpox," she admitted, quietly so neither Clydia nor the children could hear. "It no longer exists in my time."

Seldrake raised one thick, light eyebrow at her. "Did the magicians of your day whisk it away?"

Larryn closed her eyes, pain stabbing through her. He would never believe her. She supposed she couldn't blame him. Still, it hurt. "Never mind," she murmured. "I bow to your superior skills, Your Grace." She looked away so she would not see any amusement on his face. "Please take a look at this child."

Seldrake knelt at the boy's side. Little Bevin's eyes widened as though in fear. "Are you going to bleed me?" he whispered in a scared voice.

Seldrake did not look up at Larryn as he said, "Only if it becomes necessary, lad."

Bevin sat up. "Please, Doctor Larryn, don't let 'im. I saw my mama bleeded and she fainted. Please!"

Larryn bit her lower lip. She didn't want to antagonize Seldrake—but she would not let him use such a barbarous attempt at a remedy on this frightened child. Tactfully, she said, "We'll see."

Seldrake stood. "The rash's pustules do not seem as virulent as those I have observed in smallpox. Should this be merely measles, how do you treat the disease in your time?" Again, his voice took on a sarcastic note, but Larryn chose to ignore it.

"More or less the same as in yours. It's caused by a virus. We give inoculations to prevent measles, and smallpox, in the first place." Unsure whether he would be familiar with inoculation, she glanced at Seldrake. He appeared puzzled. "We inject such a mild dose of the disease into a person that it doesn't harm them but instead rallies the body's own defenses to prevent the illness in the future."

Seldrake frowned skeptically. "The only inoculation I know of has to do with plant grafts, not disease control. But even if what you say were true, what would happen to someone who did not receive inoculation?"

"We do pretty much as you probably do here. We just make the patient comfortable. So that's what we'll do now."

"Fine," Seldrake said. "And we shall keep this child isolated. At least here, measles is highly contagious, although the effects are less dire than those of smallpox or plague."

Larryn nodded. "Are there any herbs from your garden that we can use to treat the illness?"

Seldrake's blue eyes widened, as though he were surprised that she requested his advice. "Saffron," he replied. "It is used in the treatment of both measles and smallpox."

"Great," Larryn said. "Now, let's move little Bevin off by himself and hope that none of the others develop measles."

That evening after supper, they sat in Seldrake's study. Adele had left to check on the children, including Bevin.

"Have Adele and you had measles?" Larryn asked Seldrake, who lounged in a leather chair, clad in one of his loose white linen shirts and britches without stockings. One of his well-muscled legs was crossed over the other, and he appeared more relaxed than she ever recalled seeing him.

"We both had the disease as young children," he replied, and took a sip of red wine.

In fascination, Larryn watched his lips purse over the rim of the crystal goblet. She had an urge to wipe away the moistness left on his lips with her fingers.

She quickly took a sip from her own glass—and noted that Seldrake watched her as well. A tingle of sensual awareness meandered through her, and she cleared her throat. "Since I returned here to find Bevin ill, I haven't had time to speak with you about all that happened to me at court."

That threw cold water on whatever he was thinking, for he straightened in his chair. It centered Larryn's thoughts, too.

"What was that?" Seldrake sounded suspicious, and Larryn felt like punching the pillow of the brocaded settee on which she sat.

"Nothing much. I was almost thrown down some stairs. Then I interrupted the king, who actually hadn't sent for me at all, when he was involved in some rather . . . well, pleasurable activities. Before that, I spoke with Lord Browne, who made it clear he knew of your actions in saving children and demanded that I tell him more. When I didn't, he seemed quite put out. Could be he was the one who tried to kill me both times—who knows?"

Larryn watched as Seldrake's eyes grew wider. He set down his goblet on the carved table beside him so hard that Larryn was afraid he had broken its stem. In a moment he stood, tall and forbidding, beside her settee. "No more." His voice made it clear he intended no contradiction. "You must return to wherever you came from. I will not have you endangered due to me."

"It's not my decision whether to return. And if I'm endangered because of you, the least you can do is trust me." Larryn attempted a scowl as dark as his.

"It matters not whether I trust you." He took her glass

and placed it on the table beside his. When he returned to her side, he reached down and took her hand. His grip was warm and firm, and she had no choice but to allow him to pull her to her feet. "Someone," he continued, "wishes you ill. I will not have you injured, or worse, while you are in my charge."

"I'm not in your charge," Larryn contradicted. "I happen to be your prisoner, your guest, whatever. But I'm here because I think I need to be. And I want you to trust me. I have to help you—"

"You say that frequently, Larryn, but I do not need your help."

"You do, whether you know it or not." She glared up at his face, totally conscious of how close together they stood. Her breasts nearly touched the breadth of his substantial chest, and a wave of desire for this utterly masculine, utterly unsettling man before her nearly made her knees buckle. But she would not be the one to back down.

"I need no one's assistance, certainly not a woman's, who—"

"I'm a human being, not just 'a woman'!" Larryn practically shouted. "Can't you get it through your thick seventeenth-century skull that being female is not a debilitating disease? Just understand, Seldrake, that I am not here to betray but to—"

She couldn't finish, for her mouth was stopped by his. Seldrake's kiss held all the frustration that he must be feeling, for it was long and rough and inescapable.

Not that she wanted to escape. She pressed herself close against him as her lips opened to allow his tongue inside. His hands moved up to the bare skin at the back of her neck, then down inside her neckline, causing shivers to zoom through her. She pressed closer, feeling how aroused he was even through the many folds of her skirts and underskirts.

"Larryn," he muttered against her mouth, but it was her turn to silence him. She scraped the base of his front teeth with her tongue, then plunged it deeper even as he reached around to insinuate his hand into the front of her bodice. He found one nipple, teased it with his fingertips. She whimpered and moved until her breast fit into his welcome hand.

Her own hands ranged at the back of his loose shirt, feeling his heat, the strength of his sinewy, rippling muscles. But she did not want to touch linen. She longed to feel his bare flesh. She moved down, seeking the lower edge of his shirt, instead finding the trim, taut muscles of his buttocks encased in his britches.

The touch of her hand caused Seldrake to thrust his pelvis forward, a hint of his power and the pleasure that lovemaking with him would provide. His arousal was even more apparent as it pushed against her, and Larryn moaned.

"Come to my bedchamber," he whispered raggedly into her ear.

She nearly said yes. She wanted to say yes. But her mind flashed back to the argument they had been having before he sought to win it by kissing her. "Do you trust me?" she managed. "Will you tell me how to help you?"

His hand, which had been tenderly exploring her breasts, stopped moving. "I need do neither to make delicious love to you," he replied.

"Oh, yes, you do!"

"Do you not understand," he said through gritted teeth, "that other women—"

His words brought Larryn to her senses as abruptly as if he had tossed her into the Long Water at Hampton Court— where at least one, maybe more, of his lovers hung about.

Other women, indeed! This man had undoubtedly slept around like others of his time. Maybe he'd even been untrue to his beloved Charmian, though Larryn would never ask. But she had no interest in a promiscuous man. Despite the recent embers of passion not yet cooled within her, she had no interest at all.

She pulled away and stood glaring up at him. "Answer this, Seldrake," she said, her chest heaving from emotion. She followed his gaze to find that the top of her dress ex-

posed her straining nipples, and she nearly stamped her feet
in anger as she pulled the offending material up as far as
it would go—which was woefully little.

"Answer what?" Other than his erratic breathing, there
was no hint that he had been making love to her moments
before.

"Do you trust me?"

He was silent. His gaze had shuttered.

Larryn closed her eyes. She had her answer. "Well,
then," she whispered, attempting to keep her voice steady
despite her urge to cry, "can you think of any reason that
you would ever ask me for help?" *Like, when you die soon,*
she thought with a wave of sorrow, *and your ghost reaches
out to me in the future. . . .*

She hadn't mentioned that little item to him, nor would
she. Except for his sarcasm, he refused even to consider
that her claims of being from the future were real.
Therefore, he wouldn't believe her anyway.

"I need no help from you, Larryn, although it is most
gracious of you to offer." His voice was as toneless as if
he were speaking to a total stranger.

"I see." Larryn hesitated, then turned toward the door.
"Well, then, I think it's time to say good night."

It was also, she thought a while later as she sat on her bed,
time to say good-bye.

Caddie, on her lap, tried to lick away the tears that rolled
down her cheeks. That made Larryn smile as she cried, and
she hugged the squirming puppy closely to her.

She did not belong here. Her life was in danger, and she
didn't know why. The duke refused, despite all she had
tried to do to assist him, to believe she would protect him.

He had made it clear that, alive and well, he had no intent
to request help from any woman, let alone one he would
not trust. But he obviously thought she was just one in a
line of women he could control and bed.

Well, she wasn't. And if he didn't believe in her,

wouldn't even give her a hint of how she might help him—
then what was she doing here?

Falling in love with a phantom, a little voice shouted
inside her head. Falling for a man who didn't exist in her
time, and who didn't really want her here.

"Forget it," she said aloud. "I don't belong here." Caddie
wriggled and ducked her head beneath Larryn's hand to get
her to pet her. Larryn obliged distractedly. "What do you
think, Caddie?" she asked. "Should we go home?"

The puppy jumped down and stood on the floor, her fore-
quarters crouched as though she were ready to leap in any
direction Larryn pointed. Her fluffy white tail wagged eagerly.

"You do? Well, then, let's try it."

From the bottom of a chest of drawers she drew the
clothing she had come with and put it on. She made certain
that her hair was fastened into its usual tight bun. She lifted
a silver candlestick containing a single candle from the table beside her draped bed and lit it from one of the tapers
blazing in the larger candelabrum beside it.

"Come on," she said to the pup. Carrying her candle, she
pulled open the door to the hallway and looked up and
down. It was empty, and only a few tapers remained lit due
to the later hour. Caddie followed as she made her way
toward the stairway.

She climbed to the roof up the steep stone steps, the little
dog panting at her heels. She hadn't been up here much
since the night she had arrived, but it looked just the
same—and similar to the way it appeared in her own time.

She didn't think Seldrake had come up here, either, except the one time he had joined her. She had been keeping
an eye on him to be sure.

"Do you think this will work?" she whispered as Caddie
frolicked at her heels. The puppy whined, then plunged
forward into the darkness on the roof.

"Caddie, wait!" Larryn called, keeping her voice low.
She went after the pup. Following her had, after all, brought
her to this time. Maybe Caddie knew something she didn't.

She heard a bark behind her. Augie had joined them. "Sssh," she whispered to the older dog, who stood at her side wagging his tail. Jewels in his collar sparkled in the candlelight. "Are you here to help?"

Augie ran in the direction Caddie had gone.

"Wait," Larryn repeated, following them. Her single candle in the darkness hardly illuminated anything, so she had to pick her way carefully. "Where are you?" she called.

And then she saw them, two small shapes with enough white on them to pick up the candle's gleam, cavorting with each other.

"Please," Larryn said, catching up with them, "what should I do? How do I get home?"

The two dogs darted away, then back again. Did they want her to follow?

She went in the direction they indicated, and then saw it—a flickering mist that wisped slowly and eerily from the edge of the flat area of the roof. "Oh," Larryn said. She had plunged through a fog to get here. If she stepped into it now . . . ?

"Is that it?" she asked the dogs who stood nearby, wagging their tails. She didn't expect them to answer. Instead, she drew closer to the mist.

Its smell was familiar: icy and torrid at the same time. This had to be her way home, to her time.

She stopped beside it, and tendrils reached out, snaking about her feet. She could feel the slimy coolness, the burning heat. She recalled her journey here as the mist continued toward her. Caddie sat down beside her as though waiting to be captured by the fog. Larryn no longer saw Augie.

The mist had brought her here. Larryn believed that if she stepped wholly into it, she would be transported away. Away from the vagaries and danger of Restoration England. Away from the plague and the lack of sanitation, away from an era long before antibiotics. Away from a time in which no man could accept her as an equal human being, let alone as a doctor.

Away from Thomas Northby, duke of Seldrake. The arrogant aristocrat who was nearly driving her crazy with his antique attitudes.

The man, whom despite all rationality, she had begun to love.

Love? She couldn't. She would only be hurt.

But it was too late.

If she stayed here, would she have the opportunity again to get back home? What if she could never go back, and she was doomed to remain here with a man who wanted to dominate her, to bed her along with whomever else he pleased, but who still loved his dead wife?

If she went back to her time, would she see Seldrake again as a ghost? Would she regret not having stayed to help him, no matter what the cost to herself?

"What should I do, Thomas?" she whispered brokenly into the mist.

As though he had heard her, Seldrake's voice, fuzzy and in the distance, shouted in Larryn's mind, "Larryn, no!" Only, it wasn't her imagination. She turned, and there was Seldrake just making his way across the roof toward her, Augie at his heels.

Seldrake was on the roof.

"Go back inside." The command she had intended to shout came out like a distant whisper. He would never obey. Still, she believed him safe . . . for now. This wasn't the scene she had viewed from the future. This moment was not what had brought her here—but it could, if she wished, be the moment she went home.

She turned her back on him as the mist elongated and dipped and danced before her eyes. This was her opportunity. She could return to her time.

"Larryn." Seldrake's voice behind her held no arrogance but fear for her. "I do not know what that is, but please do not go further."

"You wanted me to go home, Thomas," she said, again pivoting to face him. "This is the way."

"Do not leave," he said. "Stay here, Larryn. I beg of you."

She turned and looked into eyes that glittered moistly in the faint light of the candle he held, at his other hand, with its glittering sapphire ring, outstretched toward her.

She hesitated. Caddie and Augie both barked beside them.

She looked down, saw that the mist still swirled at her feet, but it was receding.

She lifted her foot to step into it.

Chapter 18

"LARRYN, NO!" THE cry erupted from deep within Seldrake in response to unthinkable pain.

Larryn turned. Immediately, the haze began to recede.

She took a step toward him, and the fog disappeared.

If he were not the duke of Seldrake, he would have flinched beneath the wary stare of Larryn Maeller.

" 'Twas true, then?" he demanded hoarsely. "Your tale . . . you did come here from another time?"

For a long moment, a miasma he did not comprehend had surrounded the pup Caddie and licked at Larryn's feet. For a moment, it had crescendoed, enveloping them both, and he had been certain that it would spirit the two away: dog . . . and woman.

Yet mayhap he had misunderstood what he had seen. Mayhap she would have a better explanation.

"Yes," she said. Her strong, proud chin lifted. "I just had an opportunity to return, even though I hadn't finished what I think I'm here to do. You called me back. I'm not sure if I did the right thing, but here I am." She hesitated, and then she demanded, "Why did you call me? Do you believe me now?"

"I know not what to believe." He sounded humble. He *felt* humble. He now had cause to think that this woman had come to him across centuries to assist him with . . . he knew not what.

It did not matter.

A joyous bark sounded at his feet. He glanced down. Augie was there, and the pup Caddie touched noses with Seldrake's spaniel. Both tails wagged gleefully.

Augie was obviously glad that Caddie had remained. And Seldrake . . . ?

He wondered whether his eyes would ever have closed again in sleep had Larryn disappeared into the vapor. How his mouth would have opened to take food. How he could have concentrated on saving children or—

Larryn took a step toward him. She was clad in the bizarre clothing she had worn when first he had seen her here, on this very roof. Her shirt nearly reached her throat, but her skirt revealed a scandalous expanse of her legs.

Scandalous? No. Seductive. He felt his britches tighten as he watched her, recalled how she had stirred him to near unbearable lust only a scant time earlier that very evening. And then she had been clad in the most appropriate of attire.

"Look, Seldrake." Her voice was as soft as the whisper of silk on skin. Skin . . . he glanced at her bare legs, then again toward her lovely face. "I—I guess I didn't want to go. I'm not a quitter. I'm not sure how I wound up here, but I believe from something your descendant—or at least your family's descendant—in my time showed me, that I had to come. And now that I'm here, I have to stay to see this through."

"To see what through?" He could not help watching the fullness of her lips as she spoke—lips he knew were sweeter than the tastiest of the exotic pineapple fruit he had recently tasted at court.

She shrugged her slender shoulders beneath the outrageous clothing. Mayhap if he removed it from her, he would feel less distracted from what she said. . . .

As his thoughts penetrated into his awareness, he shook his head. Distracted? What could be more distracting than Larryn Maeller, dispossessed of her clothing? Standing bared before him . . .

His groin throbbed most painfully.

"As I've been telling you all along, I think I'm here to help you. But I haven't been able to figure out how."

"And how did you learn of your mission here, Larryn? Mayhap if we study each bit of your knowledge, we can determine what you need to know."

He wished not to study her knowledge, but to study *her*. Now. For as long as it took to comprehend this mystifying woman.

"I believe you have some . . . business I'm here to help you finish. Or some emotional event I'm supposed to prevent, right here on the roof."

He had no idea of what she spoke, and yet, by the fearful look upon her face, there was more she did not reveal.

He wished to wipe her fear away. To—

His thoughts roiled yet again. What if she had stepped through that vapor? What if she had disappeared from his life, this stubborn woman who demanded that he heed her in all matters? This lovely creature who claimed to be a doctor—who insisted on scrubbing people as though their lives depended on it, and who claimed that their lives *did* depend upon such exacting cleanliness.

This woman who did not choose to obey him, the duke of Seldrake, despite being under his roof, his protection, his guardianship.

This woman who attempted to drive him mad with her contradictions, claims, and demands—and would most assuredly drive him mad should she leave him.

"We shall study the matter later, Larryn." He no longer stood at the top of the stairway but trod his way quickly to her side. "First, we have much else to explore."

"What's that?" Ah, how he loved the puzzlement to her furrowed brow, the sweet uncertainty in her musical voice.

Ah, how he loved—dare he think it? No, commanded something inside him. And yet . . .

"Come with me, Larryn," he whispered, not attempting to hide the hoarseness in his voice. "We shall first explore each other."

This was absolute madness. Larryn knew it.

She nevertheless took the duke's extended hand and allowed him to lead her down the staircase. Along the hallway.

Toward his suite.

She had known the moment the mist had begun to swirl around her that she didn't want to leave.

Sheer stubbornness, she told herself. She was supposed to accomplish something here, and she hadn't done it. She had never given up before. She was not about to now.

And if staying kept her close to Seldrake . . . ? Absolute madness.

He preceded her into his suite and closed the door behind them.

"In my time," she said, nervousness making her speak, "there is a life-size portrait of you on the wall." She pointed to a bare area behind his desk. "I was fascinated by you. I almost wished I could meet you." She managed a small, ironic laugh.

His glance at her seemed to hold surprise. "Such a portrait has been commenced. Mayhap you shall see it soon."

He led her into his bedroom. She had seen it last when she had sneaked into his suite to hunt for his journals. Then, the curtains about his carved bed had been lowered, but now they were pulled back. He closed the door behind them, shutting the dogs outside. He set his candlestick on a table beside the bed. Its flickering light was the room's sole illumination.

The idea of being here alone with him, with his bed the most prominent furnishing in the room, made her shudder deep inside with desire.

He must have felt it, as he still held her hand. He pulled

her close, into his arms. "I wish to make you glad you remained, Larryn Maeller," he whispered into her ear. He pulled the pins from her hair, and she felt it fall free to her shoulders. "*Doctor* Larryn Maeller." His voice was husky and contained no irony, as though he at long last truly believed that she told the truth.

His lips nibbled at her ear, causing her to quiver all the more. A yearning for more rocked her insides, but she closed her eyes, waiting, savoring.

In a moment, he captured her mouth with his. She threw her entire being into the kiss, as the dance of their tongues suggested a sensual joining below, even more urgent and primitive.

The duke's fingers slipped one of her blouse's buttons from its hole, then another, until he drew the fabric away from her. He hesitated, and Larryn drew back to see him studying her bra in the faint light. "What manner of garment is this?" he asked.

Her laugh came from deep in her throat. "It's a brassiere," she said. "Women of my time wear these instead of bodices for comfort and support beneath their clothes."

"And how does one remove it?"

"Like this." Larryn took his hands and pulled them to her back. She guided his fingers while he slipped the tiny hooks apart. Her breasts sprang free.

"I approve of such garments," Seldrake said, his respiration erratic. "They require less effort than unlacing a bodice."

Larryn's laugh was breathless. "I suppose so."

In moments, her breasts were cupped in his hands. He bent his head, capturing a nipple in his mouth and tugging on it gently with his teeth. Larryn gasped, her legs nearly buckling.

Seldrake caught her up in his arms and deposited her gently on the bed. Once more, he gave his attention to her breasts until she moaned with pleasure.

"What must I know to rid you of this other garment?" Seldrake muttered. Larryn unbuttoned her skirt herself, then tried to control her rising passion as she demonstrated the zipper.

Seldrake seemed fascinated, pulling it up, then down—while allowing one hand to remain busy with her breasts.

"Please," Larryn murmured. "I want to undress you now."

"Soon," he promised.

As his hand began to pull off her skirt, it stopped at the side. Larryn felt something press against her. Oh, my! She could have proven long ago that she did not come from this time. She extracted the small penlight that she had slipped into her pocket before her excursion onto the roof so long ago and so far in the future.

"This is a flashlight," she told him, unsure whether she was more irritated or glad for the interruption. She pressed the button, and a beam of light radiated from it.

Seldrake reached out and took it from her, studying it and the light that continued to shine. "Has it a candle in-side?"

"No, batteries. They create an electrical current." At his blank look, she smiled. "I'll explain it to you someday."

"Another time," he agreed in a hushed voice. He shone the light at the valley between her breasts, then downward as he finished removing the rest of her clothing.

She felt both self-conscious and incredibly aroused by his illuminated scrutiny. "You are beautiful," he muttered. He flicked the button to turn off the light, put it aside, then followed its path with his hand.

Larryn arched up to meet his stroking, nearly crying out with frustration. "My turn," she insisted, sitting up. She pulled off his loose shirt. After she untied the fastenings to his britches, she drew them off—unsurprised to learn that at least this Restoration man did not wear anything resembling briefs.

He was every bit as gorgeous naked as she had antici-pated. The slopes of his well-muscled chest tapered to the planes of his hard stomach, where a thatch of light hair began, then widened to frame the base of his erection. She smiled her admiration, then reached to stroke him, even as he began to touch her feminine core. She drew in her breath, then whimpered deep in her throat.

"I can wait no longer," he whispered. He maneuvered above her on the bed, then drew her legs farther apart. She thrust up to meet him, then cried out both in joy and in pain. Her experience with sex was limited and long ago, when she had sought love soon after the death of her sister and had thought, erroneously, that she had found it.

"I am sorry." Seldrake spoke through gritted teeth. His blue eyes were glazed with passion, but his hips ceased moving. "Do you wish me to stop?"

"No. Please." She needed to stretch more to accommodate Seldrake, but she joined in the rhythm he set—gentle at first, and then more and more powerful until, with a cry of ecstasy, Larryn erupted into the surge of fulfillment even as she felt Seldrake's shudder and heard his shout.

"You achieved . . . pleasure?"

Larryn watched Seldrake's fingers gently mold her breasts a short while later. She had been thoroughly sated, but his touch was igniting her again. Did he feel it, too? She moved a little so that she could see his deliciously masculine body.

Oh, yes. He was obviously interested once more.

"Pleasure?" she replied. "Did I ever!"

His hand grew still. "Then if this mating results in a child, I shall marry you."

A chill passed through Larryn. Of course she, a doctor, should have thought of consequences, yet all her sense had given way to sensuality.

But marry Seldrake? He hadn't said anything about love, so he might be speaking out of this era's sense of morality.

Did she love him? Oh, yes, despite all of her self-admonishments. But she was certainly not going to marry him because of his misguided sense of honor.

And his words had confused her. "I think I misunderstood you. Do you think my having enjoyed what we did has something to do with pregnancy?"

"Of course. It is a well-known fact that a woman's deriving pleasure from lovemaking results in children."

Larryn sat up and stared at him. "Is that what all men of this day think?" If so, she wondered why so many women apparently became men's mistresses. Men only wanted legitimate children, so at least in theory they would only satisfy their wives.

And though she wondered—with a pang of jealousy—about Charmian, she was not about to quiz Seldrake about his marital relations with his deceased wife. They did not, as far as she knew, ever conceive a child.

Seldrake replied stiffly, "I do not know what all men think, Larryn. But medically—"

She interrupted him with her laugh. "Medically, that's nonsense." She saw the dark look knit his shaggy brows and said in a conciliatory tone, "In my time, we understand more of what causes pregnancies. I'll explain it, if you'd like. We have good forms of contraceptives, too. I didn't bring anything, of course. And I've never been on the Pill, either. I just don't—it's been important to me not to play around."

" 'The Pill'?"

"Birth control pills. We have pills and other great medicines for all sorts of things in my time. Aspirin and other painkillers, pills to alleviate the symptoms of many kinds of illnesses or diseases, and even to prevent them. There are drugs delivered intravenously for greater speed and effect. We even have antibiotics that have made the plague and other horrible diseases virtually disappear."

Seldrake sat up, reaching for his britches, which had fallen on the floor beside them. "I have become more credulous, Larryn, after seeing you in that vapor previously. If what you describe is true, I should love to see it. To be surrounded by such miracles—a physician such as I would find it heaven. And yet . . ." He sighed heavily. "Wish though I might, I cannot put credence into such strange ravings—"

"They're not ravings, they're true!" A chill started deep inside Larryn, and she pulled the down coverlet around her. "Look, let's go slowly, shall we? I'll tell you more about my time, but not all at once. I understand it must all seem inconceivable to you—but it's incredible to me, too, to have come here. You're the reason, you know, Thomas. You begged me to help you."

He had his britches on, though his magnificent chest was still bare. He turned to face her. "*I* begged you?"

Oh, heavens. She hadn't meant for that to slip out. If he'd thought antibiotics unbelievable, what would he think if she told him his own ghost had appeared to ask her assistance?

That he would soon die. . . .

"No," she whispered, feeling her throat constrict. This man was too vital to have his life snuffed out forever.

"No what?" he demanded. "Are you about to retract your absurd assertions?" He drew himself up. "Oh, yes. On top of magical pills, I had nearly forgotten your claims to the authorities in London about vehicles in tubes below the city and contraptions that fly above. Did you make these up as well?"

Larryn closed her eyes, feeling tears well in them. "I won't retract anything I know to be true," she said with a sigh. "That includes the fact that I definitely took the greatest pleasure in what we just did."

She felt the mattress sag on its leather straps and opened her eyes once more. Seldrake sat beside her. "You are not like any other woman of my acquaintance, Doctor Larryn Maeller," he said gently. "And I viewed that odd haze upon my own roof and your light without flame. They are why I cannot completely discount all of your wild assertions. And I, too, took the greatest pleasure in our lovemaking." His tone turned teasing as his thick eyebrows raised archly. "Mayhap if we try it again, I will find it easier to believe in what you say."

Larryn found herself grinning despite the moistness on her cheeks. "Mayhap? Well, then, perhaps we should do it again soon."

"Very soon," he agreed, again shucking his britches as her grin widened into an anticipatory smile.

"Oh, Caddie, what am I going to do?"

Larryn was in her bedroom, alone. Seldrake had insisted that she leave his room, but only after he had assured himself that no one was in the hall to see her escape. He intended to protect her reputation, even if she did not worry about it.

Now, an hour after she had left him, she lay against the pillow at the head of the ornate curtained bed, hugging the puppy. She wondered when dawn would come—soon, she was sure. She hoped it was just moments away, for then she could rise and get busy with the children in the cottages—and cast her muddled thoughts from her mind.

"I need to help Seldrake," she whispered to Caddie. "But when I do, will I go back to my own time?" The little spaniel wriggled in her arms and licked her nose. Larryn laughed. "Well, of course I wouldn't forget about you."

Larryn had spent a lot of energy since her arrival worrying about her mission here. Could it be she helped him just by being here? Was she simply here to take Seldrake's mind off his beloved Charmian by being his lover?

But he still thought about his wife. And even though making love with him had been one of the most wonderful experiences of her life, it struck a sour chord deep within her.

Seldrake himself had at least one mistress already, she believed—Lady Bess Mainwaring, who had also been mistress to the king.

Seldrake did not love Larryn. And she had long ago promised herself she would not become like her sister: looking for love but settling for sex.

Seldrake had been right; she could become pregnant, though not for the reason he apparently thought. He had offered to marry her—but not because he cared. "No!" she declared, causing Caddie to cower. Larryn's laugh held a note of sadness. "I didn't mean you," she said. "You're not doing anything wrong. *I* am."

Would she stay if she could? Medicine here was primitive. She could not be a doctor. "I'd only be a chattel to him," she whispered to Caddie. "And even if he married me, that wouldn't mean I was the only woman in his life." Caddie whined at her angry and despondent tone. "That's what I say."

But being able to stay with Thomas forever . . .

That couldn't happen. It *didn't* happen, for Chloe's genealogical history of her family did not unearth another wife in Thomas's life. There had been that miniature portrait of Larryn . . . but nothing else about her.

"I don't know what's going to happen, Caddie," Larryn said aloud as the puppy sleepily settled down on the thick comforter. "I just know I won't be in the duke's life much longer."

His life. It would be cut short. She did not know why, or when, or what would happen.

That, of course, must be why she had come here to help him. But how?

She had to find out. The best way to learn, of course, was to get his cooperation. He might believe now that she came from the future. That she was a doctor. Would he accept the rest?

Someday soon she would have to tell him she had visited with his ghost. That he would die, though she did not know when or how. That the reason she had to help him was so that his spirit would rest in peace.

Her burst of laughter was sad and nearly hysterical. It startled Caddie awake. "Sorry," Larryn whispered hoarsely.

All she had to do was to tell Seldrake. Make him understand. Make him believe this, too, and get him to work with her.

"That's all I have to do," she told Caddie. "I just have to find the right moment." She laughed sorrowfully again.

• • •

Daylight had finally arrived. Larryn knelt in the garden picking herbs to mix into a paste that, Adele had told her, would help little Bevin stop itching so badly.

Caddie suddenly stood to attention at her feet. Larryn looked up—and smiled. "Thomas," she said happily as he approached along the path, Augie with him. Larryn rose as Caddie took off to chase the other dog.

"Adele told me I would find you here," he said. As he reached her side, he said more softly, "Did you sleep well?" He raised one eyebrow and looked her up and down as though assessing her readiness for further play with him.

Larryn laughed. "I certainly was worn out after my . . . exercise last night." She looked him over, too. He was in his normal state of undress for hanging around Seldrake House. The waves of his light hair framed his all-masculine face, and she had an urge to touch his hollow cheek, the sensual lips that had given her such pleasure . . . all over. She felt redness creeping up her neck and looked down at the small trowel in her hand as though it had suddenly demanded her attention.

No need to tell Seldrake the truth about her sleeplessness, for then he might try to pry its cause out of her. And she didn't want to mention her own confusion, her fears and misgivings. Not when the summer day was so bright and warm already, and Seldrake, looking as gorgeous as ever, had sought her out—hadn't he? She kept her tone teasing. "So what brings the illustrious duke to the gardens usually tended by his servants and submissive womenfolk?"

"My womenfolk submissive?" His laugh was merry, and Larryn enjoyed the deep, pleasing sound. "Not so, Doctor Maeller." He knelt beside her, and she smelled his pleasant scent of castile soap and his own masculine fragrance. "Larryn, after last evening, I have been thinking. I wish you to teach me about your time and its wonders. I will be considering what matters you can help me with, as you have oft requested. This afternoon, Adele is visiting the home of the earl of Rashley to sit for a painting—since we wish no strangers here, of course. I desire that you go with her to have a portrait of you commissioned as well."

A portrait? Larryn knew, of course, that it would be a miniature. But—"Why do you want someone to paint a portrait of me?" she asked.

A bleak expression passed over his face. "I have begun to believe your strange claims, Larryn. I know you wish to return to your own time through that damnable haze on the roof after you have done all here that you must. When you leave, your likeness shall be engraved upon my heart, and yet I wish to have a portrait of you such that I can torture myself by looking upon it."

Larryn bit her bottom lip as a wave of sorrow surged through her. The man apparently did care for her, but not enough to ask her to stay. And if he did . . . ?

"Fine," Larryn said. "I'll go sit for the portrait, especially since I know it'll torture you." She grinned at him, though she ached fiercely inside because she knew his "torture" would occur because they would be irrevocably separated.

And she would be tortured every bit as much as he— undoubtedly more.

Still, she had to allow the portrait to be painted, since she knew it *was* painted. She lifted the basket beside her on the ground that contained the herbs she had picked. "I'll go get ready."

Caddie and Augie capered at her heels as she turned her back on Seldrake and hurried toward the house.

Chapter 19

LARRYN HAD HAD no idea how bored she would get posing for a portrait. Plus, she'd had to wait while preliminary sketches were made for a painting of Adele.

And then there had been the tedious verbal sparring with the elderly but spry Lady Rashley. The earl's wife had wanted nothing more than to find out Larryn's background so she could, no doubt, gossip about it at court.

Eventually, Adele and Larryn had been able to leave. Now, they had nearly arrived back at Seldrake House. The countryside outside the coach's small green-tinted windows looked familiar.

As the coach lurched around a bend, Larryn grabbed the leather strap above the door. Adele was discussing all the important people who'd had their portraits painted by the same artist. "Antoine Johnville is so much in demand that it takes him months to complete a portrait, for he refuses no commission by anyone important, so he is in the middle of several paintings at once at all times. That is why we must be prepared for further sketches and sittings."

"And is Johnville doing one of the duke?" Larryn tried to keep her tone casual despite the excitement inside her.

If it was in the preliminary stages, maybe Seldrake would live a lot longer—long enough that the portrait she saw in her time could be completed.

Adele, dressed in a lacy peach outfit that was supposed to make her resemble Venus in her portrait, tilted her head curiously. "He has one in progress—a splendid one, as large as Thomas himself, he tells me. I do not know when it will be completed, but Johnville seems eager to please those with titles above all others, so I believe we will see it soon."

"Oh, wonderful." But Larryn's pretense of enthusiasm fell short.

Adele asked no questions, though, as the coach stopped at the entry to the Seldrake estate. The gate was pulled open wide by several servants, including Ned.

Theirs was not the only carriage in the courtyard. The one with six matching, restless horses looked familiar. "Is that Lady Mainwaring's coach?" Larryn asked Adele, her heart plummeting.

"Yes." Adele did not sound pleased. "I wonder why she is here."

So did Larryn. She patted her hair to make certain it was neatly tucked up into its chignon—since it was her usual style, she had been determined to wear it that way for her portrait. She smoothed the skirt of the green silk ensemble she had borrowed from Adele, pulling it down just a little at the top to look more fashionable than she'd wanted to in the portrait.

But she had no desire to see Bess Mainwaring. She told Adele, "I'll check to make sure the children are well hidden. You find out what she's come for."

"No," Adele contradicted. "I will look in on the young ones. I believe it more important that you learn why Lady Mainwaring has graced us with her presence."

Important for whom? But Larryn did not want to argue. She lifted her skirts and hurried inside.

Ned, who had been helping with the horses, caught up with her at the door. "Oh, Lady Larryn, thank heavens ye is here. His lordship has been asking about when Lady Adele and ye was expected. He needs ye in the study."

He needed her? A feeling of pleasure crept through Larryn as she hurried through the halls. She pushed open the door to the study without knocking . . . and stopped, her heart sinking to her toes.

Seldrake was there, all right, but hardly eagerly awaiting her—for in his arms was Lady Bess Mainwaring.

He met Larryn's eyes. "Sorry," she croaked. "Ned told me you were looking for me, but I'll come back—"

"Come here now, please, Larryn." Seldrake's tone made his words a command.

Larryn bristled. She felt mortified enough, bursting in on such a tender scene. She blinked, trying to ignore her anguish.

Lady Mainwaring turned her head only enough to gaze piteously at Larryn from Seldrake's arms. "Thank heavens you have finally arrived, Lady Larryn," she said. Her voice was hoarse, as though she had been crying. "The duke said he cannot come with me to court without his able assistant—you. Not even to help my son, Lord Terence, who is so dear to both of us." She paused, looking up at Seldrake. He nodded gravely. Bess continued, "He and another child—they were playing, I am told, but Terence was thrust into the fire. His arm was burned, and he is in such pain. . . ." Her own pain was evident in the deep lines about her eyes and mouth. "The king has put his physicians to help him, has even laid on his touch, and yet my poor Terence . . . He has need of an excellent physician, and I have begged Seldrake to come immediately."

There was a fear in Seldrake's eyes that Larryn had never before seen. Seldrake helped dozens of children. Why was he so worried about Lady Mainwaring's child?

And then it came to her. Her hand flying to her mouth, Larryn stifled a gasp. She should have realized it before.

She had believed, due to Bess's airs and all Larryn had heard at court, that little Terence Mainwaring was another of the king's many illegitimate offspring. She still believed that the boy was no son of Bess's invalid husband—what was his name? Lord Purvis? But Larryn no longer thought that the king was his father.

Terence Mainwaring had to be the duke of Seldrake's son.

At Hampton Court Palace, Bess showed Larryn and Seldrake into one of the smaller, yet still ornate bedrooms. On a raised bed lay the moaning figure of small Terence. He was a handsome child, as good-looking as his beautiful mother. A sheet had been drawn over him, and an older man with white hair that was shorter than the norm in the Restoration era paced the room.

"How is he, Lord Feversham?" Bess asked the man.

"Improving," said the old man, though to Larryn the boy didn't look well. Lady Mainwaring introduced Lord Feversham as one of the palace physicians.

She sat at her son's side. "How do you feel, Terence?" she crooned.

Tears flowed down his cheeks. "I hurt, Mama."

"You will be fine, my dear little lord." She smoothed back his hair, as dark as the ebony coil that fell over her own shoulder. She laid a kiss upon his brow, then stood. "I shall see you soon," she said with a smile. But to Larryn and Seldrake she muttered, her back to her son, "I cannot watch him this way. Thomas, you must feel for the boy as I do. Take pity. Heal him." Her head bowed, she swept from the room.

"You shall see to him, Lady Larryn." Seldrake's voice was cool, as though he were a distant stranger speaking with a medical colleague.

"Of course," Larryn said. She approached Terence, pulled the silk sheet from him—and gasped. His left forearm was red and blistered. It was slathered with some kind of white goo.

And among the boy's fortunately few blisters sat big, black blotches that could only have been leeches.

Nearly gagging, Larryn managed, "Bleeding is not the

best treatment for burns." She turned to Lord Feversham. "If you would please remove the leeches, I will begin my treatment."

The man's birdlike eyes widened as though one of the leeches had spoken to him. He turned to Seldrake, who stood at the doorway. "Your Grace, I cannot in good conscience—"

"Lady Larryn is my assistant," Seldrake interrupted coldly. "You will listen to her as you would to me."

With a furious glare, the man approached the crying child. He removed the leeches and placed them, with a flourish, into an ornate box.

Shuddering, Larryn drew closer. She examined the boy's arm. "Looks like mostly first-degree burns, thank heavens, though there is one area of second-degree. At least the leeches didn't break the blisters, but there's still the possibility of infection."

"What will you do?" Seldrake did not move from his position near the door.

What was the matter with him? He usually was in the thick of things, issuing orders.

"First, we'll need warm water and soap, to cleanse his arm after those . . . insects opened his skin. Then we'll need for someone to bring in water that's as cold as can be found." She knew better than to demand ice here practically in the middle of summer. "We'll try to get him to drink later, when I'm sure he's not in shock. Have someone boil water to sterilize it, then when it cools we'll add a little salt."

A short while later, when the warm water and soap had been brought to her, Larryn spoke soothingly to the boy. She cleaned his arm as gently as possible, aware that she had nothing but cold water to ease his severe pain. "You're such a brave boy," she told him. "And you know what? As long as we keep your arm clean, you'll be fine, as long as you don't get dried out. We'll need for you to drink—what is your favorite drink?"

"The juice from oranges," he said in a small voice.

"Then you shall have as much juice from oranges as you wish." She had no idea how easy it was to obtain oranges here, in Restoration England, but if they were available anywhere, surely the king's court would have them. She glanced at Seldrake. "The duke will see to it, won't you?"

The boy looked toward the door for the first time. His face lit up. "I did not know you were there, sir."

"You are in good hands, Terence," Seldrake said softly. "Lady Larryn knows how to make you well."

The boy's small brow knit in confusion. "But you are a physician, are you not, sir?"

"Sometimes a physician who cares too much does more harm than good." Pain shadowed Seldrake's face as he continued to regard little Terence. "I shall see to your juice." He turned and left the room.

Larryn drew in her breath. She had her answer. She had more answers than she wanted.

She knew Seldrake felt guilty that, despite being a doctor, he had been unable to save his wife. He obviously cared for small Terence—more than all the other children he treated so tenderly and patiently. Her speculation must be correct. Seldrake did not want to treat Terence for fear of being unable to help him. He didn't want to see the boy suffer.

For what father could bear the agony of his son?

That night, Larryn stayed in Terence's room. She saw no sign of infection, but the boy remained awake, tears in his eyes.

She applied cold water often. When that helped only minimally with the pain, Larryn asked Seldrake about medicines that were available. He suggested more of the white salve that she had removed to clean the burns. "It is ointment of chalk," he had explained. It was made of chalk and wax and oil of roses—harmless, although she doubted its effectiveness.

"Let's try it," she said.

It did seem to soothe Terence at first. But then the boy

began to moan. Seldrake, who sat quietly on a chair near the door, winced. Larryn knew the boy's suffering tore at him. She believed she knew why. But she nevertheless wanted to go to him. To hold him and comfort him the way she did the child.

Instead, she remained across the room, near Terence. "The salve is just fine," she said gently, "but is there anything else available for pain?"

"There is." Seldrake stood abruptly. "I shall go find some syrup of meconium. It is used oft to help restless children sleep, and it eases pain as well."

"What's in it?" Larryn asked.

"Much of it is the boiled juice of poppies, although it also contains other ingredients, such as maiden-hair, mallows, and quinces."

Poppies? It was an opiate, then. Not a great idea, even if the norm here was to dose insomniac kids with it. Still, if administered right, it might help poor Terence.

And this was an instance of a logical basis for an old herbal remedy.

"Good idea," she said. "The stuff can be addictive, though, so we'll administer only small doses for a short amount of time."

Seldrake located some. As a result, Terence slept well, and by morning, when he awakened, he felt better. The redness of his burn had begun to pale. Larryn remained with him through the next day, wrapping his injured arm in cloth soaked with cool water. He soon sat up and asked for something to eat.

Larryn was gratified at his progress. So, apparently, was his mother. Lady Mainwaring dropped in often, fussing over her son and thanking the physicians for their help, though she seemed close to choking on words of gratitude directed toward Larryn. She often took Seldrake's arm and led him to the corner of the room, where they spoke in low whispers, the duke's head bowed close to Bess's.

It was not a scene Larryn relished. It made a lump rise

in her gorge, one that no amount of this era's popular purges could ever expel.

She was pleased, though, when Lady Anne Farswell visited with young Lord Apsley. Clearly Lady Mainwaring was less thrilled with these visitors, for she turned alternately snappish and maudlin, blaming Apsley for Terence's injuries.

"I did not push him into the fire, Mama," Apsley whispered tearfully to Lady Anne. "It was Lord Simpson."

"You children were all shoving at one another carelessly near the fire," Bess snapped at him. "You should have stopped the foul game."

Sobbing, Apsley ran from the room. His angry mother declared, "You are mistaken, Lady Mainwaring. Your untoward sense of rivalry affects your good sense." And with that she walked slowly and with dignity after her son.

Rivalry? Larryn wondered what was really going on between these two. She had little time to speculate, though, before Browne came into Terence's chamber. "I trust you are receiving all you need, Lady Larryn." The stylishly clad courtier's words were appropriate; his too-familiar tone was not.

Larryn glanced toward Seldrake, hoping for, if nothing else from him, a little moral support. She still suspected Browne had tried to throw her down the stairs, maybe even had tried to run her down with a coach. But Seldrake was again deep in conversation with Lady Mainwaring. His hand clutched her shoulder.

Larryn wondered if she should take some of Terence's opium syrup for her own pain—then got hold of her senses. She knew how close Seldrake was with Bess. And how she, Larryn, was just an interloper he'd happened to bed.

She managed to chat civilly with Browne, who soon left the chamber.

The next morning, Larryn believed Terence's progress significant enough that she asked to return to Seldrake House.

She was not surprised when Seldrake said he would remain at the palace for several days longer.

Seldrake returned to Seldrake House two days later. He had felt assured earlier that young Terence would recuperate fully, since Larryn had dealt with the boy's treatment.

He had not trusted himself, for, like Charmian, the boy meant much to him.

Terence was much improved. It had been time for Seldrake to return home.

Ned greeted him in the courtyard and took the reins of his horse. "Where is Lady Larryn?" Seldrake asked.

"In the banquet house, Y'r Grace," his aging retainer replied, nodding toward the farther cottage. "She has said it is time again for scrubbing the place. And hardly a speck of dust in it yet, sir." He shook his head as he led the horse away.

Seldrake almost smiled. He had missed Larryn sorely, even her strange ways. Had she truly come from the future? 'Twas harder to doubt it now that he had seen the pup and her nearly disappear into the strange miasma on the roof, as well as that odd mechanical light with no flame. And her peculiar medical ways had, thus far, been successful.

He strode toward the cottage.

The outer chamber was empty, though he heard muffled noises. He found Larryn where the children slept, scouring the wooden floor with sand beside Clydia. The children were at the other side of the chamber, using reeds to sweep up the grains. They giggled as they swept more sand into the air than into piles for removal, obviously enjoying their chore.

Larryn's slender body was clad in a gray shift that appeared as though it belonged to one of the servants. Tendrils of her dark hair had escaped from the severe style in which she always wore it, curling softly about her damp and flushed face.

He wished to kneel down and lift her to her feet. To take her into his arms—

But not here, for all to see. He believed, after her pretense at lunacy, that her good reputation meant little to her, but he cared about it. Much. For he had thought long and hard while they were separated.

Despite all of the obstacles, he wished to make Doctor Larryn Maeller his wife.

"I have returned, Larryn," he said softly.

She turned slowly, as though she had been aware of his presence yet had felt reluctant to acknowledge it. An odd ache tightened his chest. Had she not wished his return?

"How is Terence?" she asked. Her cool gaze gave no hint that she had even remarked upon his absence.

"He does well, thanks to your ministrations." That should please her; he had acknowledged her healing skills.

"I'm glad. He seems like quite a sweet little boy. Lady Mainwaring is undoubtedly proud of him." She glared at him as though he, too, should admit his pride in the boy.

Did she know his connection with young Terence? There were reasons he had not wanted it public; Bess was, after all, Lord Purvis's wife. Yet mayhap it was best if Larryn had become aware. It should not cause any difference between the two of them.

But with no further word, Larryn returned to her task.

Blast the woman! Did it mean nothing to her that the duke of Seldrake had, before the court of His Sovereign Majesty, King Charles II, allowed her to take charge of the treatment of the child? It might be the talk of court for weeks.

And did his tender thoughts of her, during his absence, mean nothing as well? She knew naught of them, of course. But should she continue to regard him as though he were one of the leeches that she had obviously so reviled, he would not tell her of them. Not this day, and not any day.

Larryn tried to skip supper that evening, but Seldrake sent Marie-Louise to fetch her. Adele's maid was timid when it came to crossing the duke. "Please, mademoiselle," she begged in her melodic accent. "His Grace, he told me especially to bring you to him. He wishes company while he eats."

"Did he ask where Adele was?" Larryn would do all she could to cover for the duke's sister.

"Non," the French maid said. "Not exactly. I hinted she had gone for another sitting for her portrait."

"That's true," Larryn said.

Marie-Louise nodded. "I did not mention that she had departed this morning."

Larryn did not want Seldrake asking further questions of the servants. So, with a sigh, she told Marie-Louise she would dine with him.

She was dismayed to see that an intimate table had been set in a small room off the dining room. "This room is sufficient for two of us," Seldrake said when she joined him. "Do you not agree?"

She saw a sparkle in his brilliant blue eyes. A sexy half-smile lifted one corner of his lips. She did not let her gaze linger on him. Too dangerous. She did not want to think of the passion they had shared. Of the dreams she had fleetingly dreamt of him. "This room is fine." She allowed him to gallantly seat her on one of the upholstered chairs with thick, carved legs.

The room had molded ceilings and tapestries on two sides depicting ancient Greek myths. Some of the people depicted were nude. Had he brought her here to remind her of their night of seduction?

Despite a slight shiver of desire that swept through her, she cast the recollection to the deepest recesses of her mind. Instead, she reminded herself of Terence Mainwaring.

That thought cooled any residual passion within her. "So, how were things at the palace when you left? Was Lady Mainwaring pleased about her son's progress?"

Seldrake gave her an odd, searching look. "She remained most pleased," he replied.

Conversation was stilted during their shared supper of oysters, followed by duckling and beef. Larryn tried to think of safe topics, but Seldrake seemed disinclined toward small talk.

She tried not to look at him, but he had dressed for dinner in a deep brown coat with creamy lace at his throat, and his imposing figure dominated the small room.

That, plus her own wayward memories of how it had felt to kiss those lips he now so sensually wrapped around morsels of meat. How it had felt to be stroked by those hands that tore hunks of bread from its loaf.

She hardly ate. Her appetite was not for food, and she would not allow it to be for anything else.

"What troubles you?" he demanded when they had at last finished.

"What makes you think that anything does?" Larryn dabbed gently at her mouth with her napkin.

"You, madam. Since we had such a . . . pleasant interlude together several nights back, the few times we have been together you have acted as though naught had happened. As though we were as unacquainted with one another as the night you appeared unannounced on my roof."

Pleasant interlude? Was that all he deemed it? To her, it had been ecstasy. Heaven.

Smothering her anguish, she waited for a servant to clear the nearly full plates from before her, then stood.

"Please answer, Larryn." The duke's voice resounded of its old arrogance. "I wish to know what troubles you."

"You're imagining things," she replied. "Have a good evening."

But he did not allow her to get away that easily. Taking her arm, he led her outside the house. The air in the garden was chilly, for summer was over. Not that Larryn had kept track of the time she had been there, but she had heard a couple of servants discussing earlier that the year was nearing its end; September had already arrived.

Daylight had nearly waned. No one was about. It was a good place for a private conversation—but Larryn didn't want one.

"I'm tired," she told the duke. "As you know, we were busy cleaning again today, and—"

"And you require greater cleanliness than any three persons I know," he interrupted. He waved a hand as though supremely irritated, which was why Larryn was amazed when he continued, "I do not wish to find such matters, or anything else, endearing about you, Larryn, yet I do."

She froze, pleasure warring with incredulity within her.

She wondered if her eyes looked as wary as his. Whatever he saw on her face must have pleased him, though, for he took her into his arms.

She felt his breath on her lips as he bent to kiss her. She opened her mouth, wanting desperately to open herself to him once more. To pretend that there were just the two of them in the world, together, alone.

But as his lips merely skimmed hers, she shuddered and pulled back. Without thinking first, she blurted, "Tell me that you have no connection to Lady Mainwaring, and then I'll go to bed with you again."

His arms about her stiffened, then released her. "That is something I cannot, I shall not, tell you."

"Then explain—"

"I explain nothing." He turned his back and stalked toward the house.

She stood there, forlornly watching him. She had a perverse need to explain *herself*. She hurried after him.

"I told you before," she whispered as they reached the house, "my sister had many lovers. I . . . I can't, and won't. And I won't play second fiddle to a man's other lovers, either."

A servant was busy lighting candles in the entry. Seldrake pulled her into a withdrawing room and closed the door behind them. They were alone once more.

He drew himself up to his full, intimidating height. He was backlighted by the flickering candles in sconces along one wall, and Larryn had the impression of an angry giant waiting to pounce on his prey. "You may believe what you wish, madam."

Her heart fell to the floor. He hadn't denied a relationship with Bess—not that she had expected him to. "I'll believe something else if it's the truth. I just—"

A noise sounded in the hallway outside. In moments, the door opened and Adele slipped in, followed by Lord Wyford. Adele giggled as Wyford pulled her into his arms and kissed her deeply before Larryn could react.

She took Seldrake's hand. "Come on, Seldrake," she said loudly. "You owe me some answers." She hoped she had given Adele time to think.

But it was too late. Adele gasped. Her eyes widened as her gaze fell upon her brother.

If Larryn had thought Seldrake looked intimidating before, now he was downright menacing.

"Wyford, you scoundrel!" he shouted, then stepped toward the man he had just insulted.

Chapter 20

THE SCENE WAS over in minutes. Seldrake had sent the restrained but obviously angry Lord Wyford from Seldrake House. He was to return only if summoned by the duke—if ever. Adele had run, crying, to her room.

Larryn was alone with Seldrake in his study. She stood near the door, Caddie in her trembling arms. The man had gotten away not only with sleeping with another man's wife, but also with fathering an illegitimate child. And yet he banned his sister from seeing the perfectly nice man she loved.

Why, then, did Larryn still yearn to throw herself into his arms?

"Put yourself in their shoes, Thomas," she pleaded. "You were in love at least once." With Charmian. And, maybe, now, with Bess Mainwaring.

But not with Larryn. Never with Larryn.

She ignored the dagger that twisted deep in her heart and continued, "Henry is a nice man. He—"

"He is a second son!" Seldrake said with gritted teeth. "You are meddling in matters that concern you not, madam."

"My name is Larryn," she corrected him angrily.

"I care not what your name is," he said coldly. "You will no longer interfere with my family." He turned and stalked from the room.

Larryn stared at the door he closed behind him. Tears welled in her eyes, and she buried her chin in Caddie's fur. "He seemed to care for me two days ago, Caddie." Her whisper sounded strangled, even to her. "Maybe he still would, if I kept my eyes and mouth shut and my bodice low." Her bitter laugh turned into a cry of pain. With the puppy still in her arms, she sat on a settee and wept.

She didn't cry long. She didn't allow herself to. Instead she delved into Seldrake's precious, private journals again—half daring him, in her mind, to come in and find her spying. He thought no better of her anyhow.

The journals were fascinating—from a historical perspective, at least. The purported cures they contained were an amalgamation of superstition, pharmacology, astrology, folktales, and religion. And these from a family of physicians who had passed along the best of their knowledge. It was no wonder that lifespans were so low in these days, even when plague wasn't rampant.

Not that she faulted Seldrake. He practiced medicine the best he knew how. The medicines he had available had certainly assisted in making young Terence feel better. But she wondered what Seldrake would think if she could introduce him to the breakthroughs of her time.

Suddenly Caddie, who had been sleeping at her feet, sat up and cocked her head. Then, barking, she ran to the study door.

Larryn froze. Was Seldrake about to burst in and castigate her again?

But Caddie's shrill barks were more like those that Cavaliers used to report intruders. Had someone come to Seldrake House?

Larryn hurried to the study door and threw it open. A poorly dressed woman stood in the entryway, conversing earnestly with Seldrake. She soon left. Seldrake whirled. Only then did he seem to notice Larryn.

"Who was she?" she asked.

"One moment." He sounded distracted. "Oh, Ned, there you are," he called to his manservant, who had appeared on the stairs. "Please ready my coach. I have to go . . . to town."

"To London?" Larryn queried. It was growing late. That could only mean—"Is there a child—"

"Yes. That was Nessie, who keeps me informed of such children." He tried to brush past her.

"I'll come, too."

"You shall not—"

"Of course I shall. No matter what you think of me, you know I can help. And you no longer have Wyford to assist you."

His blue eyes seemed to pierce her with fury, but then they softened. "You are right, Larryn. I do need your help."

Her help! He had finally asked for it. Could this be why she was here?

"I'll go get ready," she said, full of anticipation—and trepidation. Could her days here at Seldrake House—with Thomas Northby—be numbered?

Larryn, holding the overhead strap for balance, watched Seldrake pull back the curtains at the small windows as the coach careened through the night.

"I wonder what that might be." He frowned as he turned back toward her.

She sat beside him, though they only touched one another when the vehicle took an especially hard jounce. She had squeezed tightly into the corner, knowing that any contact with Seldrake made her all too aware of his seductive presence.

"What's that?" she asked idly.

"That odd light in the distance; it will make it easier to find our way, and yet it might make us more visible in the town."

Light? Larryn peered out through the window. An orange glow lit the sky in the direction in which they were heading. It lay low on the horizon, a pulsing corona. . . .

"Oh, lord!" she exclaimed. She hadn't paid much attention to dates while she was here. Not that she would necessarily have remembered anyway, but—"I think it was early September."

"It *is* early September." Seldrake regarded her oddly.

She took a deep breath, but it failed to calm her. "I wish I'd known. I've only a basic knowledge of history at this time. If I'd realized I'd be here, I would have read up on it."

"Read up on what, Larryn?"

She glanced at the duke. His voice was admirably calm, admirably patient.

Why shouldn't it be? He didn't know what lay ahead.

"Maybe we should turn back," she said.

His features went rigid. "There are children we must save from the plague. *I* must, at least. You can do as you wish."

"What I wish is for us to remain safe. And you're about to find that there are worse things to face in London than the plague—though, fortunately, I don't think many lives are lost."

He reached toward her and gripped her arm. She was very much aware of his touch—even now, when there was so much on her mind. "Of what are you speaking, Larryn?"

She laughed wryly. "I'm speaking, Thomas, of the Great Fire of London."

London *was* afire.

As their coach followed the Thames on their approach, Seldrake became ever more aware of the massive nature of the conflagration. In the distance, he saw London Bridge in flames, even the spires of the magnificent St. Paul's Cathedral. Smoke curled everywhere above the walled city.

The streets were narrow, lined with homes in the design so common to London: set back from the lane below but built out overhead so that the front of one nearly touched the front of its neighbor across the street. Turning from one lane onto another made little difference, for all were alike, and all were congested with residents fleeing the town. Eyes haunted and fearful, they trudged in anguish, towing carts piled with meager belongings, and, on top, the women and children.

Finally, Seldrake bade his coachman to stop. He alit and shouted up at the man above the terrible noises: the cries of the people swarming about, the distant roar of the fire, an occasional blast, as though of gunfire. "I shall proceed on foot," he told the coachman. "You shall wait here, or as close as possible." The fire did not appear nearby, and yet . . . from the disaster Larryn had described, he knew this area might not be safe. "I shall come looking for you later. If you are not here, then try—" After pondering for a few moments, he gave a list of homes and landmarks of increasing distance from the heart of town where he would seek out his coach—and Larryn. "You will see to Lady Larryn, ensure she remains safe—"

"What do you mean?" demanded an irate voice beside him. He glanced down. "I'm coming with you, Seldrake."

"You are not, madam," he said in his most authoritative voice. He had been angry with the woman over the last days, more so than ever before in their brief acquaintance.

And yet he still cared for her. Very much. Too much. He would not allow her life to be endangered.

"Of course I am. I'm a . . ." To give her credit, she lowered her voice, for the crowd continued to flow past as though the two stood on a rock in the midst of a rushing stream. "I am a doctor. I can help treat the injured. Besides . . ."

She stopped. He had an urge to kiss away the triumphant and seductive smile that curved her adorable full lips.

"Besides what?" He was fully aware she wished him to quiz her. He would indulge her in this game.

"Besides, I think I remember how the fire is finally stopped. If you're nice to me, I'll tell you, and maybe we can be in on the action."

"Oh, I shall be very nice to you, Larryn." A slow smile of his own curled his mouth, and he looked her over from her small boots borrowed from Adele, up to her dark hair pulled back from her lovely face, and then back down to the top of her bodice and all it revealed.

Her flush was not due to the proximity of the fire, for the conflagration remained far away. But he felt with pride that it might be due to a fire that he stoked within her.

"Hold that thought," she whispered hoarsely. With that, she put out her small, determined hand.

He clasped it. "I do not wish for you to be in danger."

"And I do not wish for you to be in danger, either." Her lower lip stuck out most belligerently.

With a fond shake of his head, he turned. Together they wended their way through the crowd in the direction of the fire.

"Okay, I didn't say I knew much."

The heat was intense. From the screams of terrified people around them, Larryn could tell the fire was gaining on the crowded residential area in which they stood. The stench of burning wood and other materials was nearly overwhelming.

"What *do* you know?" Seldrake's words were clipped. He stared about them, as though sizing up in which direction they should flee.

Wise man, Larryn thought.

"I know that the king's brother, the duke of York, helped to save the day by insisting that lines of houses be blown up by using kegs of gunpowder. That stopped the fire's progress."

"But you know not where?"

Larryn shook her head. "The king got into the thick of it, too, I think. The royals rode around on horseback, directing fire-fighting efforts and even throwing coins to the workers to encourage them." She hesitated. "I'd imagine that, in this chaos, you won't be able to find the house with the children you came to save—presuming it's even still standing."

"Oh, I shall find it."

But first, they stopped along a narrow street where they helped poorly dressed residents shepherd their children away from the fire—or so they hoped, for tales of those in flight claimed there was no way of telling which way the flames would next shift.

And then Larryn heard screams not far away. She hurried in that direction, Seldrake at her side.

Embers and flaming ashes floated around them, occasionally igniting a timber on a nearby building. Larryn tried not to breathe too deeply; the fumes nearly choked her.

In the next, nearly deserted street, flames poured from the top of a Tudor-style house. A child stood terrified at the upstairs window while his mother shrieked up at him from the narrow street.

Larryn looked around. Nearby was an abandoned cart with a load of clothing on top. "There." She pointed.

Seldrake got the message. In moments, the cart was beneath the open window. The boy screamed as flames licked at him. "Jump," Seldrake commanded. The autocratic tone that usually so annoyed Larryn sounded welcome now. "You must. Right away."

The boy listened. Only as he leapt from the window did Larryn notice that his jacket was on fire.

In moments, he was upon the cart, still screaming. The roar of the fire and his mother's cries pounded in Larryn's ears, but she did not stop. She tore off his flaming jacket, throwing it to the ground and lifting her skirt so she could stomp the fire out. Then she tore off her skirt. She quickly examined the boy. His skin was reddened but did not appear badly burned. She wrapped the boy in the material she held.

Seldrake, his muscles straining beneath his sweat-dampened shirt like a gorgeous steed, pulled the cart, with the child and her upon it, away from the fiery houses. In a minute, he released the cart and reached up. "This area is lost. Give me the boy."

Larryn handed him the child and got down, aware that her hands hurt but concerned that she had nothing to help the crying child's pain. His aproned mother ran beside them as they kept just ahead of the fire, running down the narrow street. "Me boy! Is he all right? Willy?"

"He'll be fine," Larryn gasped, nearly out of breath, hating the smell of the fire around them. She stopped, but Seldrake's strong arm thrown about her shoulder propelled her along.

He had chosen a good way to proceed, for soon they were in an area not yet burning. He nodded toward one of the houses. "Wait here." He placed the boy Willy gently on the ground beside his mother.

He'd apparently another reason to choose this direction. Larryn noticed the red cross painted on the door, the prayer scrawled beside it, LORD HAVE MERCY UPON US! A house of plague—the house they had planned to visit?

Using his shoulder, Seldrake broke down the door. Only then did Larryn hear the sounds of weeping inside. In moments, he emerged with two more children in his arms. A third, older girl was at his side, her eyes huge from fear and reddened.

"All right," he said.

"Their parents?" Larryn mouthed.

He shook his head. Larryn tried not to think about the pain in her hands as she took one of the children from him.

This time, they joined the band of people fleeing from the fire. And Larryn had seldom been as glad to see anyone or anything as when they found Seldrake's coachman in the second location they looked.

The coach was filled on the trip back to Seldrake House. Favoring her sore, but not badly burned, hands, Larryn cuddled the two children rescued from the house of plague on her lap. Other children, faces dark with soot, eyes closed in fatigue, sat throughout the coach, wedged all about Seldrake, who also held several on his lap.

Most were children who had become separated from their parents in the melee. The coachman, knowing Seldrake's proclivity for helping all youngsters, no matter what their stations, had gathered together lost and crying little ones, promising that his master would find their parents.

Willy, whom they had rescued from the fire, had gone with his mother in a different direction. Larryn had given the mother the best instructions she could on how to treat the boy's burns.

Exhausted, Larryn nevertheless sang one song after another in an attempt to soothe small, frayed nerves, to prevent any more crying. Her repertoire of lullabies was almost nil. Though she could carry a tune, she knew the limits of her own singing voice and soon tired of "Rock-a-Bye, Baby." She sang "Somewhere Over the Rainbow," "When You Wish Upon a Star," and everything else she could recall that she thought would appeal to kids. Then she tried what she could of her favorite musical: *Phantom of the Opera*—and got some rather odd looks from Seldrake, who otherwise appeared nearly lulled to sleep by the tossing of the carriage combined with his own fatigue.

Soon, Larryn believed herself to be the only one awake. She took the opportunity to study the dozing Seldrake, in the dim light of early dawn. The waves of his light-colored hair were matted and filthy. He had removed his coat, and his cream shirt was stained and its full sleeves were torn, as were his stockings beneath his singed britches. He had a scratch at the side of his right eye, and a shadow of whiskers had begun to appear on his otherwise smooth cheeks. And he had never looked more handsome.

A smudge of dirt darkened one side of his mouth, and Larryn had an urge to wipe it away with her thumb.

She didn't, though. It would have disturbed the children on her lap.

And she certainly didn't want to awaken Seldrake. . . .

His eyes popped open and regarded her with gentle

amusement. "Is all well, Lady Larryn?" He kept his voice low.

" 'Tis all well now, Your Grace," she whispered in a slightly mocking tone.

"No more great fires in London's history that you recall? Any other matter of note of which I should become aware?"

She shook her head. "If I remember anything else, I'll tell you, Thomas."

His mouth curved in a tired grin. "I am pleased when you call me by name, Larryn."

"And I'm pleased when you do the same." She nestled back in the seat, feeling her own eyes droop shut. She wished she were able to lay her head on one of his broad shoulders. The last thing she recalled seeing before dropping off to sleep was Thomas Northby's smile.

Later that morning, after they deposited the children with Clydia and other servants to be cleaned up and put to bed, Seldrake came to Larryn's room. She had half expected him to.

She was hoping he would.

She had already bathed and donned a muslin gown. She hadn't yet slept but had gotten her second wind.

"What now?" she asked, backing away from the door after letting him in.

He, too, had changed and bathed. His scent was fresh, overlain with castile soap. He must have felt invigorated, for his brilliant blue eyes sparkled as though he faced the new day after a good night's sleep.

"I will have the word put out that we have several lost children here seeking their parents. If no one comes forward, we shall render a full search—and pray that these children have surviving family. At the same time, we have young plague survivors ready to be united with any remaining relations. We can be open in our search and claim that we came into possession of all of them in the fire."

"You're quite a hero, Thomas." Larryn smiled at the tall, brave man. He had closed her chamber door behind him and remained standing near it as she leaned against the edge of her canopied bed. He wore another loose shirt, and with the scratch on his face and his clean, damp hair cascading down his shoulders, he appeared like an elegant pirate.

"Ah, but I am not the only hero of this day, my love."

Larryn's heart skipped a beat. Had she heard correctly? His *love?*

He crossed the room. "How are your poor hands?" he asked, lifting them to his lips and kissing one, then the other.

"Just a little sore," she said, trembling. "I soaked them in cool water. I might try a little of your chalk ointment later, but they're fine. Really."

He held her close for a few moments. She nuzzled her face against the roughness of his shirt, feeling the hard planes of his muscular chest beneath the cloth against her cheek. The twining of his legs around hers made her shudder with sudden desire, and she became aware of the hard shaft straining against her stomach.

"Thomas," she whispered but could say no more. His mouth plunged down upon hers in a consuming kiss that made moist, yearning passion steam within her.

He moved her gently backward. In moments, she was stretched out on the bed. She did not recall his undressing her, but she was bared to his sensual exploration. His eyes devouring her only stoked her fever further, and she reached out to stroke the straining muscles of his arms that held him above her, the leanness of his buttocks, the strength of his thighs.

"What about the servants?" she managed to whisper. "And Adele?"

"I left word that you are not to be disturbed, that you may sleep away the day should you desire."

"Oh, I desire, all right," she said, trying to smile as her breathing grew more ragged.

Unable to tease him or herself any further, she reached down to take his erection into her hand. With a groan, he rolled her onto her back and entered her.

Larryn felt as though she were once more caught in the Great Fire of London, and only Seldrake's hard, rhythmic coursing within her could quench her flames. She wanted no softness, no courting, only this hard, impassioned joining followed by a welcome release that swept inexorably away all the tensions of the night.

Later, Larryn lay with her head against Seldrake's shoulder, her fingers exploring the wiry mat of hair on his chest. He was warm, and she reveled in the touch of his skin against hers. His scent was all masculine, and she inhaled it as though it intoxicated her.

"You are mine, Larryn," he whispered against her.

Smiling, she nodded. She wanted nothing more.

She would not worry about what it meant to be his. For this moment, she would simply stay here with him, loving him. As long as she could.

As long—

She froze, recalling what had precipitated her coming to this time, meeting Thomas Northby, her beloved duke. She pulled back to look at him.

Was this the right moment to tell him the rest?

She didn't know how much longer they had. She had to try.

His brilliant blue eyes that helped her to read his every mood were half closed in his spent passion. One opened beneath a raised brow. "Is all well, my love?"

She shook her head and sat up straight. "No, Thomas, I need to tell you something."

"Ah, then, you did recall another minor incident from the past like the destruction of London. Is it England, perhaps? Will she disappear in a cataclysm as did the legendary Atlantis?"

"It's no joking matter." Larryn was hardly aware of her own nakedness as she stood and regarded the man who had captured her heart. He, too, remained bare. She drank in the sight of every hard muscle of his upper body, the flatness of his stomach, the shape of his strong legs. He was the most handsome man she had ever seen. He was so very much alive.

For now . . .

"Thomas, what brought me here wasn't just that mist on the roof. Before that, I saw you, and—"

"And you became enamored of my portrait. You described it to me, you know—hanging in my outer chamber. You viewed me and wished to come." She reveled in the lustiness of his smile as his eyes blatantly and sensually roved over her body.

For a moment, she considered jumping back into bed with him and forgetting what she had to say.

But she couldn't.

She folded her arms over her chest, though that gesture gave her little shelter from his delightfully probing eyes. "I'm serious, Thomas. I didn't want to come here, not really. But it was partly curiosity, partly because I owed Chloe and she had set me up to see you, and—"

"Ah, yes, my distant descendant, Lady Chloe. And exactly how did she arrange for you to see me, if it was not simply my portrait that attracted you?"

Larryn closed her eyes for a moment. His prior arrogance had driven her crazy. She liked the way he teased her now—but not at this moment. She spoke as gently as she could. "Chloe had seen you every year on a particular date. She had found the miniature portrait you had made of me and knew I was destined to come here. She didn't give me much choice. Augie's collar, your sapphire ring, and your family medical journals were with the portrait, too, so I knew about them all."

Thomas's strong brow furrowed, and he sat up, leaning against the carved headboard. "I do not understand any of this. Most especially . . . how did Lady Chloe see me each year?"

She had captured his attention at last. She sat on the edge of the bed, taking his large, strong hand in hers. "This isn't easy to tell you, Thomas, but Chloe did a lot of research into her family's history. *Your* family's history. She started her research because . . . because she saw your ghost on the same date every year, starting in her childhood."

Seldrake growled his disbelief. Larryn felt his grip loosen, and he tried to draw away.

She didn't let go. Neither did she look into his face as she continued. "Her findings indicated that the reason you came back as a ghost was that you left unfinished business here. Thomas—" Her voice broke, but she made herself continue. "Thomas, she invited me to Seldrake House in our time so I could see your ghost. And I *did* see you. You begged me for help. Somehow, you recognized me. I think I'm here because I was fated to come to help you, to keep you from whatever disturbed you so on the roof, so you can rest—" She could say no more, for she began to cry.

"When," Seldrake said stonily, "did Chloe determine that I am to die?"

"Too soon," Larryn gasped through her tears. "I don't know when, but much too soon."

Chapter 21

SELDRAKE HAD NO intention of considering Larryn's absurd claims. Awhile after she had fallen asleep, and without so much as another look at her—a difficult challenge, he admitted to himself, for he could have spent hours, days, observing the lovely flesh of Larryn in her state of complete undress—he slipped on his clothing and strode from her chamber.

He had appeared to his descendant, and to Larryn, as a needful spirit? Preposterous!

He had wished to care for no woman again, after the pain of losing Charmian. And to care for a woman whose mind was as bedeviled as any inhabitant of Bedlam . . . he could not permit such a thing of himself.

There was, however, the fact that her other fantastical claims had apparently been real. . . .

Before he could consider such a dilemma further, the dogs barked below, a harbinger of callers at Seldrake House. Seldrake tarried at the top of the stairway while Ned responded to a pounding at the door.

How had the caller gotten through the outer gate?

Ned's direction was always to insist that a visitor wait

outside while he informed the duke of the caller's identity. Yet as Seldrake watched, the front door was pulled quickly aside by whomever stood outside. In barged men in the red, flaring uniforms of the king's guards.

They were led by the king's lord-in-waiting, Lord Hubert Browne.

"Greetings, Lord Browne." As he descended the stairs, Seldrake kept his voice civil but inserted the appropriate touch of outrage. "What brings you to my home unannounced, and without leave to enter?"

"The king's business." Browne's tone was curt. He was clad in a coat of brilliant blue and wide britches and the finest lace shrouded his throat. His wig was stylishly arrayed about his shoulders. "In the havoc created by the fire, the duke of Apsley, one of the king's favorites, has been abducted."

"The *duke* of Apsley, is it?" Seldrake was surprised. It was not so long ago that the lovely and skilled Larryn had aided him in tending the boy in his illness, and Seldrake had gotten no wind of his elevation then. "I had not heard that the lad was granted such a title."

"He was but recently."

"Before we discuss your presence here further, pray tell me first: What is the news of the fire? Is it conquered?"

"All but. His Majesty the king and the duke of York fought it most valiantly yesterday, during its third day of raging. Now, though embers still flare here and there, it is mostly spent."

"Good." Seldrake motioned for Browne to follow him. "Mayhap you will leave your retinue here while I offer you refreshment and we discuss your reason for venturing to my home."

Browne nodded to the half score of men who stood erect in Seldrake's hallway, lances upright in their hands. They lined up against the wall.

This did not bode well, Seldrake thought with concern. Would that he could warn Adele to disappear for the moment. And Larryn. Most especially Larryn. Seldrake himself was broad-minded, had even begun to believe in some of her absurd tales.

Except for this latest, that he would become a specter. . . .

He waved his hand at his side as though to shove away such thoughts. He did not dare allow himself such distraction now, when danger faced him in the guise of Browne and his waiting soldiers. Nor would he dare permit Larryn to voice any of her strange ideas, for such would imperil her as well.

Had Browne brought other guardsmen, too, who waited outside? The man, despite his weak chin and obsequious ways with His Majesty, was no fool.

"Bring us wine and sustenance," Seldrake ordered Ned. He threw a look to his servant that he hoped the man would comprehend: *Be wary.*

Ned had been with Seldrake, and his father before him, for many years. He was protective of the family. And he was no fool. He would warn the others.

In the study, Seldrake motioned Browne to a chair. "Take your ease," he said, seating himself in a brocaded settee. He glanced toward his desk. He had a ledger within it in which he had kept names of the identified children he had rescued from plague, in order to better determine the whereabouts of their families. Browne would not know that. He would not know of the children, either. He had come about Apsley—had he not?

"So, tell me about the new young duke. Why does His Majesty believe the boy was abducted?"

"The court has moved to Whitehall. Apsley was there when the fire began. He is not there now. His mother, Lady Anne, is beside herself. There was no reason for her son to have gone anywhere. No one has seen him. No one has any news of him."

"Then what brings you here?"

"Rumors." Browne's eyes were small and cunning, and they appeared amused as they bored into Seldrake's. Did he know of the duke's surreptitious activities, or did he merely suspect, as Larryn had described?

Seldrake had little difficulty producing an amused expression of his own. "Ah, yes, there are always rumors, are there not? What are the ones of which you speak? Has someone said that they espied me in the thick of the fire yesterday with a youngster or two in my arms? If so, that person was most alert. I went to town upon news of the fire and did what I could to rescue children separated from their families." Seldrake had learned that, whenever possible, adhering to the truth was most effective.

"Then that explains what all the other children have been doing here for the past months? You foretold the fire and were planning to save them?"

The man was toying with him, yet Seldrake maintained his composure. "What other children?"

"You need not dissemble with me, Your Grace. His Majesty has given me leave to use my men to search your home. Should I locate children taken from houses of plague, I am to arrest you. And should I find the duke of Apsley here as well—I should not like to be in your position then, m'lord." He bowed his head most mockingly, and Seldrake felt fear shudder through him. Not for himself, but because, should he be found out, so would the others. Wyford, with whom he was furious because of Adele, but the man had been his friend. Dear Adele, who only wished to aid children out of kindness.

And Larryn, a healer, a doctor, mayhap even a woman from another time . . . whatever she was, she was in great peril here from those who would not be as tolerant as he. . . . A specter indeed!

"My position is secure," Seldrake said coldly. "Search if you must. The only children you will find are those rescued from the fire." He prayed that this was so, that he could maintain the facade that all the young ones present had arrived last night.

"Show me to them," Browne demanded.

But just then, the study door opened. It was not Ned or one of the other servants expected by Seldrake, but Larryn. She was dressed in a comely costume of green silk, and she held a filled tray in her hands. Both dogs followed at her heels, apparently hoping for her to drop a treat to them. But as they noticed the stranger, Browne, they instead began to sniff at his legs.

At the temporary diversion, Seldrake approached Larryn, ostensibly to take the heavy salver from her. "What are you doing here?" he muttered under his breath.

"I've come to keep an eye on you. As I've said, I'm here to help you."

But how was he to help *her?* She might even be more at risk than he if she were not silent with her heretical claims of traveling in time and witchery. And if Seldrake were as suspect as Browne indicated, he would have no means to save her. She might die as a result of their examination of him.

He might not wish to love her, but he could not stand the guilt of yet another woman he cared about dying because he failed to save her.

Mayhap, however, *he* was the one who would die. Had she not said so?

Steadfastly, he thrust aside such insidious speculation. He would not think on it now. Nor ever.

Even if it meant no longer speaking alone with Larryn.

She turned away from him as soon as he had relieved her of her tray and placed it on a table. "Lord Browne, how pleasant to see you."

He inclined his head, whilst his gaze swept her from head to toe, the ill-mannered blackguard! But Seldrake dared not challenge him now.

"Lady Larryn." Browne continued to leer, making Seldrake wish to pummel him—until one of the spaniels climbed his leg to demand his attention. Browne glanced with aspersion at the dog, and Seldrake wondered how the man tolerated the king's many pets.

"And how is His Majesty?" Larryn asked. "Has he recuperated from his efforts to put out the fire yesterday?"

Browne looked at her oddly. "You knew of his work?"

Seldrake had remained beside Larryn. He took a step

nearer her as though to reach for a glass of wine from the table. Instead, he jostled her lightly in warning. The dogs must have thought it a game, for they began to circle Larryn.

But she either did not comprehend Seldrake's intentions or chose not to. "Everyone does. Word travels fast. And we heard of the duke of York's heroism, too."

"Yes. Well . . ."

"Won't you have some wine, Lord Browne?" she asked, turning toward the tray. That gave Seldrake a moment to regard her sternly. But her gaze was most innocent—as well as obstinate. "And the cook has also put onto the tray a bit of cheese and some oysters, I believe," she continued. "Oh, yes, and some of the sugar cakes she calls 'Jumbals.' "

"Thank you, but I fear I must conclude my business." His glance toward Seldrake was chilly. Seldrake met it with an equanimity he did not feel.

"What business is that?"

"Nothing you need trouble yourself about, Lady Larryn," Seldrake interjected.

"The business of the children," Lord Browne said, regarding Larryn steadily as though Seldrake were not even in the room.

Seldrake felt his heart stop beating. Should his own activities in rescuing the young from the plague be found out, then so be it. Even if it led to his death. . . . But no other should be blamed—or punished.

Did Larryn understand?

"Oh, yes. The duke was utterly brave yesterday," she said to Browne, "the way he insisted on going to town to help those in need. And the people requiring the most help were the children. He rescued several; did you know that?"

"Yes, I know. I should like to visit with them."

Seldrake felt his hand clench into a fist that reflected his frustration. He had much he wished to warn Larryn about, and yet he dared say nothing. Not now. Not until the time that he would, if he must, confess all to save her.

"Sure," Larryn said to Browne. "I'll show you to them, if you'd like."

"Have you not some matters upon which you have promised to assist Adele?" Seldrake spoke most carefully and decisively. Larryn must certainly comprehend his intent. He wished her to leave Browne's presence.

"I can help her later," she said, her lovely smile still intact.

He had no choice but to follow as she led Browne from the study.

Larryn saw Seldrake's frustration in the set of his jaw, the way he clenched his hand. He wanted her out of the room, out of the way.

He hadn't wanted her out of his way a while earlier, in his bedroom. . . . No. She would not think about how he'd hurt her by saying nothing. By leaving her without any indication he believed in her.

Still, even if he thought she was nuts, he wanted to protect her. But just as he could not, in front of Browne, tell her what was on his mind, neither could she tell him anything.

She had already handled the problem. She hoped.

"Right this way," she told Browne. She led him past his retinue of uniformed guards, who remained at attention, and toward the back of the huge house. At the rear stairway, she said, "We have put the children in some servants' quarters for the time being; there was plenty of room there."

She could see by the tightness on Seldrake's face that he forced himself not to display any of the surprise he felt. His eyes widened nevertheless when, after they and the dogs reached the small chambers at the back of the third floor, the children from the fire were there. Not the ones rescued from the house of plague on the previous day, though; they were in the usual quarantine in one of the banquet houses.

Five children were laughing and chasing one another

around the room. They squealed with delight as the dogs joined their play.

As Browne sat on the corner of one of the beds and began to question the children, Larryn met Seldrake's quizzical gaze. She allowed herself only the smallest hint of a smile; from an upstairs window she had seen Browne arrive and had taken Adele aside with Ned to issue instructions to be followed immediately.

In a short while, Browne looked up at them. "These children are most fortunate that you were able to assist them," he said. He didn't sound particularly pleased, and once more Larryn stifled a grin. She'd done it! She had helped Seldrake.

Perhaps dealing with these kids had been his unfinished business.

She was a little less eager now, though, to complete whatever her task here was supposed to be. What if it resulted in her being sent back to her time—and never seeing Thomas again?

Maybe it would be best. . . .

But her smugness had come too soon. "And now," Browne said, "I wish to visit with the other children—at least those who are now in no danger of the plague." His porcine eyes danced with malicious pleasure.

Larryn stood absolutely still. Maybe she was in over her head after all.

"There are no other children, Browne." Seldrake spoke firmly, glaring stonily at the courtier as though daring him to call him a liar.

"Oh, I believe there are." Browne turned so quickly that his blue coat bulged out even more around him. "I shall have a look around."

Larryn's heartbeat grew fast and erratic. She had told Adele to make sure the other children were as well hidden as possible in the two cottages, and that they were sworn to utter silence. But how silent could someone convince small kids to be?

Browne had ordered the guards to continue to search the

main house. He himself insisted on looking into the other buildings. Larryn went with him, chattering as amicably as she could about how afraid she had been of the fire, how brave the duke had been—hoping that she did a reasonable job of emulating the mindless gabbling that women in this era did—or at least that men of this era expected of them.

Behind followed the silent Seldrake. Caddie and Augie must have thought this was all part of a game, for the little spaniels yapped at the men's heels and dashed through the yard.

Browne began with the stable. He was apparently soon satisfied he would find nothing there, for he turned toward the banquet house where the children who had already passed through quarantine were held.

Please let everything be all right, Larryn prayed internally. She glanced at Seldrake, who had remained impassive. She gnawed at her bottom lip; had she instructed the servants correctly? Thomas must not be found out by this man. She wouldn't let him be punished for his kindness and bravery. She didn't know how, but she would think of something.

They all passed into the outer chamber of the cottage. Larryn held her breath, listening. Not a peep came from behind the tapestry against the wall. The dogs cooperated; they found an interesting spot near the door and sniffed at it, rather than attempting to get into the area where the children waited.

"Shall we continue?" Larryn asked after a minute. "There's a garden shed you might want to investigate, and another cottage." She hated to mention the other cottage, but by doing so, she hoped to avert Browne's interest in it.

And then . . . then the unthinkable happened. Larryn heard a muffled giggle.

She coughed loudly, hoping Browne would think the noise had come from her. But the ruse did not work. Instead, he glanced in the direction from which the noise had come—toward the tapestry that covered the cottage's wall.

Seldrake again met Larryn's eye. She knew he was warn-

ing her to back off, play dumb, anything to keep out of
this. But he surely knew her better than that.

As she'd feared, Browne swept back the tapestry, revealing the hidden door. After an icy glare at Seldrake, he
turned the knob and walked in.

Adele stood in the room surrounded by children, who
huddled around her. Her blue eyes were wide and frightened.

Seldrake stepped forward, planting himself decisively in
front of Browne.

Larryn had never been more impressed with his courage—nor more afraid for him. Shaking, she looked around
for a weapon. She was a doctor, pledged to save life, but
if she had to take a life to save Seldrake and his sister . . .

"You see that Apsley is not here," Seldrake told Browne.
"You must leave now."

"And who are these children? Other fire victims—or
might they be orphans of the plague?"

To Larryn's surprise, one of the children ran from the
group. "Lord Browne!" he shouted, then clasped the courtier about the legs.

Browne stooped long enough to sweep the boy into his
arms. "Ah, Crofton," he murmured. "I have located you.
You are well?"

"Yes, Lord Browne, but Cousin Bevin got the measles."
He snuggled against Browne's chest.

The courtier's weak chin strengthened as he managed a
half-smile toward Seldrake over the child's head. "I had
heard many rumors, Duke, as I had said. Your discretion
has been inadequate. As a result, I insisted on being the
one to come to find you out. You see, Crofton is very dear
to me. His mother . . . she was slain by the plague. She was
my mistress. I put together all the information I had been
able to learn about the children you helped, then sent a
man—Warflem—to secure your assistance. He was uncertain but believed you had rescued the lad and his cousins,
who resided in the household. I remained most concerned
until I learned that the boy was not found by the searcher

of the dead who emptied her house." He put the boy down, then approached Seldrake. Larryn drew closer, too. Browne whispered, "The boy is my son. I thank you for saving him. If you will continue to care for him until I can make further arrangements for him, I will be even more indebted to you." He raised his weak chin and drew in a long breath. "Our dispute regarding Charmian shall be forevermore behind us."

"I will most assuredly care for the child, Lord Browne." Larryn heard the relief in Seldrake's voice, though it remained stiff and formal. "And I shall be pleased for the truce between us."

"Now," Browne said, "I shall return to the guards and tell them that our trip here has been in vain, that the rumors are untrue, for unless they found Apsley or any plague victims, there are none at Seldrake House."

A short while later, Larryn stood with Adele and Seldrake as they watched the mounted guardsmen flanking Browne's coach as they exited through the iron gates.

As they disappeared at the curve in the road, Seldrake turned toward Adele, his broad shoulders sagging just a little in relief. "My thanks, sister, for your efforts at secreting our young guests."

"Do not thank me, Thomas." Adele shook her head. "I was unnerved by Browne's intrusion. Larryn instructed me what to do." She looked fondly toward Larryn, who smiled.

"I shall thank Larryn as well." Seldrake's voice was soft, and he turned toward her.

Larryn's heart skipped a beat. She wanted to throw herself in his arms in relief; he'd come out of this latest crisis unscathed.

But his voice was cool as he said, "I am most appreciative of your help, Larryn. Thank you, from the bottom of my heart." His heart. Why didn't he sound as though he had one? They had made love before. Larryn had allowed herself to love him, but he was clearly maintaining his distance from her.

"Is everything all right?" she managed.

"Of course. But I must insist that, in the future, if I indicate to you that you are to leave the room, or to feign ignorance of any matter, then you shall do so."

Larryn felt her spine grow rigid. So that was it. His need to be in charge overshadowed any feelings he might have for her. "I don't feign ignorance of anything, if I don't want to." She realized how childish she must sound, but it didn't matter. Surely by now he realized she would not agree to be subservient to him.

"Even if it saves your life? I would not have it on my conscience that you were hurt on my account."

His conscience. It wasn't as though he would really care if she were hurt.

"My life is my responsibility," she said slowly and carefully. "I can risk it, if I so choose."

She recognized his angry, arrogant look, though she hadn't seen it now for weeks. "So be it," he growled. "Then it seems I must consider my own responsibilities, to myself and to this household. I do not suppose you wish to either explain or recant the strange claims you made before Browne arrived, do you? All of them."

For the first time since Browne had appeared, Larryn felt all of the fight drain out of her. She had thought Seldrake was at least accepting that she was from another time. But after their close call, throwing his death and appearance as a ghost into the mix—it had once again fired up his incredulity.

She couldn't blame him; it was an incredible story. But what could she do?

For it was true. And if by warning him, she had lost him, then she had never had him in the first place.

Chapter 22

ON WEDNESDAY AND Thursday that week, Larryn spent most of her time with the children, both fire and plague survivors. There were about a dozen. Despite the time in which they lived, they were no different from kids of Larryn's time in their energy and curiosity.

Ignoring the slight stinging of her burned hands, she played with the children. She reassured them. She checked them over. Everyone appeared healthy.

All but the ones just removed from a house of plague were ready to be returned to relatives. The family at Seldrake House was eager to find a place for them in case Browne changed his mind and betrayed them. The fewer children remaining, the less evidence of the household's illicit pursuits.

Larryn gathered information from the kids about aunts, uncles, cousins, grandparents—anyone who, if still alive, might take them in. Adele and Seldrake did the same. So did Wyford, who was invited by Seldrake so long as he only helped to tend to the children. He stayed far from Adele, but Larryn saw the longing in the couple's eyes as they tried hard not to look at one another.

Damn Seldrake! she thought. He continuously made it clear he would keep Adele away from the man she loved.

On top of that, he had turned his back on Larryn for having told the truth; however absurd it might seem to him, he would become a ghost. It had something to do with the roof of Seldrake House, so the safest course was for him to avoid going up there again. Even if he ignored everything else she said, he had, at least, to heed that.

Since the moment she had told him what she knew of his fate, he had assiduously ignored her except to speak with her on the most surface level. He pretended that their wonderful lovemaking had never occurred. He made it obvious he still resented Larryn's having a mind of her own. And he spent a lot of time away from Seldrake House.

Adele had dropped broad hints that he was visiting Bess Mainwaring.

Larryn vowed not to think about him. He was more wrapped up in his mistress now than at any time since Larryn had arrived. She still despised men who played fast and loose with multiple women's hearts—and he certainly had toyed with hers.

But the more determined she was to forget about him, the more his hard-muscled body, his bravery in the face of a multitude of dangers, his frustratingly macho personality, insinuated their way into her thoughts.

Larryn's hands healed quickly. Early Friday morning, she ventured with Seldrake and Adele in the carriage to what was left of London. There, among the sadly burned-out buildings and even more sorrowful populace, they went from door to door in the neighborhoods the children had come from, trying to locate relatives. They wore simple, peasantlike clothing, to encourage people to speak with them.

"This task was difficult enough when we had only the plague to contend with," Adele grumbled in the afternoon as they picked their way through the homeless citizens camped about the swamps at Moorfields. It was a large, level area outside London's northern wall. Several people had suggested that they come here to seek some of the fire's survivors.

"Oh, but you won't have the plague to contend with now," Larryn said distractedly. The place reeked of fire and dampness and too many unwashed bodies. Still, she thought it smelled as much of survival. The people here, surrounded by what was left of their possessions, remained alive.

She noticed Seldrake staring at her. He whispered sarcastically so only she could hear, "Did you recall some bit of history that makes you assert this?"

"Yes," she whispered back. "The fire burned the worst rat-infested areas so there wasn't much plague after the Great Fire." She pretended to ignore his glower, but it hurt. Surely, after all this, he had reason to believe she wasn't making things up.

And if so, he would listen to her. Maybe she could, after all, help him. Though why she wanted to now . . .

Adele may have missed the words of the exchange, but she stared at them in concern. "Is all well?"

Larryn squared her shoulders. She wouldn't let either of them believe that she cared what Thomas Northby thought of her. "Isn't this place amazing?" she marveled, looking around. She meant it. The crowds were vast. People clad in the dressiest of court garb mingled with the coarsely dressed common folk. Cheap possessions were mingled with the costliest of household goods, all snatched from the grasping fingers of the fire.

On their arrival at Moorfields, they heard accounts of the king's proclamations the previous day at that very place. He had reassured the populace that the fire had been an act of God and not a plot by the country's fiendish French or Dutch enemies. He had even sent food.

And he, too, had seemed to be seeking the crowd for someone. Had he thought he might spot Apsley there?

Seldrake and his group were fortunate enough to find a few of the people they sought. And Larryn made sure that Adele always remained a buffer between the duke and herself.

By Monday, they had, amazingly, located surviving relatives of all but a few of the children. Larryn found, in the fields and in the few unburned neighborhoods, that she had a talent for interviewing people, then using the information she gleaned to track down those whom they sought.

Maybe finding the children their homes had been Seldrake's unfinished business. She was definitely helping him, though she did not see how this task could relate to the scene on the roof.

Still, in case it did, and it led to her being sent home, she no longer cared . . . much. Her heart had already broken. Staying in this time, with a chilly Seldrake no longer involved in saving children's lives, held little appeal.

Or so she told herself.

Especially since he seemed so often, once they returned to Seldrake House, to turn right around and leave again. He no longer had any interest in joining her in bed—not when he could leap right into another woman's.

She didn't need a man like him. She didn't want him.

Then why, when they were together, did she crave nothing more than to shake the man, demand that he believe in her—and burrow tightly into his arms?

Instead, she helped find little tasks that threw Adele and Wyford together, away from Seldrake's disapproving frowns.

At least one couple around here belonged together.

They, at least, were entitled to happiness.

On the Wednesday after the Great Fire, Seldrake changed his clothes late in the day.

"D'you wish to wear this waistcoat, Y'r Grace?" Ned displayed a black woolen baize garment.

"Fine." For all that Seldrake was paying attention, Ned might have suggested a silver doublet. Seldrake held out his arms and Ned arranged the garment upon him.

Near all of the children had been placed with their relations. He had several more persons to visit tomorrow who might lead to homes for the rest.

He had heard of no new cases of plague since the fire had been vanquished. Mayhap Larryn, in her wild assertions, had been correct—about that, at least. In any event, he dared rescue no more children, at least for now.

Besides, he had much on his mind.

"I shall want my coach in about half an hour, Ned," Seldrake told his manservant, who bowed his head in acknowledgment then left the bedchamber.

He had promised to go to Bess's this evening. He had been seeing much of her in this last week—she and young Terence, who might, at this rate, be the last of the Northbys, albeit from the wrong side of the blanket. Mayhap his paternity would need to be acknowledged.

For Adele was becoming as obstinate as Larryn. She insisted she would marry Wyford. If Seldrake failed to give his consent to that union, then Adele had claimed she would not wed at all.

He could force her. He had told her he would. But he was loath to take such harsh measures with his sister—even though, if he did not, she might not procreate at all.

Seldrake had cast far from him the idea of wedding Larryn. He had not demanded of her further explanation of her fantastical claims of traveling through time—or meeting his specter.

He had determined not to hear, nor even to think on it. It was far too incredible. And what sane man wished to hear tales of the brevity of his own existence?

Larryn had not seemed doleful at the lack of his attentions this past week. In fact, she had seemed near joyous in her conversations with all but him—Adele, Wyford, the children, those who might assist in finding the children's homes. . . .

'Twas a good thing, he told himself. She did what was needed. She did as he bade her—though he did not ask anything he believed she would refuse to do.

Such as to speak with him in privacy. To allow her to explain her most absurd ravings, that he appeared to her as a specter. To allow him to take her into his arms. . . .

Bess and he had been alone together much, however. Lady Mainwaring had made many demands. Those of little consequence, he had attempted to satisfy.

But still, she wanted more, for herself and for young Terence.

He would hear her latest demands, and then he would see.

All of a sudden, he heard the dogs begin to clamor downstairs. He froze. Had they another unannounced visitor? Had Browne returned, this time prepared to arrest him?

The evidence of his lawbreaking had all but disappeared with the placement of the children with their relations.

Still . . . He hurried from his chamber.

Larryn felt sure that Seldrake would want her to hide in her room while he figured out why the dogs were barking.

That was exactly why she lifted her long yellow skirts and hurried down the main stairway.

But Caddie and Augie weren't there. Only Ned was, holding the front door open. When he came inside, he appeared puzzled.

"Who was there?" Larryn asked.

He shrugged. "No one, m'lady, best as I could tell."

"Ned? Have we visitors?" The deep, masculine voice from the staircase reverberated through Larryn. She had been avoiding Seldrake as much as possible these last few days.

If rescuing the children from plague or fire, or finding their relations, was what she had needed to help with—well, that might mean that she was doomed to stay here in the seventeenth century for the rest of her own days, for she was still here.

But she was damned if she was going to remain under the frowning disapproval of the man she had come here to help.

The man that, darn her foolish heart, she had come to love.

Seldrake was dressed much more formally this evening.

He obviously intended to go out. To see Lady Mainwaring again?

It didn't matter to her. She wouldn't let it.

"The dogs are someplace else in the house," she told the duke. "We haven't figured out why they're barking."

His strong brows knit into a frown of concern. Still, he said offhandedly, "Mayhap they have spotted a blackbird in the courtyard."

"Mayhap." Larryn allowed herself to mock him, just a little. She knew he tried to make light of the matter to keep her from being concerned. But *he* was obviously concerned. So was she. Cavaliers were too small to be great attack dogs, but as watchdogs, they did just fine. Sure, they barked boisterously at blackbirds. They also barked at people they didn't know. And sometimes those they did know.

"Would you care to accompany me to the courtyard?" She extended her arm to invite him to take it.

Bad mistake. He was a gentleman. He could hardly refuse. But the contact as he held her arm nearly made her knees turn to talc.

Once again she had the traitorous urge to hug him. To plead with him to take her to bed once more.

To pretend, if only for another too-short while, that he cared for her.

She snorted aloud, and he glanced down at her. His imperious chin was raised. Of course.

"Would you care to let me in on the jest, Larryn?"

She shrugged. "I'm wondering what kind of jest the dogs are pulling on *us*."

The dogs were in the courtyard. So were a bunch of servants. Familiar servants. The dogs were no longer barking.

But they were pacing back and forth as though trying to impart a message.

Larryn figured it out a short while later when she turned back toward the house and spotted Bess Mainwaring in the doorway.

How had she gotten inside?

Larryn's heart plunged as Seldrake hurried from her side in the courtyard to the lovely Bess's. "What brings you here?" he asked as he reached her. "I had intended to visit you forthwith."

"I couldn't wait any longer, Thomas." She looked up at him with flirtation in her large, beautiful eyes, and Larryn felt like throwing up.

With dignity, she approached them. "It's pleasant to see you again, Lady Mainwaring," she lied.

"Lady Larryn." Bess's cool acknowledgment and brief glance made it clear she hardly thought Larryn a notch above servant level.

"And how are things at court?" Larryn persisted. "I heard from the duke that the king had some of his own possessions moved from Whitehall to Hampton Court during the fire, to preserve them. Have you been there lately? How is your son?"

"Terence is well now." A small smile that Larryn didn't understand curved her full lips. "He will soon be even better." She looked at Seldrake, and her smile bloomed into brilliance. "You will see to it of course, Thomas."

"You know I will do what I can." He looked so fondly toward her that Larryn wanted to run right up to her room. Better yet, to the roof, to see if she could coax back that damned mist that had brought her here.

The mist. The roof. Seldrake appearing as a ghost in the future.

Why were shivers suddenly creeping up Larryn's back? She had the feeling that somehow, she would know soon what had brought her here. So much had happened . . . but what was to come?

Would she realize her purpose in time to help Seldrake?

But she heard the dogs bark again from somewhere deep inside the house. She hadn't noticed when they had left the courtyard. They didn't know Bess Mainwaring well. Why weren't they here, barking at her?

"I have made it both easy for you and difficult for you,

Thomas." The woman was speaking in riddles. What the heck was she talking about?

"I do not follow." Obviously Thomas didn't understand her, either.

But before she had a chance to explain, a clatter of horses' hoofs sounded on the hardened dirt road outside the ironwork gate. "Open!" shouted a demanding voice.

A white horse beyond the gate nearly reared up. Its rider wore a long red coat and huge plumed hat.

"It is Lord Browne," Seldrake said.

Larryn's blood froze. Was he about to arrest them?

"I must see the duke," Browne bellowed. "It is on a matter of the utmost importance."

Larryn looked at Seldrake. He glanced back at her, as though seeking her concurrence.

Seldrake sought her opinion? Hallelujah!

But what now? Did they dare trust the man?

Decisively, though wondering if she did the right thing, Larryn nodded.

At Seldrake's command, the servants opened the gate. Browne's horse galloped into the courtyard, then stopped. The lord-in-waiting slid from his mount's back.

"I must see you in confidence," he told Seldrake.

Larryn was not about to let that go unchallenged. Wondering where Lady Mainwaring had gone, Larryn followed as the two men hurried into the house. She slid into the parlor before Seldrake could close the door. "I want to know what's going on," she demanded.

For a moment, Seldrake looked his old, imperious self. But then Browne said, "I cannot tarry here. I must tell you what I will, and then leave forthwith, for I am here without the knowledge of the king. Shall I speak now?"

His eyes on Larryn, Seldrake nodded. Once more he was trusting her.

She squashed down any wriggle of pleasure. She dared not read anything into Seldrake's small gesture.

"His Majesty," Browne continued, pacing the study in

agitation, "has been informed that you did, indeed, abduct young Apsley, Seldrake."

"What! But—"

"Allow me to finish, man. The source is Lady Mainwaring. On the morrow, a retinue of the king's men shall follow me here. If the boy is found, you shall be arrested."

"But why would Bess say such a thing? He is not here." Seldrake slammed the flat of his hand upon a table, knocking over a candelabrum, whose candles, fortunately, were unlit. "You must so inform His Majesty. I have not seen the lad since last we aided him at Hampton Court." He turned to Larryn. "Have you seen him, Larryn? Tell Lord Browne—is Apsley here?"

"No," Larryn said firmly. "I haven't seen him since I was at Hampton Court the last time, either."

But why did her pulse race and burn as though someone had lit a match beneath her skin? Something was definitely wrong. Lady Mainwaring had accused Seldrake. Lady Mainwaring had appeared here, unannounced and without being let in. She had disappeared when Browne arrived.

And Browne was so serious this visit that he hadn't even made an attempt to look down her bodice.

Was Apsley here after all, thanks to Lady Bess? But why?

"Now I must depart," Browne said. "I will be with the king's guard on the morrow. We shall search the place if the boy has not been found elsewhere." He hurried to the door of the study. With his hand on the knob, he said, "You have done me a service, Seldrake—one I have attempted to repay once more. I hope to heaven that the young duke of Apsley is back with his mother before my return here." He pivoted and left.

Larryn watched his retreat. When she turned back to Seldrake, he was sitting on his leather chair behind the table. His broad shoulders were slumped in defeat. "What is happening, Larryn?" His voice was hoarse. "I had only meant to save lives, after I could not protect Charmian. But I fear I have brought doom upon my house."

"You did only what was right," Larryn said fiercely, hurrying to his side. She put her hand on his arm. "Thomas, you have to accept that you *couldn't* have saved Charmian—not here, not in this time, without the medicines to combat the plague that won't be discovered for centuries."

She expected him to glare with his old incredulous irritation. Instead, he looked up with sorrow dulling the blue of his eyes. "Would that I could see such miracles." He sighed. "I do not know why I doubted all of your tale, Larryn. You are not of my world, and I came to accept, seeing you near disappear atop my roof, that you were from another time. If you saw me as a specter, then indeed I must become one. Shall it be soon?"

"Not if I can help it. But I'm sure the roof is the answer. Something is about to happen. I don't know why, but I'm certain of it—maybe because so much seems to be happening so quickly. Browne is involved, maybe Lady Mainwaring, too." As she expected, Seldrake opened his mouth to protest, but she did not want to hear him defend his lover. She spoke again before he could utter a word. "Please, Thomas." She moved the hand that still touched his arm until she clasped his hand. It lay lifeless. She held it all the more firmly, then tugged. "Come with me."

With a quirk of his full lips, he grinned at her. "How can I resist such a pretty invitation from a beautiful woman?" He rose, and Larryn saw with relief that he allowed her to lead him from the room.

Chapter 23

"Y OU PROMISE YOU'LL stay here?"

Larryn had insisted that Seldrake follow her to his room. She had shown him to his chair behind his large, paper-strewn desk and told him to sit down. He had obeyed, though he looked none too pleased about it.

"I shall abide here for a short while," he grumbled. "That is all I can assure you."

"You've got to stay until I come back. Whatever is going to happen will play itself out tonight. Don't ask how I know, I just do." Why else would her insides be as tight as if she'd cinched all of her arteries and veins into tiny knots? Lady Mainwaring, Lord Browne, the little duke of Apsley—they all had something to do with this drama she'd glimpsed so lopsidedly from the future, but Larryn had no idea what . . . yet.

She would find out.

"What if there is peril to you?" Seldrake growled, rising to his feet. "I cannot allow—"

"I'll be fine. Really. Just wait here. Please." She stood in front of him to block his way, placing her hand against his hard chest. She felt the tautness of his muscles beneath his clothing.

He raised himself to his full height as though to defy her. He certainly was an imposing figure. His chin was raised, and his magnificent blue eyes flashed his displeasure.

Larryn couldn't help it. She reached up, grabbed him by the neck, and pulled his head down.

He resisted for only a moment. Then his lips met hers as hungrily as she could have wanted. She moaned as his tongue plunged between her lips, causing need to spark and ignite deep within her. His arms pulled her close.

Her legs weak, she gave in to sensation. But just briefly. Reluctantly, she pulled away. "I'd like to finish this later," she said. "But I'll consider it a kiss for luck." She managed a crooked smile, then said, "Wait for me here, Thomas. Please."

And then she hurried from the room.

Where should she go? To the roof, of course. She hurried to the end of the hall and pulled open a door.

It was the door through which she had followed Seldrake's ghost so long ago. His and Caddie's. Beyond was a narrow stairway. It was dark.

She hesitated just long enough to grab a candle from one of the sconces along the hallway's stone wall. And then, holding up her yellow skirts, she began to climb.

She heard an excited bark. And then another. Where were Caddie and Augie? Had they trailed after Lady Mainwaring?

She followed the sounds. They did not come from the roof, but from beyond the landing that led to the servants' quarters on the third floor.

Maybe she was wrong. Maybe whatever was going to happen would not occur tonight—not if the roof weren't involved.

She made her way down the narrow hall with its doors to the small rooms so close together. A few candles were lit in the wrought-iron sconces along the walls, their flickering glow lending an eerie cast to the stone corridor. The hallway was warm and dank.

She didn't hear the dogs, not then. "Caddie?" she called. Her voice echoed hollowly, causing chills to run up her spine. "Augie?" Her tone grew more shrill.

She heard an answering bark from a room near the corridor's end. She rapped on the wooden door.

Behind it, she heard panting and the scrabbling of little canine feet. Taking a deep breath, she thrust open the door. The dogs leapt on her for an instant, then went tearing down the hall.

She had expected to see Lady Mainwaring. Instead, there were two people in the room: Adele and the young duke of Apsley.

"He *is* here!" Larryn breathed. Glancing around to make sure she hadn't missed Lady Mainwaring hiding behind the door, she hurried into the room. "Lord . . . er, Your Grace," she said to the young boy. "Where have you been? Are you all right?"

He nodded, but his eyes were round with terror. He wore the coarse clothing of a peasant child, and it was torn.

"He's been with Bess," Adele said. "She sneaked him in earlier today. I found him here a short while ago. I haven't been able to get the whole story from him, but I gather it's something to do with her wanting the king to notice Terence instead. Is Thomas all right?"

"He's fine," Larryn replied. "But what is this about Terence?"

"He is seeking favor with His Majesty at court," Apsley said softly, "while I am merely vermin who stands in his way."

Larryn couldn't contain her outrage. "Is that what Lady Mainwaring said to you?"

The boy gave a decisive nod that shook his curls. "I do not mean to stand in the way."

"Of course not," Adele said fiercely, giving Apsley a hug. She looked over the boy's head toward Larryn. "Bess came here just a short while ago, just as I was about to take Apsley to Thomas. She claimed that Lord Browne was on his way to Seldrake House. She demanded that I remain in this chamber with Apsley for Thomas's sake, for if Lord Browne saw Apsley here he would arrest Thomas. He had proof, she insisted, that Thomas had been hiding Apsley from His Majesty. I heard the dogs clamoring outside and was terrified for Thomas. I was uncertain what to do, so even when the dogs came we remained here for now. Even though the charge would be false, I did not wish for Thomas to be arrested for abducting Apsley."

"He didn't," Apsley cried. "Lady Mainwaring took me away from my mama in the night and I have not seen her since." Tears ran down the boy's smooth cheeks.

"She's setting your brother up," Larryn said to Adele, "though I don't know why." At Adele's blank look she explained, "She's making it appear that he's to blame. I've made Thomas promise to stay in his room for now."

"He is heeding your command?" Adele seemed amazed.

"More or less. But I'd better hurry. Do you know where Bess is?"

"She mentioned something about the roof."

As if Larryn had had any doubt of it.

"Where is Thomas?" demanded Bess Mainwaring. She stood on the flat part of the roof near the white wrought-iron rail that surrounded its perimeter. Her ecru silk gown was lower on one shoulder than on the other, and the coil of hair over her shoulder seemed to have wilted. She held a single candle in a silver holder. Its flame flickered in the mild breeze.

"Inside, where he belongs." Larryn allowed herself the tiniest of triumphant smiles—just to see the lady's reaction.

It wasn't pretty. Her large, pale eyes flashed in the candlelight as though gunpowder had been ignited by her rage. "He must come to me here. I need to speak with him. You will fetch him for me."

Larryn couldn't help laughing at the woman's imperiousness. "Oh, I don't think so. I told him to stay inside, and he promised me he would."

"He made a vow to *you?*" Lady Mainwaring regarded

Larryn as though she were the slimiest of snakes in a swamp. "He need not keep it to one of your class."

That riled Larryn. "How do you know anything about my 'class'? Did you spend years in school learning to be a doctor? Have you ever helped to heal anyone in your life? I have. All you do is stand around being decorative, having men's babies without being married to them. That hardly seems like *class* to me."

Bess's eyes had widened during Larryn's tirade—until the end. And then a smugness came over her face. "Ah, that is why you make such fantastical claims of being a doctor and a healer. It is because you are jealous that I have Terence, are you not?"

Yes, thought Larryn. "Of course not," she said.

Bess took a step closer to Larryn, holding her candle up as though to study her expression. Larryn held her own up, too.

Bess was not as beautiful in the dimness. Or maybe it was her depravity that made her seem so ugly here on the roof.

"Oh, but I am certain that you are lying, 'Lady' Larryn—also that you are not a true lady. My son, on the other hand, was promised a title by His Majesty." A shadow crossed her face. "He made that trollop Anne Farswell's by-blow a duke, but he has not kept his vow to grant Terence a title."

"Apsley? Is that why you kidnapped him?"

"What is this 'kidnap'?" Bess regarded her suspiciously.

"Snatch. Abduct. Steal." Larryn took a step toward Lady Mainwaring with each word, holding her candle out like a shield. She needed to get this confrontation over with before Thomas decided he'd waited long enough. "Did you think that by making the King's own illegitimate son disappear, you could pressure His Majesty into giving your son Terence a title, too?"

"Mayhap," Bess said with a laugh. "And mayhap I wished to teach His Majesty a little humility. He needs it, do you not agree?" She did not wait for a reply but instead said, with venom in her voice, "But that was not all I did.

I intended to leave naught to chance. I wished for His Majesty to believe that Thomas abducted his by-blow Apsley, so that Thomas might be executed for treason. That way His Majesty could easily bestow the Seldrake title on Terence."

"No, you weren't leaving anything to chance," Larryn agreed with a shake of her head. "In addition to all your scheming about the king, I'm aware that you spent a lot of time with Thomas this week. Just in case your other schemes didn't work, weren't you also trying to seduce him into naming Terence his heir so his son could legitimately inherit his title?"

She had to ask that, no matter how badly it hurt. How much time had Thomas spent making love to Bess Mainwaring over the past years? Perhaps his guilt over Charmian's death had something to do with the fact he'd had a mistress even while his beloved wife was alive. Charmian had died only a year earlier. Terence was six years old. Maybe he had stopped the affair during their marriage—and maybe he hadn't.

Thomas could not have known this woman didn't care whether he lived or died, as long as she achieved what she wanted. How much time had he spent succumbing to Bess's charms this past week? Not that he owed any fidelity to Larryn.

No matter how much that hurt.

To her amazement, Bess laughed. "I see that I surmised correctly. You love Thomas, do you not?"

Did it matter if she lied or told the truth? Probably not. But Larryn had an urge to tell someone, even this creep of a woman whom Thomas cared for. Who had borne him a child.

For she could not tell Thomas. Not now.

"Yes," she told Lady Mainwaring. "I do."

"All the better, then." Her laughter shrill, Bess Mainwaring curled her elegant fingers into claws and leapt at Larryn.

•   •   •

Seldrake could not remain still.

After Larryn departed from the chamber, he paced to and fro as though drawn first to one wall and then the other.

"I made no true vow to her," he muttered. And yet, he had said he would abide in his study for a short while.

Certainly a short while had elapsed.

He heard a scratching outside the chamber. "August?" he called out. He drew open the door, and his little spaniel rushed in. "Where is your companion, Caddie?"

Augie regarded his master, then cocked his head. He barked, as though stating a response.

Despite the twisted indecision that warred within him, Thomas smiled. And then he frowned, feeling his brows knit closely together. He was the duke of Seldrake. He was never indecisive.

Without considering why, he removed Augie's collar and his own ring and placed them on his desk. "I can heed her no longer," he stated and hastened from the study.

Larryn stepped backward and to the side to get out of the way of the lunging Lady Mainwaring. She hadn't realized she was close to an edge of the roof, but she felt the un-yielding bar of the wrought-iron rail through her skirts and against the backs of her calves.

Behind Bess, a dog barked. In a moment, Caddie was at her feet, growling at her.

Bess drew in her breath as she turned toward Caddie. "Get that beast out of my way," she hissed, kicking at him.

"No!" Larryn sped forward to try to help the puppy, but Lady Mainwaring's foot made contact. Caddie yelped. "You creep!" Larryn yelled. "It's bad enough that you kid-nap babies, but to hurt defenseless animals, too—"

"Are you so defenseless?" Bess turned back toward Lar-ryn, blocking her from going to her puppy. She held her candle up, waving it in Larryn's face.

Larryn heard Caddie's whine of pain, which infuriated her further. Using her shoulder, she pushed against Bess's arm to get the candle out of the way—and felt a sharp sting on her wrist. She looked down. She was bleeding.

Bess had drawn a dagger from somewhere—a small but nasty-looking thing with a very pointed end. She was grinning as she held it out, obviously ready to use it again. She still held her candlestick in her left hand.

Fortunately, the cut on Larryn's wrist was shallow, and it bled slowly. She still held her own candle as she backed up a step, and then another. She tried to use it as a shield, as a defensive weapon, but Bess slashed the dagger toward her again, obviously unimpressed.

"I'm not defenseless," Larryn contradicted, though she knew she was losing ground on the roof. How far was she now from the railing? It wasn't high enough to keep her from going over the edge. Would it be better to be sliced further or to fall?

"Mayhap not." But Bess did not sound convinced. "In any event, you are stupid. You believe that Terence is Thomas's son?" She laughed. "He is Thomas's half brother."

"What?" Though her mind whirled, trying to devise a plan to stop this woman from burning her with the candle, to find a way to get to Caddie, Larryn stopped moving back. "What do you mean?"

"I was very . . . close at one time to Thomas's father. Terence is his son . . . although I have not told so to my dear husband Purvis. He would be most displeased, even though he is perhaps the only one of note who does not know the boy is not his own." Her grin at Larryn radiated evil pleasure. "You, of course, are not worthy of note. But it will do no harm for you to know the truth before you die. And then, I shall kill Thomas, too, so the king will at last name Terence to the Seldrake dukedom. I grow weary of waiting for my other plans to bear fruit. And then—"

A noise sounded behind her. Augie appeared, growling at Bess.

"Look out," Larryn cried. "Augie, get away. She'll hurt you."

"She will harm no one." The deep voice of Thomas Northby resounded on the roof. Relief flooded Larryn—

until she recalled the reason she had insisted that he keep
off the roof. He would die here. Bess Mainwaring was insane. She would kill Thomas. She had said so.

Larryn had to protect him. That was why she was here.

She hid her wrist at an angle to prevent Thomas from
seeing her wound. It wasn't a bad cut, but the sight of it
might cause Thomas to do something foolish. She glanced
around Bess, intending to warn him. "Thomas, she has a
knife. You promised. Get off the roof."

"Did you make a promise to this . . . this nothing, Thomas?" Bess Mainwaring had stopped moving to glance behind her. But she only was turned for a moment before she
again advanced on Larryn. "It is of no consequence," she
said. "She will die first, then you."

Larryn could see Thomas nearly at the edge of the roof,
beside the white wrought-iron railing.

He looked incredibly handsome with his aristocratic chin
raised in defiance. His hair blew in the intensifying breeze.
So did his white shirtsleeves.

His hands were outstretched.

Larryn had seen this scene before. She had viewed it as
Thomas acted it out, by himself, as a ghost.

An icy shiver tiptoed up her spine.

"Please get off the roof, Thomas." Her voice was hoarse,
and it was probably carried away as the wind grew stronger.
It blew out her candle, but Bess's body somehow shielded
her own flame.

"Allow Larryn to return inside, Bess," Thomas said. "She
has done you no harm. It is I who must be removed since
I did not assist Terence in obtaining his title. Is that not
true?"

"Both of you must die," Bess spat. "This vile wench has
defied me. She has been in my way. This time, she must
be removed."

"This time?" Larryn blurted. "You're the one who tried
to kill me before, aren't you—by running me down with
the coach and shoving me down the palace stairs."

"They were but attempts to warn you," Bess said casually. "I wished no intrusions into my plans, and you were interfering with my time with Thomas. I intended to convince him to intercede with His Majesty on Terence's behalf such that the king would grant my son his own title."

"Did you send for me to come to court?" Larryn asked, still not clear on how things had happened. "I thought it was Browne; he acted as though he expected me."

"I summoned you, then told one of the servants to inform Browne that you were coming on some errand. He had mentioned to several of us at court that he wished to speak to a member of this household, so it seemed an ideal way to lure you without having my own name associated with your appearance. But my small tricks did no good. You took no hints. Now I no longer will endure your presence." Her voice grew cunning, and she looked at Thomas. "I wish for you to suffer, however, Thomas, before I eliminate you. Mayhap you did not know, but the wench loves you. That should please you." Her stare grew cold. "This week, when I attempted to seduce you, it was strictly to encourage you to speak quickly with the king to advance my son. I would not have even considered sharing my body with the likes of you otherwise. But you refused me, you miserable son of a pig—and you had the temerity to tell me it was because you love this nobody. You must therefore die—it will accomplish my ends all the same, for *I* will convince His Majesty to name Terence your heir."

He'd told Bess he loved Larryn? Despite the peril she was in, Larryn felt a gladness fill her heart.

"You cannot kill me, Bess." Thomas was clearly making an effort to keep his tone reasonable. "I shall be expecting your attack, and shall stop it. You must give up now."

"Never!" Bess lashed at Larryn with the knife without even looking toward Thomas. Larryn was only just able to move her arm to avoid getting cut again. She heard Thomas's sharp intake of breath. "I shall find my opportunity to kill you, Thomas, never fear. You cannot be on your guard at all times."

"Then mayhap you shall kill me, Bess," he said placatingly. "Why not simply do so now instead of—"

"No!" Larryn had to stop this. This scene on the roof had to be the real reason she had come into the past. What had Thomas's unfinished business been here? Remaining alive? How could she save him?

She had to find out, and quickly.

She'd planned before to survive. Now she was doubly sure she wanted to. He loved her, too.

She took a decisive step sideways, but Bess lunged at her once more, the knife blade nearly slashing Larryn's face.

"You cannot!" Thomas shouted. He stood behind Bess. His arm whipped around her, and he grabbed her wrist so she could not use the dagger. Bess dropped it, though she still held the candlestick. Thomas continued, "I shall not let you hurt that—"

Larryn heard no more, for Bess brought the candleholder down on Thomas's arm so suddenly that he released her. Suddenly Bess's hands were upon Larryn, shoving her with a strength that only could have resulted from madness. "No!" Larryn screamed. Something was terribly wrong here. She couldn't die. She had to help Thomas.

She heard a yapping at her feet. Augie was there, sheathed in something gray, thick, and swirling, like liquid smoke. Larryn smelled something humid, yet burning. The fog. That horrible fog that had brought her here, to the past.

She fought to keep her footing as Bess made a final lunge at her, shoving at her chest. The railing was behind her legs, not high enough. She must not fall over the edge. . . . For a moment, Augie rubbed against her as though trying to save her.

She had to keep her balance—but didn't.

From the corner of her eye, she saw Caddie—the pup was all right! And then Thomas leapt at them, his hand outstretched to grab her . . . just as Bess pivoted. "No!" Larryn cried. "Thomas, look out!"

She fought to breathe as the fog engulfed her.

She heard Thomas's anguished wail, "Larryn, nooooo . . ."

It was echoed by the mournful howl of a dog—Caddie?

And Larryn screamed as she dropped into nothingness.

Chapter 24

"LARRYN? LARRYN, ARE you all right?"

The female voice seemed to reverberate from down a long, hollow cylinder. Larryn strained to figure out its source, but her eyelids were too heavy to open.

"Larryn!" Someone took her shoulders and shook her gently. Larryn managed to crack open her eyes.

She blinked groggily. It was Chloe. "Hi," she said. "It's been awhile since—Oh, my lord!" Larryn was suddenly fully awake. Her head spun, but she sat up nevertheless. "Chloe? Am I back?"

She was seated on the roof of Seldrake House. It was nighttime, but the darkness was not as complete as where she had just been. Stars did not cause the glow, for she saw none; the night sky was too light. She didn't see the moon, either. The illumination was from—what? The gaslight along the front walk, probably. And electric lights shining from the windows of the house below, and from the neighbors' down the street. Even the distant glow against the clouds from London's myriad lights.

Nor was it as silent. She heard the sound of a plane flying in the distance, the rumble of cars on a far-off highway.

"Yes, my dear," Chloe said. "You're here now. You haven't been gone long—only a couple of days—but you did disappear. Where were you? Are you all right?"

Larryn studied the woman who had been the catalyst of so much in her life. Chloe looked much as Larryn remembered her: slight; pretty notwithstanding her age; streaked pageboy hairdo. But had she had those strain lines at the corners of her eyes before?

Larryn heard a whine beside her. "Caddie?" But when she looked over, it wasn't Caddie but Augie who nuzzled her hand.

"Is that the duke's dog?" Chloe asked.

She sounded very matter-of-fact about something that was incredible. No more incredible, though, than seeing the duke's ghost, as she had done one night a year for nearly her whole life.

"Yes," Larryn whispered. "I was back in Restoration England with him. I was there for a month, not just days, though I realize there is little correlation between time there and here. . . . You don't have to believe me, but—"

But this was Chloe. "Of course I believe you; I found your portrait, remember? I'll want to hear the whole story as soon as you can tell it. But the big question is, were you able to help the duke, as he asked?"

A moan welled up in Larryn's throat. She was back in her own time. She was no longer with Thomas Northby, duke of Seldrake.

The man she loved was once again a figment of the past.

Would she see him again here as a ghost? She hadn't accomplished what she'd intended. After all the time she had spent in the Restoration era, after all her efforts, she had failed to learn what Thomas's emotional crisis and unfinished business were—until now.

"Oh, no . . ." she wailed. Her wrist hurt. She looked down. The knife wound Bess had inflicted oozed blood, and Larryn cradled it.

"How did that happen?" Chloe asked, sitting down on the roof beside Larryn. She took a clean handkerchief from her pocket and bound it gently around the wound. "Larryn, honey, I know you'll have a lot to say, but for now just tell me what's wrong." Maneuvering so as not to press Larryn's injured wrist, she took her into her fragile arms.

Larryn appreciated the support, but for a long moment she couldn't speak. She gasped, hardly able to catch her breath as her body shook with sobs. Augie climbed onto her lap and snuggled against her, and Larryn held the small dog.

Thomas's dog. Somehow, in the last heated moments of danger, something had happened—something that shouldn't have. Larryn had come back to the present, but without her Cavalier puppy. Instead, she had Augie, the spaniel from the past.

That made her cry all the harder.

And Thomas. Was he all right? Or had Bess Mainwaring made good on her threats to kill him? Might she have harmed the others, too—Adele? Maybe even poor little Apsley? The woman had been mad. She might not even have cared that she wouldn't get away with it.

What had happened to them all? For Larryn had failed them.

Chloe continued to hold her, rocking her soothingly. Larryn leaned against her, still hugging Augie.

Finally, she was able to get hold of herself. "I—I'm sorry," she gasped. "It's just that . . . it's so ironic. So sad!"

"What is?" Chloe asked.

Larryn's smile was bitter through tears that continued to roll down her cheeks. "Thomas Northby's unfinished business, the thing that involved his emotions—the very thing he needed help with to keep him from becoming a restless ghost?" She made her words into a question, and Chloe nodded her understanding. "I don't know whether he survived the night I just left. That damned crisis—it was nothing any of us could have anticipated. He distracted Lady Mainwaring—I'll explain about her later. He brought Augie onto the roof at the right time. Caddie was already there. The two dogs—I think they had something to do with my going back there. But the supreme irony: Do you know what his big emotional event, his unfinished business, was?"

Chloe shook her head slowly, so that her pageboy just skimmed her shoulders.

"It was to save *my* life." She laughed mirthlessly. "He succeeded, but now he'll never know."

The next day, Larryn arranged over the phone to extend her leave of absence from her job. She suspected, though, that when she returned to the States, she would want to get a real medical position—one in which she would help people. Maybe she would even work with the critically ill.

She would not shut herself away from humanity anymore.

That day, though, she just wanted to be by herself.

Her wrist still stung, a reminder of her ordeal on the roof—as if she needed one. But she had treated it with antiseptic, and it was healing already.

Evening finally came. "He might be there tonight," Larryn told Chloe at the dinner table. "On the roof. I'll explain then what happened, that I'm fine, and he'll be able to rest in peace."

She would never be peaceful, though—for she would live out the rest of her own days without him.

Still, the slim hope of seeing him one more time, even as a ghost, swelled her heart. Maybe—just maybe . . .

"He appeared only once a year to me," Chloe reminded her gently. "Please try to eat, Larryn. You'll need your strength, no matter what happens next."

To appease her hostess, Larryn pushed her salad around on her plate to make it appear as though she ate more than a bite—but she doubted she fooled Chloe.

"Will you tell me about what happened?" Chloe asked.

Larryn nodded. "Soon," she promised. She excused herself to go up to her room shortly afterward.

She stood in the doorway, staring at the duke's portrait.

"I miss you, Thomas," she whispered, feeling tears well in her eyes.

At midnight, she went up to the roof and stood at the top of the steps. And remembered—"Oh, my heavens, the flashlight!" She had left it in the past, along with her modern-day clothes. It wouldn't matter in the great scheme of things—would it?

What had happened to it?

As with Thomas's fate, she might never know.

Thomas. "Will he be here, Augie?" she asked the spaniel, who had come with her. He sat beside her, wagging his tail encouragingly.

After all, although Chloe had only seen Thomas's ghost once a year, Larryn had seen it on two consecutive nights—including the one on which she had been drawn back into the past.

Did she want to go there again? Yes.

But the primitive state of medicine, the smells in London's streets, the superstition of the times, and the intrigues at court . . .

They didn't matter. What did matter was that she wanted to be with Thomas—wherever and whenever that might be.

She would tell him so . . . if she could.

And she would tell him that she loved him. She had acknowledged it to Bess, but had never said the words to Thomas. Nor had he said them to her.

If nothing else, if she saw him again here, maybe they at least could rectify that terrible omission.

She waited for ten minutes. Fifteen. And then—

Augie began to bark, then howl. He ran to the edge of the roof and nearly leapt over.

Larryn dove at him and caught him. Standing on rubbery legs, she hugged the dog close. "What is it?" she demanded, her voice shaking. "Did you see something? I didn't."

After a moment, she put Augie down again—and he promptly raced once more to the roof's very edge, barking all the while.

"Cut it out!" Larryn demanded, again grabbing him. She

held him longer this time, but still she didn't see or hear anything that would explain the dog's strange actions. No mist, no ghost . . . no Thomas, or even poor little Caddie, who had also been left in the past.

Of course, a dog's senses were more acute than a human's—smell and hearing at least. Had he heard something she hadn't?

Larryn waited. And waited. And then she sighed and said sadly to the spaniel wriggling in her arms, "It's time to go back inside, Augie."

The following morning at breakfast, Larryn finally told Chloe an abbreviated version of what had happened to her in Restoration England.

"Oh, my dear," Chloe said when she had finished. "And this Bess, Lady Mainwaring, caused all the problems? There's something about her I came across in my research—I thought she was an ancestor of mine."

"She wasn't a relative to the Seldrakes alive then," Larryn said. "At least not the legitimate Seldrakes. And she was certainly a greedy witch. Little Terence was half brother to Thomas and Adele. Bess wanted him to have everything they did, and probably more." Larryn sighed. "I need to find out what happened to everyone. Can you point me toward the resources you used to track down your ancestors?"

"Of course," Chloe said kindly. Her pageboy hairstyle drooped a little this morning, as did the pleated corners of her eyes. "Larryn, I'm so sorry about . . . about everything. I got so caught up in my own quest to find you all those years that I never stopped to think about what would happen to you. I suppose I could have anticipated this—after all, there was no record of you in the past other than the portrait."

"You didn't find out what happened to Thomas in your research, either," Larryn reminded her. "You can't depend on records from back then."

"I suppose not. But I apologize nevertheless."

Larryn smiled sadly. "No need. In fact, I should thank you. Otherwise, I could never have met Thomas. I'm glad, at least, for that." She didn't wince at the contact when Chloe stood and hugged her. In fact, she hugged her back.

Larryn learned quite a bit in her research that day, thanks to Chloe's meticulous collection of research materials. They mentioned the death of Lady Bess Mainwaring at Seldrake House under mysterious circumstances. She had fallen off the roof.

Then she had not survived that night. At least Thomas had been safe from her afterward. Bess might have lost her balance as she pushed Larryn over. Larryn hoped she had gone over the edge then, so that Thomas would never have had to feel guilty about her demise.

The materials differed about the fate of the duke of Seldrake. He had died, of course—eventually. But it wasn't clear when or how.

Some sources indicated he had disappeared at the same time as, or soon after, Lady Mainwaring's death, causing speculation that he'd had a hand in it. Others claimed he had taken his own life—which infuriated Larryn. She knew him better than that.

Still others claimed he had walked away from his wealth to provide needed medical care to the poor. *That,* Larryn could believe.

But she yearned to know what had truly happened to him. Had he been happy? Would she know for certain, if she were here the next time he appeared as a ghost?

Would he appear again as a ghost?

Augie stayed at her side the entire time. Chloe's two remaining Cavaliers also came in from time to time. They seemed very accepting of the strange dog in their midst.

But Augie wasn't eating well. The maids who fed the dogs told her so. She tried to tempt him with some dog treats, even some roast beef, but he ate very little.

That evening, Chloe had a maid bring Larryn a dinner tray, then joined her in the study, but only for a short while. "I am going to a friend's to discuss a fund-raising event for the preservation of several deteriorating buildings in our area," she told Larryn. "I shouldn't be too late."

She looked in on Larryn upon her return several hours later. "You look exhausted, dear," she said worriedly. Larryn glanced at the time. It was late, and she was exhausted. She had just discovered some interesting information on Adele—but it would wait until tomorrow.

Despite how tired she was, Larryn visited the roof that night—alone. She did not want to wrestle with Augie. She shut him in her room and held her ears as he whimpered while she headed for the roof.

Once there, she stood in the darkness for a long while, alone with her thoughts. Alone with her memories of Thomas.

And then . . . was that a haze that appeared at the edge of the roof when she had nearly fallen over? She drew in her breath and just watched.

No. It was nothing, probably just a misting over of her own tired eyes. They grew even hazier as tears welled up. Well, what did she expect—that Thomas would appear because she willed him to? Ridiculous.

Slowly, she turned toward the stairwell—and heard it. A wail of anguish, one she had heard before, in a beloved familiar voice. "Larryn, nooooo . . ." With it was the howl of a dog.

Larryn whirled and looked into the darkness of this day, incomplete due to the intrusion of lights from below and reflection from the clouds above.

"Thomas?" she whispered. "Are you here?"

Although she remained staring and listening for a long time, she neither saw anything nor heard any more.

The next few days settled into a pattern of research. Larryn learned that Adele had married Wyford. Henry was granted a title of his own by His Majesty, King Charles II, for his excellent work on championing the new central sanitary authority of London after the fire, better drainage, and an improved water supply—all of which, it was said, contributed to the cessation of plague as a major problem in the city.

Henry, earl of Wyford, and his wife, Lady Adele, lived at Seldrake House—not, apparently, with the duke of Seldrake, who had disappeared or died by then. They helped to raise Lady Adele's ward Terence after the death of Terence's mother, Lady Bess Mainwaring; the shock of her death, it was claimed, had led to the death of Terence's father, Lord Purvis Mainwaring. Terence, in gratitude, assumed the name of Seldrake. In time, he married and his family became the Seldrakes of the present.

Chloe had been right, Larryn thought. And how ironic it was. Chloe was the distant descendant not of Thomas, but of his father—and of the miserable Bess Mainwaring.

When Larryn spoke with her about it, Chloe said she recalled that her family descended from Terence Seldrake, who had been the ward of Lady Adele, but she hadn't realized why, though she remembered Bess's name. "Fascinating," she said, "though I'd love to throttle my ancestress for all the trouble she caused."

Larryn also learned that Thomas had been accused of abducting the little duke of Apsley, the king's son, and of snatching children from plague houses. Young Apsley cleared him of the kidnapping charge, but there was nothing in the books and papers addressing the resolution of Thomas's alleged defiance of the plague laws. Adele had worked to clear him, for Seldrake had died or disappeared before he could be exonerated. A courtier named Hubert Browne had assisted her.

Apsley survived that last frightening night at Seldrake House to grow into a well-known diplomat in the days of William and Mary, after the death of Apsley's father Charles II and his successor, Charles's brother, James I.

Nights, Larryn always went to the roof. Though Augie whined to be allowed to come, she was afraid the dog would prevent any manifestation of Thomas if he barked and ran around the way he had that first night.

The poor dog still wasn't eating right. He must miss Thomas and Caddie.

So did Larryn.

On each visit to the roof, Larryn heard Thomas's cry and the puppy's howl. The sounds tortured her, but she saw nothing.

On the third night, Larryn called out herself, "I'm here, Thomas. I'm fine. Really." And then she sank to the roof and cried. She couldn't bear the thought that he would remain tortured like that, possibly forever, and for no reason.

The fourth day, she knew she couldn't stand it any longer. "I have to get back there," she told Augie, who sat on her lap in the study as she poured over a book on the table before her. "I need to assure him that I am fine."

Easier said than done, she knew. She hadn't controlled the phenomenon of traveling in time before—not even that night, in the past, when she had tried to go home. That had been the closest she had come, though.

She would try to re-create the circumstances that night. And if she succeeded in returning to the past—what then? Could she bear being there, forever, in such primitive conditions?

"Absolutely," she told Augie. "As long as Thomas is there."

But would he want her? History did not show them existing as husband and wife. It did not show what had happened to either of them.

No matter. Larryn had to try.

At midnight, Larryn hurried up the main staircase, then down the hall to the doorway to the narrow stairway to the roof. She turned on the electric lights at the bottom. She took a deep breath and began walking upstairs.

"Come on, Augie," she said. "But, please, stay calm." She had put a leash and collar on Augie—an ordinary leather collar. The jeweled one had been passed to Chloe from succeeding generations; it belonged in the present.

At least with the leash, Larryn would be able to keep

Augie from tossing himself over the roof in his excitement.

The little spaniel tried to dash back and forth along the hall as they headed for the stairway. He seemed filled with as much anticipation as Larryn.

Anticipation—no. It was hope that kept her going. That and determination. She had to do something. She *would* do something to help Thomas.

To be with him . . .

She was nearly shoved over by the strong winds as she stepped onto the roof. Rain squalled against her. She had put on the gown she had worn when she returned from the seventeenth century—a yellow outfit with a low neckline and long skirt. They were especially uncomfortable in the downpour.

Beside her, Augie whimpered. "What is it?" Larryn whispered. "Do you see something?"

She didn't hear Thomas's cry. Nor did she see—

Wait. Was that something moving over in the corner?

It was the area she stared at every night—the place where she had nearly gone over the edge.

The last place she had seen Thomas. . . .

"Thomas," she said, as firmly as she could with her voice quivering. "Thomas, I want to come back to you. I need to tell you that I'm fine, that you need not go through that emotional upheaval again. Your unfinished business is complete. You saved me, Thomas."

She kept watching the same area. Was that a mist forming? It seemed to flutter back and forth—like the wagging of a dog's tail.

Larryn heard a bark from beside her—Augie's. And then she heard another—a different tone, it seemed, although it was hard to tell with the storm sounds raging about her. Screwing up her face against the cold rain that hit her like an endless shower, she continued forward—just as Augie tugged so hard and so unexpectedly on the leash that Larryn let go. "Augie!" she called, rushing forward.

And stopped.

The rain was heavy but clear. But a slithering, grasping

fog rose from the edge of the roof. It had a hot, acrid, familiar smell.

Augie stood just outside it, barking and wagging his tail.

And in it stood another dog. No, a puppy. The two animals were nose to nose, sniffing each other joyfully.

"Caddie!" Larryn cried.

The pup yipped, then returned to playing with Augie. And beyond Caddie . . .

Thomas Northby, duke of Seldrake, appeared in the fog. He stood straight and tall, wearing one of his full, white shirts and wide britches, and Larryn had never seen a more wonderful sight.

"Thomas," she breathed.

He seemed translucent, and he didn't move.

The dogs moved, though, circling one another. Augie went into the fog; Caddie came out. Then they traded places once more.

"I came here to tell you that everything's all right," Larryn began. "You don't need to be a ghost any longer, Thomas."

She realized, with a sinking heart, that she didn't need to go to the past to tell him so. She had counted on doing just that, she knew for certain that, no matter what, she wanted to be with him.

What could she do now?

"I believe," said the wonderful deep voice that Larryn had so longed to hear, "that your Caddie was most eager to return to you. She has been quite restless since your departure, but most particularly tonight."

"Augie has been restless, too," Larryn said, glad that it was raining, for otherwise Thomas would be able to see her tears. "Especially when I've let him come on the roof."

"Mayhap they wish to exchange places, to each return from whence they came."

"Mayhap," Larryn mocked, but her voice shook. She took a step forward, and then another, fearful that the fog would vanish if she drew too close—and Seldrake with it.

"And you, Larryn. Would you like to exchange places?"

"Exchange, no!" she cried. "But Thomas, I love you. I want to be with you."

"And I with you, for I love you as well, Larryn." His tone was low and wistful, and he sounded very far away.

One of the dogs barked again. The fog began to recede.

"Thomas!" Larryn screamed. "Don't go. Caddie! Augie!" In a moment, the dogs were beside her—on her side of the fog. "Thomas, please—"

He took a step toward her—just as the fog disappeared.

Thomas Northby, duke of Seldrake, remained on the roof, standing in the pouring rain.

Larryn ran to him and threw herself into his arms. "You're here!" she cried, laughing and kissing him.

At her feet, she heard a bark, followed by another. She knelt to hug Caddie, then Augie. "You did this, didn't you? You wanted to be together, too."

Thomas also knelt on the slick roof. His arms reached out to hug the wet, happily writhing dogs. When he let them go, they shook themselves and ran off together.

Thomas reached out to Larryn, and they rose together. "I believe, my love, that you left this with me to light my way." He drew her old flashlight from his pocket and turned it on. "I wish for you to show me more miracles of this world of yours."

"Of course," she said, laughing.

And then she was in his arms once more. His kiss was fierce and possessive.

"Are you here to stay, Thomas?" she whispered against his questing mouth. "In my world?"

"As long as you will have me, my love."

Epilogue

"LOOK! THERE!" CHLOE was yelling joyfully.

They were in the kitchen at Seldrake House. Caddie lay in the whelping box, and the first of her puppies had just slid out.

Like a perfect mother, Caddie turned to the puppy, bit off its sack, and began licking the tiny, wriggling creature.

"What do you think, Augie?" Larryn said. The pup's father sat on the floor beside her. He whined.

Larryn laughed. So did her husband, who drew her tightly into his arms.

"And you, my love," said Thomas Seldrake. "Shall you be as diligent in the birthing process?"

Larryn looked down at her own rounded form. They had been married for just over a year, and she was pregnant with their first child.

"I thought proper men of your day didn't discuss such things," she chided with a smile.

"Ah, but I was a physician, after all. And you are thinking of what I have learned of the Victorian era, I believe, which was only in the last century. At my time, no one thought twice of discussing the natural occurrences of living. Besides, I am no longer 'of my day.' "

"No," Larryn said fervently, "you're not, thank heavens." She nestled even tighter against Thomas, and she felt him kiss the top of her head.

The first days after his appearance on the roof had been a jumble, and she recalled them now with phenomenal plea-sure.

Chloe had been delighted to meet her distant relation. She was also highly efficient in acquiring an identity for him. "He's my nineteenth cousin seventeen times removed, or something like that," she said. Her research work on the Internet and otherwise for years had resulted in a lot of knowledge, and not only about her family. With just a little more effort, she had been able to acquire all sorts of papers needed to make Thomas an acknowledged human being in this day when credentials were so important. "And I only had to grease a few palms," she'd said proudly. He had taken the name Seldrake, like hers.

Of course Thomas was to remain at Seldrake House, she'd told him. "You have a prior claim on it," she'd said. "A much longer claim than I." Thomas had gratefully ac-cepted her help.

He was pleased that Chloe had found Augie's collar con-taining an old locket of Adele's, with Larryn's portrait se-creted inside. He had hidden them himself in the banquet house, along with his ring and medical journals, in the faint hope that Larryn might, instead of dying, have returned to her home in the future. If so, he wished her to see her portrait and the fact that he had acknowledged at last that she was a doctor. She told him that Chloe had found the other items with her portrait, too.

Thrilled, happier than she had ever been in her life, Lar-ryn diligently taught him about his new time.

He decided that it would take him too long to become a full-fledged doctor here. "I haven't more knowledge than a tot in this new, miracle-filled era," he'd grumbled. "My skills are antiquated."

But they were highly suitable for a historian. And so, he had—again with Chloe's help in acquiring credentials—

begun to teach early British history in the lower schools. His colorful descriptions and commentaries had quickly caught the attention of so-called experts in the field. He had been invited first to become a guest lecturer at universities, and then a professor.

In addition, he had gotten a contract—with an amazingly lucrative advance—to edit and publish his family's medical journals, both for their historical value and for their use in natural medicine. He was also to write several books about his era of expertise. The BBC had also gotten wind of this marvelous, newly discovered expert, and had hired him to work on several scripts for true-life historical shows for television.

In the meantime, with Larryn's help, he researched all that had happened in medicine from his time to now. "So many wondrous discoveries," he marveled.

He was equally enthralled, though, with movies and television. And airplanes. He had insisted on coming home to the United States with Larryn while she packed up her belongings and returned with him to England.

"Truly astounding," he had said of his first plane flight.

All in all, Thomas was beginning to fit in to this time.

Larryn couldn't have been more proud of him.

He hadn't proposed marriage, though, until he'd had an idea that he would be able to support a wife here. "I might impose on Chloe for a place to live," he had asserted, "but I shall not rely on anyone else to support me."

Even though Larryn would have been glad to.

Still, for the self-esteem of such a proud man, she was delighted things were working out so well. She, too, was happy, for she was working now with injured children, advising in their medical treatment and helping with their rehabilitation.

But she was happiest just being Mrs. Thomas Seldrake.

And she had, after all, helped Thomas discover and resolve his unfinished business—finding his true love and a way to be with her.

Larryn still could not completely understand all that had

happened. She was a physician, a scientist, a person who had once firmly believed that there was a rational answer for everything.

But no modern theory that she could discover, whether scientific or paranormal, could fully explain what had happened to Thomas and her.

The most reasonable hypothesis, she believed after research and endless discussions with Chloe, was that Thomas and she had gotten caught in some kind of time warp. Larryn must have gone into the past before; otherwise, how could her portrait have appeared in the locket? She had been shoved from the roof then, too, and apparently Seldrake believed she had died. The emotion of losing Larryn that way meant that when Seldrake himself had passed away, he returned, as a ghost, to that moment instead of moving on.

In that scenario, how and when had he died? Had he died young, as Bess Mainwaring had intended? Had he lived a long life and died of natural causes? Larryn had no idea.

But this time the dogs had changed places—the impetus, Larryn believed, that had changed the situation. Thomas came forward to Larryn's era several days after the incident on the roof had occurred, when Caddie returned home. Thomas therefore had not died at any time in the past. As a result, the reports of his death or disappearance had become confusing and inconclusive.

But that was just a theory. They would never know for certain. Eventually Larryn gave up trying to fully understand what had happened and simply accepted it—just the way she did her happiness with Thomas.

"I learned much from losing you, Larryn," he whispered to her late one night in the dark in their bed, a few days after his arrival, when they had finished making joyful love. "So much so that I blessed the union between Adele and Wyford. My only regret in leaving my time is that I was not there to see them wed."

"They were happy together, Thomas," she assured him. "I didn't learn all I wanted to in researching what happened after I left, but I did find references to Lord and Lady Henry Wyford and their many children, including their ward, young Terence. He was a doctor, and his wife's name was Adele. Chloe says she has many distant cousins who are their descendents; she will introduce them to us soon.

"Thank heavens," Thomas had said, and had kissed her once more. . . .

Chloe's cry brought Larryn back to the present. "Look!" she said again. Another puppy had popped out. The older woman knelt on the floor, grinning at the exciting event unfolding before her. She glanced up at Larryn, who smiled at her from Thomas's arms. "Have you ever seen anything so miraculous?" Chloe asked.

"Oh, yes," Larryn said softly, and she looked deeply into her husband's sparkling blue eyes.

Historical Note

THE GREAT PLAGUE of London occurred in 1665, killing more than 68,000 people. Although there were fewer deaths from plague the following year, more than 1,700 Londoners succumbed to the disease in 1666, the year of the Great Fire.

TIME PASSAGES

FRIENDS ROMANCE

Can a man come between friends?

❑ **A TASTE OF HONEY**
by DeWanna Pace   0-515-12387-0

❑ **WHERE THE HEART IS**
by Sheridon Smythe   0-515-12412-5

❑ **LONG WAY HOME**
by Wendy Corsi Staub   0-515-12440-0

All books $5.99